MW01006494

The terminal at McCarran International Airport stands in stark contrast to the glitz and glamour of downtown Las Vegas. All of the vendors have locked up for the night. A lone janitor is attempting to vacuum the stained, tread worn carpet, and with the exception of a handful of slot machines droning out their senseless jingles, the terminal is essentially empty and quiet.

Andrew Carlson is waiting for U.S. Senator Charles Wooten to get off PanAm's flight 1107 from Washington, DC. After it appears that all of the passengers have exited the aircraft, there's no sign of the senator. As a couple of giggling stewardesses start to walk past him, he says, "Pardon me, but have all of the passengers gotten off the plane? I'm supposed to meet someone, but I seemed to have missed him."

"Are you looking for Senator Wooten?" asks one of the stewardesses.

"Yes, as a matter of fact, I am."

"Well, you haven't missed him. He's still on the plane."

"Is he all right?"

"Not exactly, but it's nothing that a good night's sleep and a pot of coffee can't fix," she replies.

"Should I go out there and get him?" he asks, somewhat embarrassed by the situation.

"No problem. I'm sure the captain and the rest of the crew will be more than happy to help you."

"Thank you, ladies. Good night," he says to the stewardesses as they walk away.

Upon entering the aircraft, Andrew can see the senator giving one of the crewmembers a hard time about leaving the comfort of his first class seat. After spending over four hours in the air from Washington, the senator is more than a little tanked from the complimentary drinks.

As Andrew gets closer to him, the senator finally recognizes him and says, "Andy! How the hell are ya'? I thought you were going to meet me in Vegas."

3

"Charlie, you *are* in Vegas, and apparently I'm in a lot better shape than you," replies Andrew in a scornful tone. "I see that you've decided to start the celebration without me."

"Oh Andy, don't be such a hardass. I've only had a couple… well, maybe three Bloody Marys." The stewardess standing behind him rolls her eyes, and shakes her head while holding up six fingers.

"Charlie, our charter is waiting and you're holding up the show."

"Okay, okay," replies the senator apologetically. "Give me a hand, will ya? You know how these damn seats are, easy to fall into, and hell to get out of."

"On three. One…two…three! There ya go." Once out of the seat, Andrew guides him to the doorway, waves to the aircrew, then helps the senator down the ramp.

"Where's the limo?" asks the senator, slurring his words.

"We're not taking a limo. We have a chartered flight to Reno, remember?" says Andrew.

"What about my luggage?"

"Already handled. Don't worry about it," replies Andrew.

"Well, where's the plane?"

"It's in front of that hangar over there. Can't you see it?" asks Andrew as he points to a sleek, almost shark-like Beechcraft King Air 100, silhouetted in front of a lighted, open hangar. "Think you're sober enough to walk that far?"

"Look here," says the senator, as he stops, closes his eyes, and tries to touch his nose, almost falling flat on his face.

"Whoa there! Easy Charlie. You're gonna hurt yourself," says Andrew as he tries to maintain his grip on the senator's arm.

"Whaddayamean hurt myself? I'm as sober as a judge," replies the senator.

"Uh-huh. Think you can walk to the plane without breaking anything?"

"Sure! Sure. No problem. Now where did you say that plane was again?" asks the senator while squinting his eyes, trying to focus in the darkness.

Inside the hangar office, a charter pilot is nursing a lukewarm cup of coffee from the vending machine, while reviewing the weather report and flight plan to Reno.

A young man enters the office from the hangar and drops some change into the vending machine for a cup of coffee. He's wearing a pale gray flight suit and polished, black, military-style boots.

"Hope you like it weak and piss warm," mumbles the pilot without looking back.

"You know, I can't tell you how many times my uncle has called the company to have them come out and fix it. But all they do is refill it and collect the money," replies the young man with an air of disappointment in his voice.

The pilot glances at him, then says, "Funny, but I don't think I've seen you around here before. Been here long?"

"My name's Higgins, Bill Higgins. Actually, I prefer to be called William, but everyone calls me Bill, so I just go with the flow."

"So, who's your uncle?" asks the charter pilot.

"Benny Parsons. He's my mother's brother. As a matter of fact, Uncle Benny was the one who taught me to fly." Higgins starts walking toward the pilot and points to a framed black and white photo on the wall and says, "Look. This picture was taken back in the summer of 1953. That's Uncle Benny, me, my dad, and my mom." Higgins pauses a moment, smiles, then continues. "I think the paint was still wet on that sign when this picture was taken."

"Uncle Benny started Hard Eight Air Freight with three war surplus Douglas C-47's and a Curtiss C-46A Commando. All of them were still painted in military olive drab. I helped him paint over all the military markings, but it would be a couple of years before he could afford to completely repaint them."

Now, the charter pilot is smiling and says, "Your Uncle Benny and I flew C-47's together in Korea. He named his plane Hard Eight Air Freight. He obviously liked it enough to name his charter business after his plane. My name is Harold Murphy, but during the war everyone called me Murph. So I named my plane..."

"Murph's Turf! When I was growing up, Uncle Benny used to talk about you all the time," replies Higgins.

"You've got a pretty good memory, Bill. Sorry, I meant to say William."

5

"It's okay," replies Higgins. "Everybody does it."

"Do you still fly?" asks Murphy.

"Not as much as I used to. I served a couple of tours in Southeast Asia for Air America in the early 60's. That got a little hairy from time to time, but the money was good, and it helped pay my way through law school. Now, Uncle Benny lets me help out around here whenever I can."

"I don't know what I'd do if I couldn't fly," says Murphy. "I hope I never have to find out."

"I'm guessing that's your Beechcraft King Air 100 out there."

"Yep. Brand spanking new," replies Murphy proudly. "She doesn't have a hundred hours on her yet. We're still working the bugs out."

"She's a beaut." Higgins pauses a moment, then says, "Hey! Would you mind if I took care of your pre-flight for you?"

"I don't know about that. She's our pride and joy. Like I said, she's brand new. Maybe some other time." Murphy turns his attention back to his flight plan and weather report.

While taking a sip of his coffee, Higgins looks out the window and spots two men walking across the tarmac toward them. "I don't suppose you're waiting for a couple of passengers, are you?"

"As a matter of fact, I am," replies Murphy.

"Well, they're almost here, and by the looks of it, one of them looks like he's pretty well lit." Once again Higgins says, "Let me take care of your pre-flight while you take care of your passengers. Then all you'll have to do is power up and head out to the wild blue yonder."

"You mean the wild *black* yonder. No moon tonight, along with a fair amount of cloud cover. Kind of unusual for this time of year."

"Yeah, but you've got that King Air out there. You'll be cruising over it in no time."

"You know? If you weren't Benny's nephew," Murphy pauses, shakes his head, and says, "Oh, what the hell. Go ahead and do the pre-flight, but be careful. If you scratch or break anything, your ass is mine. Got it?"

Higgins snaps to attention and gives him a mock salute. "Yes sir. I'll take care of everything. I'll do the walk around, fire up the engines, check the oil and fuel pressure, reset the altimeter."

"Don't bother with the altimeter. It's already set."

"Sure thing. I'll check the radios, transponder, radar..."

"Don't bother testing the radar either. Some module was on back order, so I'll be flying without it." Murphy is beginning to feel more than a little frustrated. "Look Bill, William. Just follow the pre-flight checklist, okay? It's in a leather pouch tucked in the map pocket on the back of the co-pilot's seat."

"Will do. Take your time, and I'll get your baby ready for takeoff." Higgins walks over to Murphy and shakes his hand. "Everything is going to be okay. Besides, I'm hoping you'll take me up in her one day."

"We'll see," replies Murphy.

As Andrew and the senator finally reach the hangar, Higgins opens the door for them while keeping his back to the light. The senator glances up momentarily, barely catching a glimpse of Higgins' face. The intensity of the harsh, blue fluorescent lighting from the office causes the senator to grimace and turn away. But there is something familiar about the young man's face.

While Murphy deals with his passengers, Higgins performs a quick walk around, checks the tires, flaps, stabilizer, and rudder, then climbs into the cabin, and settles into the pilot's seat. After scanning the instrument panel, Higgins reaches behind the co-pilot's seat and finds the leather pouch exactly where Murphy said it would be. He primes the fuel pumps, fires up the two powerful turboprop engines, then checks to make sure all of their readings are in the green. Next he flips to the back of the manual to find the location of the electrical fuse panel. Once open, he replaces the fuses for the radios and the emergency transponder. After he secures the fuse box, he adjusts the altimeter.

"Everything okay up there, Bill?" asks Murphy, while peering in from the cabin door.

"Yep!" replies a startled Higgins. "Everything's in the green."

"Well then," says Murphy, "Would you mind giving me a hand with the senator? He's definitely had his limit, and then some."

"Tell me captain, how many stewardesses are there on this flight?" asks the senator. "I'd like another Bloody Mary before we take off."

"I'll get right on it," replies Murphy. "Bill? Grab the senator's hand and pull while I push." As Murphy starts pushing the senator up the ladder, he groans, "Come on, Senator. At least try to help us get you in there."

Once Higgins and Murphy get the senator into the cabin, Higgins guides him to his seat, with Andrew taking a seat behind him. While Higgins gets the senator settled and secure in his seat, Senator Wooten struggles to read the nametag on his flight suit. "W.H. Higgins. Have we met somewhere before? Your face seems faintly familiar."

"I don't think so sir," replies Higgins as he hurriedly tries to buckle him in place. "I'm sure I'd remember."

"It'll come to me, I'm sure. It always does," says the senator as he slowly succumbs to his overindulgence of alcohol, drifting off to sleep.

As Higgins starts to exit the plane, Murphy taps him on the shoulder and says, "Thanks for taking care of the pre-flight for me. Tell ya what. I've got another charter next Tuesday. If you're not busy, wanna fly back to Reno with me? I've got a couple of high rollers who'll want to try their luck in Vegas. You'll be gone a day, maybe two at most. We can share war stories, and I'll even sign off on your seat time."

"Sure. That'd be great." Murphy reaches out and shakes Higgins' hand. Then Higgins says, "I'll button her up for ya. Have a safe flight."

"See you Tuesday, Bill, ah, William," replies Murphy.

Higgins secures the cabin door, then stands off to the side, just past the wingtip, so Murphy can see that he's clear. Higgins waves to Murphy, and he waves back while throttling up the engines.

Higgins turns away from the prop wash as he walks back to the hangar. Once inside, he sits down at the desk, turns on the radio and adjusts it to McCarran's tower frequency.

As Murphy maneuvers the aircraft down the taxiway, he radios the tower. "McCarran tower, McCarran tower, this is November One Seven Four Tango Alpha, requesting clearance for departure on runway One Five North. I repeat, One Five North."

"Roger that One Seven Four Tango Alpha. This is McCarran tower. You are clear for takeoff on runway One Five North. Winds are calm. Scattered cloud cover. Visibility ten miles plus. Have a safe flight."

"Roger that McCarran tower. November One Seven Four Tango Alpha on rollout to Reno International."

"How long will it take us to get there?" shouts Andrew, trying to be heard over the roar of the engines.

"We should be on the ground in Reno in about two hours. Just sit back and relax. We'll be there before you know it."

Andrew slides back into his seat and attempts to get some desperately needed sleep. The senator is already snoring almost as loud as the engines.

***

About thirty minutes into the flight, Murphy senses that something's wrong. What few lights are visible on the ground don't look quite right; as though he were below his designated altitude. He glances at his altimeter, and it's indicating that he's at the proper altitude. For his own peace of mind, he decides to contact air traffic control and get an altitude check. "Southwest Regional ATC. Southwest Regional ATC. November One Seven Four Tango Alpha requesting an altitude check. Repeat, November One Seven Four Tango Alpha requesting an altitude check. We're en route from Las Vegas to Reno. Heading is North/Northwest. Air speed is Two Two Zero knots. Indicated altitude is One Zero Two Zero Zero feet. Repeat, One Zero Two Zero Zero feet."

But just as Southwest Regional Air Traffic Control begins to transmit, the plane's radio goes dead. *"What the hell?"* Murphy says out loud to himself, rousing Andrew with his frustration.

"Is there a problem?" asks Andrew.

"Yeah, my radio just up and died. It was working fine, then all of a sudden, it just quit. I'm going to put the plane on autopilot, and see if it might have blown a fuse." Just as Murphy turns on the autopilot, the plane encounters some turbulence, jarring the senator out of his sleep.

"What was that?" asks the visibly shaken senator as he tries to sit up.

"Just a little turbulence, nothing to be concerned about," says Murphy.

"What are you doing over there? Shouldn't you be in the pilot's seat?"

"I have the plane on autopilot while I check for a blown fuse. Our radio is out."

Meanwhile, Southwest Regional ATC is frantically trying to contact them. "Southwest Regional ATC to November One Seven Four Tango Alpha. Pull up! Pull up! You're too low! Increase altitude by One Five Zero Zero feet immediately! Emergency! One Seven Four Tango Alpha. Emergency climb! Emergency climb!" Silence. "One Seven Four Tango Alpha. Respond." Again, silence.

Once the pilot opens the fuse box, he discovers not one, but three fuses are blown. *What the hell is going on here?* All three fuses have amperage values below the required value of their port. The pilot growls in a threatening tone, *"Heads are going to roll when I get back to Reno."*

"William Henry Higgins!" blurts out the senator confidently. "I knew it would come to me. I knew I had seen that man before."

"Who?" asks Andrew. "You mean the man at the hangar?"

"Yes! He's the young man who helped us get the swing vote on our military contract."

As the pilot snaps the proper fuse in place, the radio suddenly barks to life with the warning from Southwest Regional. "Emergency climb! Emergency climb! One Seven Four Tango Alpha. Do you read?"

Murphy looks up just in time to catch a glimpse of the growing mountain's menacing silhouette blocking out the stars around it. Realizing their imminent doom, his last words are, "Oh shit."

November One Seven Four Tango Alpha disappears from radar, and all communication is lost. Southwest Regional ATC continues calling out to them, but there's no response.

Back at the hangar in Las Vegas, Higgins smiles, and turns off the radio. He picks up the phone and makes a long distance call. After the third ring, someone answers.

"Yes?"

Higgins says, "It's done."

"Any chance of survivors?"

"No sir, none," replies Higgins.

"Good. See you back in Washington on Friday, noon, my office. Don't be late."

"Thank you, sir. I'll be there."

"And Bill?"

"Yes sir?"

"Welcome to the Core." With that comment, Higgins hears a click, followed by a dial tone.

TLC: Chapter 2
Homeland Security Complex
Secret Service Division
Friday afternoon,
May 13, 2011, 1500 hours local time

Thomas Andrew Jackson, simply known to his friends and associates as AJ, joined the Marine Corps shortly after graduating high school. His father had been a Marine, just like his father before him. In fact, his father said their lineage could be traced back to President Andrew Jackson. Unfortunately, AJ's father was one of the two hundred and twenty Marines killed in the Beirut barracks bombing in 1983. He was only ten years old when he lost his dad.

For the past twelve years with the Marines, AJ had been a squad leader in the Special Operations Group. Their missions varied from search and rescue, search and destroy, forward observation, intelligence, etc. While most of those missions are still classified, AJ and his team's performance have been outstanding, garnering a number of citations and commendations.

However, after twenty years of active service, he felt it was time for a change. But he also had some reservations as to how his background and training could be applied to civilian life. His CO was also retiring and suggested he consider going to work for either the DEA or Secret Service. After some soul searching, AJ decided to apply to the Secret Service.

AJ stands at just over six feet tall, two hundred pounds, medium short brown hair, green eyes, and clean-shaven. His face has a chiseled look, not rugged, but his cheekbones, jaw, and chin are clearly defined. There is a sense of purpose in his appearance. His shoulders are proportionate to his body, but also squared off, obviously due to his training and exercise regimen. His arms and legs are muscular, but not overly apparent. In fact, once dressed up in a suit, he looks like a trim and fit professional businessman. But the suit is just a cover, camouflage, for a man who can kill you in a heartbeat without breaking his stride or losing his composure.

AJ has been with the Secret Service for about three months when his supervisor calls him into the office. "AJ?" says Mr. Weathers, "I know you haven't been with us very long, but I have a special assignment for you. It's not exactly high profile, but you'll be in charge."

"What's the assignment?" asks AJ inquisitively. "How many agents will I be responsible for?"

"None," says Mr. Weathers. "You'll be on your own."

"Say again?" he asks with a surprised look on his face. "I'll be on my own? What kind of assignment is it?"

"You're going to be Senator William Henry Higgins' personal bodyguard, and driver."

"What? You're giving me a babysitter's job?" he responds sarcastically.

"Watch your mouth, son!" barks Weathers. "First off, you should know the senator asked for you by name." AJ is obviously not happy about the situation, so Weathers tries to take on a more subtle approach. "AJ, I'm more than familiar with your background. This job requires someone who understands the chain of command. Someone who is accustomed to working with superior officers, yet someone who can think on their feet, and take command of the situation if and when necessary."

"I didn't know the senator was military."

"He's not, but he is a very powerful and influential man on The Hill, and he's accustomed to telling people what to do. That's where your understanding the chain of command, and working with superior officers comes into play. But at the same time, you'll need to keep your ears and eyes open."

Weathers continues, "We've heard through the grapevine the senator may be making a play for the Presidency, and with that, who knows who or what might start crawling out of the woodwork. I need someone on the inside who can keep a watchful eye on the senator. Make no mistake about it. This is a very important assignment. And should Senator Higgins make a public announcement about running for the Presidency, you'll already have a leg up on everyone else, and you'll be in charge of his security team."

"You're not blowing smoke up my skirt, trying to make me feel better about this detail, are you?"

"Now, why would I do that?" asks Weathers.

"Because no one else wants this job either?"

"AJ," sighs Weathers, "Like I said, Senator Higgins asked for you by name, so this really isn't a request. Besides, this job could lead to more rewarding opportunities."

"How does the senator know anything about me?"

"I have no idea."

"Okay, okay, but I don't have to like it."

"Look at this way. You'll be your own point man. Just give it a little time. It'll be okay," says Weathers reassuringly. "You'll see."

***

Robert Monroe Weathers spent thirty years in the United States Army, retiring at the rank of Colonel. After graduating from West Point Military Academy, he was the first African-American to jump into the intelligence sector. He was a key asset in cracking many of the coded messages between the USSR and the People's Republic of China during the Cold War. His superiors were constantly impressed by his dedication and perseverance. Once he was on a project, he was worse than a "bull dog", staying with it until it was resolved. In fact, his tenacity earned him the nickname "Bull Dog Weathers".

Before his retirement date was set with Army Intelligence, both the CIA and Secret Service were trying to woo him to their respective agencies. He initially joined the CIA, but after two and a half years of service, he requested and received a transfer to the Secret Service.

Because of his high security clearance, no one seems to know why he requested the transfer, and he's never volunteered any information in that regard.

TLC: Chapter 3
Higgins' estate
Monday morning
May 16, 2011, 0800 hours local time

AJ drives out to Senator Higgins' estate in Maryland the following Monday morning. And what a place it is. A large concrete wall, at least ten feet high, surrounds the estate. There are security cameras placed in strategic areas, and the wrought iron gates are remote controlled, as well as operated through a keypad at the entrance. The gates are massive in their design, not in an ostentatious sense, but more from a security aspect.

AJ stops at the gates and pushes the call button for the intercom. A voice comes over the speaker, "State your name and your business here."

"Jackson, Thomas A., Secret Service, ID number Sierra, Sierra 55191. I'm here to see Senator Higgins," he replies. There is no response, but then the gates begin to move, and AJ proceeds through them.

Once through the gates, the driveway winds its way toward the home, allowing AJ a brief glimpse of the house from different perspectives along the route. It's Country French style, with its arched top windows, French doors, are quite different from what AJ had expected.

AJ parks his charcoal gray, government issue, Crown Victoria behind the senator's limo, which is parked near the front door. AJ adjusts his collar, tie, and jacket as he approaches the front door, carrying his personnel file in a manila envelope under his left arm.

As he reaches for the doorbell, the butler opens the door. "Good morning Agent Jackson. The senator is expecting you in the library," says the butler. "My name is George Washington Harris, and I'm the Head Butler."

"Well, good morning to you Mr. Harris."

"Everyone calls me George, Agent Jackson."

"Well, everyone calls me AJ, Mr. Harris."

"Very well. If you will call me George, I will call you AJ."

"Good morning, George," he replies. Both men smile, then George leads AJ to the library, and introduces him to Senator Higgins.

Senator William Henry Higgins is a tall man, about six feet two, two hundred and fifty pounds, gray hair, blue eyes, clean shaven, very cultured, a smart dresser, and a lively step for a man well into his sixties.

As AJ and the senator walk toward each other to shake hands, AJ presents Senator Higgins with his file. Without examining the contents, the senator casually tosses it on his desk and says, "I've already read your file, Thomas."

"It's AJ, sir," he replies.

"Of course, of course. AJ," says the senator. "I don't know how much your supervisor has told you about me, but I've been on Capitol Hill for almost forty years. I've seen, and been a part of, a lot of history during that time, but I believe I still have a lot to offer this country of ours."

"Our country has taken the dregs of the world, the leftovers, the misfits, and we've become a world power. We've made medical breakthroughs, improved our way of life, flown to heights that no other country has been able to achieve. We were the first to split the atom, the first to break the sound barrier, the first to touch the ocean's floor, and the first to walk on the moon."

"But we've sat on our laurels for the past twenty years, and the rest of the world is nipping at our heels. Japan has taken over a large portion of our automotive industry, and now South Korea is trying to take another bite out of it. China controls our steel industry. Even our own major companies and corporations have moved their production facilities to Mexico, or overseas, because their labor and manufacturing are cheaper."

"We've become dependent on foreign oil, while our own oil fields lie dormant. We've allowed ourselves to become slaves to those we have either conquered by war, or helped with economic aid and/or sanctions. We are fast losing our world dominance, and if something isn't done soon." The senator pauses a moment, then says, "Well, so much for being on the soapbox this morning. What did Weathers tell you about me?"

"Well, Senator, you pretty much covered it," he replies a little nervously.

"Do you like to hunt?"

"Excuse me?" asks AJ with a puzzled look on his face.

"Do you like to hunt? You know…pheasant, quail, geese, duck."

"I can't say that I've had much of an opportunity, sir. My father died when I was young, and the Corps has been my life since I was eighteen. The only thing that I've had in my crosshairs has been the enemy, and most of the time, they were shooting back."

"Well, that's one of the nice things about game hunting. They don't shoot back. Do you own a shotgun?" asks the senator as he walks toward his ornate, hand carved gun cabinet and motions AJ to follow him.

"As a matter of fact, yes, I do; three of them."

"What kinds are they? Brownings, Remingtons, Berettas?" The senator opens the case and pulls out one of his prized over and under Brownings. The stock is hand carved, while the receiver is extensively engraved with portions of it inlaid in gold.

"Well, one of them is a Remington, an 870. I also have a Benelli M3, and an FIE LAW 12."

"Are they sporting shotguns?"

"Not exactly. They're classified as assault weapons, sir. While the 870 is a pump, the other two are semi-auto, although the Benelli is selectable between semi-auto and pump action. The 870 and Benelli hold eight rounds each, while the FIE holds nine. All three are equipped with modified actions, and night sights. They're not pretty, but they perform their functions well."

"Well, we have to make do with two rounds," says the senator smugly. "Tell me. Have you ever shot clays?"

"Clays, sir?"

The senator gets a big smile on his face and says, "They're discs made of clay and are thrown by a trap machine to simulate a bird in flight. I have a range out back. What do you say we take a crack at a few?"

"Sir, aren't you needed in Washington?"

"Nah, today is an off day. Besides you and I need to get to know each other better."

"Well, I'm game if you are, although I'm not really dressed for it."

"You're fine, but I need to get out of this monkey suit. I'll have George show you where the range is. George. George!" George comes rushing down the hall in response to the senator's calling. "George, pick out one of the Remingtons for Mr. Jackson, along with my Browning and take them down to the range. And tell Jeffrey that I need him in the hut to operate the trap machine."

"Yes, sir." replies George. As the senator heads upstairs to change, George removes the Browning and a Remington from the cabinet and places each one in a lined soft case. Then he opens the lower cabinet and takes out four boxes of shells and places them in a range bag.

"Didn't he say we were just going to fire off a couple of rounds?" asks AJ.

"I'm sure he did," replies George, "but this is his version of a couple of rounds."

"And who's Jeffrey?"

"He takes care of the senator's vehicles, along with other odd jobs around the estate. He's a young man originally from Chicago, and a bit of a perfectionist I might add, at least when it comes to cars."

"Where's the range?"

"I'll show you, just follow me."

"Wait a minute, George. I need to get something from the car. I'll be right back." AJ sprints out to his car, opens the trunk and pulls out a long black case, then sprints back to the house, where he catches up with George.

"This way, AJ," says George.

"I'm right behind you," AJ replies as the two of them exit the French doors from the library.

They walk past a couple of flower gardens and out buildings before finally arriving at a clearing. The range consists of what appears to be a quarter circle broken down into five evenly spaced shooting positions along the arc. Centered out in front of the arc is a small bunker-like hut. A portion of the hut is underground to allow the shooters a clear view of their target, as well as minimize the potential injury of the operator.

18

George hands AJ the Remington and watches him try to figure out how to break the action to load it. George can hardly contain himself. Finally, George says, "Grip the butt stock with your right hand, then push the lever to the right with your thumb."

"Oh! I see. Thanks, George," says AJ, feeling embarrassed and blushing a bit. George reaches into his pocket and hands AJ two rounds that he loads into their respective chambers. "I guess it's pretty obvious that I've never handled one of these before."

"I just hope your aim is better than your familiarity with the gun."

"Why don't we just find out?" says AJ with a cocky smile on his face.

"Why not indeed? Jeffrey? Pull!" Suddenly, there's a loud THA-WACK and an orange disc flies away from the hut, climbing up and off to the left. AJ snaps the action closed, shoulders the weapon, takes aim, and fires. The first round appears to just graze the target, causing the disc to wobble erratically and change its course, but the second round turns the disc into dust.

"Not bad!" exclaims the senator as he walks up behind them. "Not bad at all!" AJ breaks the action, ejecting the spent casings from the still smoking barrels. George bends over, picks up the spent casings, and places them in his pocket. There is a surprised look on his face as well, and while the senator notices his expression, says nothing.

"No sir, just beginner's luck," replies AJ smiling.

"Well, we'll just have to see how long your beginner's luck holds out," says the senator. "Shall we begin?" AJ nods his head, and the senator explains how the exercise works.

The senator and AJ take turns firing from each of the five positions. Both of them shoot quite well, with the senator finally edging out AJ by a couple of points.

"Well done, AJ. Well done!" says the senator as he hands his shotgun to George, who in turn places it back in its case. "It's been awhile since I've had some worthy competition. Are you sure you've never done this before?"

"Yes, sir, quite sure," he replies. "But target shooting has its similarities as well as its differences. In the field, I generally used an M-4 or an AK-47. You have to learn how to lead your target, adjust for range and windage, in an effort to make every round count."

"Well son, I think you've done a pretty good job of learning how to lead your target. Does the Remington feel right to you? If not, you can try another, if you wish."

"Yes, sir, this one is fine. The first two rounds felt different from the rest, almost like the loads were more powerful, or the type of shot was different. But it was probably more due to George here trying to catch me off guard, and not getting the butt firmly against my shoulder in time before I fired." George looks down, as though he is embarrassed about something.

"You're probably right about that," says the senator. "Tell you what. Some of my colleagues are coming out this weekend for a little target practice. After a couple of warm up rounds, we usually set up a friendly wager or two. I'm certain we could get a little competition going. Would you consider partnering up with me? We could clean up! And I'll cover the bets. What do you say?"

"Do you mind if I take a rain check? I have a few things to take care of this weekend."

"I understand," says the senator. "On a different note, I'm sure you'd like to get a feel for this place. George, here, has been my right hand man for almost as many years as I've been in office. I'm sure he knows this place better than anyone else, me included." George smiles and nods his head in agreement.

"Thank you, Senator. I have to admit that I was feeling a little nervous about meeting with you today. But getting some fresh air and squeezing off a few rounds, I feel much better now," he replies, while handing the Remington to George.

George takes the Remington and places it in its case, and starts walking back to the house. AJ walks over to the tree where he had propped his shotgun, slings it over his shoulder, and starts to follow George.

"Is that one of your shotguns?" asks the senator.

"Yes, sir. It's my Remington. I thought that if I was shooting badly enough with yours, I might at least save face using mine."

"Well, that obviously wasn't the case now, was it?"

He nods his head and says, "Fortunately. I better catch up with George."

"Very well. We'll get back together after lunch, and I'll give you my itinerary for the week," says the senator.

"Back in the library at 1300, I mean 1 o'clock, Senator?" he asks.

The senator smiles and says, "1300 hours will be fine."

"1300 hours it is, then. See you there, sir," replies AJ as he jogs back toward the house.

When AJ catches up with George, he can tell George is a bit uneasy. "Do you mind answering a couple of questions for me, George?"

"I suppose," the butler replies while focusing on the pathway ahead of him.

"Whose idea was it to start me off with a pair of field load number 6's? Was it you or Higgins?" he asks.

"I have no idea what you mean," George replies without looking up.

AJ reaches into George's coat pocket and removes the two spent casings. "Then, what are these doing in your pocket?" George doesn't answer, but he's definitely a bit worried. "Oh, and another thing. Why were you feeding me 7½'s while you were giving the senator 9's?"

George stops dead in his tracks and says apologetically, "I was doing my job. The senator hates to lose. He felt that by catching you off guard on the first couple of rounds, it might give him a bit of an edge. And as far as giving you 7½'s and the senator 9's, well, it was just another way of trying to stack the deck in the senator's favor."

"Was that your idea, or his?"

"His, sir," replies George feeling humiliated and embarrassed.

"George, I've already said you can call me AJ. I just wanted to know that's all, and honestly, I kind of knew the answer already. I just needed to hear you say that. I believe you."

George breathes a sigh of relief. "I must admit that you are a truly gifted marksman, sir."

"Come on. Let me help with those." AJ smiles, takes one of the gun cases from George, and follows him up to the house.

The past few weeks have been uneventful for AJ. He's driven the senator to and from Washington almost daily. The limousine is a government spec Lincoln Town Car with all the standard fare; bullet proof glass, reinforced frame, body, and door panels, GPS monitoring, satellite communications, Secure Channel cell phone, 2-way radio, etc. But it's also a slug to drive. While the engine and transmission have been beefed up to some degree, the car still weighs over 6,000 pounds. That's a lot to ask of a relatively stock engine. 0-60 takes almost ten seconds, and top speed is about 100-105, but who in their right mind would want to go that fast in a stretched Lincoln? AJ is getting bored.

Upon AJ's arrival at the estate, he's surprised to find the senator's limo still in the garage, rather than parked out front. He assumes Jeffrey, Higgins' detailer, probably overslept or was otherwise occupied. AJ gets in the car and turns the ignition key, but the limo won't start. Suspecting the battery is probably dead, he pops the inside hood release. But just as he's about to reach under the hood for the secondary release, he notices a small smudge on the hood near the hood ornament. He knows the car is thoroughly cleaned and wiped down every night, and the senator's detailer is a perfectionist. He'd have never missed something so obvious. While there are other vehicles at the estate, AJ decides to take the senator in his personal vehicle, a newly acquired, bright yellow Hummer H2.

As he escorts Senator Higgins out to his vehicle, the senator asks indignantly, "Where's the limo?"

AJ replies, "Your limo wouldn't start, so I thought we'd take mine instead." He opens the rear passenger side door for the senator, assists him into the vehicle, then closes the door behind him. Walking around toward the driver's side of the SUV, he pauses at the rear of the vehicle, pops the rear hatch, and removes a moderately sized black bag. He then continues on to the driver's side of the vehicle, gets in, and places the bag on the front passenger seat.

The senator is amazed by all of the appointments in AJ's vehicle. It has a sumptuous leather interior. There are video monitors mounted in the back of the headrests, and Headline News is on the monitor. He can faintly hear the familiar voice of the news commentator coming from a pair of wireless headphones lying on the other passenger seat. In the dash is a GPS display panel with trip computer, and there are two digital scanners mounted neatly underneath the dash, their LED's chasing each other across their faces. Located on the passenger side, next to the dash, is a pedestal mounted laptop computer, and it appears to be online with a web service. He also notices the engine sounds a bit rough, angry, definitely not factory tuned.

Once AJ starts heading into Washington, the senator asks, "What the hell is this? These damn things aren't cheap, and I know most of this stuff isn't standard equipment, and it certainly isn't government issue. And the last time I checked, I don't think you could afford one of these things on NCO or Secret Service pay."

"Well, Senator," he replies, "you're correct on all counts. This vehicle was originally built for a major drug lord in South America. DEA acquired it in a drug bust before it could be shipped out of the country. It had less than 1,500 miles on it. My former CO is now with the DEA and was in charge of the bust. He owed me a favor."

"A favor, huh?" chides the senator.

"You can relax, Senator. We have all of the amenities of your limo. We have bulletproof glass, Kevlar mounted in the floorboards and doors, GPS, satellite TV, Internet access, leather seating, plus we can go off road, if necessary. I believe there's even a mini bar behind the seat, sir."

"What kind of favor?" asks the senator.

"I saved his life in Iraq."

"Oh," replies the senator.

"Sir? Would you mind buckling up? I've never had any passengers in here before, and since this thing's a little top heavy, I might accidentally jostle you around a bit," AJ says to the senator, all the while watching him in the rear view mirror to make sure he complies.

The senator doesn't like seatbelts, never wears one in the limo. He hates the feeling of being tied down. But over the past few weeks, he has learned to trust AJ, even though he thinks that AJ's request is testing his limits of cooperation.

But AJ has an ulterior motive in asking the senator to buckle up. He senses that something bad is about to happen, and he doesn't want to worry about the senator bouncing all over the interior of his SUV.

AJ reaches over to the radio/GPS monitor, and touches a button that switches the display from GPS to a camera mounted at the rear of the vehicle near the roof rack. It provides an excellent view of the traffic behind them. He starts trading glances from what is going on ahead of them, to looking for any vehicles making sudden or suspicious movements behind them.

It doesn't take long for him to spot a black suburban with blacked out windows. It's weaving in and out of traffic, positioning itself closer to them. With that, AJ reaches over and unzips the bag he had placed in the passenger seat earlier.

"Senator?" Higgins looks up to AJ's call. "I don't mean to alarm you, but we seem to have picked up a tail. I know you're pretty good with a shotgun and your sporting clays, but just how good are you with a handgun?"

The senator sits upright and says, "Son, I served in Vietnam before most Americans even knew that country existed. I was a pilot for Air America. Handguns were about the only thing they'd let us carry back then. I can hold my own in a firefight."

With that comment from the senator, AJ reaches into the bag, and pulls out a rolled up, black webbed duty rig that holds a Beretta M9, along with a pouch holding another 2 magazines.

"Here, take this. If we get stopped, and the shit hits the fan, whatever you do, don't get out of the vehicle. You're relatively safe in here. If I have to get out, I'll activate the OnStar emergency alert system, and help will be on the way, pronto. But I say again. Do not get out of the vehicle! Have I made myself clear?"

"Crystal!" replies the senator, as he pulls the Beretta from the holster and racks the slide, loading a round into the chamber.

AJ eases off the accelerator to put some distance between them and a panel van immediately in front of him, just in case he needs to make some sort of emergency maneuver.

Without warning, that very van locks up its brakes, sliding into a broadside position in front of them. The side door of the van slides open to reveal a man in black fatigues, secured within the doorway with some kind of harness. He gets off two rounds of 00-buckshot, striking the windshield directly in front of AJ. Luckily, the bulletproof glass does its job. But the attack really pisses him off, so instead of attempting to stop or maneuver around the van, AJ floors the gas pedal. The Hummer lunges forward as though it had been struck from behind, and before the shooter can move, AJ's Hummer slams head-on into the side of the van, almost rolling it on top of the Hummer. AJ hits the brakes, causing the van to literally leap off the Hummer. And as the van begins to roll, it bursts into flames. Seconds later, the van explodes, killing everyone inside.

Out of the blue, a soft female voice comes over the OnStar Emergency System. "OnStar Communications. Our system indicates you have been in an accident. Is everyone okay?"

"Miss? I'm declaring an emergency. Check my file and look for Sierra, Sierra 55191. I need you to call the number attached to that code," says AJ in an authoritative voice.

Now that he's stopped, the suburban stops in the center lane at an angle about five or six car lengths behind AJ's Hummer. Three men jump out with their AK-47's blazing. The senator instinctively ducks for cover. AJ shifts into reverse, and floors the throttle again, this time aiming for the suburban, and any of the gunmen that might get in the way.

"Sir? I don't think I like your tone, and you haven't properly identified yourself. We have specific protocol that must be satisfied before I can review your file," she says curtly. "Do I hear gunfire? I see that your vehicle is moving again. Are you attempting to leave the scene of an accident?"

AJ manages to hit one of the gunmen while the other two dive for cover; one behind a car, the other behind the outside guardrail.

"Ma'am? I *really* need you to call the number attached to Sierra, Sierra 55191. This is an emergency!" While AJ continues his charge toward the suburban, the gunman next to the guard rail takes aim at the senator and gets off a few rounds, striking both the doors and the glass, but again, no penetration. The senator stares at the shooter as he goes by, but only the gunman's eyes are visible.

"Sir! If you do not properly identify yourself, I will be forced to call the local authorities, and tell them you are attempting to flee the scene of a crime, and I may be forced to immobilize your vehicle to facilitate your capture," demands the operator.

AJ yells out, "Brace yourself!" then slams into the Suburban's right front fender, hitting it so hard the Suburban's front wheel snaps off. The hood folds up like an accordion, almost obscuring the driver, who evidently isn't wearing his seatbelt. The force of the impact throws him over the steering wheel, and into the windshield, snapping his neck in the process.

"Sir? My sensors now indicate that you have been involved in yet another accident!" The operator hears nothing but silence now. "Sir? Sir? Are you all right?"

The second impact dazes AJ momentarily, and the two remaining gunmen decide to move in to finish them off. The first gunman approaches the driver's side, rifle at the ready. He stands a few feet away from the door and stares at AJ's motionless body.

Cautiously, he moves toward the door, then slowly reaches for the door handle. As the door latch releases, AJ kicks the door open, grabs the hot barrel of the gunman's AK-47 with his left hand, forcing it upward just as the gunman pulls the trigger. AJ shoots him twice in the upper chest, with a third round to the throat. The gunman releases his grip on the weapon, while he staggers backwards, drawing his last breaths, literally drowning in his own blood. Finally, he falls backwards to the pavement.

The last gunman, seeing AJ come to life, flings open the front passenger door and attempts to shoot AJ from behind. But the senator gets off two quick rounds, both striking him in the head. AJ sweeps his weapon to the passenger side just in time to watch the last gunman collapse onto the pavement. Both AJ and the senator look to each other, then both sighing with relief, lower their weapons.

Once again, the operator calls out, "Sir? What's going on? Who are you? And is everyone all right?"

"Ma'am? My name is Thomas Andrew Jackson. My password is Liberty. Will you please call the number attached to the code Sierra, Sierra 55191? In case you're wondering, you'll be putting in a call to the United States Secret Service. To answer your question as to our condition, yes, we're alive, but there are least six dead bodies out here on the highway that need to be picked up as soon as possible. I'm also willing to bet we've got quite a traffic jam out here, and it's morning rush hour. What do you say?"

"Yes sir! Yes sir! I'm calling them now. Is there anything else I can do for you?" pleads the operator.

"As a matter of fact there is. What's your name?"

"My name? It's ah, Debbie, sir," she replies rather hesitantly.

"Well, Debbie? I think my vehicle is going to need a tow. Better make it a flat bed. No, you better make that three flat beds and a fire truck," he says.

While the OnStar operator puts in a call to the Secret Service, several hundred morning commuters have already made calls from their cell phones, and now the sky is swarming with both police and news helicopters, plus police cars, ambulances, and other emergency vehicles are closing in from all directions.

AJ asks the senator to remain in the Hummer, more or less out of sight from the media, while he stands next to one of the bodies, both arms raised, his Beretta in one hand, and his Secret Service ID in the other. The senator can see AJ on one of the monitors in the Hummer, courtesy of Headline News. What a cluster! The turnpike is locked up for miles in both directions. It is quite a sight.

Minutes later, Secret Service agents arrive by helicopter. Three of them begin trying to determine the identity of the shooters, while two others escort the senator toward the helicopter.

As they pass by AJ, who is having his burned hand attended to by a paramedic, Senator Higgins stops, shakes AJ's good hand, and says, "Thank you. You saved my life. I'm sorry about your Hummer, though."

Both look back at the Hummer, riddled with bullet holes, broken glass, and mangled body parts. AJ then looks at the senator, smiles, and says, "I haven't owned it long enough to hate it yet. Besides, yellow really wasn't my color anyway."

The senator returns the smile, then leaves with the two Secret Service agents to board the helicopter. A second Secret Service helicopter lands a few minutes later and picks up AJ to take him to Washington for debriefing.

TLC: Chapter 5

Mr. Weathers meets the helicopter on the roof of the Homeland Security Building. As AJ exits the helicopter, Mr. Weathers starts asking questions. "What in the hell happened out there?"

"Everything started going south the moment I discovered the senator's limo wouldn't start. I bet if you send some agents to the estate, they'll find that someone has tampered with his vehicle."

"Well then, how did they know you and the senator were in your vehicle?"

"Obviously, someone has the senator's house under some sort of surveillance."

"Have you been performing regular electronic sweeps?" inquires Mr. Weathers.

"Yes and no, sir."

"What do you mean, yes and no?"

"Yes, I perform the sweeps every day, but I perform those sweeps at different times of the day. I don't want anyone to know when I'm going to do them."

"Good," says Mr. Weathers. "What about phone taps?"

"Checked every day, sir."

"What about deliveries? How are they handled?"

"Deliveries are met at the gate, and someone with security stays with them until they leave." answers AJ.

"What happened to your hand?"

"It's just a couple of minor burns from grabbing the barrel of an AK-47. It's nothing, really." AJ pauses for a moment. "Sir?"

"Yes, AJ?"

"What really bothers me is why. This was an assassination attempt on a U.S. Senator, in broad daylight, and in public. It was obviously well planned, and executed. If I had been driving the Crown Vic, or any other car from the senator's estate, you'd be scraping our bodies off the pavement instead of theirs."

AJ continues, "To my knowledge, the senator hasn't made any formal announcement about his plans to seek the Presidency. In fact, he hasn't even mentioned anything to me about that. There have been no threats on his life that I'm aware of. Everything seems to be normal, absolutely nothing out of the ordinary. So, why, and why now?"

"Well, AJ?" sighs Weathers. "That's why you're out there, to protect the senator, and to find out why."

"Now that we know the senator's life is in danger, what about a team, sir?"

"Unless the senator requests it, and the President authorizes it, you're the man, AJ. And I just got off the phone with the senator, and he has complete confidence in you."

"Who does he think I am, the Terminator?"

"Well, it's not every day someone takes out seven assassins and only discharges his weapon three times," remarks Weathers with a grin on his face.

"Let's not forget the senator fired two rounds, taking out one of them, and I totaled my Hummer in the process of taking out the others."

"Yes, thank goodness it *was* your Hummer. Just think of all the paperwork you'd be filling out right about now. And let's not forget about the investigation, the review board and…" You can tell Weathers is starting to get under AJ's skin, and he's enjoying every minute of it. "By the way, when did you get a Hummer, and what possessed you to get a yellow one? Do you enjoy standing out in a crowd?"

"Well, maybe I *should* have been driving the Crown Vic," counters AJ, sounding more than a little perturbed. "Then we wouldn't be having this conversation, and *you* would be filling out a lot of paperwork, buried up to your eyeballs in investigations and the review board," replies AJ, trading barbs with Weathers. "And, for your information, I just picked up the Hummer over the weekend. It was confiscated in a major drug bust, and my former CO owed me a favor. It was certainly cheap enough, and I couldn't afford to complain about the color. Okay?"

"Enough of this bull shit! See what the other agents have learned about your dead assassins," says Weathers. "I'll leave the two agents with the senator for now, and let you try to make some sense out of all this. But no screwing around. Now get out of my office and get back to work!"

"Yes, sir!" barks AJ as he heads for the door. "By the way, sir, who do I talk to about getting my Hummer replaced?"

"You have insurance, right?" asks Weathers flippantly. "I suppose you should talk to them, don't you? I'll bet GEICO can't wait to hear from you."

"Okay, Bob. I'll give you this round, but your time is coming. You can trust me on that," he says. Weathers hates being called Bob, and you can almost see steam rising from his balding head.

"Out! Get out and get back to work!"

***

AJ requisitions a car from the motor pool and drives out to the Bethesda Naval Medical Hospital, where the bodies of the assassins have been taken.

He makes his way down to the morgue to meet the agents who have begun trying to find out who they were, before doctors begin performing autopsies on them. This time, the agents introduce themselves.

"Agent Jackson? I'm Special Agent Michael Rollins, and this is Special Agent Steven Anderson, and Special Agent Wesley Niles."

"Well, what do we have?" asks AJ.

"For starters, we have seven dead bodies," says Agent Niles with a smirk on his face.

"Amazing! We have an agent who can count. Look smart ass. That was Senator Higgins' and my ass those guys were shooting at, and you don't see me laughing. So, do you want to try that again?"

"Sorry sir. I was just trying to lighten the situation a bit," replies Agent Niles.

"Business first, levity later. Now, one more time. What do we have so far?"

"Not much, sir," says Agent Rollins. "The three men in the van are crispy critters. The lab doesn't know if they'll be able to tell much about them. The bodies were burned so badly, there's not much left for a DNA sample."

"Okay, what about the van they were driving?"

31

"It was stolen two days ago from a dealership in Virginia. The dealer didn't even know it was missing until we called and inquired about it," says Agent Anderson.

"How do they know it's only been missing for two days?" asks AJ.

"Because that was when it was delivered to the dealership," replies Anderson.

"Good work. Okay, what about the suburban?"

"Nothing yet, sir. We're kinda puzzled on that one, too," says Niles.

"What do you mean?" asks AJ.

"Well sir, for starters, the license plate is a phony. The numbers aren't registered with DMV or NCIC. The VIN tag by the windshield is bogus, too. It's a GM plate, but the numbers and letters don't match up to any GM make or model. Plus the numbers stamped on the chassis, engine, transmission, and rear axle, have been disfigured. Someone really knew what they were doing. It's going to take a while to figure that one out."

"Make sure you keep somebody on it," says AJ. "Hopefully, that'll lead us somewhere. Now, what about the other bodies? What do we know about them?"

"Not much at this stage of the game, sir. No IDs of any kind were found on them," says Rollins.

"What about fingerprints, scars, tattoos, haircuts? Any of idea of their nationality?" asks AJ.

"I doubt we'll get anything back on their fingerprints. All of them seem to have been disfigured by acid or a similar substance. But by their haircuts, and general overall appearance, we believe they're American, sir," says Anderson.

"Almost certainly military, too," says Niles.

"What about tattoos?" asks AJ.

"Well, most of the men had tattoos at one time, but it appears they were surgically removed. All we know is the tattoos were located in almost exactly the same place on all of the assassins, except one," says Anderson.

"Where? Show me."

AJ and the three agents enter the morgue, and uncover the nearest body. On his right upper arm is evidence of a surgically removed tattoo.

The area is approximately four inches wide and a little over an inch high. AJ moves his arm around, trying to get some sort of reflection or shading for any clues that might help him determine what the tattoo might have been. "Nothing," he says disappointingly. "Whatever the tattoo was, it must have been removed some time ago."

The agents start uncovering the other bodies, and AJ checks them one by one.

"Nothing. Nothing!" Suddenly, AJ stops dead cold at the side of the assassin he had shot, staring at his face.

It's obvious something has struck a nerve with him. AJ turns around, and bolts out of the morgue, leaving the three agents puzzled and surprised. The agents strike out after AJ, attempting to catch up with him.

"What? What's wrong?" yells Rollins.

"Nothing," says AJ, shaking his head as he continues to charge down the hallway toward the exit.

"Don't give me that. You know something. What is it?" asks Rollins as he finally catches up to AJ.

As Rollins reaches out and touches AJ's shoulder, AJ turns around, grabs Rollins by his shoulders, and pins him to the wall, yelling, "I knew that guy! I helped train that guy! We shared the same foxhole, the same canteen. I was even at his sister's wedding. He was reported missing and presumed dead about a year ago. And I just killed him!"

"Where did you train him?" asks Rollins.

"Don't you get it? He's a Marine! They're all Marines! Or at least, those four men were," replies AJ, his voice filled with anguish and emotion. He releases Agent Rollins, takes a couple of steps back, then strikes out down the hallway again. As agents Anderson and Niles join Rollins, Rollins yells out, "Why didn't the last guy have a tattoo?"

"Because David hated needles!"

***

Lance Corporal David McKenzie was just a normal kid wanting to make a better life for himself. David came from a broken home. From a very early age, he had seen and heard his

33

parents get into vicious arguments and fights. One night, their dad came home drunk. That in itself was not unusual. But on this particular night, it appeared their father had been in a fight, and by the looks of it, he had probably lost. His left eye was almost swollen shut, his nose was swollen and bloody, and both hands were bruised and bleeding. His shirt was torn and half out of his trousers.

As he staggered into the house, their mom met him at the door and tried to help him to the bathroom and tend to his wounds. But he would have none of that. He told her to get away, that he could take care of himself. As she continued to try to get him to the bathroom, he backhanded her across the face, knocking her off her feet, and slamming her to the floor. Her left arm struck the kitchen table on the way down, breaking it just below the elbow.

David's brother, Tim jumped up and charged his dad, screaming at the top of his lungs. David was right behind him, while Lisa tried to hide behind the sofa, sobbing and crying out for her mother. Once the boys finally subdued their father, David dialed 911.

That would be the last time they saw their father alive. David was twelve years old when his father left them, leaving his mom to care for him, his younger sister, Lisa, age ten, and his older brother, Tim, age fourteen. Six months later, the police came by the house and asked their mom to accompany them to the hospital. Their father had evidently gotten drunk again and into another fight. But this time, someone drove his nose into his brain and killed him.

Tim, was constantly getting into trouble after that. He got in with a bad crowd, and soon he was smoking, drinking, and getting into fights, just like his dad. By age sixteen, Tim had dropped out of school, and every cop in town had him in the backseat of their squad at one time or another.

Then, one day Tim didn't come home. David, now fourteen, got on his bike and started looking for him. David knew all of Tim's so-called friends, and he sought out each and every one of them, but no one would admit to having seen Tim that day.

It was getting dark, and David had just about given up hope, when he remembered a place where the two of them would go when they just wanted to be alone. It was an old abandoned shack near the railroad tracks.

As David approached the shack, he called out Tim's name, but there was no response. It seemed eerily quiet, and David was starting to feel very apprehensive about going into the shack, but he knew he had to make sure Tim wasn't in there. As he entered the shack, he could barely make out a figure slumped over in the corner, almost invisible in the shadows. David called out, "Tim? Tim? Is that you?" But Tim said nothing. Then David saw the needle stuck in his arm. Tim was dead.

***

AJ can't get David's face out of his mind. *"Who were the other Marines with him? Were David and the other men working undercover on some sort of covert operation? And if so, who were they working for? And why were they trying to kill the senator?"* He decides that it's time to sit down and have a serious talk with Senator Higgins. As he walks toward his car in the parking lot, he sees the sun starting to set. *"Damn!"* he says under his breath. *"Talk about a wasted day."* He gets in the car, and as he approaches the intersection that would take him back to Washington, he suddenly veers back toward the expressway. *"Lisa! I wonder if she's heard from David over the last year."* AJ drives toward Brookmont.

***

Lisa Marie McKenzie/McNee is married to Sean Patrick McNee and lives in Brookmont with their two young sons, Timothy and David, named after her brothers, of course. Lisa and her brother, David, had always been close, but became even more so after their father and Tim had died. They were almost inseparable.

David and Sean were the same age, played football together, with David as quarterback, and Sean as one of his primary receivers. The two of them formed a unique bond, which later included Lisa.

With the exception of David, Lisa feared all men, and it was only because of the bond which David and Sean shared, that she

35

entertained the thought of going out with Sean. Initially, you really couldn't call them dates, because it was just the three of them. I guess you'd call it hanging out. But David could see that Sean was growing fond of Lisa, and Lisa seemed to be warming up to Sean, so the three of them started double dating. David never really had a steady girlfriend, but he also never had a problem finding someone willing to go out with him.

By the time David and Sean graduated high school, Sean and Lisa's relationship had solidified, and David felt comfortable leaving her in Sean's hands. Shortly after she graduated high school, Lisa moved in with Sean. Then, a little over a year later, Sean and Lisa were married, with David in his dress Marine uniform, standing in for their dad. David had been a member of AJ's squad for a little over 6 months, so it was natural for him to invite AJ to Lisa's wedding. AJ would also be invited to both of her son's christenings. But AJ would also be there when Lisa got the news that David was missing and presumed dead.

TLC: Chapter 6

AJ pulls up in front of Lisa and Sean's brownstone. The lights are on, and he can see an occasional shadow moving by the windows. They're home. AJ is trying to think of an excuse as to why he'd drop by without any apparent reason. He doesn't want to arouse suspicion too soon into the conversation. After all, the last time he saw her was David's funeral at Arlington Cemetery. Now, he's about to tell her the same thing again, but this time, there's a body with three bullet holes in it, and he's the one who put them there.

AJ walks up to the front door, hesitates for a moment, takes a deep breath, then rings the doorbell.

"Mommy! Mommy! Someone's at the door!" yells little Tim.

Lisa goes to the door, turns on the front porch light, then peeks through the curtain to see who's there. "AJ!" she exclaims, as she hastily unbolts the door and opens it. "What a pleasant surprise! Come on in! What brings you all the way to Brookmont? Aren't you still in the Corps?" He walks in, and she wraps her arms around him, giving him a big hug. "I haven't seen or heard from you since the funeral. How have you been?"

He says, "I'm no longer on active duty, and I've joined the Secret Service. I realized I was getting older, and getting up at 0400 every morning had long since gotten old. I figured I'd find out what sleeping in was like." AJ forces a smile as does Lisa.

"Come on in and have a seat. Have you eaten? I was just cleaning up the dishes from dinner. There's still plenty to eat, and most of it is still warm."

"Thanks. It has been a long time since breakfast, and I haven't enjoyed a good, home cooked meal in years." He pauses a moment, then says, "Sure, why not?"

"Well then. Come on into the kitchen, and let's see what we can whip up." Lisa grabs him by the left hand, and AJ winces from the pain. "What happened to your hand?"

"Oh, it's nothing," replies AJ. "I burned it on the job. Nothing serious."

"How? Let me see. Oh! What did you do? It looks like you grabbed a pipe or something."

"Stay alive," he says with some degree of disappointment.

37

"What are you talking about? What happened?" she asks.

"First, I need to ask you a few questions, and I need you to be totally honest with me," he says, while looking Lisa straight in the eyes.

"Of course," she replies. "What's wrong?"

"I need to know if you've heard from David since the funeral."

"What? Are you crazy? David is dead. You know that," she replies sarcastically. She also appears to be hurt and angry.

"Lisa, the correct phrase is missing and presumed dead. No bodies were ever found. Not one."

"Are you trying to tell me that David is alive?" she asks while turning away from him, raising suspicions she might be hiding something.

"Lisa, I need you to look at me and tell me the truth," he says, as he gently grabs her arm, and turns her back to face him. "Has David been in contact with you since the funeral?"

"What are you doing? Let go of me. David is dead!"

"You're right. David *is* dead."

"What? What do you mean?" asks Lisa with a surprised look on her face.

"Were you watching TV this morning?"

"Off and on, why?" Then her eyes open wide as she realizes what he is about to tell her. "You were in that shootout on the expressway this morning! The news said seven terrorists attempted to kill a senator, but failed. It was a mess! There was one vehicle on fire, and two others seriously damaged. Traffic was tied up for hours. Did you have anything to do with that?"

"Yes. I was the man protecting the senator."

"What about the terrorists? What happened to them? Who were they working for?"

"They're all dead, and we don't know who they were working for, or what they expected to benefit by killing the senator."

"So, what does that have to do with David?"

"David was one of the terrorists."

"What? You're lying! You're lying! David is not a terrorist! He loves his country!" Little David and Tim come running into the kitchen crying, with both of them clinging to Lisa's legs.

"Then, Lisa? Someone set David up to look like a terrorist. You've got to tell me everything David told you. I need to get to the bottom of this. It's the only way I'll be able to clear his name."

"Wait a minute. You said all of the terrorists were dead, and you were protecting the senator. Was anyone else with you, besides the senator?"

"No, it was just the senator and me. All of the terrorists wore black clothing and hoods that covered their faces. Three of the terrorists charged the vehicle. David was one of them, and I shot him."

Lisa's eyes begin to fill with tears, and she starts shaking her head in disbelief, sobbing and crying out, "No, no, no! I am not believing this!"

"I'm sorry Lisa, but I had no idea it was David, and it was either take his life or lose mine. I'm trained to survive, just as David was."

"Get out of my house!"

"Lisa, I need your help. I need to know everything David told you about what he was doing, and who he was working for," he pleads.

"Get out of my house! Now! You murderer! Get out! Get out!"

"Lisa? Right now, you're the only lead I have in finding out what all of this is about. I can't help you or David unless you help me. If David becomes labeled as a terrorist, they will not allow his body to be interred at Arlington. In fact, his cross will be removed and destroyed. You know he wasn't a terrorist, and I know he wasn't a terrorist. But I've got to be able to prove it. I owe him that much."

Suddenly, the power goes off. Little David and Tim start crying even louder. Through a window, AJ can see the neighbor's lights are still on. "On the floor, now!"

"Why? What's happening?"

"You're about to have some uninvited guests bearing some very unpleasant gifts," he says while pulling out his Beretta, releasing the safety. "Do you have a safe place to hide?"

"There's a closet under the basement stairs."

"Good. Take the kids down there, and do your best to keep them quiet. Your very lives may depend on it."

"What are you going to do?"

"I'm going to let them know that we don't want anything they're selling. Now get out of here, and let me take care of business," he says firmly.

As Lisa gathers up the boys, and heads for the basement, AJ crawls to the bathroom located in the hallway between the kitchen and the dining room/living room. From that vantage point, he can see both the front and back doors.

He pulls out his cell phone, and just as he starts to dial 911, someone opens up on the back door with what sounds like a suppressed H&K MP5. Splinters and debris go flying! A man kicks the door open and fires another random burst, while sweeping the room with the attached spotlight and laser.

AJ fires two rounds into his chest, but the gunman just flinches from the impacts, and continues to fire. Realizing he must be wearing a bulletproof vest, AJ fires three rounds at kneecap level, with at least one round hitting the mark. The gunman drops to the floor in agonizing pain. Now with the light out his eyes, AJ fires another two rounds striking the gunman in the head.

No sooner has AJ finished off the first gunman, a second one takes out the front door, then dives into the living room, landing behind a couch. AJ fires two rounds into the couch where he thinks the man should be. The gunman pops up and unleashes the entire magazine toward him. AJ tucks back into the bathroom and balls up behind the cast iron tub, flinching as the rounds strike the tub, sending shards of shattered porcelain into the air, along with wood splinters, shattered tile, and mortar dust.

But then, the second gunman makes a fatal mistake. Out of ammunition, and assuming he has taken out AJ, he remains upright while changing out the empty magazine. AJ rolls out of the bathroom and squeezes off three rounds at him. All three find their mark. One hits near the top of his vest, the second nicks his jugular vein, and the third grazes his temple. His arms go limp, dropping his weapon. He staggers a moment as he attempts to remain erect, before finally collapsing behind the couch. AJ visually checks both doors to see if anyone else might be about to come in, but all that can be heard is a neighbor's dog barking his head off.

AJ crawls over to the second gunman and finds him lying in a pool of blood, gasping for air. He's dying. AJ asks him, "Who are you? Who do you work for?"

The gunman looks up at him, and whispers, "TLC."

AJ says, "What?"

The gunman is losing consciousness due to the rapid loss of blood. As his hand slowly slides away from his wound, he mutters, "T...L...Ceee."

AJ shakes his body in an effort to awaken him, but it's too late. He's gone. AJ rises to his feet, and heads down to the basement. It is pitch black down there, cluttered, damp, and musty. He reaches into his coat pocket and pulls out a small flashlight. He can hear the children whimpering and finds the door under the stairs. AJ says in a calm voice, "It's over. You can come out now."

Lisa slowly opens the door and sees him standing there in silhouette. "Are you okay?"

"I'm fine. Grab what you think you're going to need for the next couple of days, and let's get the heck out of Dodge."

"What are you talking about?" she asks. "We can't leave here. What about the kids? I'm going to need a change of clothes for the kids and me, pajamas, toys..."

"Lisa, we don't have time to do all that. We've got to go. Now! I can't protect you here. Besides you don't have a front or back door anymore, and there are two dead bodies upstairs."

"Aren't the police coming?"

"I'm sure they are, but I don't know who else is coming with them. Lisa? Don't you get it? Two guys just shot up your house! They didn't come here for me. They came here to take care of you."

"What about Sean? What am I going to tell him?"

"Let me worry about that. Lisa, please. Just go on upstairs, grab a couple of things, and let's get the hell out of here. Now!"

Lisa gives him a stern look, then grabs each boy by the hand and stomps her way up the stairs. When she gets to the top of the stairs, she lets out a shriek. "Oh my god! Look at this mess! Everything's ruined! What am I going to tell Sean?"

AJ walks up behind her, rests his hand on her shoulder and says in a calmer tone, "It'll be all right. Just go on upstairs, grab some of the kids' things, and let's get out of here, okay?"

While Lisa and boys go upstairs, AJ rushes out the front door towards his car. Once he gets in and starts it, his headlights shine on another Crown Vic a couple of houses down. It has a government plate on it, G17399. He writes the number down for future reference, then backs the car into the driveway next to the house, close to the back door. He hits the remote trunk release and opens the back doors. As he passes the open trunk, he realizes something is missing. His black bag. *"Oh shit!"* He says to himself.

As he walks past what's left of the back door, he sees Lisa struggling toward him hidden behind what appears to be a blanket stuffed with the children's clothing and toys. He asks, "What in the hell are you doing? Moving? Where are the kids?"

Without warning, Lisa seems to trip, falling forward onto the bundle, and to his surprise, he can see duct tape covering her mouth. Suddenly, a third gunman pops up behind her and opens up on him! AJ tries to duck behind the refrigerator, but one of the rounds manages to nick his left arm before he can fully cover himself.

He quickly pulls out his Beretta again, then remembers he hasn't changed out the magazine! His mind races. *"How many times did I fire? Two, then three, two, two again, then three. Twelve rounds! Only three left, I better make this good."*

He peeks out from behind the refrigerator to see the gunman is waiting for him, baiting the gunman into firing another burst. Then AJ hears the tell tale sign of an empty magazine. While the gunman struggles to reload, AJ steps out from behind the refrigerator, marches toward him, and fires two rounds into his face. As the shooter drops to the floor, AJ reaches down, rips the tape from Lisa's lips and asks, "Are you all right?" She nods her head. "Well then, can we get the kids and get the hell out of here?" He reaches down, takes her hand, and helps her to her feet. While walking up the stairs, AJ swaps in a fresh magazine, and pockets the empty one. Both of them grab one of the boys, then hurry back down the stairs, hop in the car, and make their escape.

Rounding the first corner, they're almost run off the road by four police cars with lights flashing and sirens blaring, followed closely by a couple of ambulances. Less than a block behind them, three more cars with hideaway emergency lights come flying by, but no sirens. The cars appear to be unmarked. AJ says to himself, "*If it were just one unmarked car, it might have been a supervisor or a detective, but three unmarked cars back to back? No, the last three cars weren't cops.*"

"Where are we going?" asks Lisa.

"I've got to find someplace safe for you and the kids. But first, we've got to make a little side trip."

"Side trip?"

"Yep, there's something I need to pick up."

"And where might that be?"

"The government impound yard."

"Really? This should be interesting."

About a half hour later, AJ pulls up to the gate of the government impound yard. The guard approaches the driver's side of the car, flashlight in his left hand, and his right hand on his side arm. "Identification please. State your business."

AJ shows his ID and says, "Jackson, Thomas A. Secret Service, ID number Sierra, Sierra 55191. My Hummer was brought in here earlier today. I left my jump bag in there, and I need to pick it up."

"That Hummer was yours? Man! That thing looked like it was in a war! So, you're the guy who popped all those terrorists. My hats off to you, sir," says the guard. "You'll find your vehicle on row M, space number fifty-six. Be careful sir. We have a couple of dogs roaming the yard for added security. They shouldn't bother you, though."

"How's that?" asks AJ.

"Well, sir? You're coming in the front gate, rather than over the fence. The dogs don't like people who come over the fence. Goes against their nature," he says with a smile. "Do you mind if I ask you a question?"

"I guess not. Go ahead."

"Why yellow?" asks the guard.

"Simple. It was on sale," AJ replies.

"Makes sense, I guess. Just be careful out there. And keep an eye out for those dogs."

"Thanks. Will do."

AJ drives into the impound yard, finds row M, and sure enough, his Hummer is sitting in space number fifty-six. The Hummer looks worse than he remembered, sitting there in the dark, bathed only in the faint glow of the yard's halide lights.

Peering through the passenger side window, he can see his jump bag still sitting on the seat where he had left it. He grabs the door handle, but it's locked. Then he realizes he left the keys with the towing company at the site of the incident. Someone had locked the doors as a security measure. Luckily, AJ has a spare set hidden inside the right rear fender.

Reaching blindly underneath the fender, AJ finds the keys, but he also finds something else. He reaches into his coat pocket and pulls out his trusty flashlight. Lying on his back, he eases underneath the Hummer to get a better look at his discovery. It appears to be a metal box, roughly two inches by two inches by six inches. There are no visible screws or identifying marks on it. There are two wires coming off the box. One of these wires seems to go to the fuel tank. At first, he thinks that it's a bomb, but if it were, why didn't somebody just trip it while they were on the expressway? It would have been a lot easier to accomplish, along with sparing the lives of seven men. Then he realizes that it must be some sort of transmitter or transponder. The wire leading to the fuel tank probably used the fuel pump wire as an ignition source. The other wire coming off the box had to be the antenna. *"So that's how they found us."* AJ says to himself.

The transmitter is held in place by a powerful magnet. He takes out his pocketknife, clips the ignition wire, and pries the unit from the inner fender panel. The unit falls on his chest. *"Damn this thing is heavy for its size."*

Suddenly, AJ can hear the panting of a dog, and it's getting closer! He's looking all around trying to determine where the dog is coming from, but sees nothing. Then, from out of nowhere, AJ is startled by a firm jab to his groin. He slowly lifts his head and looks down toward his legs to see what appears to be a Doberman/Rottweiler mix with its muzzle buried in his crotch. The dog looks up at AJ, shows his teeth, and begins a very low growl. AJ says to himself, *"Damn! He's got to weigh over a hundred pounds and half of that's gotta be teeth!"* Then, both the dog and AJ hear another dog barking in the distance. The dog turns toward the barking, then charges off in that direction.

AJ takes advantage of the situation by quickly rolling out from under the Hummer, and breathing a sigh of relief. He unlocks the passenger door, grabs the bag, and tosses the transmitter into it. Just as he is about to close the door, he remembers giving the senator his backup piece. He looks in the backseat, but doesn't see it. Then he checks between and under the front and back seats. Nothing. *"Well, I hope the senator took it with him,"* he says to himself, and gives the Hummer one final sweep.

Returning to the Crown Vic, AJ pops the trunk release and drops the bag into the trunk. As he opens the driver's door, he sees Little David and Tim sound asleep in the back seat. After he gets into the car, he eases the door closed, in an effort to not wake the kids.

Lisa says, "You don't have to worry about them. They usually play so hard during the day, that when they go to sleep, a bomb wouldn't wake them up." With that remark, Lisa tries to force a smile, but AJ can see the hurt in her eyes.

Back on the road, he's racking his brain trying to think of a safe place for Lisa and the kids. Then it strikes him like a bolt of lightning. The perfect place, the perfect vengeance. Where else? *"Robert Weathers' place, of course!"*

AJ says, "I need to get you somewhere safe, so you can put the kids to bed, and get yourself some rest."

"What about Sean? I still haven't contacted Sean."

"Where is Sean?"

"He's out of town on business. He's not due back until the end of the week."

"We've got to find you a land line, so you can give him a call. Do you have his hotel number or a cell number to contact him?"

"Can't I just use my cell phone, or yours and call him now?"

"We can't afford to chance it. They may have a tap on your line."

"Who are *they*?"

"*They* are the ones David was working for. *They* are the ones who tried to kill the senator and me today. *They* are the ones who shot up your house, and tried to kill all of us. I don't know who *they* are yet, but I'm going to find out," says AJ with a determined tone in his voice.

TLC: Chapter 8

AJ pulls up in front of Mr. Weathers' house, and says, "We're here."

"Where exactly is here?" asks Lisa.

"Robert Weathers' place. He's former Army intelligence, but now, he's my boss. I need to warn you though. He's got a mean bark, but he's essentially harmless. Not much bite if you know what I mean."

"Yes, I understand. Kind of like David, right?"

As AJ gets out of the car, and picks up Little David from the back seat, he says, "Right, but louder, much louder." The two of them walk up to Mr. Weathers' front door. AJ rings the doorbell, waits about ten seconds, then rings it again. Finally, he sees a couple of lights come on in the house.

Weathers sees AJ through the peephole in the door, and starts swearing before he gets the door open. "AJ? Do you have any idea what time it is?"

"It's way past their bedtime sir. Where do you want me to put them?" he asks as he walks past Weathers holding the door.

Lisa follows him into the house, smiles at Weathers, and says, "Hello."

"What? What the hell are you doing? What is this all about? Who are these people? And what do you mean, where do you want me to put them? This is my house, not a hotel. AJ, answer me!" he bellows.

Lisa says to AJ with a smirk, "You're right. He is louder than David."

"What? Who the hell is David? AJ? I want some answers. *Right now!*"

As Mrs. Weathers enters the living room, she says, "Honey? What's all the commotion about?" She spots Lisa and Tim and says, "Oh my! What a cute little boy. He must be tired." Little Tim is unconscious, thank goodness.

"Hi. My name is Lisa McNee. This is my son Tim, and AJ's holding little David."

"You're out awfully late, aren't you?" asks Mrs. Weathers.

"Yes ma'am," answers AJ. "So far this evening, we've confronted three well-armed men that remodeled her home, and I

47

think I found a GPS transponder on my Hummer. And that doesn't include the fact that earlier today, I was shot at, totaled my Hummer, killed a friend and fellow Marine, and I may have uncovered some type of government conspiracy or cover-up."

"AJ?" says Weathers, "That's enough about business. I don't talk about business in this house. Let's go outside and get some fresh air, then tell me what you have. Let me grab my coat."

As AJ hands little David over to Mrs. Weathers, Lisa shouts, "AJ! You've been shot!"

"What? You mean this? No," he says with a smile and a light chuckle. "It's just a scratch. Hardly touched me, see?"

Sure enough, under closer inspection, Lisa sees that even though the bullet had torn through his jacket and shirt, the bullet had just barely broken the skin. AJ had been lucky.

As Mrs. Weathers and Lisa head upstairs to one of the spare bedrooms to put the little boys to bed, Lisa says, "I'm going to tend to that as soon as we're done up here."

AJ nods his head, then he and Weathers walk out the front door, and down the steps to AJ's car. He begins telling Weathers everything he had discovered. "I drove over to Bethesda Naval Hospital and met with Agents Rollins, Anderson, and Niles. As I was debriefing them, we discovered that it appears most, if not all, of the assassins were ex-military, and at least four of them were Marines. Three of the four men had tattoos surgically removed, and by their size and shape, they were the approximate size of the USMC tattoo."

"And what about the fourth man?" queries Weathers.

"Lance Corporal David McKenzie was the fourth man, sir. He was in my squad for a time. We developed a bond of sorts. A little over a year ago, he was transferred to another unit. A few months later, he was reported missing and presumed dead along with four other Marines due to a training accident. David would never betray his country sir. He loved his country."

"David," says Weathers. "Isn't that the name of one of her boys?"

"Yes, sir, Lisa is David's sister. I believe that whomever David was working for, suspected he had been talking to Lisa, and decided to take care of any loose ends. I just happened to be

48

there, or she'd be the one on the floor in a pool of blood, along with her two boys."

"Have you questioned her yet?"

"I was in the process when they arrived to remodel the house."

"Are they all dead?"

"Yes sir, but before one of them died, I asked him who he was working for. He said something that sounded like TLC. I noticed a couple of other things, too."

"Such as?"

"Both attacks have been with an odd number of men. Then as we were leaving the house, there were three unmarked cars with hideaway warning lights following about a block behind the police cars and ambulances. That makes seven, three, and three. Do you think that means something?"

"Could be," says Weathers. "Maybe, maybe not. What makes you think the three assassins worked for the government?"

"How about the fact they were driving a Crown Vic with government plates?"

"I don't suppose you wrote down the tag number, did you?"

"Yes, sir, I did," he replies while pulling a piece of paper from his inside coat pocket. "It's G17399."

"Hmmm. All odd numbers again," says Weathers. "Maybe your idea of everything relating to odd numbers is a clue. You said something about a transmitter?"

"Yes, sir. In the course of all the confusion surrounding the attack this morning, I left my jump bag in the Hummer. Once I realized I'd left it there, I drove out to the impound yard to retrieve it. I keep a spare set of keys hidden on the vehicle, and I discovered the transmitter while trying to find my keys."

"Do you have it with you?"

"Yes, sir, right here," says AJ as he reaches into the bag, and hands it to him.

"Yes, this is government issue, all right," replies Weathers. "Do you mind if I hang onto it and see if I can find out who signed for it?"

"What do you mean?"

"These things aren't cheap, even by government standards. This is an inventoried item. So, if it's inventoried, somebody

49

checked it out. And if someone checked it out, we can find out who it was."

Weathers continues, "Well, AJ? It looks like you've done a pretty good job today. And you've certainly discovered enough stuff to keep me busy for a while. I'll start on the transponder first thing, and I'll have my secretary run this tag number to see which department the vehicle is registered to. And then I'll see what I can dig up on that TLC thing."

As the two of them start walking back up the steps to his house, Weathers pats AJ on the back and says, "Now, I think it would be a good idea if we all tried to get some sleep, don't you?"

"Yes, sir, thank you sir," says AJ as he starts to follow Weathers into the house.

"Well then, AJ? I guess I'll talk to you tomorrow. Goodnight," says Weathers while closing the door on him. AJ stands there for a moment, staring at the door. As he starts down the steps, he hears the door open once again. He turns and starts back up the steps when Weathers says, "AJ? You will be out at the senator's estate by 0800 hours tomorrow, right?"

"Yes, sir."

"Good. I'd hate for you to be late for work, especially after all of this running around you've been doing tonight. Hurry home and get some rest. If tomorrow is anything like today, you're going to need it. Goodnight." Weathers closes the door once again, and turns off the porch light, leaving AJ alone in the darkness.

AJ slowly walks down the steps to his car, gets in, and starts the car. He looks out the window, staring at the front of Weathers' house. He watches the lights go out on the second floor, sighs, then drives off.

TLC: Chapter 9
AJ's apartment
Tuesday morning
June 14, 2011, 0030 hours local time

AJ finally makes it back home. His two-bedroom apartment is somewhat sparse. Having been with the Marines for over twenty years, there had been no need for much in the way of furniture, or personal items.

The Marines had been his life 24/7. It was either military fatigues or dress uniform. Okay, so there were the occasional weekends out with the guys or girls, but how does anyone screw up casual wear?

The Secret Service was a real stretch for him, at least in the clothing department. Suits had to be coordinated with shirts, ties, shoes, and socks. Thank goodness for J.C. Penney's and Sears' mix and match.

The first few months were an absolute nightmare, but overall he held his own. While you wouldn't call AJ a neat freak, his apartment certainly looks better than most other single men would have. It must have been some of that military training and organization etched into his brain.

The living room consists of a simple cream colored couch and matching chair, coffee and end tables, a couple of generic table lamps, a modest stereo, and an LCD flat screen TV. The master bedroom is home to a pair of nightstands, dresser, and king size bed. You can still bounce a quarter off the mattress. While there are few pictures on the dresser and one of the nightstands, the walls are painfully bare. The second bedroom is a combination office and workout room.

AJ makes his way to the bedroom, pulls off his jacket, takes a look at the bullet hole, even pokes his finger through it, sighs, then tosses it on the bed. He removes his tie and shoulder rig, then unbuttons his shirt. While standing in front of the mirrored closet door, he takes it off and studies the blood stained bullet hole. He says to himself, *"I wonder if there's enough sleeve left to make a short sleeve shirt out of it?"*

Once down to his boxers, he wanders down to the bathroom, and turns on the shower. While waiting for the water to get hot, he opens the medicine cabinet, and takes out some alcohol, a couple of 3x3 pads, and ointment for his wound, laying them neatly on the counter. He tests the water temperature, drops his shorts, and steps into the shower. As he leans against the shower wall, the water cascades over his face and down his body, allowing the tingling effect to relax and massage his muscles. Afterward, he dries himself off, then walks over to the counter to tend his wound. He dabs the alcohol onto one of the pads, cleans the wound, then applies the ointment, but leaves the wound exposed to help speed the healing process.

AJ slips on some shorts, heads back to the bedroom, and retrieves the empty magazine from his jacket along with his Beretta. He returns to the second bedroom, and opens the closet door to reveal a significant inventory of weapons and ammunition. There's a Steyr AUG, a Colt M-4, and a Colt M16A2 with an M206 grenade launcher. Both Colts are equipped with Trijicon ACOG scopes. There's an H&K MP5 with collapsible stock, suppressor, forearm spotlight, and pulse laser, plus an H&K MP5K with pulse laser. For long-range targets, there's a Remington M700 Police Sniper's Rifle in .308 caliber, with a Swarovski Auto Ranging Scope. And finally, there are two shotguns, a Benelli M3 Super 90 select fire 12-gauge shotgun equipped with ghost ring night sights, and an FIE LAW-12, also with night sights and spotlight.

The handgun department is a little less intimidating. There are two Beretta M9's, two 92FS Centurions, all with night sites, and a rare 93R, fully automatic model along with a half dozen 30-round magazines next to it. AJ opens the drawer below the handguns, and pulls out a cleaning kit, then settles down at the desk to thoroughly disassemble and clean the Beretta.

His mind wanders back to the attack on the expressway, remembering the expression of surprise and fear in David's eyes, as he staggered backwards after AJ had shot him. He still can't get over the fact he shot and killed David. AJ shakes his head and continues cleaning his weapon. Finally, around 0130 hours, he goes to bed, but David's face still haunts him. Eventually, sheer exhaustion kicks in, and he falls asleep. But at 0600 hours, he's rudely awakened by his alarm clock.

AJ's morning routine begins with a trip to the can, followed by a cold splash of water to his face. He stares into the mirror trying to focus on his face. *"Damn boy. You look worse than the south end of a north bound mule,"* he mumbles to himself. *"Train wrecks look better than this."* After this little bit of self-criticism, he staggers to the kitchen, goes to the refrigerator, pours himself a glass of juice, and a bowl of cereal. Then, as he starts his coffee pot, he says under his breath, *"One of these days, I've got to learn how to operate that damn timer."*

While eating his cereal, he walks back to the spare bedroom, and steps up on the treadmill. He starts with a moderate walk, and once he's finished his cereal, he moves up to a jog, then finally up to a full run. It's now 0620 hours. AJ moves over to the 4-point workout station and gives each point a five-minute workout on his arms, shoulders, legs, and back.

At 0645, he brushes his teeth, shaves, then takes a quick shower. By 0700, he's getting dressed, and by 0710, he's heading out the door to start another day.

***

While he fights with the morning traffic, AJ is trying to think how he's going to approach the senator about yesterday's fiasco. As he passes by the place where the incident occurred, he sees caution signs, and yellow tape, with the words "Crime Scene-Do Not Cross" stretched between the barricades. There's also a lone police car, with its lights flashing, in an attempt to keep traffic away from the outside lane where the van had rolled and burst into flames. You can clearly see the burn marks on both the pavement and guardrail.

AJ arrives at the senator's estate at 0800 hours, and notices the senator's limo is not parked out in front of the house. AJ parks close to the front door. As he bounds up the steps, he's met by the head butler.

"Good morning AJ," says George.

"Morning George. Is the senator all right this morning?"

"Yes, he's fine, but he's decided to take the day off. He felt the two of you had some important things to discuss, and he thought it would be easier to do it here, rather than on the road. He's waiting for you in the library."

"Thank you, George," he says as he walks toward the library.

AJ finds the senator standing in front of the large windows overlooking the courtyard, gazing at the view. As he enters the room, the senator hears him, turns and says, "Good morning, AJ. How are you feeling today?"

"Good morning, Senator. I was about to ask you the same question."

"I'm just fine, especially considering the alternative. You handled yourself quite well out there yesterday. I'm afraid to think what might have happened had I been with someone else, or even in the limo for that matter!"

"Sir, I'm flattered, but we're all trained to do our job to the best of our ability. Had we been in the limo, I probably would have tried to dodge the van, instead of ramming it. We would have been involved in a completely different scenario. Being in the Hummer definitely offered us an advantage the limo would not."

"I couldn't agree with you more. While I was at the hospital getting checked out, I had some time to reflect on the situation, and I decided to find out who made that armored car of yours. I made a couple of phone calls to some friends with the CIA and the DEA, and found out it was built by Eberhardt & Keyes Coachbuilders, Ltd. in New York. They've been making custom limousines and bullet proof cars for over fifty years. They began modifying the Hummer H2's as soon as they started coming off the assembly line. And when GM announced they were discontinuing the entire Hummer line, they picked up every H2 they could find."

"Eberhardt & Keyes had a few of them in different stages of conversion when I called them. They remembered your vehicle, and pulled the spec sheet on it. Do you know what a World Products 454 is?"

"Yes sir, I do. World Products is a company out of Ronkonkoma, New York, I think. They build custom engines. The factory engine in the Hummer H2 is a 6.0-liter V-8 that puts out about 325 horsepower. World Products modifies the engine by boring and stroking it from 6.0 liters to 7.4 liters, which is the equivalent of 454 cubic inches. Horsepower jumps from 325 to over 500, and…"

"Spare me the details," says the senator. "Anyway, there's one that's almost finished, and they're going to build it to the same specs as yours, except mine will be black, of course. I don't want to attract any undue attention. Wouldn't you agree?"

"Absolutely," replies AJ. "But..."

"AJ, I'm sure you've got a lot of questions to ask, so why don't we just cut to the chase."

"Yes, sir. Thank you, sir. Yesterday, there were seven men bent on trying to kill you, us. We know at least four of them were ex-military, Marines sir. I haven't had a chance to get any updates on all of them, but one had been listed as missing and presumed dead due to a training accident. I'm willing to bet all of them will be listed in a similar manner."

"One vehicle was stolen from a dealership two days prior to the attack, and the other vehicle had an altered VIN and a counterfeit license plate. We're running checks on the weapons, too, but it won't surprise me if we come up empty handed. This was a well organized, well financed, and professional attempt on your life, sir. It was meant to be public, and graphic. Almost like it was supposed to be sending a message."

"Well, AJ? I've heard a lot of statements, but I haven't heard any questions, yet."

"I just felt it was important to make you aware of what we know, and the overall gravity of the situation, so it might help explain the importance of the questions I'm about to ask."

"Well, go ahead. Get to it."

"Sir, I've never heard of an assassination attempt on a U.S. Senator, at least to this extreme, in my life. We've heard rumors you're planning on running for the Presidency. If you are, it might explain why someone wants to take you out of the running."

"And if it's not?"

"If you're not, then we've got to start beating the bushes for some answers."

With that, Higgins walks over to the doors of the library and closes them. Then as he walks back toward his desk, he stops by the credenza to refill his coffee mug. "Would you like some coffee? It's fresh, and by the looks of those bags under your eyes, you could probably stand a jolt of caffeine."

"Thank you, sir. Maybe later." replies AJ.

As Higgins returns to his desk, Higgins says, "Please, have a seat. This is going to take awhile."

"First of all, yes, I'm going to run for President. But, right now that's just between you, me, and a handful of other people. We're still a couple of weeks away from making it public. And yes, those assassins were sent to take me out of the running as you so eloquently put it. But you'll be surprised to know they weren't sent by a foreign power, or a radical paramilitary group. In fact, in a roundabout way, they work for the government."

"Excuse me, Senator?!" exclaims a surprised AJ. "What in the hell are you saying?"

"Actually, it's a little more complicated than that. Tell me, AJ. Just how much do you know about our government?"

"What do you mean?"

"Let's start back a little over two hundred years ago. The people of this country were essentially misfits, castaways, or those who dared to openly criticize their homeland's system of government or sanctioned religion. But all of these people came together under a handful of patriotic men, men of vision. Those men wrote and signed our Declaration of Independence. This, of course, created a furor in Western Europe, and wars erupted. Yet our thirteen colonies prevailed, and ultimately gave birth to these United States of America."

"Soon, our Constitution was written, and our system of government went from a collection of dreams and ideas, to a work in progress. But even when all of these things were in place, there was a small group of people who actually ran this country. They called themselves the Core. To these men, the Core meant: The basis from which all things begin. They were patriots first, businessmen and entrepreneurs second. They were men who wanted to help this country grow, prosper, and become more powerful."

"The Core kept records up until the beginning of the Civil War. At that time, it was feared that if outsiders found out about the Core, anyone related to it would either be hung or shot, so for a time, they went underground. This was indeed an unusual and dangerous time, because there were members from both the North and the South working together in an effort to keep this country in one piece. It is believed the Underground Railroad was started by and financed through the Core."

"But then there are other rumors they were responsible for the substandard boilers put onboard the great paddle wheelers on the Mississippi, Missouri, Ohio, and Allegheny Rivers. This not only caused the destruction of the paddle wheelers themselves, but their cargoes as well. They are believed to have financed renegade bands of men to sabotage the railroad tracks both north and south of the Mason/Dixon line, which also slowed the advance of men and materiel to the front lines."

"Even the Battle of Gettysburg is suspected of being caused by misinformation distributed by the Core. Both the North and the South were led to believe their opponent was weak and ill prepared for such an engagement. It was hoped that by causing all of these things to occur, both governments would see the continued wholesale and senseless slaughter of our young men and massive loss of materiel, were physically and financially unsustainable."

"Then, when the Civil War appeared to be at its worst, members of the Core decided that in order to reunify the United States, President Lincoln had to die. Never before had the Core ever proposed the death of anyone. And it was the first time that something put to a vote came close to being a tie. So to prevent any future votes being locked in a tie, the Core always had an odd number of members who were active at any given time. Should a meeting be called, and an even number of members attend, members would draw straws to determine who would abstain from voting. All decisions were made by a simple majority. These rules are still a part of the Core to this day."

"Proposals brought before the Core were initially done anonymously, in an effort to prevent favoritism and to ensure the proposal stood solely on its own merits. Members were forbidden to discuss these proposals before or after the meetings. Anyone caught disclosing the origin of a proposal was immediately censured for a period of not less than one year. He was barred from attending meetings, or visiting with other members of the Core. And since this caused an even number of members, someone always lost their ability to vote by default. This further reduced the tendency of someone talking about a proposal due to peer pressure."

"A second violation resulted in his permanent removal from the Core, and he was forbidden to mention anything about the Core to anyone, under the penalty of death."

"But the most important law of the Core is that no member can ever be President of the United States, Vice President, or Speaker of the House. Members of the Core have to be equals, regardless of their position in or out of the political or business arena."

"This is bullshit, right?" asks AJ.

"AJ? You said that you wanted to know who wanted to have me killed, right?"

"If that's the case, that means you're a member of the Core," says AJ in disbelief.

"Yes. As a matter of fact, I am."

"Just how long have you been a member of the Core, Senator?"

"How long has no relevance. Let's just say that I've been there long enough to have had an effect on the history of our country."

"Well, Senator? If you've been a long-standing member, don't you realize that you're attempting to break a cardinal rule of the Core? You're attempting to write your own death warrant."

"Actually, what I'm attempting to do is break the Core."

"Wait a minute, Senator. If the Core is supposed to be guiding our country along a supposed righteous path, why do you want to break it?"

"AJ? Have you ever heard the term, power corrupts? In the beginning, the Core did indeed guide our country along a righteous path, as you put it. But as we approached the Twentieth Century, the Core started to change. Its focus became more self-serving, often at our government's and the people's expense."

"Remember the U.S.S. Maine? It was suspected she had been blown up by Spain in 1898, and so began the Spanish-American War." Higgins pauses a moment, then says, "It was staged, AJ. It recently became public knowledge the explosion was caused by a spark igniting the suspended coal dust in one of the coal bins."

"There were companies on the verge of bankruptcy that would benefit from a war. Firearms and cartridge manufacturers had invested millions of dollars in new technologies, such as smokeless powder, brass cartridges, spiral cut bores for improved accuracy, and the introduction of the machine gun."

"That war showed them what worked, what didn't, and what improvements needed to be made. Of course, other companies and businesses flourished because of the war, such as the steel and coal industries."

"Even the railroads and the shipping industry benefited from the increased traffic of goods across the country. So, in a roundabout way, members of the Core saw themselves as creating increased business and prosperity for our country. But they forgot about all the Americans who died or were wounded on foreign soil. They were the true casualties of war."

"How about Pearl Harbor? Most people believed President Roosevelt knew in advance the Japanese planned to bomb Pearl Harbor. If he did, it was only a hunch. America's reluctance to address Japan's aggressive action in China, and her neighboring Pacific island nations, fed Japan's belief that it could dominate the entire Pacific. But the Core was well aware of communications between Japan and Germany. They could also foresee the airplane, carrier, and submarine as being instrumental in winning the war in the Pacific. Why do you think all four of our carriers were nowhere near Pearl when it was attacked?"

"Boeing, Douglass, North American, Republic, Grumman, and others, all had planes on the drawing boards, just begging to be built, but Congress was still reeling from the aftermath of the Depression, and frankly didn't see a need for advanced military hardware."

"Almost all of our battleships were leftovers from the War to End All Wars. Most of our soldiers still carried bolt-action rifles from the same period, and there were less than one hundred battle ready tanks in our army inventory, and none remotely compared to the technology, mobility, and lethality of the Nazis."

"The United States was ripe for the picking. Our only advantage was that we had major ocean boundaries between our adversaries and us. While the Core didn't conceive the war, it did withhold information that might have delayed or even thwarted it."

"Senator, you're talking ancient history here."

"What? You want something more up to date? How about these little tidbits? In 1961, President John F. Kennedy inherited former President Eisenhower's plan to drive Communism out of Cuba. This was a combination of Cuban nationals working in conjunction with the CIA. I'm sure you recall how badly the Bay of Pigs operation was, and by the looks of things, the impending war in Vietnam and Southeast Asia wasn't looking very good either."

"In 1962, the United States, working through the CIA, had a handful of people offering training and financial support for some little known countries called South Vietnam, Cambodia, Thailand, and Laos. Our official goal was to prevent Communism from taking these countries over. The French had already gotten their collective asses kicked over there, and our attempt wasn't looking any better. We needed more manpower, military hardware, aircraft, etc."

"Remember, yesterday I mentioned I had been a pilot for Air America? I was working for the CIA. We all were. We were told that the United States was eventually going to get involved in a war in Southeast Asia, and these countries would play a pivotal role in the name of Democracy vs. Communism. We needed to collect all the intelligence we could, and make as many friends as possible, before the war broke out."

"Again, our military industry had hundreds, if not thousands of products and ideas that needed a battle arena to introduce and test those products. Plus there was money to be made in certain illicit trading deals from these countries."

"We're not talking about drugs here, are we, Senator?"

"Well, you can never have too much silk, rice, counterfeit watches, and hand-made basket goods, now can you?" replies the senator.

"Both President John F. Kennedy and Attorney General Robert Kennedy believed these operations to be unwinnable and wasteful, and foresaw them to be very unpopular with the American public. Both Kennedys were very powerful men, from

60

a very powerful and influential family. Members of the Core tried to reason with the President, but he wasn't willing to budge. Threats were made, but were left unheeded. To drive the point home that the Core was serious, they arranged the supposed suicide of Marilyn Monroe."

"The Core had long been aware of both John's and Robert's affairs with Ms. Monroe. The Core had photographs, and 8mm videotape of their trysts in the Bahamas, and the Virgin Islands. There was even a penthouse in Las Vegas where both Kennedys had been seen and taped with Ms. Monroe."

"When presented with some of those pictures and intelligence, both Kennedys backed down for a while, but soon, President Kennedy decided that he could, and would, take on the Core. He did not believe the Core would dare try to assassinate the President of the United States, much less a Kennedy. He even threatened to go public about the Core. Kennedy had just written his own death warrant, and it was carried out in Dallas, Texas on November 22, 1963."

"Robert backed off once again, at least for a period of time, but then began investigating the Teamsters Union, and Jimmy Hoffa. He was trying to get to the Core without attacking them head on. The Core initially saw Robert as more of a nuisance than anything else, but one of our associates overheard a conversation between Robert and a Treasury official, that he planned to expose the Core with information obtained from Hoffa. The very next week, when Robert announced his desire to run for the Presidency, TLC. Hoffa's fate was also sealed, although his TLC wouldn't happen until July of '75."

"Excuse me?! What did you say?!" exclaims AJ, in disbelief of what he had just heard.

"TLC?" repeats the senator. "Have you ever heard that term before? Have you any idea what it means?"

"Well, I don't think it means tender loving care," replies AJ sarcastically.

"No, quite the contrary. It means Terminate Life Cycle. It's the term we use instead of kill, murder, execute, neutralize, etc."

"Sorry sir. I'm not sure I follow," says AJ with some disgust.

"Each member of the Core has their own operatives. No one knows all of them. If the Core determines that a TLC is necessary, lots are usually drawn at random to see which of us will provide operatives for it. The number is always odd, and in most cases, the minimum number of operatives for a TLC is three."

"Once a member has submitted an operative for a mission, his name is removed from the lottery for a year, or until everyone has invested at least one of their operatives on a TLC."

In most situations, the neutralization process is supposed to look like death by natural causes, or some sort of tragic accident. Only in very few instances should it need to be public and/or graphic, such as with the Kennedys."

"So, I guess you're telling me that Ted Kennedy's plunge into the Chappaquiddick was a TLC."

"As a matter of fact, it was," replies Higgins. "The Core had known for some time that Ted was having a series of affairs. At least his liaisons were not as high profile as those of his brothers John and Robert. We had plenty of documentation, from notes, letters, phone calls, photos, even video. But Ted had been staying out of the limelight for the most part."

"One day, in July 1969, while cleaning out some of Robert's memorabilia, Ted uncovered his file on the Core, and he started snooping. One of our members overheard a conversation between Ted and another senator about the Core. It was decided that Ted needed a little TLC."

"Three operatives were assigned to handle the operation. They were instructed to make sure that he was inebriated and had a female companion, preferably someone other than his wife. It seemed that Ted was more than happy to cooperate in the matter."

"On July 19, 1969, Ted was observed getting into a car accompanied by a young woman, plus it was blatantly obvious Ted had been drinking. Once he was on the bridge, a sniper took out the left front tire. Ted lost control of the vehicle and plunged into the water."

"Honestly, the Core expected Ted to drown, at least that was the plan. Of course, we all know he didn't, but what did happen was far better than anything we could have hoped for. He panicked, and fled the scene. But what you, and the public, didn't know, his female passenger was still alive, at least until one of our operatives finished her off. Ted's political life was ruined for the most part, and while he remained a member of Congress, he posed little threat to us to his dying day."

"Senator, what you're talking about here is premeditated murder. In fact, assassinating the President of the United States, along with other government officials would be considered high treason! What happened to patriotism, working together for the common good, and building a better and stronger America?"

"AJ, I'm just beginning to scratch the surface here. Remember Kent State, May 5, 1970? Thirteen wounded, four dead? Here's how that one went down."

"A certain senator, who will remain nameless for now, had a daughter enrolled at Kent State. This senator had a pretty strong following in the senate, and had openly opposed a bill the Core was trying to get passed. Regardless of what they tried, the senator refused to change his mind. On the morning of May 5th, he found a note at his desk advising him to watch the news. To his horror, the headline story revolved around the shootings at Kent State."

"Shortly after turning on the news, his daughter called. She was crying almost uncontrollably. It turned out that she was okay, but her best friend had been shot and killed as she stood beside her."

"Wait a minute! There were hundreds of students at that rally! How could either of them been sorted out from the crowd? And in the heat of the moment, how could a single shooter, shooting freehanded, kill one, but not kill, or at least wound the senator's daughter?"

"Well, there's always a certain amount of risk involved in most of these operations, but we do our best to minimize any collateral damage, unless it suits our needs. In this particular instance, we were able to stack the deck in our favor."

"First off, the shooter was in a building above the crowd, giving him a bird's eye view of the area. While he had a Colt M-16 rifle, it had been modified for sniper duty, and equipped with a high power scope."

"Secondly, both the senator's daughter and her friend had been sprayed with dyes invisible to the naked eye, without their knowledge. Special filters were required to see the dyes, and the

63

scope was so equipped. This would ensure the senator's daughter would be in close proximity to the target to witness the kill."

"After having received our message, the senator changed his position, and our bill passed with minimal hassle."

Then Higgins' voice begins to tremble and there are tears in his eyes.

"Senator?" asks AJ. "What's wrong? Are you okay?"

"I had just been elected to my state senate post when the Kent State incident occurred," says the senator. "My niece was his daughter's best friend! While those seventeen lives were ruined that day, an entire nation would be forever changed."

"I didn't know anything about the Core, or its part in the incident. In fact, I would not know anything about, or be approached to join the Core for another five years. Even after I became a member, my focus was on the good we could do. I guess I was still pretty much an idealist, even after my tour in Southeast Asia."

"I was going through the archives when I came across the entries regarding the Kent State incident. The plan was very cold and detailed, just like a military operation. Casualties were expected. In fact, they anticipated closer to fifty students being shot or killed in that operation. That was the beginning of the end for me. I knew there had to be some changes, so I began trying to bring back what I called the Old Core."

"I arranged a meeting with the members and read aloud our history from its humble beginnings through our current days. In a roundabout way, I was trying to shame them, open their eyes to what we had become. Some of the members were interested and listened attentively, while others talked about their golf scores, their new boat, or latest stock acquisitions. I did my best to maintain my composure, but I was boiling inside. I felt dirty and ashamed, and I left that meeting disillusioned, helpless."

"I've since dedicated my life trying to make a difference within the Core. Sometimes, I have succeeded, while others I have been soundly defeated. I've finally come to the conclusion that there is only one way to resolve this."

"Paint a bull's eye on your chest?" says AJ sarcastically.

"No. Take down the Core. Expose it for what it is, and what it stands for. Expose its members, and let the chips fall where they may."

"But, Senator. Since you have been a member all these years, you could be impeached, sent to prison, or worse. Assassinated!"

"I'm willing to take that risk, AJ. Besides, you've shown me what you can do. Now I need to show you what I can do. All you have to do is watch my back."

"Senator, you're asking me to do the impossible, sir. We were lucky out on the expressway. I don't think they'll be inclined to make the same mistake twice. You really need more security, at least three, maybe four more men. I could ask Mr. Weathers..."

"No! Absolutely not!" barks the senator. "Not until I make my intentions public! I'm not about to ask for any favors from the Secret Service or the President, and I'm certainly not accepting any."

"Well, Senator? Tell me about the security staff in house. Who are they, how many do you have, and what is their level of training?"

"They're from a local security company. Lehman, I think. Their primary function is to keep an eye on the monitors for the security cameras. They will occasionally catch thrill seekers coming over the wall, looking for souvenirs, or trying to take a picture or two. Most of the guards carry side arms, but I'm not really sure how much training they've had."

"Do you, or they, have an armory on site? You know, a cache of weapons, rifles, shotguns, etc.?"

"I own a few handguns, and my shotguns," says the senator, as he points to the beautifully hand carved gun cabinet in the corner of the library.

"Senator? You've got a huge house and grounds to secure, and nothing to do it with. Tell me about your operatives, your assassins."

"What do you mean, tell you about my operatives?" asks the senator in a somewhat threatened tone.

"How many do you have? Where are they, and how soon can you get them here?"

"You don't expect me to answer that, do you? I can't afford to expose my operatives to you or anyone else. They're anonymous, remember?"

"Senator? If I don't get some help soon, and I do mean soon, both of us may become anonymous! We've got to get organized. I need at least four men here with some form of military training, preferably Ranger, Special Forces, SEAL, Delta, whatever. They must be willing to take orders from me without question, yet have a good head on their shoulders, with the ability to think on their own if and when necessary. Next, we need to acquire a substantial amount of weapons and ammunition, without raising a lot of questions or red flags."

"What kinds of weapons are we talking about?"

"For starters, we're going to need a half dozen H&K MP5 submachine guns for close quarter protection. We should also have a half dozen Steyr AUG's with 16-inch barrels. This weapon can provide both close quarter and moderate standoff range protection. They're compact, almost as small as the MP5's, and they're easy to conceal. Next, we'll need a half dozen shotguns. I prefer the Benelli M3's, in that they offer both semi-auto and pump action capability. And finally, we could use at least one, although I would prefer two, Barrett M82A3 Precision Sniper Rifles. We'll also need an assortment of smoke, stun, and tear gas grenades, along with gas masks for our own protection. And we're going to need some form of night vision capability as well.

"Damn, AJ! How do you expect me to remember all this?"

"No problem, sir. I'll put it on a flash drive. That way, you can keep it with you. I'll include the specific equipment I want for each weapon, such as magazines, optics, lasers, flashlights, silencers, etc. And I'll also include the type and amount of ammunition needed for each weapon."

"Are you planning on starting World War Three?" asks Higgins.

"Actually, I'm hoping to prevent it."

"Seriously, AJ. Where do you expect me to find all this equipment?"

"You told me earlier that you have connections with the CIA, DEA, and the military. Surely, somebody owes you a favor or two. But, you also need to keep in mind that getting this hardware needs to be kept secret. It's absolutely essential no one knows you're acquiring this little arsenal."

"Are you kidding? With a laundry list like this, they're going to think that I'm trying to start my own third world country!"

"Perfect. That's exactly what you're going to tell them."

"What?"

"If anybody asks, you're helping a small third world country acquire some arms for their leader's protection."

"You don't think anyone is going to buy a bullshit story like that, do you?"

"Senator, my job is keeping you alive. That laundry list will help me do my job. Your job is to fill that list without raising any eyebrows. Isn't that part of politics? You're the head of the Appropriations Committee, right?" With that, AJ gets up and starts toward the doors leading to the hallway.

"Now where are you going?"

"I'm going to pay a little visit to your in-house security team to see if they can explain how someone managed to get on the grounds, disable your limo, and get out again, undetected."

While AJ walks down the hallway toward the security room, his cell phone rings. It's Weathers. "Good morning, Mr. Weathers. Any updates regarding yesterday's incident?"

"Good morning, my ass! So far, we've been able to substantiate that all four of the shooters were ex-military, and yes, all were either believed killed or missing in action, presumed lost, or at least unrecoverable. Two of them were on the same exercise with Corporal McKenzie. The other two were supposedly victims of a terrorist bombing attack in Iraq. We're still working on the other three bodies, but getting sufficient DNA from them, especially after your little barbeque, is proving somewhat difficult."

"What about the Suburban?"

"We lucked out on that one. One of our technicians found an unaltered VIN on the chassis. It was originally part of the government motor pool here in Washington. It disappeared about two years ago. The last service entry was 3 June 2009; normal maintenance stuff. It was part of the general inventory, and would be assigned to any department or agency that needed an additional vehicle on a temporary basis, such as covering another unit out for service."

"Who was it assigned to when it disappeared?"

"The IRS."

"And those people bitch when we can't find a gas receipt. Anything from NCIC on the weapons?"

"Nothing local, but Interpol says the AK47's were manufactured in Romania, and were fully automatic versions. They're relatively new, and were supposed to have been part of a military contract that somehow found its way to the Black Market."

AJ walks outside and leans against his car. "So, what you're telling me is we really don't know any more now than we did yesterday," he sighs. "What about the three men who attacked us at Lisa's house last night?"

"There's nothing I can tell you about three men who don't exist."

"What do you mean, don't exist? Lisa's house is riddled with bullet holes, and there's blood all over the place from those three guys! How do three stiffs just up and disappear?"

"Somebody got there ahead of the cops and said it was under DEA jurisdiction. The locals never got a chance to enter the house."

"How could DEA get there so fast?"

"They didn't," replies Weathers in disgust. "I spoke to a friend of mine with the DEA, and he said he knew of no operations going on at all last night. I had Martha call NSA, ATF, and the FBI, and nobody knows anything about a shootout in Brookmont last night, other than the locals who got turned away at the door."

"But I've got to tell you, there's a lieutenant down there who is pretty hot right now. He was asking one of the agents all kinds of questions, but all the agent would tell him was to back off, they had everything under control."

"When the lieutenant demanded to know the agent's name, things got a little dicey for a couple of minutes. But then the lieutenant got a call from his chief ordering him and his men off the property. He said that he couldn't see much, although he could see at least one body in the living room. And yes, there were bullet holes everywhere."

"Did you ask this lieutenant if he would recognize the agent if he saw him again, or could he identify him from a photo?"

"Oh, he'd welcome the chance. He said he'd love to meet this guy off the clock anytime," replies Weathers.

"So, I guess you're telling me we have no evidence, no bodies, nothing."

"Yep, that's about the size of it."

"Well, what about the tag number I gave you last night?"

"I didn't think that your assassins would be caught dead running around in a delivery truck."

"What?"

"Your government tag number is registered to a 2007 Ford Econoline 3/4 ton delivery van assigned to the GSA."

"This thing is getting more interesting every minute. Stolen vehicles, vehicles with altered VIN's, vehicles with switched tags. I wonder what we're going to find next?"

"I was able to track down which agency checked out that transmitter you found on your Hummer."

"Great!" replies AJ enthusiastically. "Now we're starting to get somewhere."

"Not really. In my former line of work we called this a red herring."

"Sir? I'm not sure I follow. What do you mean?"

"For starters, it is a GPS transmitter, and it is an inventoried item. It was checked out about a month ago, by the DEA, for the purpose of maintaining surveillance on a well known drug dealer."

"In other words..."

"In other words, the DEA evidently forgot to remove the transmitter before releasing the SUV. It hasn't been active in over a week."

"A red herring," says AJ with an obvious sound of disappointment in his voice.

"Right. Oh! I think I've found out what TLC stands for."

"Terminate Life Cycle," says AJ.

"Yeah. How did you know that?"

"It's a long story. I'll tell you more about it when I get back to the office. But I wouldn't ask too many questions about TLC if I were you."

"Why is that?"

"Bad things seem to happen to people who ask too many questions about it." AJ pauses a moment, then says, "Look, I'll tell you everything I know once I get back, okay?"

"All right. So, when are you coming back to the office?"

"Right after I raise a little hell with house security."

"What about the senator?"

"He's okay, just a little banged up. Nothing serious. He's decided to take the day off and should be safe at home, at least for today. But you and I have a lot of things to talk about."

"Okay, give me a call when you're heading this way. See you in a bit," says Weathers as he ends the call.

70

TLC: Chapter 11

AJ goes back into the house and down the hall to the security room. He starts to knock on the door, but as he grabs the doorknob, he discovers that it's not locked. He casually enters the room and closes the door behind him.

With his back to the door, he scans the room. Directly in front of him are three manned workstations, each with nine monitors, in three rows of three. Each workstation has a computer and a multi-line telephone. Off to the left are two uniformed security guards sitting around a table. One has his feet propped up on the desk and is reading a newspaper, the other a magazine. To the right is a doorway leading to a break area where he sees another guard preparing something to eat. Amazingly, no one has even glanced in his direction or acknowledged his presence.

AJ walks up behind one of the guards watching the monitors, pulls out his Beretta, places it to his head, and shouts, "BANG! You're dead! You're all dead!" AJ scares the one reading the newspaper so bad he loses his balance and falls over backwards! The second guard drops his magazine, and tries to stand up while frantically trying to extract his weapon from its holster. AJ walks over to him and presses his Beretta to his chest, saying, "Mister, I said you're dead. Dead men don't move." There is fire in AJ's eyes, and it's obvious the guard is physically and mentally shaken.

The guard from the break room rushes to the doorway and says, "What in the hell is going on here?"

"Who's in charge of this bunch of misfits?"

"I am," says the guard standing in the doorway. "What's this all about?"

"What's your name and rank?"

"Brian Jamison. I'm their supervisor," he replies.

"Why are you here, Jamison?"

"What is this? Twenty questions?"

"Answer the question. Why are you here? What's your purpose?"

"We're here to protect the senator and his property, sir!"

"Well, you're obviously not doing a very good job, are you, Jamison? All of you just died."

"Sir, I don't think that this was a fair test of our abilities," says Jamison.

"Have you ever served in the military?"

"Yes, sir!"

"Where and when?"

"Iraq, sir, 2009."

"Army? Marines?"

"Army, sir!"

"Were you a grunt?"

"No, sir, motor pool."

"Are you a mechanic?"

"No, sir. I drove a truck."

"Then, you didn't see any action, now did you, Jamison." AJ sounds disgusted and begins to turn away.

"Yes, sir! I saw plenty of action," snaps Jamison.

"Now how would a jockey see action?" barks AJ.

"On the battlefield, there are only two ways to get supplies to forward bases and outposts; fly it in, or drive it in. If you have to leave your post to retrieve supplies that land outside the LZ, you risk losing those supplies, plus you're exposing your men to the enemy."

"That leaves having it brought in by ground transport."

"Sounds logical, so what's your point?" asks AJ.

"While your ground troops are safe behind their lines, the men and women driving in with their supplies are the ones at risk."

"Not only are we exposed getting to our destination, oftentimes, we have to return the same way. Double jeopardy."

"My last convoy cost us twelve GI's killed or wounded, including my co-driver, Corporal Terrence Newsome. I took some shrapnel in my right leg, but Terry was KIA. Sixteen vehicles were lost or seriously damaged. Once we got home, I was discharged on a medical, nerve damage." About that time, his right leg begins to shake.

"What's that?" asks AJ.

"The docs call 'em tremors. They say it's nothing serious, but I have to be careful when I drive. And I can't afford to sit in one position very long either."

"Sorry to hear that," says AJ, more than a little embarrassed.

"I'm used to it."

"Well, we're going to have to step up security around here, starting today."

"What's all this about?" asks Jamison. "Everything's been fine up until…"

"You call this fine? I just walked through an unlocked door into the heart of the senator's security center and killed all of you."

"But sir. You can not consider this a fair test of our…"

"Jamison! Are you and these men on the clock?"

"Yes sir, but…"

"Well, if you're on the clock that means you're supposed to be protecting the senator, right?" AJ is waiting for an answer, but Jamison is just staring at him. "I say again, if you're on the clock, you're supposed to be protecting the senator, right?"

Jamison looks down, obviously embarrassed, and says, "Yes, sir."

"Okay, now that we have that out of the way, let's see what we can do to fix it. Is there a policy and procedure manual around here somewhere?"

"Not that I've seen."

"You're kidding, right? Do you have an office?"

"Yes, sir. Right this way," says Jamison, as they walk back into the hallway, over to the next room which is also unlocked. AJ gives him a stern look. "I'll make sure we keep both doors secured from here on out."

"That's a start," replies AJ.

The office is very small, not much larger than a broom closet, almost like an afterthought. There is a small metal desk, a computer, multi-line phone, two chairs, two filing cabinets, and a small bookcase.

"Nope, no manual, sir. Just the daily log and some personnel files," says Jamison.

"Well, we're going to have to come up with one right away. How long have you worked here?"

"This is my third week, sir."

"Well, how long have you worked for this security company?"

"This is my third week, sir."

"You can cut the 'sir' crap. I was a sergeant in the Marine Corps. Most people call me AJ."

"Well AJ, you can call me Brian."

"What were you doing before you came to work for the senator?"

"Outside of my military training, I don't have much to fall back on. After I was discharged from the Army, I tried driving a cab for a while. But the problems with my leg made it practically impossible to work a complete shift. On one occasion, I almost hit another car while pulling away from the curb. I had just dropped off a fare, when out of the blue, a spasm in my leg jammed the accelerator to the floor. Scared the shit out of me."

"I bet." AJ pauses a moment, then says, "Look, I want to apologize for being so hard on you in there, but we've got some serious problems. Some will be easy to fix, while others...Well, some of them are going to take some time. And time is a luxury we just don't have."

"Can you tell me what's going on, and what you're expecting of me and my men?"

"Well, for starters, you know the senator and I were ambushed yesterday."

"Yes sir, and from what I heard, you were a one-man army."

"We were also pretty lucky out there. But the problems started long before we even left the estate."

"What do you mean?"

"Someone was able to tamper with the senator's car after it had been cleaned and prepped for our trip into Washington. That means someone was able to get in, disable the car, and get out without being detected. The down side is Jeffrey had Sunday and Monday off, so the car was serviced Saturday. That gave someone a window of opportunity from Saturday evening until early Monday morning."

"Well, that spreads the incident over six shifts."

"They also knew we switched to my Hummer, a vehicle I just picked up over the weekend. Monday was the first time I drove it here. Add to that, they knew the time we would be leaving, and our route."

"So, what are you thinking?" asks Jamison.

"Well, it's got to be one of two things. Either they have a pretty sophisticated means of monitoring everything that goes on around here, or they have someone on the inside."

74

"What's your gut feeling?"

"I hate to say it, but I believe it's someone on the inside," says AJ.

"I agree. So what kind of changes do you want to make? Where do we start?"

"First, you need to have electronically controlled, keypad-style door locks put on both the security room, and your office. Everybody gets their own code. Only the supervisors and I will have access to this office. Both keypads will have data loggers on them, so we can determine who is here and what they're doing." Jamison is writing down the information. "Got all that?"

"Electronic keypads with data loggers. Yep. Got it."

"Good. Before I 'killed' all of you, I scanned all the monitors and noticed there was no camera monitoring the entrance to either room. I want one installed tomorrow and set up with a video recorder. The camera should be a color unit with an infrared illuminator and an independent backup power supply, so it can see in the dark, and operate in the event of any type of power failure."

"Color camera, illuminator, time lapse re...cor...der...Okay."

"Don't forget the backup power supply, and it's got to run both the camera and the video recorder."

"I got it, I got it."

"What about the other cameras?"

"What about them?"

"Are any of the cameras being recorded on a regular basis?"

"No, but any of them can be. There is one recorder at each station that can record any camera by the simple flip of a switch."

"And what happens if you need to record more than one camera at that station?"

"Right now? A single monitor can display up to 4 cameras simultaneously. But other than that, we're screwed."

"Well, call up whoever handles your company's video security and tell them we need every camera on a recorder, preferably digital, and I want it done yesterday."

"I'll do my best, AJ."

"How many men are on a shift?"

"Usually five, including the supervisor. Everyone takes turns watching the monitors and walking the grounds."

75

"Why are there six men on today?"

"The first guy you killed watching the monitors? He's in training, just started yesterday."

"Sorry about that. How much do you know about the rest of the guys on your shift?"

"Such as?"

"Have you reviewed their files? Do any of them have military backgrounds? Any special skills? Firearms training? Self defense?"

"Well, the guy that did the back flip at the table is also new and claims to be a black belt in three different disciplines of martial arts," Jamison says with a smile.

"So that's what that was!" replies AJ sarcastically.

"Well, he's young and trying to impress the other guys."

"And it's guys like that who can get you killed when the shit hits the fan. You need to sit 'Kung Fooey' down and get the straight scoop on him, or he's out of here."

"I hear ya."

"Anything else?"

"Well, everyone has to qualify with their side arm, baton, taser, and pepper spray, or they can't carry them."

"I noticed at least two of your guards, including your martial arts specialist, weren't carrying anything."

"Obviously they must not have qualified then."

"Oh boy," sighs AJ. "Cannon fodder."

"Excuse me?" asks Jamison with a perplexed look on his face.

"Back in the sixteenth through nineteenth centuries, men who couldn't shoot or fight were placed on the front line as bait for the opposing forces first volley of cannon and/or rifle fire. As the opposing force was either reloading or preparing to make the next volley, your seasoned troops and cannons took out their front line."

"That had to be pretty brutal," says Jamison.

"Well, if they can't make a good enough score to qualify with a weapon, they better get qualified, or they'll have to find another place to work. Everyone who walks the grounds must be armed and know how to use them." AJ sighs again, shaking his head. "This is going to be harder than I thought. What do you know about the other supervisors?"

"Most of them seem to have their heads on straight. All of them seem to be pretty intelligent and take their jobs seriously."

"I have a better idea. How many supervisors are there?"

"Six, plus a swing man from the main office."

"When do the shifts change?"

"Each shift is 8 hours: 7 to 3, 3 to 11, and 11 to 7. Everyone has to be on site fifteen minutes prior to their shift to debrief the person they're relieving. All shifts rotate with one week on each shift. We get two days off on days and evenings, and a long weekend after completing the graveyard shift.

"Okay, call them up, and tell them we're having a meeting Thursday night at 2100 hours. And tell them it's mandatory."

"That's kinda sudden, isn't it?"

"Remember? Time is a luxury we don't have."

"Well, I guess there's no time like the present. I'll start calling them now."

"Good. Keep me posted on your progress, and be sure to let me know if anyone gives you any static, okay?"

"What if someone can't make it?"

"Tell them I'll be happy to meet with them on an individual basis. That way I can give them my undivided attention, and I can guarantee I'll have theirs," says AJ with a wicked smile.

"Somehow, I don't think that would be something I would want to look forward to."

"You've survived this one, so far," says AJ. "You have a lot of objectives to carry out, so I'll leave you to it. Any questions?"

"No, I think I have it covered."

AJ gets up and starts to head for the door, stops, turns around and says, "Oh, by the way. I want a list of the security personnel who worked from this past weekend through yesterday. Call me when you have it ready, and I'll tell you where to send it."

"Will do."

"One more thing. I want the files on all of the supervisors at that meeting Thursday night."

"That shouldn't be a problem."

"Very well, Brian. Carry on," he says as he heads down the hallway. AJ puts in a call to Weathers. "Sir? I'm on my way. I should be there in about thirty minutes."

TLC: Chapter 12

AJ arrives at the Homeland Security Complex at 1300 hours to meet with Mr. Weathers for a debriefing about his conversation with Senator Higgins. As he approaches Mr. Weathers' secretary, he says, "Good afternoon, Martha."

"Good afternoon, AJ," she replies. "Mr. Weathers has someone in with him right now."

But through the door you can hear Weathers say, "Martha, tell AJ to come on in. There's someone he needs to meet. I want to introduce him to his new partner."

As AJ opens the door, he says, "What partner? Yesterday, you told me that I was working this detail alone, and now I have a partner?"

"Well, AJ? A lot of things have happened since yesterday, and I've decided that you need a partner," says Weathers. "Let me introduce you to..."

"Julie Anne Robinson. When did you join the Secret Service?" he asks in a less than pleasant tone.

"So, you remember Ms. Robinson?" asks Weathers.

"Yes, I do," he replies with a stern look on his face. "First question, sir. Who's in charge of this operation?"

"Why, you of course, AJ," says Weathers with a perplexed look on his face. "Why would you ask such a question?"

"Because if we were still in the military, she would be my superior officer, sir."

"Well, AJ, neither of you are on active duty with the military anymore, and both of you are currently working for the Secret Service," says Weathers. He then looks at Julie and says, "AJ is the point man on this operation, and you will take orders from him, unless I say otherwise. Do you have a problem with that, Agent Robinson?"

"No, sir," she replies with a provocative smile on her face.

"See?" says Weathers as he leans back in his chair. "Happy now? I was about to go over her file when you arrived. Care to sit in with me while I review it?"

"Not really, sir. The reason I came down here was to go over my findings about, well, you know, TLC and the Core."

"What do you mean, tell me about the Corps. The Marine Corps?"

"Not the Marine Corps, sir, but a group of men who supposedly control the government and call themselves the Core."

"What's the Core?" asks Weathers.

"Well, I thought you knew something about the Core, since you knew what TLC meant. By the way, what's Agent Robinson's security clearance?"

Weathers looks in her file and says with a smirk, "It's higher than yours. What do you have?"

While AJ begins bringing Weathers up to date with his conversation with Senator Higgins, part of AJ's mind starts to reminisce about his relationship with Julie.

***

Julie Anne Robinson, that is, Lieutenant Julie Anne Robinson, studied law at Radcliffe College, where she was also involved in the Navy ROTC program.

As she approached graduation, she received job offers from several law firms across the country, from New York to Los Angeles, but she longed to travel. After graduating from Radcliffe, Julie joined the Navy's JAG (Judge Advocate General's) Office. Her father had been in the Navy, and she wanted to contribute part of her life for the things he had instilled in her. Plus it would allow her the opportunity to see the world at the Navy's expense.

At five feet ten inches, one hundred twenty-five pounds, red hair, dazzling blue eyes, a slightly turned up nose, a wholesome smile, fair skin, shapely body, and a pair of gorgeous long legs, Julie is a sight to behold.

During her tenure with the Navy, she worked on numerous cases, from mishaps at sea, to pilot error and equipment malfunctions, from hazings to murder. Rarely did any of her cases surface for public review, so her legal escapades never brought her fame or notoriety. But she was an excellent attorney. Julie was thorough in her research, and she always pushed others to find the answers to elusive questions. She always wanted to know the truth, no matter what.

Whenever Julie wasn't working on a case, she enjoyed tagging along with the NCIS, and eventually transferred over to NCIS. That's when her investigative skills really began to develop. That was also about the time she met AJ.

***

Bosnia
March 18, 2006
2130 hours local time

Two squads of Marines were dropped behind enemy lines to recover a pilot and his RIO (Radar Intercept Officer) in Bosnia. Military intelligence said the drop zone was safe, and once they were on the ground, they would be met by two Bosnian sympathizers. They would lead them to the Navy pilot and his RIO, then assist with their escape back to friendly soil.

Things started going bad as soon as they hit the ground. It was a night drop, and they were immediately caught in an ambush. One helicopter was destroyed, leaving the second helicopter to take off with the downed helicopter crew, and two wounded Marines. AJ and the remaining Marines provided cover fire, until the second helicopter could get airborne and make its way back to base. After the helicopter was safely out of range, AJ and his men slipped away into the darkness.

Once safely hidden away in a bombed out industrial building, AJ discovered their only radio had been shot up in the firefight. Now, they really were on their own, at least until they could find another means of communication.

AJ and his team still had a mission to fulfill, so the next morning, they began scouting around to see what they could come up with. Luckily, they stumbled across some Bosnian sympathizers who led the Marines to the aircrew. The pilot was in pretty good shape, but the RIO had broken both legs when he landed in a pile of rubble. He was conscious, but weak and appeared to have some internal bleeding. The squad's medic bandaged and sedated him the best he could, but said the RIO

80

needed medical help ASAP. AJ had initially planned to pack it in during the day, and attempt to make their escape after dark. But those plans would have to change if he expected to get everyone back home alive and kicking.

AJ and his team hid in the back of a large delivery truck driven by the sympathizers. As they approached one of the checkpoints, AJ and two other Marines slipped out the back and took out the guards manning the checkpoint. Afterwards, they changed into the guards' uniforms and waited for the next military vehicle to show up.

They worked the checkpoint for about an hour before a 6x6 finally pulled up to the checkpoint. The driver and co-driver were rendered unconscious, then AJ and his team drove the truck to the Bosnian border without incident.

However, when they attempted to cross the border, they were confronted with friendly fire. AJ had used the truck's horn and lights to transmit an SOS signal, which no one picked up on until after the truck had been hit with an RPG.

A Stryker 8-wheeled armored vehicle was dispatched to assess the damage and capture any remaining survivors. When the squad leader discovered they had fired on friendlies, medics were rushed out to care for the wounded until a medevac helo could get them to the nearest field hospital. Two Marines and the RIO died as a result of the incident. AJ and another Marine were wounded.

The Officer of the Day and the Base Commander immediately began working on a cover story and wasted little time in filing charges against AJ. AJ was being accused of gross incompetence and negligence, and the incident was being reviewed for his court-martial. That's when Julie met AJ.

He was still in the hospital, recovering from shrapnel wounds to his left leg and arm. Luckily, the shrapnel didn't sever any major arteries, muscles or tendons. What began as a cold and callous interrogation slowly began to give way to a more personable and impassioned understanding of what was going through AJ's mind during the operation. It became obvious to Julie that AJ's decision to risk a daytime escape in order to save all hands and complete the mission was indeed the right one. What started out as case of incompetence against AJ, ended with him receiving the Silver Star, a Purple Heart, and a Battlefield Commission he would later turn down.

However, the Base Commander and the Officer of the Day did not fare so well. Julie's investigation uncovered evidence revealing the BC and OD deliberately tried to withhold information, which included witness tampering, and would prove AJ's attempt to alert the base of who they were. The BC was transferred to a non-combat zone, and the OD demoted and transferred to Alaska.

Once AJ became ambulatory, he was transferred to England for R & R. It just so happened that Julie had friends in England, plus she had some time to kill between cases. While fraternizing between officers and NCOs is frowned upon, neither of them initially saw their relationship that way.

But things have a way of changing over time, and soon they began to fall in love. Both of them tried to rationalize their relationship as being primarily platonic, but they were only fooling themselves. Finally, Julie was the one who broke it off, although it literally tore her apart emotionally. She knew she loved AJ, but as long as they were in the military, their relationship would only cause trouble for both of them.

AJ took it pretty hard, too. But he had no idea what was going through Julie's mind. He took it as a slap in the face, so he went cold turkey on her. No letters, no phone calls, nothing. That was five years ago, and now, out of the blue, here she is.

***

"So, now you know about as much as I do," says AJ.

"Do you have any idea of how big the Core is?" asks Weathers.

"No, sir, but I intend to find out."

"What about backup? Do you think Senator Higgins will provide you with the men you're going to need to protect him?"

"I gave him until Friday. After that, we'll need to bring some people in."

"Well, at least you'll have Julie with you tomorrow, that'll be a help."

"I'm not so sure. He might perceive her as a threat that we can't count on his ability to deliver. I suggest we wait a couple of days and see what happens. If he comes up short, I'll insist he take her on. But if he fills the bill, well, we'll just have to figure something else out."

"I'm not too crazy about this, but there is some logic in your thinking."

"Look. We still have plenty of things that need to be done. Julie and I and can go back to your house and talk to Lisa."

"Who's Lisa?" asks Julie.

"Lisa is David McKenzie's sister," replies AJ. "Oh, never mind. I'll explain it to you on the way over there."

"That's a good idea, AJ," says Weathers. "Maybe what we need is a woman's touch with her. Someone who is not as close to the situation as you."

"What situation?" asks Julie.

"Didn't you watch the news yesterday?" he asks, as the two of them leave Weathers' office and head for the elevator.

Once in the elevator, the two of them find themselves alone with each other for the first time in almost five years. He's trying his best not to look directly into her eyes, because he can feel himself weakening and longing to wrap his arms around her, and draw her up to him. But what he doesn't know is that Julie is desperately trying to get him to do just that. From the moment the elevator doors close, AJ hasn't stopped talking, but Julie hasn't heard a single word he's said.

While driving out to Mr. Weathers' home, he tells Julie about the attack at Lisa's home the night before. It's somewhat easier for him to talk to Julie this way, since part of his concentration is now on traffic. But every time he glances over to her, he can't help but notice those beautiful long legs jutting out from her taut skirt, and just a hint of cleavage peeking out from her blouse, and those luscious lips, just begging to be kissed.

Julie, on the other hand, is checking out the scenery to help prevent her from doing and saying the things going on in her mind. While she has gone out with a few guys over the years, none of them were serious, and never lasted very long. AJ holds her heart, body, and soul, only he doesn't know it, at least not yet.

AJ pulls up to the curb in front of the Weathers' home, then walks around and opens the door for Julie. As she sweeps her legs out of the car to exit the vehicle, AJ can't help but notice that her blouse pulls away from her body, and gives him a very inviting view of her breasts. While it appears totally innocent on her part, Julie had deliberately loosened the upper button on her blouse as AJ was walking around the car to open her door. She is determined to get his attention and break down his resistance to her. It's working. He points to the steps that lead up to the Weathers' home, then stays a step or two behind her as they ascend them to the door, all the while his eyes are fixed on her swaying hips. AJ is in agony. Those old feelings are rising to the surface.

Mrs. Weathers answers the doorbell, and invites them into her home. "Good afternoon AJ, and who's this lovely young lady?"

"This is Agent Julie Robinson, Mrs. Weathers," he says. "Is Lisa in?" The boys are in the living room watching TV, playing and screaming as little ones often do.

"Yes, Lisa and I are in the kitchen trying to decide what we want to prepare for dinner. Come on back." The three of them go to the kitchen and find Lisa standing in front of the pantry. "Lisa? Look who's here. It's AJ, and he brought a friend, Ms. Robinson, I think."

"Please, call me Julie," she says, forcing a smile. Lisa turns briefly, nods her head, then turns back, and continues to scan the pantry.

AJ walks up behind Lisa, slowly turns her around, hugs her and says, "Lisa? Julie works with me, and she needs to ask you some questions about David. I felt it might be a little easier talking to a woman about this. Why don't you and Julie go upstairs so you can have a little privacy? Mrs. Weathers and I will watch the boys."

"Just promise me one thing," says Lisa in a broken voice, with tears streaming down her cheeks. "Promise me that whoever set David up, pays for this with his life. Promise me. Promise me!"

"I promise," he replies, holding her tight to his chest. As AJ stands there holding Lisa in his arms, Julie begins to see a totally different side of him. The AJ she had known before was somewhat brash, carefree, yet focused on his job, and his men. While he was a different person whenever he was around her, she still felt he was not the sensitive type. She had obviously been mistaken.

AJ walks with Lisa and Julie to the staircase, then stops at the base of the stairs while the two of them continue on. Julie closes the bedroom door behind them, then asks Lisa to sit on the bed, while she sits at the dressing table. She removes a micro recorder from her purse, presses the record button, then says, "This is Agent Julie Robinson, interviewing Mrs. Lisa McNee, sister of Corporal David McKenzie. It's Tuesday, the 14th of June, 2011, at 1630 hours, and we're at the home of Mr. Robert Weathers, supervisor with the Secret Service." She presses the stop key, then listens to the recording to make certain the recorder is working properly. Once satisfied that it is working as it should, she once again presses the record key, and says, "Mrs. McNee, Agent Jackson tells me he was with you at Corporal McKenzie's funeral last year. Is that correct?"

"Yes," says Lisa, as she tries to fight back the tears.

"Is it also true, that since the funeral, you have had contact with Corporal McKenzie?"

"Yes, I have."

"Were you surprised to hear from him?"

"Of course I was surprised! Actually, shocked would be more accurate."

"So, you weren't aware he had faked his own death?"

"Of course not! My god! I was devastated! I had already lost my mother, father, and our older brother. He was all the family I had left. I could hardly bear it. David was much more than just my brother."

"When did you become aware that David, Corporal McKenzie, was still alive?"

"It was Little Tim's birthday, last November. David sent him a birthday card, and a gift certificate to Toys 'r' Us. At first, I thought maybe he had set it up sometime in advance, prior to his death, but that wouldn't have been David."

"How was the card delivered?"

"It was dropped in the letterbox in our front door."

"Was there a stamp or return address on the envelope?"

"No, no stamp and no return address. It was obviously hand delivered, because it was dropped off before the mail had run that day."

"Did David make any other attempts to contact you?"

"Yes. About a week later, I came home after running a few errands, and found a message on the answering machine. It was David."

"Do you have caller ID, and was there a number left for you to get in touch with him?"

"Yes, I have caller ID, but the number wasn't listed. The display read Private."

"What did David say in the message?"

"He said that he was alive, and he would try again at the same time the next day."

"Well, did he?"

"Yes, he did."

"So, what did he tell you?"

"He said that he, along with other members of his squad, had been approached by some people from the government, but outside the military. He was told that by working for them, he would be able to do things for the United States, that otherwise could not be done. But for them to be able to work effectively, they either had to 'die' or be listed as 'missing and presumed dead'."

"So, their exercise in the North Sea was staged to look like an accident. If he was supposed to be dead, then why was he contacting you? Surely he knew he was risking his cover?"

"I'm sure he knew that, but there were things starting to bother him. Things that made him question who and what these people were."

"What do you mean?"

"For starters, since he had been working for them, he had seen only two other members of his squad. When he asked where the others were, he was told they were out on a training exercise, or on a mission."

"So?"

"He and the other two squad members were in training, too. They were learning about electronic surveillance, unique ways of killing people, all kinds of stuff," replies Lisa. "He asked himself how the other squad members could be out on a mission if they were supposed to be in training? He stopped by their barracks a few days later and discovered all of their gear and personal effects were gone, their room vacant, almost like they'd never existed. When he approached his training officer about it, all he said was that they had washed out, and were returned to regular duty."

"But how could that be if they had been listed as missing and presumed dead, along with the rest of them?"

"It didn't make any sense to David either. He gave me their names, home towns, and a couple of friends' names, and asked that I try to confirm or deny his suspicions."

"Well, did you?"

"Yes, I did. Their status as missing and presumed dead had not changed."

"What did you do next?"

"I waited for David to call me."

"Well, did he?"

"I didn't hear from him again until sometime in March. I almost hung up on him when he called. His voice sounded so different, strained. He said he felt like he was being watched. He told me he knew the other team members were dead, by the way things worked around there. He really sounded spooky. I don't know any other way to describe it. He also said he wasn't going to call me anymore, because he was afraid something might happen to me and the kids. Just before he hung up, he said he was sorry for the pain he had put me through, and that he loved me. Then he said goodbye. That was the last time I heard from him."

Tears are streaming down her face again, and her words are breaking up, while trying to maintain some degree of control. Julie turns off the recorder, walks over to Lisa, sits beside her, and holds her hand. Lisa finally loses it, and begins to cry uncontrollably.

Mrs. Weathers and AJ can faintly hear Lisa's crying over the din of the boys playing around. As he turns to go upstairs, Mrs. Weathers touches his arm and says, "AJ? Why don't you let nature take its course? Lisa's had a troubled life. Between an

87

abusive father, the deaths of her older brother Tim, her mother, and now David, along with raising two boys, a husband who spends more time on the road than at home, the poor girl needs to vent, or she's going to lose her mind. It needs to get out, so she can cope with what's coming next."

"And what's that?" he asks.

"Tomorrow…Tomorrow is coming."

"And what is that supposed to mean?"

"No one really knows what tomorrow's going to bring," she says with a smile on her face. "One can hope it will be joy and happiness, but it could just as easily be sorrow, pain, and misery. You pray for the best, but prepare for the worst."

"Robert and I have been married over thirty years, and not once has he told me anything about what he does, but I have always had faith in him and what he was doing. He's a kind and gentle man, but when he went to work for the CIA, I noticed a gradual change in his behavior. He started to become more reclusive and secretive. What he was doing for them was taking a little part of him every day. I did the best I could to try to help him get it back, but I seemed to be fighting a losing battle."

"One day, Robert came home early and found me in the kitchen, crying. In all the years we've been married, he had never seen me cry before. He rushed over to me to see what was wrong, and saw that I had dropped a dish in the sink, and it had shattered into a million pieces. He said to me, "Honey, it's only a dish." And I said to him that I wasn't crying over the dish. It was only the trigger that made me cry, not the cause."

"We sat down at the kitchen table and talked for almost an hour. I could tell he understood what I was saying, because I could see the tears welling up in his eyes. The very next day, he put in a request for transfer to the Secret Service."

She begins to smile again, then says, "Actually, it was more like an ultimatum. Even the Director of the CIA tried to talk him out of it, but he told them they could either transfer him, or he was going to take early retirement."

"You know? I still don't know what he does for the Secret Service. He doesn't volunteer, and I don't ask. But you know what? I got my Robert back. I got my husband back. That's enough."

Mrs. Weathers and AJ are still watching the boys, when Lisa and Julie finally come back down to the main floor of the house. AJ stands up, and Lisa walks over to him and gives him a hug and a kiss on the cheek, then says, "Thank you." Lisa glances at the clock on the wall, and says, "Where did the time go? It's almost dinner time, and we still don't know what we're going to have yet."

As Mrs. Weathers gets up from the couch, she says to AJ, "You and Julie are going to stay for dinner, aren't you?"

"Thank you Mrs. Weathers, but I've already asked too much of you and your husband, and I would not dare to presume we should have dinner with you tonight."

"Nonsense! I haven't had this many people at my dinner table since the holidays!"

Then Lisa says, "AJ's right. You already have a house full with me and my kids. It's been a hectic day for all concerned. Maybe some other time, perhaps." Lisa is looking at Julie, and Julie is looking at AJ.

Looking at both Lisa and Julie, Mrs. Weathers realizes what Lisa is trying to say. "Very well, AJ. Why don't you take Julie out for a nice quiet dinner? We'll get together another time, okay?" She can see Julie's eyes light up, so she knows she did the right thing.

As AJ and Julie prepare to leave, he asks Lisa, "Have you tried to contact Sean?"

"Yes, I have."

"What did you tell him?"

"I told him the house was going to need some remodeling before we could move back in," she replies.

"How did he take that?"

"I'm not really sure. There was nothing but silence on his end of the line."

"Oh well," says AJ. "Are you going to call him back?"

"Maybe tomorrow, give him a chance to let it soak in."

"You two need to get going before all the good places get packed!" says Mrs. Weathers.

"Are you trying to get rid of us?" asks AJ.

"What do you think?" replies Mrs. Weathers.

"Okay. Okay. I can take a hint."

"I was beginning to wonder," says Lisa.

As AJ opens the door, they discover that it's raining heavily. "Damn! Where'd this come from?" he exclaims. "My umbrella's in the trunk! Wait here while I get it and unlock the doors."

"Don't be silly! I won't melt," says Julie, as she covers her head with her suit jacket. "In fact, I'll race you to the car! One, two, three, go!" as she runs down the steps to the car.

"But Julie! The car's locked!" he yells, as he tries to catch up to her.

Both of them are soaked to the bone as they jump into the car. Julie is laughing like a schoolgirl, but she certainly doesn't look like one. The rain has made her blouse almost transparent, revealing her firm breasts and erect nipples, through her lacy bra. AJ is having a hard time taking his eyes off them, yet Julie acts as though nothing is out of the ordinary. She looks over at AJ, then looks down at her breasts, and says, "What? It's not like you haven't seen them before."

"I just don't remember them looking that good! That's all," he says with a smile.

"I'll take that as a compliment," she replies. "Now, can we go somewhere and get something to eat? I'm starving!"

"We can't go into a restaurant with you looking like that. You might get arrested for indecent exposure!"

"Well, surely there's a decent restaurant that has takeout near your place, right?" she says with a devilish smile.

"Chinese okay?" asks AJ.

"Mandarin?"

"Absolutely," he says.

"Perfect!" she replies.

"Tell you what. I'll call it in, drop you off at my apartment, then I'll pick up dinner. Okay?"

"Works for me."

TLC: Chapter 14

AJ pulls up to the front of his apartment building, jumps out of the car, opens her door, and escorts Julie into the building. The two of them take the elevator up to the fourth floor to his apartment. While AJ is standing at the door fumbling with his keys, Julie is standing right in front of him, with those gorgeous breasts of hers almost blocking his view. He glances up at her face, and sees that she has this demure look about her. She's teasing him, literally destroying his concentration, and she's loving every minute of it.

"Yes!" he says, as he finally finds the right key, unlocks and opens the door.

As Julie enters the apartment, she says, "Wow! Who's your maid?"

"No maid," he replies. "I'm hardly ever home, except to eat and sleep."

"This place is so spotless, it's almost sterile. No parties?"

"No time."

"That's a shame," she remarks.

"Not really," he says. "I have plenty to keep me busy."

"What about tonight?"

"Why don't we just concentrate on getting you out of those wet clothes, into something dry, then I'll pick up dinner. What do you say?"

"Okay. Where's the bathroom?"

"Down at the end of the hall. The bedroom is the first door on your right. I'm sure I've got a shirt or something you can wear. I'll be right back shortly."

As Julie walks toward the bathroom, she's unbuttoning her rain soaked blouse. Once she reaches the bathroom, she turns around and faces AJ, pulls the blouse out of her skirt, exposing her breasts, then slowly closes the door behind her. AJ is standing there, literally in shock. Julie is teasing him mercilessly, and now he's got to leave her to pick up dinner!

AJ rushes over to the Chinese carryout to pick up their order, but it isn't quite ready, so he goes to the bathroom to take care of business. While standing at the urinal, he can't help but notice the condom dispenser in front of him. *"Hmmm. I should*

91

probably get a couple of these, just in case," he says to himself. He reaches into his pockets and finds that he has no change for the machine. He quickly washes his hands, then goes to the counter. A little old Chinese lady is standing there, and as he pulls out a five-dollar bill, he asks for some quarters.

"You have hot date?" the lady asks with a heavy Oriental accent.

"Pardon me?"

"You have hot date?" she asks again.

AJ is embarrassed by the question and blushes a bit, like a kid caught with his hands in the cookie jar.

The old lady smiles and says, "You need to order Moo Shoo Pork. Special sauce make girl very hot! Make her want you! Moo Shoo Pork look like Chinese burrito. Gets her juices flowing! Makes her very hot!"

"Ma'am, I don't think that's going to be a problem," he says with a sheepish grin.

"Try it! You see! Make her very hot!"

It's obvious this little old lady has his number, and it doesn't appear she's going to give up very easily, so AJ finally relents and says, "Okay. I, ah, we'll try the Moo Shoo Pork."

"Good choice! Try it. You see. Make her want you. Make her very hot!" she replies, while exchanging his five dollar bill for quarters and singles.

"Thank you. Thank you," says AJ.

As AJ returns to the men's room to buy the condoms, the oriental lady's husband comes up behind her and asks, "What's with the silly accent? And what was all that about Moo Shoo Pork making his girlfriend hot?"

The little old lady replies in perfect English, "Some bum ordered Moo Shoo Pork almost an hour ago and never showed up. I'm sick and tired of throwing away perfectly good food, so I wanted to see if I could talk him into buying it." Her husband shakes his head in disbelief, and disappears back into the kitchen.

***

While AJ is out picking up dinner, Julie takes a quick shower, wraps herself in a towel, then goes to AJ's bedroom to find something to wear. She remembers buying him a silk shirt while they were in England together, and she's curious to see whether or not he's kept it. After all, it's been five years since she last saw him.

As she goes from one shirt to the next in his closet, she is starting to get worried that maybe he's thrown it away. She starts raking the hangers across the rod faster and faster, until one of them falls from the rod. As she bends over to pick it up, she spots the sleeve of the shirt she's been looking for in the hamper. She smiles, feeling relieved, and starts pulling the shirt from the hamper. When she spots the blood stained bullet hole, she gasps.

Suddenly, Julie hears someone at the door. It's AJ fumbling with his keys while trying to hold their dinner. She rushes to the door, and as she opens it for him, AJ loses his balance, and almost falls into the room.

Instinctively, she attempts to catch their dinner before it hits the floor, and loses her towel in the process, exposing herself in all her splendor.

"Thanks! I needed that," he says with a smile.

She stoops down, picks up the towel, wraps it around herself once again, and says sheepishly, "No problem. Glad I could help." As AJ takes their dinner into the living room and places it on the coffee table, she asks, "How's your arm?"

"What?" he asks, as he motions her to sit on the couch, while he sits on the floor across from her. He starts dividing the entrees onto their Styrofoam plates, occasionally sampling an item here and there, then passes a plate on to Julie.

"Your left arm," she says as she begins to eat hungrily. "While I was looking for a shirt to wear, I noticed the shirt I had gotten you was in the hamper. When I pulled it out, I discovered what appears to be a bullet hole along with some blood around it."

"Oh, that," he says, as he begins to eat. "That happened while I was at Lisa's house. Remember I told you about the three guys that tried to kill us?"

"Yes, I do. But you forgot to mention that you got shot," she says rather bluntly.

"Look. It's nothing. Just a scratch, that's all. See? And as far as the shirt goes, I'm taking it to the cleaners tomorrow to see

93

if they can make a short sleeve shirt out of it. I think there's enough material, don't you?"

"You don't have to do that on my account. It's just a shirt. Mmm! This is good! What is it?" she asks while sampling the Moo Shoo Pork.

"Well, if it's just a shirt, why did you go to the trouble of trying to find it?" He has her! *"She has no comeback!"* He says to himself.

"Actually, it was more out of curiosity than anything else," she replies while continuing to eat voraciously.

"Really? You know we bought a few other things together. Why that one? Why that particular shirt?"

She drops her head, obviously embarrassed. "Okay, you've got me. Look, I was going to tell you later, but I guess now is as good a time as any. The day we bought that shirt, I felt closer to you than I ever had before. AJ? I love you. I've loved you from that first day I saw you all bandaged up in the hospital. I didn't care if you were innocent or guilty. Well, I hoped you were innocent. Anyway, I don't know how to put my finger on it, but I just knew." She pauses long enough to take another bite. "Mmm! This is really tasty! What did you say this is?"

"Wow! That's a little heavy. Then why did you drop me like a live grenade back in England? I thought we were getting along just great." He pauses, then says, "I didn't say what it is."

"You know how the military is. I was an officer, you were a noncom. They would have frowned about our relationship from the very beginning. And even if we had been able to get married, our relationship would have been strained by your job and mine." She stops long enough to wolf down the last bite of her Moo Shoo Pork. "Is there more of this over there somewhere?"

"Maybe, but I was willing to give it a try." He takes a bite of his Moo Shoo Pork, then says, "Uh-huh," as he hands her another one.

"You know? I was actually hoping you would have accepted that Battlefield Commission they offered you. I saw that as a glimmer of hope we could have gotten together, as equals." AJ is shaking his head. "Don't you see?" she continues, "We would both have been officers, and there would have been nothing the military could do to prevent us from getting married. But when you turned it down, it made me feel like you cared for your men and your country, more than me! I was jealous. And hurt. I didn't know how to compete." She pauses for a moment and takes another bite. "This is really good! Have you ever tried this before?"

"Julie? Why didn't you tell me? I really had no idea, no clue that was how you felt. No, this is the first time. A little old Chinese lady recommended we try it."

"You had no clue," she says disappointingly. "Who do you think I am? Do you think I jump into bed with every client I defend?" She takes another bite, then asks, "Has she ever recommended you try anything before?"

"No!" he exclaims. "Of course not. But..."

"But what?" she asks in an aggressive manner. "You don't believe I jump into bed with just anyone, or no, the little Chinese lady has never recommended anything to you before?"

"Yes! I mean no. Damnit!" he says getting frustrated. AJ pauses a moment to collect his thoughts. "Yes, I believe you when you say you don't just sleep with anyone, and no, the little old Chinese lady has never recommended anything to me before."

"Good! I'm glad we got that cleared up," she says. "Now, what is this we're eating?"

"Promise me you're not going to laugh."

"About what?"

"What I'm about to tell you," he says. "Promise."

"Okay," she replies with a look of curiosity on her face.

"The little old Chinese lady asked me if I had a hot date," he says embarrassingly while staring down at his plate.

"Now, why would she ask you a question like that?"

"Because I came out of the bathroom asking for quarters."

Julie has this perplexed look on her face for a few seconds, but then the light comes on, and she bursts out laughing. While trying to catch her breath she asks, "What does that have to do with what we're eating?"

"I guess Moo Shoo Pork is supposed to be some kind of aphrodisiac."

Julie is literally howling now. "Are you serious? She actually said that?"

"Well, not in so many words. She said it would make you want me, make you hot for me." Julie is laughing to the point of tears.

"Look," he says cautiously, "I, ah, had never met anyone like you before, and, ah, well, you know."

"What?" she asks as she's trying to regain her composure.

"While I was in high school, when all the other guys were busy trying to be jocks, and all that stuff, I really didn't do much with girls," he says reluctantly. "Oh, I went out on a few dates, and I guess you could even say I had a girlfriend or two, but, well... I... ah…"

"AJ? What are you trying to say?"

He takes a deep breath, sighs, then confesses, "Until I met you, I had never really had what I would call a serious relationship with a woman before."

"You're kidding, right?" she says in disbelief. "But AJ, you're a Marine. You're tall, handsome, you're smart, you're focused, you're confident..."

"Bullshit!" he says. "The Marine Corps teaches you discipline, determination, and gives you the skill and ability to kill just about anyone or anything that gets in your way. There's nothing in the Marine Corps manual that tells you anything about male/female relationships."

He pauses a moment to catch his breath. "Oh, women see the uniform, and go gaga," as he becomes animated and rolls his eyes. "But none of them were really focused on me, the man *in* the uniform. I've had my share of one-night stands, and I guess, in some respects, I'm probably just as guilty as they were. And while there might have been some lust or passion involved, there was no warmth, no substance. Hell, I'll bet over half of them never even knew my name."

"Well, did you know theirs?" she counters.

"Touché! You see? I just can't win," as he sighs and shakes his head.

"Win what?"

"A conversation with you," he replies.

"It's not a contest, AJ," she says with a smile. "Besides, I'm a damn good attorney. I'm supposed to win."

"Can I ask you a question?"

"Depends on the question."

"Is the Moo Shoo Pork working?" he asks smiling.

"Well, I guess there's only one way to find out," she says with a seductive look on her face.

"Hmm," he mumbles, then carefully begins to work his legs out from under the table, gets up on his knees, then starts to lean over the coffee table to give Julie a kiss. But, as luck would have it, he knocks over his drink, and that creates a domino effect with everything else on the table. Julie shrieks, jumps up, and loses her towel again. She tries to cover herself with one of the pillows, and she's laughing hysterically. AJ frantically tries to keep everything on the coffee table, all the while cursing under his breath, and shaking his head.

"AJ," she says while trying to regain her composure, "you're supposed to eat it, not wear it."

"Well, I guess that's one way to spoil the mood."

"Oh, AJ, you give up too easily. Look, I'll help you clean this up. Then we'll take a shower, so I can get you cleaned up, and then we'll see what happens next, okay? Come on. Let's go."

TLC: Chapter 15

AJ's apartment
Wednesday morning
June 15, 2011, 0600 hours local time

Julie awakens to the aroma of fresh brewed coffee. She stretches her arms above her head and yawns. As her eyes begin to focus in the morning light, she notices that AJ's room is quite stark, just the bare essentials. No pictures adorn the wall. No awards, diplomas, medals. Nothing. Just bare walls. The room is neat by all other accounts, but it's missing character. It doesn't look lived in. Now she starts to hear the clatter of pots, and pans, the sizzle of fried eggs and bacon, and the faint smell of... No way! Homemade biscuits?

As she starts to sit up, she realizes she is completely nude. Then, as she recalls last night, a very satisfactory smile shines upon her face. She hasn't felt this good in over five years! She also notices her clothes are folded neatly on the back of the chair, and even her shoes have a fresh shine to them.

She finds a shirt AJ left by her side of the bed for her to wear. She slips it on, then wanders into the kitchen to find AJ humming to himself, as he's cooking away. She reaches around him from behind, snuggles her head next to his, and says in a soft, seductive tone, "Good morning."

"Did you sleep well?" he asks with a smile on his face, while still focusing on their eggs.

"Well, I certainly did after," she says in a sultry voice, as she nibbles on his ear.

"Are you wanting to start round two already? We haven't had breakfast, and the coffee isn't ready yet. Don't you need any caffeine?"

"You can be my caffeine," she half whispers in his ear, as she starts rubbing her hands up and down his arms, then onto his firm chest, down to his taught abdomen. Then as she nuzzles his neck with her nose, she eases her hands down below his waist. It's obvious that at least a part of him is ready for round two.

"Look! Let's at least eat the eggs and bacon while they're hot," he says, while trying to resist her advances.

"Who are you trying to convince, me or 'him'?" she asks as she continues to kiss and fondle him.

"Julie, if this were the weekend, you couldn't drag me out of the bedroom. But it's already after 0600, and we both need to get ready for the day. I need to get you back to the office, and then I've got to be out at the senator's estate by 0800, or my ass will be in a sling."

"You look! I don't know about you, but I haven't enjoyed making love like that for a long time! I'd kinda like to know I wasn't dreaming last night. How about you?" she asks sounding hurt and unappreciated.

"I'm afraid you're going to have to wait until tonight for a repeat performance, because I've really got to get moving," he says. "The senator's a pretty punctual kind of guy, and if I want to stay on his good side, well, I need to be there on time."

"Oh, all right. But I'm holding you to that repeat performance tonight."

"Should I place another order for Moo Shoo Pork?" he asks jokingly.

"Only if *you* need it."

With breakfast out of the way, and Julie's had some time to reflect, she asks, "Well, what's on the agenda for today?"

"As I mentioned earlier, I need to pick up the senator and take him to Washington, and that will pretty much kill the day for me."

"What about me?"

"Well, did Lisa give you any leads last night?"

"No, not really. I suppose I could check out the names of the men in David's squad, and see what their backgrounds and specialties were."

"You might want to do a search on how many men have been listed as missing in action and presumed dead over the last three to five years. I'd probably concentrate on the Army and Marine Corps, and I'd be looking at those with Special Ops training. Oh! I know. If I gave you Lisa's address, you could snoop around and see if there might be any clues everyone else missed."

"Perfect! Leave me with the dirty work!"

"Look. You were the one who worked with NCIS, not me. Let's just see how good you really are." he says as if he were challenging her.

"Okay, you're on." she says, responding to his challenge. "What's the address?"

"511 North Addison. I think it's the fourth or fifth house on the left, off Main Street. It should be pretty easy to spot. I would imagine it's surrounded by yellow caution tape and barricades."

"I think I can find it," she says reluctantly. "Anything else?"

"Not right now, but I'm sure I'll think of something."

"I bet you will. Think we'll have a chance to get together for lunch?"

"I wouldn't count on it," he says. "Remember? I'll be on the Hill."

"Oh yeah, right. The Hill," she replies sarcastically and turns away.

AJ reaches over and gently lifts her chin and turns her face toward him and says, "Tell me something. Do you really think I enjoy driving the senator around all day in a stretched Lincoln? Do you think I get my jollies following him from one session to another, then another?"

"Sometimes I feel like the school monitor, or your garden-variety wallflower. I stand in the shadows within earshot, just in case something happens. I'm not part of any conversations, other than saying the words, "Yes, sir" to his, "Follow me," or "Let's go." Believe me. I'd much rather be out in the field, using my head, my training, leading my squad to a specific goal. Get the job done, and get out. I'm used to being the adversary. But here, I feel like I'm a sitting duck."

"I'm sorry AJ. Since you put it that way, I have a better understanding of how you feel. As a matter of fact, I've learned more about you in the last twenty-four hours than I did the entire time we were together in England. And yes, it's all good." She smiles, then reaches over and gives him a long, deep kiss. As she starts to back away from him, she says, "You've gotta tell me something."

"What's that?"

"When did you learn how to make homemade biscuits?"

"Oh. These? These aren't homemade," he says with a light chuckle. "These are Pillsbury frozen biscuits. But don't they smell and taste like homemade? Really, I wouldn't even know where to start."

Again she laughs, "AJ, you're honest to a fault, you know that?"

"What?"

"Oh, never mind. It's not important," she says. "Who gets the bathroom first?"

"Well, ah," he hesitates.

"Thanks. You're such a doll," she says as she heads off to the bathroom.

"You're welcome," he says under his breath.

TLC: Chapter 16

AJ drops Julie off at the Homeland Security Building and takes off to pick up the senator. As Julie gets off the elevator on her way to her desk, she runs into Mr. Weathers.

"Good morning Agent Robinson. You're here a bit early aren't you?" he asks.

"AJ dropped me off on the way to the senator's estate. I thought I'd do some research on the men in Corporal McKenzie's squad, along with any military personnel who have been declared missing and presumed dead over the last three to five years," she replies.

"Julie," says Weathers, "that's what the interns are for. Jot down the information you need and give it to Martha. She'll give it to a couple of the interns downstairs. What else did you have in mind?"

"Well, AJ suggested I go out to Lisa's, I mean, Mrs. McNee's house to see if I can dig up any clues that might have been overlooked," she replies.

"Now that sounds like a good idea," says Weathers. "We never did sign a car out for you, did we."

"No, sir, not yet."

"Here are my keys. It's on Level Three, space number seventy-seven, just to the left of the elevator. It's a dark blue Crown Victoria, tag number G 17179."

"Thank you sir, but that's really not necessary," she says. "My car is parked on Level Four. I don't mind using it."

"No, I insist. You're on company business. Just be sure you take everything you need, camera, fingerprint kit, gloves..."

"Sir, I have everything in my briefcase right here," she replies as she tries to get Mr. Weathers to pocket his keys.

"Agent Robinson," he says in a firm tone. "If you want to stay on my good side, I suggest you take these keys, and get out of here, before I move your office down with the interns. Do I make myself clear?"

Julie snaps to attention and says, "Yes, sir! Thank you, sir. Right away, sir." She takes his keys and, in quickstep, hurries back to the elevator. As she passes Martha's desk, Julie asks, "Geez! Is he always that cranky?"

Martha replies, "You think that's cranky? You should have heard him *before* his third cup of coffee!"

Julie exits the elevator on Level Three, and sure enough, his car is just a couple of spaces from the elevator. She gets in, adjusts the seat, steering wheel, and mirrors, then starts the car. Once at the exit, she pulls out the address information for Lisa's house, and heads out.

***

Traffic is moderately heavy, although having spent the previous six months driving in LA, she's used to it. Traffic on Main Street is considerably lighter, but when she turns onto North Addison, she's confronted by a man wearing an orange jumpsuit and a yellow plastic hard hat, waving a stop sign in her face. There's a bulldozer and a back hoe where Lisa's house is supposed to be.

As she lowers the driver's side window, the man with the stop sign walks up to her and says, "Lady, you can't get through. We're tearing down a building, something about a gas leak."

Julie gets out of the car, takes out her Secret Service ID and asks, "Who's in charge here?" as she starts walking toward the demolition site.

"Ma'am, you don't understand. There's a gas leak up there someplace!" the man exclaims.

"Well, if you have a gas leak, where are the people from the gas company? Shouldn't they be out here shutting off the main? Don't you think tearing down a building might cause a minor explosion by itself?" she says sarcastically. "Now, once again, who's in charge? I want a name, and I want to see some paperwork authorizing this demolition, and I want it now." She puts her purse down on the hood of a truck across from what used to be Lisa's house, takes out her phone, and calls AJ.

"Look lady. I don't know from nothin'," he replies. "My job is to keep people from gettin' into the demolition site, that's all. But I can tell you that those three guys over there ordered the demolition," as he points to another Crown Vic with government plates. She puts down the phone, and starts digging for her digital camera from her purse. While the camera is powering up, the driver can tell Julie is up to something, so he starts backing up

103

the hill. She focuses the camera toward them, and gets off a couple of shots before they get out of camera range. Then she turns toward the house and takes a couple of pictures of the demolition.

Suddenly, she hears the faint sound of AJ on the phone, "Hello? Hello? Julie? Are you all right? Answer me!"

She picks up the phone, and says, "AJ? Remember when Lisa was telling you what she had told Sean about their house needing a little remodeling before they could move back in?"

"Yeah?"

"Well, they're actually going to need to look for a new house."

"What do you mean, and what's all that noise?"

"Well, you're not going to believe this, but I'm standing in front of the lot where Lisa's house used to be. And the sound you're hearing? That's a bulldozer and a back hoe finishing it off."

"What? You're kidding, right?" he says disbelievingly.

"AJ? You did say 511 North Addison, right?"

"Yeah."

"As of right now, it's officially a vacant lot."

"What the hell happened? Who authorized it? Who's in charge?" he asks.

"There was something said about a gas leak, but other than that, I don't have any answers, yet. However, I'll get to the bottom of this. I did spot a car with government plates on it, and according to the guy that I spoke to, one of them had given the authorization."

"Did you get a tag number?"

"Better than that. I got a picture of the car, the tag, and with a little luck, the occupants."

"Great job Julie. Just for that, I'm gonna buy you dinner tonight!"

"Let me guess. Moo Shoo Pork?"

"Is that a question, or a request?"

"I'm sure you'll figure it out," she says smiling.

"Okay, okay. Think about what you'd like, and I'll be happy to take you there."

"We'll see. What time and where should we meet?"

"Well, you've seen my place. Do you want to stay at my place again, or do you want to go yours for the evening?"

"I do need to go to my apartment, take a shower, and get some fresh clothes and a few other things. But I'm still not settled in my place yet. Most of it is still in boxes from the move, so if you don't mind, I'd like to sleep over at your place again. Maybe I can get you to volunteer to help me unpack over the weekend, and I'll treat you. How does that sound?"

"Well, I'm not cheap, but I can be had. Deal."

"All right then. Let me get back to questioning these people over here, and maybe I can get some names and paperwork about this. Talk to you later."

"Okay. Just be careful."

"I will. Bye." After ending her call to AJ, Julie turns to the man with the stop sign and yells, "Hey you! Traffic control."

"Who, me?"

"Yes, you. What's your name, and who's in charge?"

"My name's Gus, Gus Kowalchek. The foreman's name is Artie Franks. He's the one on the bulldozer."

"What's the foreman doing operating equipment?"

"Those suits in the car wanted the job done now. And the guy who was supposed to be operating the bulldozer didn't show up for work this morning," says Gus. "From what I could hear, those suits were threatening to put the squeeze on Artie if he didn't hurry up and get the job done."

"Do you happen to know where Artie keeps his work orders?"

"Sure! Artie's a real putz when it comes to paperwork. He usually leaves it all on top of the dash. Collects it at the end of the week to turn it in. He's always losing something. And I'm always tellin' him to put that stuff somewhere safe, like in a briefcase or somethin'. But he never listens to me."

"Which truck is his?"

"You're standin' next to it, lady."

"Oh! I see," she says, sounding a bit embarrassed. "Thank you. I guess you should get back to whatever it was you were doing."

"Sure thing lady," he replies, as he starts to walk back down the hill. "Oh, by the way, what you're lookin' for won't be on the dash board."

"I'm sorry?"

"The work order for the demolition is in the glove box. It's a three-parter. White goes to the customer, yellow goes to the office, and the foreman gets the pink," he says. "I don't think the suits bothered to pick up their copy."

"Really?" she asks. "You know, I should probably pick it up for them, since we both work for the government."

"Fine by me," he replies. "I just worry about traffic." Gus walks back to the intersection.

Julie returns to her car, drops her purse on the seat, and pulls out her brief case. Then she walks around to the passenger side of the truck, in an effort to conceal herself from the foreman or anyone else watching the area. She opens the door carefully, places her briefcase on the seat, and pulls out a pair of latex gloves, a plastic bag, and her fingerprint kit.

She notices a couple of clean prints she believes are probably Artie's, so she brushes them and pulls them for her file. She also finds a couple of gas receipts, and bags them for backups. While she's digging in the glove box, she finds the work order. Sure enough, the address is 511 North Addison.

The work order reads: *"Abandoned home, unable to locate homeowner, structure unstable, and uninhabitable. Property seized by HUD with permission by the U.S. Government due to homeowner failing to pay delinquent taxes on said property. HUD recommends its immediate demolition. HUD Order # D-35779. Process immediately. Dated: 14 June 2011."* The order is signed, but illegible.

Julie carefully tears off the top copy, places it in the bag, peels off her gloves, puts the bag and gloves in the briefcase, and then closes it.

As she starts to back up to close the door, she turns and finds Artie standing behind her. "Shit! You scared the living daylights out of me!"

"Somethin' I can help you with, Miss?" asks Artie with a snide look on his face.

"No, thank you. Gus said you might have a map in your glove box, but I couldn't find one," she says as she starts to walk away.

Artie grabs her by the arm and asks, "Are you sure that's all you were lookin' for?"

Staring directly into his eyes, she says sternly, "Artie? Unless you want me to embarrass you in front of your men, I'd suggest letting go of my arm, right now."

"And just how do you propose to do that?"

"Why don't I just show you?" Julie lays her briefcase on the back of the truck, turns, and knees Artie in the groin. As he bends forward in reaction to the hit, she grabs him by the same arm he had held her, gives him a quick spin, and flips him to the ground, flat of his back.

Julie stands over him and says, "When a lady asks you to let go of her arm, I suggest you do it. The next one might not be as nice as me." She smiles, picks up her briefcase, and casually walks back to her car, leaving Artie on the ground, curled up in a fetal position.

As she starts the car and prepares to back out onto Main Street, Gus walks over to her and says, "Lady, that's the funniest thing I've seen all day! Wait'll I tell the other guys that Artie got beat up by a skirt!" Gus walks out onto Main Street, stops the oncoming traffic, and motions to her that it's safe to back out.

Julie backs out onto the street, stops next to Gus, and says, "My pleasure." She decides that since she's on this side of town, she'll stop by her apartment, take a quick shower, and put on some fresh clothes. While she's at it, she'll pack some clothes for tomorrow, along with a few personal items.

Cruising down the road reminiscing about last night, she casually looks up to the rearview mirror and sees what appears to be the same Crown Vic she had seen in front of Lisa's house. The car is slowly gaining on her, and now she can clearly make out the shapes of three men in the car.

Julie moves over into the inside lane, and the car eases into the same lane two cars behind her. Just ahead, she can see that the light ahead is turning yellow. While there is still oncoming traffic, she moves out into the intersection, and once the light goes red, she cuts off an oncoming car that almost T-bones her. The oncoming driver stabs the brakes, and honks his horn, while shouting obscenities at her. Although Julie couldn't hear him, she could well imagine what he must have been saying. From her rear view mirror, she can see the other Crown Vic stuck at the light behind the other two cars. She smiles to herself and continues on her way.

However, a few blocks later, they're right back on her bumper. Traffic is moderate, moving along about 30-35mph. They're much too close to be left behind again, so she starts thinking how she can lose them. She moves over into the outside lane, then makes a right hand turn. They follow. Julie makes another right turn at the next intersection. Again, they follow. She eases up to about 40mph, and they remain on her tail, definitely closer than the recommended distance for their speed. Julie makes another right turn, and now they're back on Main Street, heading back toward Addison.

Off to her right, Julie spots a patrol car at the next traffic light. She can't believe her luck. She starts slowing down, hoping the light will change from green to yellow. The car behind her is really close, and the driver is obviously focused on her and doesn't see the patrol car. Sure enough, the light changes from green to yellow. At the last possible moment, she guns it, and makes it through the intersection as the light changes to red. The tail continues to follow Julie, blowing the light. The police car leaps into action with lights and siren blaring. From her rearview mirror, she can see the driver's frustration as he pounds his fist on the steering wheel, and reluctantly pulls over to the curb. With that, Julie decides she's probably better off heading back to the office.

While still relishing her victory, Julie calls Weathers. "Mr. Weathers? I guess it was a good thing you had me go out to Mrs. McNee's house this morning."

"Really? How's that? What did you find?"

"Well sir, the house has been demolished," she replies. "Three men driving a car with government plates gave a demolition crew a work order, supposedly from HUD, to tear down the house. I suspect it's a phony order."

"What makes you think that, Agent Robinson?"

"Well, for starters, the order was written yesterday, and they were out there tearing it down by 0800 this morning."

"And?"

"Have you ever heard of anyone or anything working that fast in Washington?"

"Are you implying the wheels of commerce move slowly here?"

"Sir, you said it, I didn't."

"I see your point."

"Well, do you have anything on the three men?"

"Yes sir. I was able to take a couple of pictures of the car, the tag, and I think we might even be able to make out a face or two, as they tried to back away."

"Is that all?"

"No sir," she says. "I was also able to get the top copy of the work order, along with some sample prints of the foreman. I'm hopeful the other prints on the work order will show up on NCIC. If these are men working for the Core, they could be ex-military, and if they are, their prints should show up somewhere."

"Very good, Agent Robinson. I'm impressed. Anything else?"

"As a matter of fact, I believe I do. After I left the McNee residence, those same men started following me. I was able to trick them into getting stopped by one of Brookmont's finest, at the intersection of Main Street and Washington. I think if you contact the Brookmont Police Department, you might find out the name of the driver."

"What did you do?"

"Well sir," she says rather smugly, "he was evidently paying more attention to me than his surroundings, and I tricked him into running a red light in front of a cop."

"Julie, you didn't," he says disbelievingly. "Good job, Julie, I mean, Agent Robinson. Good job."

"Thank you, sir. I should be at the office in a few minutes. Want me to come up to your office and fill you in?"

"Certainly. I'll have a couple of the interns up here to take care of your prints, and photos, and I'll have one of them call Brookmont PD, and see if they are willing to give us any info on that stop. What was that intersection again? Main and..."

"Washington, sir."

"Washington. Okay, got it. See you in a few."

Just as Mr. Weathers ends the call with Julie, his private line
rings. Before he has a chance to say "Hello", the voice on the
other end of the line says,

"What in the hell are you doing down there?"

"I beg your pardon?"

"Do you know that we've lost ten key operatives, and almost
exposed the identities of three others, all of this in just over forty-
eight hours?"

Weathers covers the mouthpiece of the phone, pushes
Martha's intercom button and says in a commanding tone,
"Martha, trace the call on my private line. Do it now."

Weathers replies indignantly, "Who is this, and how did you
get this number?"

"Who I am is of no importance, but who I represent? Well,
that's another matter entirely," replies the voice.

"Well, if you've lost ten of your key operatives, then you
better start training them better, or you better have a whole lot of
them. And as far as exposing the identities of the other three
operatives? You might tell them to try observing traffic signals,
especially when there's a cop present."

"We are trying to maintain the balance of our country, our
way of life," says the voice.

"Trying to take out a U.S. Senator in broad daylight, and
trying to kill an innocent woman and her children, are not what I
would call very humanitarian things to do, would you?"

"We know why you left the CIA," says the voice.

"I have a better view from my office?" replies Weathers with
an air of sarcasm in his voice. "A better benefit program?" He
pauses a moment. "Oh, I know. They don't charge me any extra
to cover my wife."

"How *is* your wife, Mr. Weathers?" asks the voice. "Have
you spoken to her today?"

"What do you know about my wife?" asks Weathers with
some aggression in his voice.

"Mr. Weathers, we're accustomed to getting what we want,
regardless of what must happen for us to get there," says the
voice.

"Leave my wife out of this. If you've got a problem with me, you better talk to me!" says Weathers in a commanding tone.

"But, I am talking to you, Mr. Weathers," says the voice calmly. "You're just not listening. Think about it. We'll talk again... Soon. Oh! And say "Hello" to your wife for me, okay?" Then, the line goes dead.

Martha calls back on the intercom and says, "Sorry Mr. Weathers. There wasn't enough time to get a trace. The only thing we could determine was that the call was made by cell phone."

"Damnit!" yells Weathers. "Martha? Put in a call to my wife. Now!"

"Yes, sir, Mr. Weathers."

Weathers opens the lower right hand drawer of his desk to reveal his Beretta 92FS Centurion secured in a black Sherpa paddle holster. He removes it from the holster, checks the loaded chamber indicator on the right side of the slide, verifying a round is in the chamber. He presses the mag release, and checks the magazine to confirm that it's at fifteen round capacity, then slams the mag back into the butt of the pistol. He stands up, slips the holster onto his waistband, and holsters the pistol. He then rushes over to the closet, grabs his suit jacket, and puts it on as Martha says over the intercom, "I have your wife on line one."

He rushes back to the desk, picks up the phone while pressing line one and says, "Betty? Are you all right?" with a sense of urgency in his voice.

"I'm fine Robert. What's wrong?" she asks innocently.

"Have you received any unusual phone calls, seen any strangers around the house, anything out of the ordinary, anything at all?"

"No, Robert, nothing. As a matter of fact, Lisa, the boys, and I just got back home from a trip to the grocery store."

"They went with you?"

"Why, of course! They've been cooped up in the house for two days. The boys needed to stretch their legs, plus Lisa and I needed some fresh air."

"Betty, I don't think you understand the situation. There are men looking for Lisa and the boys. Honey, I know you mean well, but if they're seen in public, there's a good chance someone is either going to try to kidnap or kill them, along with anyone else who happens to get in the way. These people are cunning and ruthless. Death means nothing to them."

"Robert! You're scaring me!" she says with fear in her voice. "You've never talked to me this way."

"Honey, we've never been in a situation like this before. And I'm sorry to talk to you like this. But this is serious. I don't want anyone getting hurt, especially you. So, please. Keep them in the house. No one leaves the house unless it's absolutely necessary. I'm coming home now."

"Robert? What's wrong?"

"I'll tell you about it when I get home, okay? Now, I'm going to hang up and call you right back on my cell phone." Weathers is already dialing the number on his cell phone when he hangs up the office phone. The phone barely rings once when Mrs. Weathers answers the phone again. "Still with me?"

"Yes," says Mrs. Weathers.

"Good. Now, I want you to stay on the line, and have Lisa pick up the poker by the fireplace. I need you to go to every room, check to make sure all the windows and doors are locked, and there's no one else is in the house."

"You think someone is in the house?" she asks with a sudden change in her voice.

"Honey, just do it, okay?" he says desperately. "And keep the phone on."

"Robert, I'm scared!"

"I know, but I can't take the chance of someone being in the house with you. But honey, I'm on my way." No sooner had he uttered those words when he suddenly remembers he doesn't have a car. While standing in front of the elevator, waiting for the doors to open, his luck wins out. Inside the elevator is Julie. Weathers steps into the elevator and says, "Where did you park the car?"

"The same place I picked it up this morning. Why?"

"We've got to go to my place. Betty, Lisa, and the kids may be in trouble," says Weathers, as he pushes button number three.

"What's going on?"

"Someone just called me on my private line and threatened Betty and me. I've got her checking the doors, rooms, and windows to make sure they're all secure." Weathers starts talking to his wife again. "Betty? Are you still there? Is everything all right?"

"Yes, everything looks okay so far. We've checked the living room, bath, kitchen and dining room. We're going upstairs now to check the bedrooms."

"Okay, honey. Take your time and all of you stay together," he says reassuringly. "You're doing fine."

Weathers shifts back to Julie. "Call the police and have them send a unit over to my house. Tell them to kill their lights and sirens at least a block or two before they get there, and stay outside, unless I tell them otherwise, okay?"

"Yes, sir." she says as she dials 911. While Julie is talking to the police, and Weathers is talking to his wife, the elevator stops on Level Three, and the two of them head for the car. Julie beats him to the driver's side of the car and says, "Keep talking to your wife, and I'll drive. Just hang on!"

"Okay, but I'm going to show you a couple of shortcuts to dodge traffic, so pay attention. The last thing we need to do is get run over by a semi or into a dead end!"

"Look. You concentrate on keeping your wife calm, and I'll concentrate on getting us there, okay?" Then she says to the police dispatcher on the phone, "That's right, 1539 Adams Street...Good! We're in a dark blue Ford Crown Victoria with government plate number G17179. We should be there in about ten to twelve minutes. Call me when your officers are in position. My number is 555-2171. Thanks." Julie then looks at Weathers and says, "The dispatcher says they have two cars en route, estimated time three to five minutes. They'll stand by on opposite ends of the block until we arrive."

"Did you hear that honey? The police will be near you in just a few minutes," Weathers says reassuringly to Betty. "Julie and I are on the way, too. How are you doing?"

"We're okay. So far, so good. I'm checking the bathroom now." There's a brief silence. "Robert? Everything appears to be okay upstairs. I guess the only thing left is the basement."

"Betty? Don't go down to the basement. I want you and Lisa to find the heaviest thing you can, and block the basement door.

It's too dark, and there's too much clutter down there to deal with. Just block the door and wait for me, okay?"

"That sounds good to me. Hurry home Robert. I'm scared. So are Lisa and the boys."

"I know. Just hang on a little longer," he says calmly, while his insides are doing somersaults. As Julie reaches the street, she leans over to turn on the lights and siren, but Weathers grabs her hand and says, "The way we're going, we'll be better off without them. Just drive."

Julie nails the throttle once she gets onto the street. Weathers says, "Julie, the real art to getting somewhere in this traffic is to be smooth. If you come up on people too fast, they invariably panic and hit the brakes, which means you either have to brake or dive into another lane. Either way costs you time and effort. Calm down, read what's going on ahead of you and plan accordingly. Got it?"

"I know what I'm doing."

"Don't argue with me, Julie. I've been driving in this traffic for over three years. I know how they think, act, and drive. Trust me." He pauses a moment, then says, "Now at the next block, take a left."

"Yes, sir, got it."

"Once we make the turn, go up three blocks and make a right. We'll go up another three blocks, then make another right. That should get us past the bottleneck in that construction zone and the one way. After that go one block, make a left..."

"Hold it! I can't think that far in advance. I'm concentrating on traffic, plus I'm worried about your wife, Lisa and the boys! I'm sure you know where you're going. Just give me a block or two warning so I can make the necessary lane changes, okay?"

"Sorry, you're right. I'm wrapped up in this, too. You're doing fine. Whoa! Look out for that truck!"

"I see him! I see him! Just talk to your wife, okay?" yells Julie. "Let me concentrate, will you?"

"Oh! Yeah. Betty? Betty, you still there?"

"Yes, Robert. We're still here. Lisa and I are trying to move the buffet from the dining room to block the basement door."

"Good idea, dear."

Julie's cell phone rings. It's the police department. "This is

Agent Robinson...They are? Good! Just have them stay put until we get there. We're about," she looks at Weathers, as he holds up five fingers, "five minutes out...Thank you."

Weathers says, "Betty? The police are on either end of the block. We'll be there in about five minutes. Think you can hang on that long for me?"

"Yes, dear, I believe we can, but please hurry."

The next five minutes seem like an eternity, but finally they make the turn onto Adams Street. Julie flashes the high beams to alert the police they've arrived, and all of them converge in front of the house, blocking the street in both directions.

Two officers follow Julie and Weathers into the home with guns drawn, while the other two officers stand by the cars, awaiting further orders. As they enter the house, Weathers motions for one of the officers to go upstairs and recheck the area. Weathers and the other officer move the buffet, then Julie and the officer turn on the basement lights, and proceed downstairs. Weathers joins and consoles his wife, Lisa and the boys in the living room.

At first, everything appears to be okay, but then Julie hears a slight squeaking noise, and discovers the basement door leading to the alley is ajar. Cautiously, Julie and the officer approach the door. The officer positions himself with his back against the outside wall, pistol held with both hands, centered, and pointed downward, safety off. He motions for Julie to swing the door open, while stepping back from harm's way in the process.

As she opens the door, the officer steps into the doorway with his weapon aimed outward, sweeping from left to right, but nothing crosses his path. Once the officer says "Clear", Julie examines the door. She can see some telltale scratches around the keyway of the deadbolt.

The officer who had gone up to the second floor yells out, "Clear!"

Hearing that, Julie calls out, "Mr. Weathers? You might want to come down and take a look at this."

As Weathers makes his way down the stairs, he asks, "What is it? What did you find?"

"It looks like someone picked the lock on the basement door, sir." Julie shows him the scratches on the deadbolt and tells him they had found the door open. The police officer radios the other two officers to check the alley behind the house, then puts in a call for an evidence team and a detective.

Weathers and Julie go back upstairs and rejoin Mrs. Weathers, Lisa and the boys. Weathers asks, "Betty? While you were checking out the house, did you notice anything missing or out of place?"

"No dear, I was so scared, the only thing I was worried about was finding someone in the house. I'm sorry."

"Honey, there's nothing to feel sorry about," he says while lifting her head up and smiling at her. "You're safe, and that's all that matters." She smiles, then wraps her arms around him and gives him a big hug. "Now, let's see if there's anything missing, shall we?" Betty nods her head in agreement, and they begin their search of the house.

Weathers goes to his study and starts to look things over, when he notices a thick nine by twelve-inch manila envelope on his desk. It has his name and address on it, but no return address. He walks back to the door and says, "Betty? Did you put any mail on my desk today?"

Betty comes to the base of the stairs, and says, "What did you say, dear?"

"Did you put any mail on my desk today?"

"No, I haven't. The only things that came in the mail today were a couple of bills."

With that, he says, "Thank you," then closes the door behind him. He goes back to the desk, opens the lower right hand drawer, and pulls out a pair of latex gloves, his fingerprint kit, and a small ultraviolet light. He scans the envelope with the ultraviolet light to see if there might be any type of residue or powder, but sees nothing. Then he lightly dusts the envelope to see if there are any fingerprints, again, nothing.

There's a slight bulge in the center of the envelope, similar in size to a jewel case for a CD. Weathers gently runs his fingers around the edges of the envelope to see if there is anything attached to the underside of the envelope, again, nothing.

He decides to sit down at his desk, and taking a deep breath, carefully picks up the package. The envelope appears to be fairly thick, possibly a file or dossier, along with a disc. He places the

116

envelope back on the desk, then reaches into the center drawer and pulls out a knifelike plastic letter opener. He holds the envelope firmly with his left hand, as he deftly opens the end of the envelope with the letter opener.

Julie and Mrs. Weathers have searched the balance of the house, but nothing appears to be missing or out of place. Just as they're about to sit down, the doorbell rings. Mrs. Weathers starts towards the door, when Julie says, "Mrs. Weathers, please sit down. I'll take care of this. You've been through enough today."

"Thank you dear, but it's my responsibility, my house."

"It's no problem Mrs. Weathers. I'm sure it's the police, and they're going to want to see the basement and ask your husband a lot of questions. I'll handle it."

A man is standing at the door with his ID in hand, and two others are making their way up the steps behind him. They're wearing white coveralls and carrying what appear to be large metal tool boxes. When Julie opens the door, the first man asks, "Mrs. Weathers?"

"No, I'm Agent Julie Robinson, Secret Service," she replies. "Mrs. Weathers is in the living room. She's worn out from all the excitement she's been through this afternoon. Hopefully, I can answer any questions you might have."

"We'll see. I'm Detective Bartoli," he says rather smugly. "Gaines and McNally are part of our Evidence Division."

"Please gentlemen, come in."

"We understand that you had a break-in, is that correct?"

"That's correct."

"Was anything stolen, damaged, or broken?"

"Mrs. Weathers and I haven't found anything out of the ordinary, so far. But, Mr. Weathers has been upstairs for several minutes. He may have found something."

"Well, would you mind showing the evidence team the point of entry? Then you and I can talk to Mr. Weathers."

"Fine," she replies. "If you'll follow me, please?" She walks them to the door that leads to the basement. "At the bottom of the stairs, turn right. You'll find the point of entry at the back of the house." Julie returns to the living room, where she and Detective Bartoli head up the stairs to find Mr. Weathers.

117

When Mr. Weathers hears them coming up the stairs, he quickly slides everything back into the envelope, and drops it into the lower right hand drawer. He lays the fingerprint kit and ultraviolet light on top of the envelope, then peels off the latex gloves and closes the drawer, just as Julie knocks on the door.

"Mr. Weathers? Detective Bartoli would like to speak to you about the break-in. May we come in?" asks Julie.

"Come in Julie, the door's open," replies Weathers as he rises from the desk and approaches the door. Julie opens it and enters the room, followed by the detective. "Detective Bartoli, is it? I'm Robert Weathers. Have you found anything?"

"Mr. Weathers, I just got here, so no, sir. We haven't found anything, yet. But I do have a few questions I'd like to ask you," says the detective.

"Shoot, detective. What would you like to know?"

"Well, Mr. Weathers, how did you know that someone was in the house? I realize that I just walked in the door, but I didn't notice any telltale signs of an alarm system. Is there one in the house?"

"You're very observant, detective. Tell me. How long have you been on the force, may I ask?"

"I've been here about five years, but I was with the NYPD for almost twenty years," he replies.

"Twenty years in New York. Why didn't you retire, and head down to Florida?" asks Weathers.

"I hate gettin' sand in my shoes. Besides, most of the people down there are either blue hairs, Cubans, or Puerto Ricans," replies the detective with some disgust.

"I think your view is a little skewed, don't you?"

"What do you mean by that?"

"I agree there is a fairly large presence of retirees, your 'blue hairs', and I will even agree to a heavy concentration of Puerto Ricans and Cubans in the southern portion of the state. However, I'm not inclined to agree they are the dominant population."

"Well, that may be. I'm not the fuckin' census bureau. But I still hate gettin' sand in my shoes."

"Then all you have to do is stay off the beach," replies Weathers.

"That's easy for you to say. The fuckin' place's got water surrounding it on three sides!" says the detective.

"Kind of like New York City, right?" replies Weathers.

"Yeah, right. But at least you can see land on either side of ya."

"And you don't have to worry about getting sand in your shoes," reiterates Weathers.

"Right."

"Did you know that there are over eight million people crammed into just over three hundred square miles that constitute New York City, and that about sixteen million people are spread out over fifty-four thousand square miles of Florida? While Florida has about twice the number of people, it has over one hundred and seventy-five times the land mass."

"Who the fuck do you think you are, Mr. Rogers or somethin'?"

"No detective, just making conversation," replies Weathers smirking a bit.

Julie is dying. She can hardly contain herself. She turns and walks away from the detective, past Weathers. As she moves behind the desk, she notices what appears to be part of a glove sticking out of the lower drawer. Then she spots the faint, but distinct rectangular outline of fingerprint dust on the blotter. She hadn't noticed it while standing next to the detective. She just hopes the detective hasn't seen it either.

"By the way, detective, what part of New York City did you work?" asks Weathers.

"Well, I, ah, started out in Queens, but most of it was in Brooklyn," he replies hesitantly.

"That explains it." says Weathers.

"What?" asks the detective with a confused look on his face.

"Your mouth, detective." says Weathers sternly.

"What do you mean, my mouth?" asks Detective Bartoli, rather defensively.

"I mean what's coming out of it, detective," replies Weathers. "We're both professionals, you and I. Do you think using profanity makes you sound professional? Are you trying to impress me with your gutter talk? Did any of the books you read in the academy use profanity?" Bartoli is shaking his head.

119

"You know? I'm the victim here, but you're talking to me like I'm some low life scumbag on Skid Row, or some pimp on the strip. Did I interrupt your lunch, or is it that you don't like talking to an educated Black man?"

Detective Bartoli is beginning to see he may have bitten off more than he can chew with Mr. Weathers.

"Detective? The way I see it, you've got two choices. You can either straighten up your act, or call your supervisor and tell him to send me someone who knows how to act like a professional. What's it going to be?"

"Please, Mr. Weathers, don't say anything to my supervisor. I don't need another report in my file. I'll either get canned or sent to God knows where. I just want to do my job. I'm a good cop, Mr. Weathers. I may be a little rough around the edges, but I'm a good cop."

"I'll bet you are, detective," says Weathers. "But you're going to have to work on those rough edges if you want to get anywhere. I'll tell you what. Why don't you wait for me downstairs? Ask my wife, politely, for something to drink. I need to speak with Agent Robinson for a minute or two, then I'll be right with you. We'll start over, and I'm sure everything will be all right."

"Yes, sir, thank you, sir," replies the detective as he starts backing out of the room.

"Oh, would you mind closing the door behind you?" asks Weathers.

"Not at all, Mr. Weathers."

"Thank you, detective. I'll be down directly."

As Weathers and Julie hear the detective walking down the stairs, she half whispers, "What in the hell was that all about?"

"Tell me, Julie. When you're performing an investigation or interrogation, what's the first thing you do?"

"Take control of the situation. You ask the questions. The person you're questioning provides the answers."

"Exactly. I couldn't afford to let Detective Bartoli take control of the situation, because I didn't want to have to lie. Here. I have something to show you."

He sits down at his desk, opens the lower right hand drawer, pulls out the envelope, and lays it on the blotter. "By the way, thank you for not saying anything about the fingerprint dust on the blotter."

"I figured you had your reasons, and you'd get around to telling me what's going on. So, what's going on?"

"I believe a member of the Core called me, and wants us to back off protecting Senator Higgins."

"Why?"

"I think the answers are right here," he replies, as he tilts the envelope, spilling its contents onto the blotter.

"What is all this?"

"I don't know. I had just opened it when I heard you and the detective coming up the stairs. But if I had to guess, I'd say it probably has something to do with Senator Higgins and the Core."

"Well then. We need to get AJ over here as soon as possible."

"Not so fast Julie. We don't know where AJ's allegiance lies right now."

"Don't be ridiculous," she says emphatically.

"Keep your voice down," whispers Weathers. "Humor me for just a little while, okay? Things have been happening so fast. We've got to stop, catch our breath, and regroup. Remember? The senator asked for AJ specifically, and he's told him all kinds of things about the Core, its structure, its power, and its purpose. How do you know that the senator hasn't recruited him into the Core, and AJ's one of them now?"

"Mr. Weathers, that's pure fantasy. I know AJ. He'd never go to work for a subversive group like that."

"That's what AJ said about David McKenzie, too. Julie, you haven't seen or heard from AJ in over five years. How can you say you know him? People change, and not always for the better. Besides, Senator Higgins is a very smart and shrewd man. There's no telling what he's told AJ."

"Okay, I'll play along for now, but…"

"Just give me a little time to sort through this stuff."

"No sir. We're going to sort through this together, or I'm going to let AJ know what you're up to," she says with a serious look on her face.

"Are you threatening me?"

"No sir. Actually, I'm trying to help. Two people can sift

through this twice as fast. And if you're intent on keeping AJ out of the loop, I want to resolve this as quickly as possible."

"When are you going to see AJ again?"

"Tonight," she replies with a smile.

"And you're going to be able to keep this under wraps."

"As far as the break-in goes? No sir. I'm sure he's probably already aware of that. But the envelope and its contents? Yes, sir. For now, this is just between you and me. I don't suppose I could borrow your car for the night, could I?"

"Well, I am already home, and the day is pretty much shot to hell. I really don't see any point in driving back to the office for you to get your car, either. So, yes you can use it tonight, but tomorrow, we're going to get you into a company car, got it?"

"Yes, sir, I got it. Would you like me to pick you up in the morning?"

"I'm not so sure I want to take the contents of this envelope to work. I'm pretty confident we can do most of our research right here. Do you have a laptop?"

"Yes, I do. But sir, they've already broken into your house once. What makes you so sure they won't do it again?"

"They've already made their point. They want us to process this information, so why don't we do just that? Go on home, get cleaned up, and do whatever it is you two want to do. I'll see you in the morning around 0900?"

"That'll work," she replies. "Sir? Don't you think you should go downstairs and talk with Detective Bartoli?"

"Yes, yes, I'll head downstairs in a minute," he says while stuffing the file and disc back into the envelope.

"Are you going to work on any of that tonight?"

"I'm not sure at the moment," he replies. "Betty took all this pretty hard. I'll probably spend the evening with her, helping her cope with it all. And frankly, I'm not in the proper frame of mind to start sifting through all this right now, either."

"Tomorrow it is, then," she says as she heads toward the door.

"Oh, Julie? Don't forget to write up your reports. I prefer to have them turned in daily." Julie has a distressed look on her face, and as she starts to respond, he says, "On second thought, I'll allow you a reprieve for today. But consider this the exception, not the rule."

Julie breathes a sigh of relief, and says, "Thank you, sir. But just so you know, I already have them recorded for reference. I'll take care of it tomorrow."

"We're going to get along just fine," he says with a smile. "Now, get out of here, and let me deal with Detective Bartoli."

"Okay, I'll see you in the morning," she replies as she walks down the stairs.

"Have a good evening, and tell AJ I said hello," he says following her down the stairs.

"I will. Bye Mrs. Weathers, Lisa. See you tomorrow," she says as she heads out the door.

Mr. Weathers walks over to Detective Bartoli and says, "What do you say we try this again?"

TLC: Chapter 18

It's 1730 hours when AJ calls Julie. "Hi! I just wanted to let you know that we're on our way back. It'll probably be close to 1930 before I make it back to the apartment. Are we still on for this evening?"

"Of course, silly. You think I'm going to let you off the hook that easily?"

"Other than discovering Lisa's house had been torn down, did anything else exciting happen today?"

"Oh shit! I forgot to tell Lisa about that."

"Why? Did anything else happen today that I should know about?"

"A couple of things come to mind. I was tailed by those guys from Lisa's house, twice. Somebody threatened Mr. Weathers and his wife, and then somebody broke into their house."

"And you didn't call me?"

"If I had, would you have been able to break away and come to their aid?"

"Probably not."

"Exactly, so what's your point?"

"I just hate being left out of the loop, that's all. Well, did they steal anything?"

"They haven't discovered anything missing so far. And I'm sure he'll have the house checked for bugs and wire taps after the cops leave, but he honestly doesn't expect to find anything. As best we can tell, the house appears to be clean."

"That just doesn't make any sense. Why break into a house if you're not going to steal or plant something?"

"I agree, unless you're just trying to show someone you can."

"You also said that someone threatened Weathers. Any ideas?"

"We don't know anything for sure, but we suspect it's probably someone inside the Core. By the way, can the senator overhear what we're saying?"

"Nah. I have the privacy window up. He's been on the phone ever since we got in the car."

"Well, that's good, but why don't we continue this discussion once we get back to your apartment. I don't suppose you have an extra key hidden away anywhere do you?"

"I do, actually. When you get off the elevator, turn right and go down to the end of the hall. You'll see an in-wall cabinet for the fire hose and fire extinguisher. Open the door and lean the extinguisher over. You'll find my key taped to the underside of it."

"That's pretty clever, at least until they decide to change out the extinguishers."

"Hmm. I hadn't thought of that."

"Well, that doesn't happen very often. I think they're supposed to go in for a pressure test and a recharge every five years."

"Remind me to check the inspection sticker when I get home."

"No problem. I'll do it for you when I pick up the key."

"Thanks, I'd appreciate it. Oh! Do you want to go out for dinner, or do take out again?"

"It's really been a long day. Why don't we just eat in? Something simple."

"Like?"

"Anybody around here make Chicago style pizza?"

"I think I might know of a place. How do you like yours?"

"Stuffed. I really enjoy spinach, pepperoni, black olives, mushrooms, and cheese of course. Lots of cheese. I suppose you can add just about anything else you want, except onions or bell pepper. They give me..." she whispers, "bad breath and...gas."

AJ starts to laugh to himself, "Gotcha! Chicago style, stuffed, spinach, pepperoni, olives, mushrooms, and lots of cheese. Hold the gas!"

"That's black olives! And don't you forget it!" she says giggling.

"Yes ma'am! Black olives it is!"

"AJ? If I didn't love you so much, I'd...I'd...I don't know what I'd do to you."

"Don't worry, I'm sure you'll think of something."

"You can count on it! By the way, do you have any wine in the house?"

"No, like I said, I don't party, and I've never considered myself a wine connoisseur either."

"Don't worry then. I'll take care of the wine. You do have wine glasses, don't you?"

"I'm sure I've got something around the house that'll pass for wine glasses, okay?"

"As long as it doesn't have a handle on it, I guess it'll do," she says reluctantly.

"Come on. I'm not that far removed from mainstream society, am I?"

"Well, the jury is still out on that subject." There's a long pause, then she says, "No, AJ. You're not that bad. Just playing with you."

"Whew! That's a relief. So, around 1930 hours then?"

"It's a date!"

"See you then, bye."

"Bye, AJ."

Just as AJ ends the call, Senator Higgins lowers the privacy window and says, "AJ? You've been pushing yourself pretty hard these past few days. Nothing's really going on for the next day or two in Washington, so why don't you take tomorrow off? You certainly deserve it. I have a couple of meetings tomorrow about your 'laundry list', and they'll be picking me up. But Friday, I'd suggest you wear something a little more casual. I'm sure I'll have a few surprises for you by then."

"Sir? Are you sure? Don't get me wrong, I'm certainly grateful and all, but this is, after all, my job."

"Look, AJ. After I make my formal announcement about running for the Presidency, you're going to be busier than a one-armed paperhanger. So, I'd just say 'thank you', enjoy the day off, and be prepared for a busy day, Friday. Okay?"

"Well, Senator? Thank you. I'll try my best to rest up and be ready for whatever comes Friday."

"You're welcome, AJ. Now, I'm probably going to be on the phone for the duration, so I'm going to raise the window again. Nothing personal, you understand."

"No sir. No problem at all," he replies. AJ starts to call Julie and tell her the good news. But at the last moment, he decides to wait and surprise her at dinner tonight.

The rest of the trip appears to be uneventful, but AJ and the senator are being tailed by a dark blue Ford panel van. Inside are

126

three Core operatives. They're equipped with all sorts of electronic surveillance and monitoring devices. While the senator's cell phone uses a unique encryption coding system which prevents his calls from being monitored, AJ's phone is not so equipped.

Once back at Higgins' estate, AJ stops in front of the mansion, where George is standing at the curb to open the senator's door. AJ lowers the privacy window, turns and says, "Sir, are you sure about my taking the day off tomorrow? I really think I should be with you when you start talking about my weapons list to these people."

"Nonsense. I'll be fine. Besides, most of the people I'm going to meet prefer to maintain their anonymity."

"Are you saying that some of these people are members of the..."

"Now AJ, don't put me in a position to have to lie to you, okay? You want me to keep this as low profile as possible. I believe your words were not to raise any 'red flags' about this little arsenal you want. Well, the only way I can acquire it, is to go to the highest level possible. That's all you need to know for now."

"Yes, sir. I was just trying to help, that's all."

"I know, but this is one time your assistance is not required. In fact, it could be a bit of a hindrance. Believe me. You'll have your hands full come Friday."

"Well then, Senator. I guess I'll see you Friday."

"Friday, 0800 hours, sharp," says the Senator, as he exits the limo.

"Yes, sir. I'll be here." AJ then drives the limo over to the garage, where Higgins' detailer is patiently waiting to get started on his evening duties. As AJ gets out of the car, he asks the detailer, "Do you have a phone book I could borrow for a few minutes?"

"Sure thing, AJ. Whatcha lookin' for?"

"I need to find a place that makes a good Chicago style stuffed pizza."

"Man, there's a place over there on 33rd, just off the expressway. Now they make a fine pizza!"

"So, you know about Chicago style pizza?"

"Dude, I'm from Chicago, actually Cicero. But yeah, I know about Chicago style pizza. And that's about as close as you're gonna get around Washington."

"I don't suppose you'd happen to know the name of that pizza place, do you?"

"Sure do!" he replies with a smile.

"Well?"

"Oh! Sorry. It's called Chicago Style Pizza," replies the detailer with a grin spanning literally ear to ear.

"You know, I've been here almost a month now, and while I've seen you a couple of times, I can't seem to remember your name."

"My given name is Jeffrey, Jeffrey Samuels, but my street name is Doo Whopp," he says proudly.

"Do what?" says AJ.

"No...Doo Whopp! Like in music man, like in music. I may detail cars during the week, but I spin music on the weekends. I don't make much money at it, but it's a lot of fun. Chicks dig it."

"Man, you oughta come to one of my gigs. Sometimes a couple of girls'll be dancin' in front me, you know, dancin' that sexy stuff. Then all of a sudden, they'll flash their tits, or bend over and..."

"That's okay, Jeffrey, I mean Doo Whatever," says AJ shaking his head, as he turns and starts to walk toward his car.

"Man? Are you makin' fun of me?" he asks while acting a little aggressive, yet obviously hurt.

AJ stops, turns back, faces him and says, "No, Jeffrey, just playing with you. I appreciate the tip."

"Ain't that the same thing, makin' fun, and playin' with me?"

AJ walks back to him and says, "Jeffrey, you're a fine detailer. You do wonderful work. And I'm sure you're a good DJ, too. Making fun of a person is usually someone trying to intimidate or embarrass another. Playing with a person is exactly that. You play around with your friends, right? Kid each other?"

Jeffrey is looking down and away from him.

"Right?" AJ asks again, smiling, as he's trying to get Jeffrey to look at him.

"Yeah, I guess so," says Jeffrey, half smiling, yet still looking down.

128

"Tell you what," says AJ. "When's the next gig, Doo Whopp?"

He looks up at AJ, and smiles, saying, "Well, there's one Friday night, but I don't think you'll want to go to that one."

"How come?"

"Well, it's a bachelor party, and there's gonna be a couple of strippers there, so things are probably going to get a little...ah... shall we say...interesting?"

"I gotcha. Definitely not something you'd want to take a date to."

"Not unless you're willing to share," replies Jeffrey smiling.

"I like you Jeffrey, but not that much," says AJ. "Now see? You're playing with me!"

"I suppose...I think I have a gig next week that'll be more main stream, if you know what I mean."

"Well, keep me posted."

"Will do, man," replies Jeffrey. "Hey! Do you know what kind of wheels the senator's getting tomorrow? He told me to pick up a ladder. What in the hell am I gonna do with a ladder?"

AJ smiles and says, "Yes, I do, and yes, you're going to need a ladder."

"Well?"

"Oh! If the senator has chosen not to tell you what's coming, I certainly don't want to spoil the surprise. You'll find out soon enough."

"Man? I hate that! Nobody tells me nothin'," says Jeffrey while shaking his head.

"All right, all right. I'll give you a couple of hints, but that's all, okay? But if you tell the senator I spilled the beans, we're both screwed, got it?"

"Sure! Great! Whatever, man!" replies Jeffrey with his eyes open wide with excitement.

"You're definitely going to need the ladder, and you're going to love the gadgets and toys inside. Even the undercarriage will be easier to clean. You're going to love the motor, and the thing can go off-road if necessary."

"Damn! The boss is getting' an SUV?" asks Jeffrey in disbelief.

"Sorry, Jeffrey. I can't tell you anymore than that. If I said anything else, well, I'd have to kill you."

Jeffrey starts waving his arms in front of him, while backing away. "Okay, okay, I get your drift. I'll see it tomorrow. I'm cool, I'm cool."

AJ smiles, shakes his head, then turns and starts walking to his car. As he reflects on what he'd just said to Jeffrey, he stares at the dull gray Crown Vic. He sighs as he recalls his brief, shining moment with his Hummer. While starting the car, he pulls out his phone and makes a call. "Hi. Is this Chicago Style Pizza? Good. I'd like to place an order."

***

Jeffrey "Doo Whopp" Samuels is a twenty-something Black male from the suburbs of Chicago. He got his start detailing cars with his father, who worked for a shop on the South Side. His father insisted he finish school and make a better man of himself. His father had dropped out of school at an early age, and discovered that many of life's opportunities would pass him by, simply because he wanted to take a short cut. He did not want that to be his son's legacy.

Jeffrey finished high school without incident, and had enrolled at a local vo-tech center. Initially, everything seemed to be going well, until one night after class, he accepted a ride from one of his classmates. The car turned out to be stolen, and the owner of the car had been nearly beaten to death.

When the police spotted them on the Dan Ryan Expressway, a chase ensued. Several cars were damaged before they were finally pinned against a guardrail. Jeffrey was listed as an accessory to both the beating and theft, both of which were felonies. He would endure the hardships of Cook County Jail for almost three weeks, until the victim was well enough to go downtown and name his classmate as the sole culprit in the act. Jeffrey was unceremoniously released, given his personal belongings, and shown the door. No apologies, no excuses.

Even though Jeffrey was able to prove that he was, in fact, a victim in the incident, he was suspended from school. He was

130

fired from his part time job, and to add insult to injury, no one else was willing to offer him a job.

The Samuels had family in the Washington area. They felt a change in surroundings might help set things straight. His aunt was widowed, and her house needed some attention. So a deal was struck between Jeffrey and his aunt. He would first try to find a job, any job, and help around the house, in exchange for room and board.

At first, Jeffrey was having no more success finding a job in Washington than he had in Chicago. He was getting desperate to find something, when he answered an ad about a lounge looking for a DJ. Even though he had never done anything like that before, he felt there couldn't be much to it.

When he arrived at Sal's Place, he was in for a big surprise. For starters, Sal was short for Sally. He and Sally hit it off right away, and she helped him learn the art of being a DJ. She even came up with his street name.

Jeffrey was relieved to have a job. Plus working as a DJ at night afforded him the ability to work on his aunt's house during the day, as well as look for a more permanent full time job, doing what he knew and loved most, detailing cars.

One day, Jeffrey answered a blind ad in one of the local papers. He called the number listed in the ad, and a man began to ask him the usual questions: name, address, phone number, previous employment, etc. Then, the man asked about what he liked about detailing.

Jeffrey spent several minutes telling the man how he had watched his dad work on cars, and how it had affected his life. His father had shown him how to tell when a finish needed a total rework, or just a touch up. He showed him how to tell when a buffer was needed, or the gentle touch of a hand.

The man suddenly cut him short, gave him an address, and told him to be there at 10am the next morning. Before Jeffrey had a chance to ask him about what he should bring, the man hung up.

The next day, Jeffrey caught a cab to the address the man on the phone had given him. It was a half-hours drive, and almost cost him every penny he had on him. The cab dropped him off in front of what appeared to be a vacant warehouse.

The service door was ajar, so he stuck his head inside and said, "Hello? Is anybody in there?" There was no response. As his eyes adjusted to the dim light inside the warehouse, he could see a black Lincoln Town Car, along with a large manila envelope on the windshield with his name written in big bold letters. He opened the envelope and found a brief letter that told him to detail the Lincoln to his personal standards. There were no specifics, other than the car needed to be ready by 5pm.

He found an electrical panel near the door, and began flipping switches. There was a large tool chest with the tools, compounds, waxes, and glazes he had mentioned to the man the day before. He placed his boom box on the bench next to the tool chest, tuned in a local jazz station, and turned up the volume.

After that, he placed the four pedestal mounted halogen lights around the car. While the sides of the car seemed to be in pretty good shape, all of the horizontal surfaces, the roof, hood, and trunk, had suffered from acid rain, and the lenses on the headlights had been hazed by someone using harsh chemicals, probably ammonia-based, on them.

After completing his inspection of the exterior, he set to work cleaning the interior. He vacuumed and shampooed the carpets, cleaned, then treated the leather. From there he moved to the engine bay, inspected the battery, belts, hoses, and fluids. He steam cleaned the engine compartment, then he moved on to the trunk. From that point, he scrubbed and cleaned the wheels and tires, then covered them with plastic.

Now, the real work began. Jeffrey had his work cut out for him with the car's exterior. Time seemed to fly, as he worked tirelessly to bring the car's finish back to life.

Just as he had finished and was about to stand back and admire his work, someone flipped the master switch, killing the power to the lights and music. From the darkness a voice said, "Time's up. Someone will contact you in the next day or two. You'll find another envelope just outside the door as you leave. In it, you'll find sufficient funds to cover your expenses for the day. Good day, son." With that, the man opened the door, briefly outlining his silhouette against the afternoon sun, then closed it behind him.

Jeffrey felt as though he had been used. There was no "Thank you," or "Nice work". *"Someone will contact you in the next day or two,"* kept going through his mind. *"Someone my ass!"* he said to himself, as he snatched up his boom box, and walked slowly to the service door.

As promised, there was an envelope by the door, and much to his surprise, a cab was waiting to take him back home. But the real surprise came when he opened the envelope and found five crisp one hundred dollar bills inside. "Holy Shit!" he yelled. Suddenly, there was a spring in his step, as he strutted toward the cab. Senator Higgins has a new detailer.

Julie stops by her apartment, picks up a few things, and still manages to beat AJ back to his place. The key is exactly where he said it would be. While she's there, she checks the inspection tag on the extinguisher. The extinguisher is good until October 2012.

Once inside AJ's apartment, she puts the wine in the refrigerator, and sets a couple of candles on the coffee table. She places her overnight bag on the bed, and pulls out a very sexy and revealing negligee, laying it neatly on the bed. Putting her hands on her hips and smiling, she says to herself, "*Let him try to ignore me in this!*" She also catches a whiff of body odor, makes a face, and heads for the bathroom, shedding her clothes on the way down the hall.

Considering all the running around and excitement over the past 24 hours, she decides to take a lounging bath. She turns on the water, then goes back to the bedroom to get her bath oil. Settling into the hot soothing water, she begins to relax, sighs, and says to herself, "*Just 10 minutes or so, and I'll be all right.*" Julie falls asleep almost immediately.

Suddenly, she's jarred awake by the doorbell. The water has cooled, and according to her watch, she's been out for almost an hour! While trying to rinse herself off, and drain the tub, she cries out, "Just a minute!" The doorbell rings again. She jumps out of the tub, frantically trying to dry herself. The doorbell rings again. "I said just a minute!" She rushes to the bedroom, whips on the negligee, and takes a passing glance at the mirror to check her face and hair. The doorbell rings yet again. "I'm coming!" As she swings the door open, she says demurely, "What do you think of this?"

"Damn lady! You look fine! You need to order pizza from us more often. But it's still gonna cost you twenty-nine fifty, plus delivery." says the delivery boy, with his eyes open wide, gazing upon Julie's near naked body.

Julie shrieks and slams the door. "You didn't properly announce yourself!" she says from the other side of the door. "I was expecting my boyfriend."

"Lady, with a bod like that, I'll be your boyfriend!"

"Well, I don't think my boyfriend would approve," she replies. "Besides, one is enough for me."

"Tell me. What's he got that I ain't got?" asks the delivery boy trying to act tough, as AJ eases up behind him.

"How about a badge and a gun?" says AJ as he sticks his finger in the delivery boy's back near his right kidney.

"Shit man! Today just ain't my day. I finally find me a good lookin' chick, and she's got Five-O for a boyfriend!"

"No, not Five-O. Secret Service. You know what that means?" as he jabs the delivery boy with his finger again. "I could cap you right here, right now, and nobody would do a thing about it."

"Please mister! I was just foolin' around. I didn't mean anything by it. Please don't shoot me. Here! You can have the pizza. No charge! Just let me go, and I promise you'll never see my candy ass again. I swear!" pleads the delivery boy.

"How much did say that pizza was again?" he asks while giving the delivery boy another jab near the kidney.

"It's your lucky day! You're our...ah...ah...fiftieth customer today! So, your...ah...pizza and delivery are...ah...free!" stutters the delivery boy, as he looks up toward the ceiling, grimaces, closes his eyes, and prays that AJ won't shoot him.

"You know? Come to think of it, I could have sworn I had to pre-pay with my credit card before you guys would even deliver this far out," he says angrily.

With that, AJ spins the young man around, sticks his finger in the young man's face and yells, "Bang!"

The delivery boy's eyes and mouth open wide, as he drops the pizza, then sprints down the hall to the stairway.

"Hey! Wait up! You forgot your tip!" yells AJ.

"Keep it!" yells the delivery boy already halfway down the stairs.

AJ stoops over, picks up the pizza, and looks inside to see what kind of shape it's in. He walks over to the door and knocks. As Julie slowly opens the door, he says, "Do you have this thing about exposing yourself to people whenever you open a door?"

Julie blushes as she lets him in, then closes the door behind him. "I thought it was you, and of course, I wanted to surprise you,"

"Well, I'm surprised all right," he says as he looks at her clothes strewn down the hallway, and wet footprints coming from the bathroom. "Are you, by chance, reliving your dormitory experiences, because I don't recall this type of behavior back in London."

"AJ? I've been wearing the same clothes for two days. I was hot, tense, tired, and just wanted to relax in the tub for a few minutes. I guess I really didn't know just how tired I was, because I fell asleep for almost an hour. When the doorbell rang, and I realized what time it was, I naturally assumed it was you. And yes, I wanted to surprise you. Just, not quite like that," she says as she drops her head, embarrassed.

AJ reaches out, lifts her head, and says, "I really do appreciate the thought, and honestly, you're a sight to behold." Just as she thinks he's about to kiss her, he says, "Now let's see just how good this pizza is. I'm starving! How about you?" Julie is speechless, stunned by his sudden change of direction. Staring at him in disbelief, AJ continues, "Where's the wine? Did you find any decent glasses?"

Julie is on the verge of tears, when he suddenly turns and pulls a small bouquet of flowers from his jacket. She smiles and bursts into tears at the same time. She rushes to him, gives him a big hug, and says, "You really are an asshole, but I love you anyway."

"Now can we have some pizza?" he asks. "I really am hungry."

Julie steps back, flashes her breasts at him and says, "Which do you want first? Pizza or dessert?"

As he places the pizza in the oven, he asks, "What should I set the temp for? What about the wine? Should I bring the wine?"

"AJ? Are you coming, or not?" she asks demurely, while standing in the bedroom door.

"I'm coming! I'm coming!" He kicks off his shoes, peels off his jacket and shoulder rig, leaving a trail of clothes as he heads toward the bedroom. Julie giggles, then runs and jumps into bed, with AJ right behind her. She squeals when he grabs her, and the two of them begin to laugh while they tussle in the bed. Gradually, laughter turns into moans of pleasure as they begin to kiss and caress each other. Soon, they are in the throes of making love. Once again, the two of them are in heaven.

***

"My god! That was wonderful!" she says almost out of breath. "I guess last night wasn't a dream after all!"

"If it is, I hope I never wake up," he replies, breathing heavily. "I guess it's a good thing I have tomorrow off. Want to sleep in?"

"Oh AJ, I can't. I'm supposed to meet up with Mr. Weathers tomorrow and go over what happened today."

"Well, since I have tomorrow off, mind if I tag along? Maybe we could do something afterward. What time are you supposed to meet him?"

"0900, but you know how debriefings are, long and boring."

"Want me to drop you off?"

"That's not necessary. I have his car." She pauses a moment, thinking. "Tell you what. We'll get up early in the morning, have breakfast, maybe a little more dessert," she says smiling. "Then, you can go back to bed, and get some rest. Maybe we can meet up for lunch. How's that?"

"I suppose," he says, obviously disappointed.

"AJ? We've got the whole weekend to spend together. We can go out and do the town, or we can stay in, and do each other. Now how bad can that be?"

"Oh, all right. You win. Hey! What's that smell?"

"Smells like cardboard. Burning cardboard! AJ? What temperature did you set the oven on?"

"200...250...Hell, I don't know!" About that time, the smoke detector starts beeping. "Oh shit! Open a window! Quick! Before we have the fire department up here!" The two of them are scrambling around the apartment. Julie is trying to open the windows, while AJ pulls the smoldering cardboard box out of the oven, dumps it in the sink, and runs water over it to put it out.

Just as things start to calm down a bit, the phone rings. AJ picks up the phone and says, "Hello?"

"This is ADT Security. Our system indicates your smoke detector has gone off. Is everything okay?"

137

"Yes, everything's fine. I had put something in the oven, leaving it in the box, and I guess I had the temperature up too high," he says embarrassingly. "It won't happen again."

"Okay sir. Just for the record, I need your name and your password," says the operator.

"My name is Thomas Andrew Jackson, and my password is Liberty."

"Thank you Mr. Jackson. Are you sure everything is okay?"

"Yes ma'am. Everything is fine. Sorry to cause you folks any headaches."

"It's no problem sir. We're here to help. Have a good evening."

"Thank you, and you do the same. Good night."

"Good night, and thank you for using ADT."

The two of them stare at each other and begin laughing.

"Well, so much for having Chicago Style Pizza tonight," he sighs.

"Got anything in the fridge?" she asks.

"I think there's some leftover Chinese from last night."

"Don't tell me there's still some Moo Shoo pork left over."

"No, I think all we have left are some oriental vegetables, rice, and some sesame chicken."

"Well, I must admit, I am hungry. Think there's enough for both of us?"

"I'm sure we'll make do. Want me to heat it up, or would you prefer to do the honors?"

"I'll do it. I think we've both had enough excitement for tonight."

"Sounds good to me," he replies. As Julie walks past AJ, he gives her a smack on her fanny.

"Hey! What's that for? That really smarts!" she says as she tries to rub the sting out of it.

"Just because," he says smiling. "Just because."

TLC: Chapter 20
Wednesday evening
2100 hours local time

Just a few blocks from the White House, Senator McCarthy has called for an emergency meeting of the Core to discuss the week's events. Senator Joshua McCarthy has the floor.

"Gentlemen, I'm sure you're aware our attempted TLC of Senator Higgins was a dismal failure. Plus, it appears that our effort has only served to strengthen his resolve about running for the Presidency."

"At the cost of ten of our operatives, so far," mutters Walter Phillips, CEO of a major banking institution.

"Mr. Phillips. Is there something you'd like to share with all the members?" asks Senator McCarthy, while giving Phillips a stern look. Phillips shakes his head. "I didn't think so. Very well. As I was saying, since Senator Higgins has ignored our advice, it looks like we're going to have to look at other alternatives to resolve this issue. I have word that Senator Higgins plans to announce both his retirement and his decision to run for the office of the President of the United States, at a party to be held on the Fourth of July."

"What a grandstander," says Phillips.

"One more comment from you, Mr. Phillips, and you may find you're scheduled for a TLC!" bellows Senator McCarthy to a visibly shaken Phillips. "Since the direct approach has failed, I think we should look at more subtle means of termination. The party is scheduled to be at the Watergate Hotel. It will be black tie, and by invitation only." He looks down at Phillips, anticipating him making another comment. Just as Phillips is about to open his mouth, he looks up and sees McCarthy staring at him, and quickly changes his mind. "While we'll only need one operative to carry out the TLC, I suggest we use at least five operatives to guarantee its success."

"We have at our disposal, a newly developed toxin that gives the illusion of a heart attack, and is virtually undetectable, even by an autopsy. It's activated by alcohol, so it could be triggered almost immediately at the party, or remain dormant for several days. Best of all, there's been no antidote developed for it as yet,

139

and regardless of the dosage, tests have shown it to always be fatal."

Major General Woolbright asks, "Just how is this toxin delivered?"

"A microscopic needle, about the size of a wasp's stinger, attached to a pressure sensitive bulb, is used to deliver the toxin. We already have rings, and other devices in our inventory, capable of delivering it. Great care must be taken with this toxin however, since anyone receiving the slightest prick with this toxin will die."

McCarthy continues, "I see that we have fifteen members present. I now call this proposal to a vote. How say you? Those in support, say aye." The vote is unanimous.

"Mr. Phillips! Since you have such a desire to speak out this evening, I have a job for you." Phillips is startled by his request. "Come on. It's not going to hurt," says McCarthy as he picks up a silver serving bowl. "You're going to have the honor of selecting the five members who will be providing the operatives for this task."

"Senator McCarthy, sir," says Phillips pleadingly. "I don't think that I'm qualified to..."

"Get up Phillips! Be a man. All you've got to do is draw five names," says McCarthy. Phillips is trembling as he gets up and approaches McCarthy. He looks into the bowl and is stunned to see only five slips of paper, and one of them has his name on it! McCarthy steps in front of Phillips, with his back to the other members and whispers to him, "Just call out the names. Save yours for last, and I'll save your sorry ass. Screw it up, and I'll personally make sure you won't live to see the sunrise. Got it?" Phillips' face goes pale.

Phillips draws the first name. "Senator Howard Long." A muffled conversation begins among the members.

"Gentlemen, please! Mr. Phillips is trying to call out the names for this operation," says McCarthy.

"If I get selected again, I won't have any operatives left!" says Senator Long.

"Sorry about that, Howard. What are the odds?" McCarthy says sympathetically, but with a smile on his face. "Go on, Phillips. Who's next?"

140

"Mr. Richard Connelly," says Phillips with a tremble in his voice. Mr. Connelly owns a large computer software company that supplies programming software for both the IRS and the military. Connelly sighs, and shakes his head.

"Phillips? Step it up. We don't have all night. I'm sure we all have other things to do."

Phillips reaches into the bowl and pulls another name. "Mr. James Hudson." Mr. Hudson is the CFO for one of the largest oil companies in the United States.

"What's going on here, Joshua? I've already lost one of my best operatives on the first attempt, and I almost had another one's identity exposed yesterday," he says aloud.

"I've got nothing to do with it," says McCarthy. "Phillips is pulling the names, not me."

Phillips is sweating bullets as he draws the next name. "Senator Alex Burgess."

"Now see here Joshua." roars Senator Burgess. "You're taking my last seasoned operative! This thing is rigged!"

"How dare you accuse Phillips like that!? He had no way of knowing I was going to call on him." says McCarthy. "Draw the last one, Phillips. Do it now!"

Phillips takes a long look at the last piece of paper, then he says in a broken voice, "Wa-Wa-Walter Phillips." Suddenly there is silence.

"Now see? How could you accuse Phillips of rigging this lottery? He just drew his own name, and I know for a fact that he too, only has one veteran operative left."

"I want to see that bowl Joshua!" says Senator Burgess as he charges toward the table and bumps into Phillips. Phillips loses his balance and bumps into the table, effectively knocking the bowl onto the floor. To everyone's amazement, including Phillips, several pieces of paper float away from the bowl, as it bounces off the carpeted floor.

"Gentlemen! Gentlemen! Please take your seats." pleads McCarthy. "Walter? Are you all right? Here. Let me give you a hand."

Phillips starts to reach for McCarthy's hand, but remembers what he had said about a ring being able to deliver the toxin. He can see that McCarthy isn't wearing a ring on his right hand, so

141

he takes it. After he pulls Phillips to his feet, McCarthy brushes off his shoulders, then pats Phillips on the back. Phillips feels a slight twinge as McCarthy says, "That was quite a tumble! Are you okay?"

Phillips whispers to McCarthy, "I thought you said that you were going to save my ass."

McCarthy smiles, and says, "I just did." He motions for Phillips to take his seat.

"Now gentlemen," says McCarthy, "I expect to have the names of your operatives, along with their files, no later than noon tomorrow. I hope you will provide those operatives who have had experience with this type of covert delivery system. For those who can't, we'll arrange to have them sent to the farm for a few days to give them the opportunity to learn the proper way to use this system. After all, failure is not an option, only death. Now, before we adjourn, is there any other business that needs to be addressed?" Silence. "No? Then, good night."

As everyone starts to leave the room, McCarthy walks over to Phillips and says, "Sorry I was so rough on you, but you know how I am. I hate interruptions, and this really was serious business." Phillips nods his head without looking up. "Tell you what. Want to go out for a drink? I'll buy. What do you say?"

"Apology accepted," Phillips replies. "But it's getting late, and Leslie wants me to review her speech about homeless children in Washington before she presents it to the Women's League tomorrow. You know how it is."

"Sure, I understand. Rain check then?" asks McCarthy.

"How about Friday? I'm closing a deal on a military contract for a new type of weapons delivery system. Supposedly worth billions!" says Phillips.

"Friday it is then," replies McCarthy as he reaches out to shake his hand. Again, Phillips hesitates for a moment, then shakes his hand.

***

Senator Joshua Abrams McCarthy comes from a long line of politicians. His father had been a state senator for over 30 years, as his grandfather had been before him. Shortly after having

142

been elected governor of Massachusetts, his father had a fatal heart attack on his yacht in Chesapeake Bay. While his father was Irish Catholic, his mother was Jewish, hence his name. Joshua was her grandfather's given name. Abrams was his mother's maiden name.

Joshua is tall, about six foot two, two hundred and thirty pounds, in his late forties, with just a hint of gray in his hair, very distinguished. He's very alert, intelligent, and handsome.

Men are attracted to him because of his wit, and his knowledge of what's happening in and around Washington. Other men fear him and see him as a predator, looking for one's weaknesses, lulling them into a false sense of security, then moving in for the kill when they least expect it.

Women, on the other hand, find him charming and irresistible. Many have fallen for him and paid the price. Pictures have occasionally hit the local papers, but Joshua always manages to come through, none the worse for wear. Surprisingly, his wife, Michelle, seems to be oblivious to his dalliances, and appears to remain firmly by his side.

Besides women, Joshua has one other weakness, cars. Not just any car, but cars that are unique, exotic, fast, and of course, expensive. While he is chauffeured during the week in his stretched Lincoln, he may be coddled in a Bentley Continental Flying Spur, along with his wife, for an evening on the town. Or he might fly solo in his Ferrari 575 Barchetta, Mercedes SL65AMG Black Series, BMW M6, Lamborghini Gallardo LP 560-4, or his newly acquired Aston Martin DBS. Joshua is living the dream of most playboy wannabes.

His political contacts provide him with suites at five star hotels from New York, to Boston. One staunch supporter keeps an open reservation on a cabin for him in the Poconos, while another has a beach house overlooking Chesapeake Bay, near the marina where Joshua moors his father's yacht.

One of his uncles was a U.S. Senator, and while in college, Joshua was his aide. His uncle made certain he met the right people, rubbed the right elbows, etc. He had majored in business, with minors in political science and law. But his home run came when he married Michelle.

Michelle Louise Marston comes from a family of old money derived from the railroad and steel industries. She is beautiful, smart, and very active in upper crust social circles. Michelle has an exotic European look about her, possibly Greek or Italian. She's about five foot nine, with long, silky, rich black hair, and large brown eyes that seem to melt men's hearts, as well as brain cells the moment they gaze upon her. She has the body and legs of a swimsuit model. Every movement is smooth and graceful, in short, poetry in motion. While on the surface, she has the beauty, grace and poise of a swan on a motionless lake, beneath the surface cruises the cunning, power, and jaws of a great white.

She graduated with honors in law at Harvard, along with minors in organization and management. She quickly immersed herself in her father's law firm in New York, assisting with corporate mergers and buyouts. But being the only child, she believed that one day, she would eventually take her father's place in the Core.

Her great, great, grandfather was one of the pioneers at the beginning of our industrial age. While he was a sharp businessman, he was also ruthless. What he couldn't buy, he stole. Tales were told that the skeletons in his closet would fill a cemetery the size of Forest Lawn.

At the turn of the century, the Marstons' business ventures carried a lot of weight in political circles. Shortly after the end of World War II, her grandfather sold off the railroad business, and by the time the steel industry started to falter, Michelle's father had already begun to diversify into other types of industry and business, many of them outside of the United States.

A young financial advisor by the name of Joshua McCarthy had warned him that foreign steel manufacturers, along with the greed and corruption within the Steel Workers Union, would be the American steel industry's demise.

Joshua also saw new and promising industries coming onto the market, and made recommendations to Michelle's father. He and Joshua's uncle saw Joshua as a good match for Michelle, as well as a future member of the Core. You see, Mr. Marston and Joshua's uncle were both members of the Core. Between his uncle's and Mr. Marston's collective clout, Joshua's seat in the

144

Senate was secure. He would become one of the youngest U.S. Senators to date.

***

McCarthy walks out to the parking garage and gets into his car, an Aston Martin DBS, and starts it. He blips the throttle a couple of times, listening to the growl of the V-12 coming to life. Smiling, he makes a call. "Bill? We're set. Howard, James, Alex, Richard, and Walter will be sacrificing their last experienced operatives on your supposed demise. Plus, Walter just became our first human guinea pig on this new toxin my people have developed. Only they think there's no antidote. The problem is, we won't know just how effective it is until Friday unless, of course, Walter decides to imbibe before then."

"Well Joshua, that would certainly be a perfect alibi for you, wouldn't it?" asks Higgins.

"Yes, but I want to see the expression on his face when it hits him. I want to be the last person he sees on the face of this earth, and I want him to know that I did it to him," says McCarthy with a wicked grin.

"Damn Joshua! Remind me not to get on your bad side."

"No problem, Bill. Gotta go. I have a date with Elizabeth."

"I thought your wife's name was Michelle."

"It is! Talk to you tomorrow," replies McCarthy as he roars out of the garage.

TLC: Chapter 21
Wednesday evening
2330 hours local time

AJ is lying in bed next to Julie, who has fallen fast asleep. His mind is racing from all of the excitement this week, especially being reunited with Julie. He says to himself, *"After five years, what are the odds of us both working for the Secret Service, both getting stationed in Washington, and then being assigned as partners. What are the odds?"*

At first he's smiling about his good fortune, but then he starts to realize just what *are* the odds? Something's not right. He slips out of bed and slips away to the other bedroom, carefully closing the door behind him. Sitting at his desk, he turns on the desk lamp, opens the file drawer, and pulls out a copy of his file. When he gets down to the part about the rescue attempt in Bosnia, he finds what he's looking for. *"Lieutenant Julie Anne Robinson is appointed legal counsel for Master Sergeant Thomas Andrew Jackson, 5 April 2006."*

He knows that Weathers is thorough in his research. After all, his career in the military was dependent on it. *"If this information is in my file, then it will most certainly be in hers. There's no way in hell our pairing is a coincidence, so what does Weathers have up his sleeve? And come to think of it, Julie's no dummy either. Surely, she would suspect something. This is grade school stuff. Anybody with half a brain could figure this out."* Suddenly, it hits him. *"Julie and Weathers must be working together. They have to be. Against me. But about what? What do I know? Shit!"*

AJ starts pulling weapons off the wall and loading them into an assault bag. He grabs the suppressed MP5, then he picks up and breaks down the Steyr AUG. Next, he picks up several magazines for both weapons, and places them in their proper pouches within the bag. He makes certain his earmuffs and safety glasses are properly stowed, then sets the bag on the desk. Slipping back into the bedroom, he grabs some clothes, along with his tactical vest, and returns to the other room. Once dressed, he scribbles a quick note, sticks it on the refrigerator, and eases out the door.

AJ's apartment
Thursday morning
June 16, 2011, 0600 hours local time

Julie awakens to the beeping sound of the alarm clock. She
stretches her arms, then rolls over to find that AJ is not in the bed.
She also doesn't smell anything cooking. The apartment is quiet.
Thinking he might be in the bathroom, she slips on her robe, and
tiptoes quietly down the hallway to the bathroom. But the
surprise is on Julie. The bathroom is empty. In fact, AJ is
nowhere to be found. Wandering into the kitchen, she finds AJ's
note stuck on the refrigerator. It says, *"Gone out to get some
fresh air, and vent a little frustration. Back in a bit."* Julie is
puzzled by his comment about frustration, but rather than dwell
on it, she begins to get ready for work.

Since Weathers isn't expecting her before 0900, she's taking
her time getting ready, occasionally checking her watch,
wondering what's happening with AJ. She tries calling him a
couple of times on his cell phone, but her calls go straight to
voice mail.

Just as she's about ready to leave, she hears someone at the
door. It's AJ. As he walks through the door, he looks up to see
Julie, then immediately looks away, and closes the door behind
him.

"Where'd you go?" asks Julie. "I was hoping we'd have a
repeat performance before I headed out to meet Weathers this
morning. What's with the bag? Do I smell spent gun powder?"

"My! You're full of questions this morning, aren't you?" he
says rather sarcastically.

"AJ? What's wrong? What's going on?" she asks innocently.

"Funny. I was about to ask you that very same question."

"What are you talking about?" she asks.

"Evidently, you and Weathers must think I'm as dumb as a
rock," he says in disgust.

"AJ? Will you stop talking in circles and tell me what's going
on in that thick skull of yours?"

"Okay, here goes. First off, how long have you been in the
Secret Service?"

"About six months. Why?"

147

"Where were you stationed before being assigned here in Washington?"

"L.A., but what's that got to do with anything?"

"When did you first have contact with Weathers?" he asks coldly.

"A few weeks ago. I wanted to transfer to Washington. I know a few people out here."

"You mean me, don't you?" he asks.

"I had no idea you were in Washington. And I sure as hell didn't know you were in the Secret Service, or even working under Weathers for that matter," she replies with some resentment in her tone. "It was as much a surprise for me, as it was for you, when you came through that door. But, I guess I'm the only one who thought it was a good thing." She turns away, walks into the living room, and sits down on the couch.

AJ can see Julie seems to be genuinely hurt by his questions, so he begins to soften his approach. "Julie, there's a lot more going on here than meets the eye. You've seen your file, haven't you?"

"Of course I have. So what?"

"Is there any mention of you defending me in Bosnia?"

"You know there is. What does that have to do with anything?"

"Who is our immediate supervisor, and what's his background?" he asks with an intense look on his face.

Julie starts to answer, but then pauses, and begins thinking things through. "Oh shit! Of course! It's so obvious! Why didn't I see that?"

"What? Do you honestly expect me to believe that you have nothing to do with this?" he asks is disbelief.

"AJ? With God as my witness, I swear I knew nothing about any of this."

"You swear?"

"Yes, I swear."

AJ can see tears welling up in her eyes.

"AJ, I'm telling you the truth," she says, as she drops her head and begins to sob.

AJ weakens. Kneeling before her, he says, "I believe you. But Weathers definitely has something going on, and I'm going

148

to find out what it is. I'm sick and tired of being everybody's pawn."

As he starts to get up, she grabs him and says, "Hold on. There are some things I need to tell you before you go John Wayne on me."

"Oh! So you have been holding back." he scoffs.

"It's about yesterday," she sighs. "Weathers made me promise not to say anything. But under the circumstances, I'm going to do something I've never done before. I'm going to break a promise. But AJ, you've got to promise me you won't do anything or admit to knowing anything I'm about to tell you."

"Tell me what?"

"Promise!" she cries out.

"Okay. I promise," he says as he sits down beside her.

"Remember when you said it didn't seem to make any sense breaking into Weathers' house and not steal or plant anything? Well, they did leave something."

"What?"

"They left a large manila envelope with a disc and what appear to be some files."

"What's it about?"

"We're not sure. That's why I'm going over to Weathers' house this morning. We're going to start looking it over and see what we can come up with."

"Well, let's get going!" he says enthusiastically. "If two can do it twice as fast, surely one more will only speed things up."

"Wrong. For starters, you're not supposed to know anything about it. Secondly, Weathers thinks you may be working for Higgins now."

"Well, I am. He put me there, remember?"

"No, what he means by working for him is that you're now working for the Core."

"But Higgins wants to break the Core."

"Does he? Does he really want to break the Core, or does he want take it over?" she asks.

"Remember? They killed his niece at Kent State."

"I don't know, but something just doesn't feel quite right about all this."

149

"You're telling me. It's beginning to feel like you need a program to tell who the good guys are in this mess."

"Well, for right now, I'm beginning to think it's just you and me," says Julie. "I'm not so sure if I fully trust Weathers in all this, especially after realizing he had to know of our previous relationship and playing dumb about it."

"So, what do we do now?" he asks, obviously frustrated about the situation.

"I'm going over to Weathers' house so he and I can start figuring out what's in the file, and that disc. Oh. That reminds me. Can I borrow your laptop? Mine's still packed away, and I told Weathers I'd bring one."

"Yeah, mine's in the other bedroom, next to the desk."

"Hey, cheer up," she says. "I'll bring it home tonight, and I'll see if I can either slip the disc away from him, or at least copy what's on it. That way, you and I will have something to work on tonight. What do you say?"

"Now, that sounds like a plan. You better get out of here, or you're going to be late. Weathers hates it when people are late."

"Okay, I'm going. But first, you've got to tell me what you were doing while I was asleep."

"Nothing important. I'll tell you about it tonight, okay?"

"Oh, all right. Just be that way," she sighs, as she starts towards the door. "I'll talk to you later."

"Don't forget the computer," he says with a smile.

"What am I thinking?" she asks, as she turns around and starts walking toward the other bedroom.

"Well, I don't know what you're thinking, but I'm thinking I ought to give you one of these," he says, as he grabs her about the waist, snatching her toward him, then planting a long, lustful kiss on her lips. She resists momentarily, but then literally melts in his arms, wrapping her arms around him. As he slowly breaks away from the kiss, he gazes into her eyes, and says, "Please, be careful out there. I've dreamed of no one but you these past five years. And now that we've been given a second chance, I don't want to lose you again. I care more about you than you can possibly know. Julie? I love you."

Julie's heart is about to burst. Even when they were together in England, AJ had never said those words, not once. Tears are welling up in her eyes, but they are tears of joy. "Now, look at me. See what you made me do? I'm ruining my makeup," she says in a broken voice.

AJ pulls out a handkerchief, gently blots her cheeks, and says, "No, you've never been more beautiful."

Julie reaches up and draws him to her, then begins kissing him passionately. AJ can sense she's trying to guide them toward the bedroom, and starts to unzip his fly.

He breaks her lip lock long enough to say, "What do you think you're doing? You're going to be late."

"Oh, haven't you heard? There's a major gaper's block at a construction site on the expressway. Traffic is backed up for miles," she says, as she begins to unbutton her blouse, and slips out of her skirt.

"Well, you know, there are a number of side streets you could take to get around it," he says whispering in her ear.

"No, too late. I'm already caught up in the gridlock," she replies as she pushes him down on the bed.

"That's too bad," he says smiling. "You could be stuck for hours."

"You're telling me." she says with a devilish smile.

"Stop!"

"Why? What did I do?" she asks.

"Call Weathers now, and let him know you're going to be late. You don't want to see his dark side. Trust me."

"Boy! You really know how to spoil the mood."

"No, I'm not trying to spoil it. But the sooner you get that call out of the way, the sooner you and I can get down to the business at hand."

"What makes you think I'm going to use my hands?"

"Look. I'm serious. Weathers can be an absolute asshole if you don't keep him apprised of your situation. I know. I've been there."

"Oh, all right," she says disappointingly, as she slides off of him, reaches into her purse, and pulls out her phone. She's surprised to see she has a message waiting, so she calls her voicemail. It's from Weathers. *"Julie, something's come up, and I've got a few things I need to do. I'll call you later."*

"Hmm. Now that's interesting."

"What? Who was it?"

"It was Weathers. I guess I should have checked my phone earlier."

"Well, what did he say?"

"He said something came up and would call me later," she replies with a puzzled look on her face.

"That's perfect! Now we can go over and pick up that envelope and see what's in it," he says excitedly.

"Not so fast. As far as I know, he's expecting you to be at work, and if anyone shows up at the house, it should only be me. We don't want to be raising any suspicions, now do we?"

"You're right, as usual."

"Besides," she says in a sultry voice. "We still have some unfinished business of our own to tend to, don't you think?"

"Well, we could always save it for later."

"Yeah? And what are you going to do with that tent in your pants?"

"You helped put it there. So, I think the least you could do is help me resolve it, don't you?"

"Sure thing. The bathroom's at the end of the hall. Why don't you just hop in the tub and take a cold shower. That should do the trick."

"Come on Julie. I was only kidding. Please?" he begs.

"Okay, but you better not try to make a habit out of this," she says smiling.

"Me? You were the one who started it."

"AJ? Do you want to argue the finer points of this situation, or do you want to have wild, ravenous sex?"

Weathers is sitting on a park bench across from the Lincoln Memorial, reading the Washington Post. An Army lieutenant walks up to him and says, "Colonel Weathers?"

"Yes, lieutenant?" he replies.

"General Woolbright and Senator Higgins are waiting for you over there, sir," says the lieutenant, as he points toward two black Suburbans parked at the curb.

"Thank you, lieutenant." Weathers follows him to the curbside of the second vehicle, where the lieutenant opens the door for him. Once inside, the lieutenant closes the door, then walks up to and gets in the lead vehicle. Weathers finds both Woolbright and Higgins on their cell phones talking away. Higgins and Weathers make eye contact, yet Higgins continues with his conversation. It's evidently with one of the vendors for the party.

"No, no, no! I want fresh Maine lobster flown in. I don't want any of that California crap. This *is* the East Coast, isn't it? You could almost drive up to Maine and pick them up yourself! Get it right, or I'll find someone who can! Got it? Good!"

General Woolbright seems to be having problems of his own. "What do you mean they've found another glitch with the weapons system? We're already $200 million over budget on the damn thing. They've had two failed demonstrations, as well as being 18 months behind schedule! What is it this time? Aw... Come on! You've got to be kidding! Call SynTec Automation Systems and tell them they've got until this afternoon's shakedown cruise to get that helicopter prepped and on the flight line. And if the damn thing screws up this time, I'm going to have their collective balls on a platter!" Then he calms down a bit and continues, "Now look. I'm going to be in and out of meetings most of the day, so unless you've got some good news to tell me, I don't want to hear from you or anyone else. I'll check in throughout the day, so hold my calls, okay? Thank you Beverly."

Woolbright looks at Weathers to see that he has a surprised look on his face. "What?"

Weathers asks, "You were talking to a lady like that?"

Woolbright replies, "That's no lady. That's my secretary. You should hear her talk!"

Weathers shakes his head and says, "So, Senator. What's on the agenda today?"

"You know, this fella AJ? He's got a lot of balls. Don't get me wrong. I like him. I like him a lot. He's intelligent, manages to keep a cool head about him when the shit hits the fan and all. But, have you seen this?" he asks as he hands Weathers a piece of paper.

Weathers scans the paper and says, "What is this? Are you putting together some type of strike force or something?"

"That, Bob, is AJ's idea of protecting me."

"Well, if you've got the right manpower, you could hold off a small army with this kind of hardware. Wait a minute...A Barrett? He actually told you he wanted a Barrett?" asks Weathers.

"Look again," says Higgins. "He wants two of them."

"If the Core decides to plan a full out frontal assault, and you've got this kind of firepower, they haven't got a chance."

"You and I both know the Core won't try that kind of thing again," says Higgins. "They got their asses kicked. In public! Besides, my intelligence group tells me they're going to hold off until the party at the Watergate Hotel."

"Have you told him that, yet?"

"AJ? No. He's still trying to play this as a military operation."

"If the Core fails to complete your TLC at the party, they still may try a frontal assault before it's over."

"If everything goes as planned at the party, my opposition within the Core won't have any seasoned operatives left. And even if they did, by the time I finish feeding information to AJ, he'll be my one man army."

"Senator, AJ is a Marine. He eats Rangers for breakfast," says Weathers, then looks over at General Woolbright and says, "No offense, General."

"None taken, Colonel," replies Woolbright.

"So, tell me Bob. Should I get this equipment, or not?"

"Senator, if I were you, I'd get it. If you don't, you'll be telling AJ you really don't trust his judgment. Besides, when all this is over, you can give it to some poor third world country to protect their leader."

"Funny. That's exactly what AJ said," says Higgins smiling.

"What's the latest on getting manpower?" asks Weathers.

"I've got four men coming in from Secure-1 Executive Protection Services, Ltd. They train professional bodyguards. You just call them up, and tell them what you want. They review their roster, and they'll send you a complete file on their candidates. I told them they had to be ex-military, preferably with some sort of Special Forces Training, heavy experience in hand-to-hand combat, edged weapons, and light military firearms.

"What about the other one?" asks Weathers.

"He'll be one of my operatives."

"Senator? AJ is going to check them all out. You know that."

"What do you mean, check them out?"

"You know perfectly well what I mean. He's going to want to check their files, run their fingerprints, the works."

"Well, wouldn't he be running all that through you?"

"Probably, but he's pretty sharp, just like you said. If your operative is a Marine, all he'll have to do is ask a few questions about his outfit, tours, officers, etc., and he'll be able to conduct his own investigation. He's got plenty of contacts of his own to verify whether they're who they say they are, or not."

"Damnit! You're right, of course. I hadn't thought of that," says Higgins in disgust. "Now I'm a man short." He pauses a moment while shaking his head, then asks, "What do you suggest?"

"I assigned a partner to AJ the day after your attempted assassination. Has he mentioned anything about it?"

"No, he hasn't. What's his background?"

"Her background, Senator. His partner is a woman," replies Weathers.

"You're kidding, right? A woman? Well, what's her background?"

"For starters, she's not the hardened military type, if that's what you're asking. But she's smart, and very capable with firearms, as well as hand to hand. She served in the Navy's JAG Corps, and spent some time with NCIS."

"Bob? If I didn't know better, I'd say it sounds like you're trying to set me up."

"Look, if you let him bring in his partner, it might make things easier for you to bring your operative in later, when things settle down a bit. Just make sure he's got a good cover. But above all, make sure he's not a Marine, okay?"

"Sounds like double jeopardy to me."

"How's that?" asks Weathers.

"A partner who is both a woman and a lawyer. Damnit Bob. You sure know how to pick 'em." says Higgins as he lets out a chuckle, then slides back in his seat.

"Back to my original question. What are the plans for today?"

"For starters, Ainsworth, with the CIA, says he can handle the MP5's and the Steyrs. And Rickman, with the DEA, says he has a couple of Barretts we can use, along with the shotguns he wants. The General, here, has offered to help me take care of the ammunition, grenades, night vision, and gas masks, so we'll be going out to the army depot to pick them up, and see what else we can find. Oh, and if we have time, we're going up to New York to pick up my new limo."

"I didn't know you were getting a new limo. What's wrong the old one?"

"After seeing the punishment AJ's Hummer took, I decided I need something that offers a bit more protection. Eberhardt and Keyes is supposed to have mine ready by the time we get up there."

"You're telling me that your new limo is a Hummer?" asks Weathers in disbelief.

"Yep, and I'm working on a little surprise for AJ, too."

"What kind of surprise?" asks Weathers.

"You'll see."

TLC: Chapter 23
Marston-McCarthy International Legal Services
Manhattan, New York
0930 hours local time

Michelle is reading over a proposal regarding a corporate takeover of BioGen Research by an undisclosed major medical group when her cell phone rings. After the third ring, she glances at the display and recognizes the name and number. "This better be important, Avery. I'm busy."

"Your husband was pretty busy last night," says the voice on the other end.

"Tell me something I don't already know. He had a business meeting last night," she says as she flips a page of the proposal.

"Yes, and that lasted a whole thirty minutes. But then he drove over to The Whittier Hotel and had a liaison with a Miss Elizabeth Reynolds. They seemed to be quite close. Is she, by any chance, related?"

Michelle slams the file closed and snarls, "Cut the crap! What did you get on the bastard last night?"

"Well, it appears that Elizabeth is quite athletic, and your husband was pretty resilient in his ability to assist her with her workout."

"Did you get it on video?"

"Oh yes. And, thank goodness I brought an extra tape! Your husband was in rare form last night. I think he was going for a record. Four hours and seventeen minutes. Even I was exhausted."

"Please, Avery, spare me the details," she replies tersely. "When can you deliver a copy?"

"I'm transferring it to disc as we speak. I could have it to you later this afternoon. Have you told your father what you're up to? By the way, what exactly are you up to? We've been tailing your husband for months. You've got more than enough evidence to divorce him, and ruin his career."

"Look! You take care of your business, and I'll take care of mine, okay? You're getting paid, rather handsomely, aren't you? Do you have a problem with that? Or should I start looking for someone else?"

"Now Mrs. McCarthy, you…"

"It's Ms. Michelle Marston! I suggest you remember that," she says coldly.

"Yes, Ms. Marston."

"Anything else? I'm really busy."

"I'm not sure. Right after the meeting, he made a phone call to a government secure number."

"Have you been able to hack into their frequency yet?"

"Their frequency isn't the problem. It's their encryption code. Just when we think we're making progress, they change it. We were able to get the number he was calling, but it was nothing but static and buzzes after that."

"Well, have you been able to trace the number?"

"No, that's why it's called Secure Line. Ms. Marston, we're dealing with the federal government here. We could get into a lot of trouble if we're caught snooping where we don't belong."

"Just what in the hell am I paying you for? You've been watching him for almost six months, and you can't hack a simple phone line?"

"Ms. Marston, we're dealing with a government designed, monitored, and controlled wireless communication system. Secure Line spends millions to maintain the security and integrity of their system. For Christ's sake! Even the President is dependent on this system!"

"I'm not paying you for excuses, I'm paying you for results! I know he's up to something over and above his little love affairs, and I'm going to find out what it is."

"But Ms. Marston. We have access to his computer, as well as making videotapes of his amorous liaisons. You'd think we were shooting a documentary! We have GPS transponders on every car, with the exception of the Aston Martin. And we should have that one online before the week is out. We know where he is practically anytime, anywhere. His every movement is recorded including where and how long he stops. You've got enough dirt on him now to bury him."

"I'll tell you when I've got enough! I want you to find out who he's calling, and what they're talking about. And don't call me again until you do!" Michelle terminates the call.

TLC: Chapter 24
Robert Weathers' home
0930 hours local time

Julie rings the doorbell at the Weathers' home. Mrs. Weathers answers the door and says, "Julie? What a surprise. Didn't Robert call you? He had to go out, and I'm not sure when he's coming back."

"Hmmm. That's odd," she says innocently as she pulls out her cell phone. "Oh! He must have left me a voice message. I guess I should have checked it before I came over. Well, since I'm here, there is something in his study we were going to work on today. You don't think he'd mind if I took it with me, do you?"

"Oh, I'm sure if the two of you were going to work on something, I doubt he'd mind," replies Mrs. Weathers. "I only hope you know where he left it, because I hardly ever go in there."

"I believe I do. I'll only be a moment."

"Take your time."

Julie walks up the stairs and enters his study, closing the door behind her. She sits down at his desk, and pulls out the lower right hand drawer. Sure enough, the envelope is still there. She opens her briefcase, and places the file inside. As she's about to close the drawer, she notices another envelope with Senator Higgins' name in the return address portion of the envelope. Just as she's about to pick it up, her phone rings, startling her. It's AJ. She answers it. "AJ? You scared the living daylights out of me! What do you want?"

"Did you get it?"

"Just put it in my briefcase."

"How long before you can get back to the apartment?"

"Well, I was thinking about taking Weathers' car back to the office and picking up mine."

"Okay, I'll meet you there. I've got a couple of things I want to check out anyway."

"Such as?"

"Nothing concrete. They're just hunches right now. I want to see how they play out."

159

"Okay. Do you want to work on the file while we're there?"

"Why not?"

"Sounds good to me. I'm going to talk to Lisa for a moment, then I'll be on my way."

"Meet you there. Bye."

"Bye," she replies.

As Julie walks out of Weathers' study, she can hear someone's muffled crying. She follows the sound to Lisa's bedroom, and knocks on the door. "Lisa? Is everything all right?"

Julie's knock at the door startles Lisa. While wiping her face to clear away the tears, yet still sniffling, she says, "Just a minute." She stands before the mirror, trying to straighten up her makeup, then walks over to the door and opens it. "Oh, hi Julie. It's nothing, really. Just the excitement, the stress, and all. Plus the boys have been perfect little tyrants, as usual. And keeping them indoors hasn't helped our nerves any."

"Look. AJ might buy a bullshit story like that, but I'm a woman. So, what's up? Talk to me."

Lisa turns away and begins to cry again. "I just got off the phone with Sean. He's leaving me and the kids."

"Why would he do a thing like that? Certainly not over what happened to the house."

"Oh, he still doesn't know anything about the house being demolished. No, he's leaving me because he found another woman, no kids, and no emotional baggage. Plus, she's got money, too. He's been seeing her for some time, before David was born," she says, trying to hold back the tears, the anger, and the hurt.

"Well, that bastard!" says Julie with anger in her voice. "No, I should have seen it coming," she says. "After seeing what my dad did to my mom, and how self destructive Tim was, I had pretty much made up my mind I was destined to go through life alone. I was afraid of men, and what they could do to me. The only man I ever really trusted was David, at least until he introduced me to Sean. Then I began to trust again."

"We'd been having personal and financial problems since Tim was born six weeks premature. His lungs hadn't fully developed, so he lived in an incubator for almost a month, with some sort of medical supervision 24/7. Our insurance hardly scratched the

160

surface. Plus we had just bought the house, so most of our savings went to cover the down payment. Sean lost his job because he was taking time off from work trying to take care of Tim and me. He was unemployed for almost two months. We thought we were going to lose the house."

"But then this salesman's job came up, and things started to look better. He had to be out of town a lot, but the money was good. I took on some seamstress work, so I was able to work at home, and take care of Tim. It made me feel like I was contributing to our situation, and allowed us to buy a few frivolous things from time to time."

We were finally getting back on our feet, and actually a little ahead of the game, when I became pregnant with David. Sean was spending more time out of town, and even when he was home, things weren't quite the same. He always seemed a bit moody. Nothing I did seemed to satisfy him. Something was wrong with the house, or Tim was getting underfoot. The slightest thing would set him off."

"Then, there were the phone calls. He would always try to sneak away out of earshot. But sometimes he wouldn't know I was close by, and I could see him smile, or hear him laugh a little. Whoever was on the other end of the call had more of an effect on him than I did."

"Now look at me. David is dead, Sean is leaving me for another woman, our house and personal belongings are gone, and all I have is what I was able to gather up the other night. I don't even have a toothbrush! My life is shit! The whole world is shit! What did I do to deserve this?" Lisa starts crying again, and her entire body is shaking from her emotional release. Julie feels helpless.

"Lisa, while I've never been in your exact position, I do have an idea how you feel. You've got some serious questions that need to be addressed."

"Oh yeah? Like what?" she asks while sniffling and crying.

"Do you still love Sean? If the answer is yes, then you're going to have to fight for him. But if the answer is no, then you're going to have to fight for your children and yourself. The fact that he's bringing his affair out into the open, tells me he's already made up his mind where his allegiance lies. Languishing in self-pity isn't going to solve anything. I know. I've been there." Julie pauses a moment, then continues.

"Lisa, you're a beautiful young woman. You're smart, bright, and you have two darling," Julie makes a funny face, "young children. Any man with half a brain would be lucky to have you. Don't sell yourself short, either. But you are going to have to make some decisions. And now is the time to make them."

"There's something I'd like to know," says Lisa.

"What?" asks Julie.

"Do you love AJ?"

"Yes. Yes, I do," replies Julie, feeling a little embarrassed. "And that's the very thing I've been talking about. AJ and I first met about five years ago, when we were both still in the military. I was an officer and he was a noncom. We fell in love, but I allowed the military to dictate our future, rather than what was in my heart. While I have no idea what has brought us back together, I'm not letting go this time. I will fight, with every fiber of my being, to keep him. So, yes, I love him."

"I'm glad to hear it. You're right. I do have a lot of things to think about, and I will. I'm not going to be anybody's victim anymore," she says with confidence and conviction.

"Good for you. Now, I've got to run. AJ's waiting for me at the office. But first, I want you to promise me one thing."

"What's that?"

"If you ever need someone to talk to, about anything, I want you to promise you'll call me. Here's my cell phone number. Call me anytime. I mean it. Okay?"

"Okay, I promise. Now get out of here before you lose AJ again."

"I'm going. I'm going," says Julie as she heads down the stairs.

"Oh, Julie?"

Julie stops, turns, and faces Lisa. "Yes?"

"Thanks for listening."

"Like I said. Anytime." Julie smiles, continues down the stairs, and out the front door.

Julie gets in the car and starts heading toward the Homeland Security Complex. Knowing she's at least ten to fifteen minutes behind schedule, she calls AJ. "Hi! You're not going to believe this."

"Oh, I don't know. Try me."

"I'm running a little late. Lisa and I had a little heart to heart chat, and before I knew it...Well, you know," she says embarrassingly. As she's talking to AJ, she glances at the rear view mirror to primp her hair, and notices a familiar looking vehicle behind her.

"I can believe it."

"AJ? Where are you?"

"I'm about two blocks from the office. Why?"

"Remember those guys who were following me yesterday?"

"Yes."

"Well, they're back."

"Julie? Where are you?" he asks with a sense of urgency in his voice.

"I'm on the way to the office, probably about five, maybe six minutes out."

"Do you know what space belongs to Weathers?"

"It's on Level Three, Space number seventy-seven. It's close to the elevator. My car is on Level Four. I don't remember the space."

"Don't worry about your car right now. Have they made any aggressive moves toward you?"

"No, they seem to be hanging back. I don't think they know I've seen them."

"Good, let's try to keep it that way. Hopefully, they'll let you get into the garage before they try to do anything."

"Now there's a scary thought. They're going to assault a government agent *in* the garage of the Homeland Security Complex," she says sarcastically.

"Who knows? Maybe all they want to do is talk," he replies cynically. "I'll be next to the elevator when you pull in. As soon as you park, lie down on the seat and cover your head. If they decide to shoot, it's usually where they can see their target. If

163

they try to open a window or get out of the car, I'll be waiting for them. And should the shooting start, crawl out on the passenger side, okay? I want the car to be between you and them, not between you and me."

"Got it!"

"Whatever you do, don't stop unless you absolutely, positively have to. Stay to the outside, and try to be the lead car if at all possible..."

"AJ, I've done this before. I understand the game, okay?"

"Julie, this isn't a game. They're playing for keeps."

"I know," she says while wringing her hands on the steering wheel.

"Tell you what. Leave your phone on, so I can hear what's going on. If you get pulled over for any reason, be sure to say where you are, exactly. I'll be on my way to you, and I'll do my best to have the cavalry with me," he says reassuringly. "But I'll need to know where I'm going."

"No problem!" Julie pauses a moment, weighing the situation, then asks, "Do you really think we're going to get into a firefight? In the garage?"

"I certainly hope not. But, if we do, I've got my black bag with me."

"Black bag?"

"You know. My assault bag? The one I had with me this morning? Never mind. Just remember. As soon as you pull into the parking space, lay down! I don't want you to be in the direct line of fire."

"You'll think I'm part of the upholstery!"

Julie manages to stay in the outside lane all the way down to the Homeland Security Complex, and the car tailing her is still on the inside lane two to three cars back from her. As Julie slows down to turn into the parking garage, she sees the car speed up. Suddenly she sees what appears to be the barrel of a gun stick out of the open window. As she ducks in an attempt to dodge a hail of bullets, she hears BBRRAATT!!!! She screams, as at least a dozen rounds shatter the glass on both the driver and passenger side of her car! In her panic, she floors the accelerator instead of the brakes and careens head-on into one of the steel reinforced

164

concrete pillars guarding the entrance to the garage, narrowly missing pedestrians scrambling to get out of her way.

The force of the impact crushes the front end, causing the air bags to deploy, dazing her in the process. AJ could hear the sound of suppressed gunfire, shattered glass, Julie's scream, and the crash through Julie's phone. Plus he heard the crash from down below. He shoulders the MP5, drops his bag behind the elevator shaft, then starts running down to the entry level of the garage. As AJ gets his first glimpse of the car, he sees Julie slumped over the steering wheel and deflated airbag, along with the dust from its deployment still hanging in the air. He cries out, "Julieee! Julieee!"

Once he reaches the car, AJ yells at a gawker talking on his cell phone. "Hey you! Dial 911! Do it now and get an ambulance and the police rolling! And tell them we may have entrapment. That'll get the fire department down here, too." Julie appears to be unconscious. He tries to open the door, but the impact has jammed the fender against it. He tries the backdoor, but it's also jammed. He rushes to the passenger side of the car and manages to force the front door open, then eases himself inside. Even with all the pulling, shaking, and jerking, Julie hasn't flinched.

AJ gently touches the side of her neck to see if she has a pulse. Thankfully, she does, and now that he's close to her, he can also see she appears to be breathing normally. Julie moans as she slowly starts to come around. AJ says calmly, "Julie, don't move. You might have a concussion or a neck injury. You're safe for now. I've got an ambulance, fire department, and police coming, so please don't move. They'll be here any minute."

She gives a weak reply, "Whatever you say."
AJ tries to take her mind off of her predicament by teasing her. "You didn't happen to get the tag number off the car that did this, did you?"

"You've got to be kidding, right?" she asks emphatically.

"Ah! Ah! Don't move. Everything is going to be okay. Just be still until the paramedics get here." Both of them can hear sirens in the distance now. "See? I told you. Now just hang on a minute or two longer, and we'll see about getting you out of here. Now don't go away. I'll be right back."

AJ eases out of the car, and pushes through the crowd of people gathering around the scene. He steps out into the street, waving his arms to attract the attention of the paramedics in the ambulance.

As soon as the ambulance pulls up to the curb and stops, AJ starts talking to one of the paramedics as he bails out of the ambulance. "I'm Agent Jackson with the Secret Service, and the lady in the car is Agent Julie Robinson, my partner. She was forced off the road by another vehicle and hit a concrete pillar head-on. She was wearing her seatbelt, and the airbag deployed as well. She appears to have been unconscious for about a minute. I checked her pulse and respiration, and both seem to be within normal limits. She's regained consciousness, and she appears to be alert, coherent, and aware of her surroundings. I've also had her remain in the impact position to reduce any additional trauma. But both doors on the driver's side are jammed, so we're either going to need to use JAWS or take her out on the passenger side."

"Damn! You're full of information, aren't you," says the paramedic. "You've done this before, or just watch a lot of TV?"

"Former Marine. All of us have some basic medical training to help keep us alive in the field."

The paramedic yells out, "Hey Mike! Grab a C-collar, and put the backboard on the stretcher! Sounds like we've probably got a head and neck injury. I've got the jump bag."

"I'm on it, Dan!" Mike yells back.

"Look, Dan. How far back is the fire department? We need to get her out of there as quickly as possible!" yells AJ, as he tries to raise his voice over the noise of the surrounding turmoil.

"I don't know, man. I have enough to worry about without trying to keep up with the FD. All I know is they're probably tied up at a wreck on the expressway. Bad one, too. A jack-knifed semi and at least a half dozen cars are tied up. So far, there are two confirmed dead, at least seven injured, three of them critical. The cops are trying to clear a spot big enough to land a chopper, but it's not looking good. So, right now, it's going to be just us chickens!"

"Great," says AJ. "Then I guess we'll just have to take her out the passenger side."

"Sounds like it," says the paramedic. "Tell me. Do you always run around with a machine gun?"

"Only when necessary," replies AJ.

"Crowd control?" Dan asks with a grin.

"Like I said, Dan, only when necessary."

Several agents have rushed out of the building to assist AJ in keeping bystanders away from the wreck, as well as securing the area. A female agent is talking to Julie.

Once at the wreck, Dan slides into the backseat and starts his assessment of Julie and her possible injuries. Dan carefully checks her head and neck for any potential problems. "Wow! That's a nice little goose egg you got there!"

"Ow! Thanks for bringing that to my attention!"

"Sorry," Dan replies.

AJ opens the front passenger door and eases back into the car next to Julie and says, "Hi. I see you're still here."

"Well, there seems to be something blocking any potential forward motion, and my door is jammed shut. So, I guess you could say that I'm kind of a captive audience. Wouldn't you agree?" she says sarcastically.

"Very funny. Julie? When Mike gets here with the stretcher, he's going to put a C-collar on you to immobilize your head and neck. Strictly precautionary, mind you, but better safe than sorry."

"When am I getting out of here? I'm starting to feel a little uncomfortable, and I think I broke a nail."

Dan says, "Once Mike gets this collar on you, he'll come in from the passenger side, and together, we'll perform a quick visual and physical assessment. Once we've got that out of the way, we'll ease you onto a back board." AJ gets out of the way to allow the paramedics to extract her from the car.

Scanning the crowd, AJ spots a familiar face, and yells, "Hey! Niles! Over here!"

Niles rushes over to AJ and says, "What in the hell happened? Is she going to be okay? What's she doing in Mr. Weathers' car?"

"Never mind all that right now," says AJ as he hands Niles his MP5. "Here, take this and take the elevator up to the third level and look for my black bag. It's behind the elevator shaft on the left side, near the rail. Drop it off with Weathers' secretary and ask her to put in his office for now. Tell her I'll pick it up later, okay?"

"Yes, sir! I'll take care of it personally." says Niles.

"I know you will, because I just made you responsible."

"Oh...Yes sir, I see sir," he says sounding a little embarrassed.

"Niles? Just loosen up a bit. You'll be all right," he replies smiling while patting him on the shoulder. "Have you seen Agent Rollins?"

"Yes, sir. He's right over there," pointing toward the street near the ambulance.

"Thanks, Niles," replies AJ while changing his focus to Rollins. "Agent Rollins!" yells AJ while waving to get his attention, then motioning him to come over.

"Is Agent Robinson going to be okay?" asks Rollins.

"Barring any internal injuries? Yeah, I think she'll be fine. Thanks for asking. I'm putting you in charge of the scene, at least until the cops get here. See if you can find any witnesses who saw what happened. Get any information you can, and get our forensics team down here right away. And have someone check out street cams. Maybe we'll get lucky and find some decent head shots."

"Do you think this is related to what we've been working on the last couple of days?" asks Rollins.

"Probably, and that's what you're going to find out."

After what seems like an eternity, Julie is lying on the backboard, with AJ at the head, carefully pulling her from the car. Once Julie and the backboard are on the stretcher, Mike begins securing her to the backboard, starting at her feet, and working up toward her head. Dan checks the reaction of her pupils, asks about her ability to focus, then checks her blood pressure and pulse again to see if there have been any changes since being removed from the car.

"Everything looks good so far," says Dan. "Once we get you in the ambulance, it's a short ride to the hospital. I'm no doctor, but by all indications, except for a few bumps and bruises here and there, I think you're gonna be okay. The biggest thing we're concerned about though, is head and neck trauma. Thank goodness you were wearing your seatbelt, and the airbag deployed."

"Thanks," she says nervously. As Mike and Dan start rolling her toward the ambulance, she looks at AJ and asks, "Are you coming with me?"

"You bet!" he says as he starts walking beside her. Suddenly, he stops and says, "Where's your briefcase?"

"It was on the passenger seat before the accident, but who knows after the impact."

"I'm going back to the car, and see if I can find it. You guys go on ahead. I'll catch up. I'll only be a minute."

"Okay, but we'll only wait a minute," says Dan. "Dispatch has already called wanting to know why we're not already rolling. They have another call for us to take."

"Well, if I'm not there by the time you get her loaded up, take off without me. I'll get there any way I have to. Now go!"

Making his way back to the car, he can see the woman, who had been talking to Julie earlier, inside the car. He can also see that she's preoccupied with something in her lap. She hasn't noticed AJ walking up behind her. Peering over her shoulder, he can see that she's trying to open the briefcase. "Can I help you miss?" he asks.

"You startled me!" she gasps. "Ah...no, I was just checking to see if her briefcase was secure."

"Funny, but it looked to me like you were trying to open it," he says. "May I see your ID please?"

"Of course," she replies, as she starts to exit the vehicle. Suddenly, she tries to hit AJ in the face with the briefcase, while simultaneously kneeing him in the groin. In spite of the pain inflicted by her attack, he manages to wrestle the briefcase away from her. But once she loses her grip on the case, she turns and bolts into the crowd, making good her escape. AJ makes a half-hearted attempt to chase her, but the pain is just too intense.

He yells out, "Rollins!"

Rollins turns and sees that AJ appears to be hurt, rushes toward him, and asks, "What happened to you?"

"Do you know the name of the female agent talking to Julie just a moment ago?" he asks while grimacing from the pain in his groin.

169

"What agent?" asks Rollins.

"The one in the gray suit, white blouse, nude panty hose, about five foot five, five six, about a hundred and ten, probably a size five, maybe a six, straight, medium length dishwater blonde hair, and plain, blunt toed, black shoes with two inch heels. She also has a gold bracelet on her right wrist, and gold one-inch loop earrings."

"What color were her eyes?" asks Rollins.

"I couldn't see her eyes, because she was too busy trying to close mine with Julie's briefcase."

"What?"

"You're telling me you didn't see what just happened?"

"No, what happened?"

"I was walking with Julie to the ambulance, when she asked me to go back and get her briefcase. But when I got to the car, this female agent was trying to open it. When I asked her what she was doing, she tried to hit me in the face with it, and kneed me in the groin!"

"Damn! That's gotta hurt." says Rollins shaking his head, fighting a grin.

"No shit!" replies AJ, as he holds the briefcase in front of him with one hand, while massaging himself with the other.

"Careful AJ, I may have to arrest you for lewd and lascivious behavior," says Rollins smirking.

Suddenly both of them hear the WHOOP! WHOOP! of the siren, then watch the ambulance pull away from the curb. Once rolling, the siren goes into full song.

Rollins says, "Well, it looks like you just lost your ride."

"That's the story of my life. Guess I'll just have to drive myself to the hospital." AJ and Rollins start walking toward the garage elevator.

"Want me to take you?"

"Now, how are you going to do that, especially since you're in charge of this scene?

"You're right, of course. How about Niles?"

"No, I'll be all right. Besides, if Julie checks out okay, and they decide not to keep her overnight for observation, she's going to need a ride, too. But I do appreciate the offer."

"No problem, just trying to help, that's all."

"That reminds me. I need to call Weathers and tell him what happened," AJ says while pressing the elevator button.

"Now that's a call I hope I never have to make."

"Goes with the territory, Rollins," he replies as he enters the elevator. "Look, I'll keep you posted on Julie's condition, and I expect you to keep me updated on anything you find out about this, okay?"

"You got it," replies Rollins as the doors close. AJ calls Weathers on his way to the third floor of the parking garage.

"Yes, AJ? What's on your mind this morning?" asks Weathers, sounding a bit bored or annoyed.

"Someone just tried to kill Julie."

"What? When? Where?" he asks emphatically.

"Just a few minutes ago. She was being tailed by three men in a Crown Vic coming from your house, and they shot at her as she was about to pull into the parking garage here at the office. She crashed into one of the pillars at the entrance. As best we can tell, it doesn't appear she has any broken bones. But we won't know about any head, neck, or internal injuries until they have a chance to check her out at the hospital," he pauses. "Sir, I'm afraid your car is totaled."

"Forget the car. Have you told anyone else of your suspicions?"

"No, sir, I haven't."

"Good. Who's in charge of the investigation?"

"Right now? I put Rollins in charge. I'm getting ready to head for the hospital, myself."

"Which one?" asks Weathers.

"Washington Memorial."

"I'm leaving now. I'll meet you there."

"Sir? There's one more thing."

"What's that, AJ?"

"Someone tried to steal Julie's briefcase."

"Now, why would someone want to do that?"

"I think we need to talk about that in private, sir."

"I'll get there as fast as I can."

"See you there, sir. Goodbye."

"What was all that about?" asks Higgins. "Somebody have an accident?"

"Yeah, except it was no accident," replies Weathers with anger in his voice. "Someone within the Core just tried to kill one of my agents."

"You're kidding!" says Higgins. "How do you know it has anything to do with the Core?"

"Get off it, Bill! You know damn good and well the Core was behind it." Then Weathers says to the driver, "Stop the car and get me a cab."

"Is she all right?" asks Higgins with a cynical look on his face. "Don't you think you're overreacting, just a little bit there, Bob?"

"Driver. I said stop the damn car. Now!" demands Weathers. "Look. Who else would have the balls to attempt to kill a Secret Service Agent in front of the Homeland Security Complex in broad daylight?"

"Ya got me there, Bob. I don't suppose this is the same agent you have partnered up with AJ now, is it?"

Weathers is silent, pondering the conversation he's having with Higgins. *"How did he know the agent was female? Unless..."*

Just as he's about to say something, Higgins says, "I'd think twice before asking the question that's on the tip of your tongue there, Bob." Higgins pauses a moment, then says, "Lieutenant? Stop the car and get the Colonel a cab."

AJ rushes into the emergency room and calls out to a nurse. "Nurse! Julie Robinson. Car wreck. She probably arrived less than 10 minutes ago. Where is she?"

"You'll have to check at the desk over there," as the nurse points toward the nurse's station, which seems to be just this side of sheer pandemonium. "We've had a number of people brought in from the wreck on the expressway. We don't have names on most of them just yet."

"No, no, no. She wasn't involved in the wreck on the expressway," he replies. "She was involved in a shooting in front of the Homeland Security Complex."

"You just told me she was in a wreck. Now you say she was involved in a shooting?" she says with a confused look on her face. "Now which is it?"

"Both, actually."

"Well, you're still going to have to check at the desk. I'm sure she's in here somewhere."

"Ma'am, you don't understand. She's a Secret Service agent and someone just tried to kill her!"

"Well, you're still going to have to check at the admissions desk. I'm sure they can help you."

Just then, AJ spots one of the paramedics from the accident. "Mike! Mike! Over here!"

Mike looks up to see who is calling his name and spots AJ waving his arms. Mike acknowledges his calling, and motions AJ to come toward him. "Hey man. Sorry we had to leave you over there, but dispatch was raising hell with us."

"No problem. Getting Julie here was your first priority anyway. Do you know where she is?"

"Yeah. They've already sent her up to X-ray."

"Do you know which cubicle they've set her up in?"

"Yeah. The one over there in the corner."

"Thanks Mike. I appreciate all your help."

"Just doing our job. I hope she's okay. Gotta go."

"Me too!" replies AJ. "Me too." He sits down in Julie's cubicle, waiting for her return.

Almost an hour goes by, when AJ hears Weathers' distinctive voice asking a nurse where Julie is. When the nurse points toward the cubicle, Weathers can see AJ standing there, staring at him. He walks over to AJ and asks, "How's she doing?"

"I have no idea, sir," he replies in a somewhat strained voice. "They had already taken her up to X-ray by the time I got here."

Weathers can detect some pain in his voice, and asks, "AJ, are you all right?"

AJ turns away from the opening and massages his groin and says, "That little bitch who tried to steal Julie's briefcase really did a number on my balls!"

"Well, you should probably have it checked out. If you ever plan on having any kids, you'll want to make sure they're not ruptured or anything," he says smirking a bit.

"Very funny," replies AJ sarcastically. "I'm going to walk up to the front desk and tell them I need to have my balls checked out? They'll probably call security on me. They'll think I'm some kind of a nut case or a drunken pervert!"

"Well, we are talking about your balls, you know."

"I'll get over it."

"Okay, they're your balls." Weathers pauses a moment, then says, "You know? We're probably going to be here awhile. Why don't you have a seat, take the load off?"

"I don't understand what's taking them so long. She was already up there when I arrived, and I've been here almost an hour. Damnit!" says AJ, obviously worried and frustrated.

"Look, son. These things take time," says Weathers. "Besides, I heard on the radio there was a wreck on the expressway not far from here."

"Yeah, yeah, I know. There are a lot of other people in here besides Julie. But, right now, she's the only one I'm worried about. Do you understand?" AJ pauses for a moment, then his voice changes tone. "You know? We need to get some things out in the open, and I think now is as good a time as any."

"This sounds pretty serious," replies Weathers. "Should we be talking about this in here?"

"Do you honestly think anyone can hear us in this mad house?"

"If it has anything to do with national security, we need to take it outside."

"I don't know if it does or not, but it has everything to do with you, Julie, and me."

"I was wondering how long it was going to take you two to figure it out. By the way, who was the first? My money's on Julie."

"Well, I hate to burst your bubble, but I was the first. Julie's focus was more on me, I guess."

"Hold on a minute. What are you talking about?" asks Weathers with a perplexed look on his face.

"Come on. Give me a break. You know she defended me on that incident in Bosnia," he replies.

"Yes, and she did an outstanding job of saving your bacon over there. She displayed excellent investigative skills. Not only did she interview the pilot and the surviving Marines on that mission, but she sought out, found, and interviewed practically everyone on the line that day."

"She found out a noncom told his lieutenant he thought whoever was driving the truck was trying to contact them by Morse code. His lieutenant radioed the Officer of the Day, advising him to have everyone hold their fire, because he thought there were friendlies in the truck. However, the OD disregarded the message and ordered a battery to fire on you. When Julie confronted the OD of her discovery, he openly threatened her. Did she ever discuss any of that with you?"

"No, she didn't. What did he say?"

"I don't know. It never got out of her department, but I can assure you, that's why he got demoted, and shipped off to Alaska."

"Well, he should have been the one on trial, instead of me."

"You're probably right. You know, I can't believe that you and Julie didn't hit it off five years ago, especially since you two seem so close now."

"What are you talking about? I did fall in love with Julie five years ago. We spent three weeks together in London while I was recovering from my wounds. I thought everything was going great, but then out of the blue, she ditched me."

"You're not trying to pull an old man's leg are you?"

"Not at all. You've seen both our files."

"Yes, I have, but neither of them say anything about your personal lives."

AJ is stunned. Weathers is right. While the files clearly define their professional careers and their interaction, there is nothing about their personal lives in them. "Sir, I must apologize. Somehow, I had it in my head you were fully aware of our earlier relationship, and was somehow trying to use us against each other."

"AJ, you're paranoid. Plus you have an overactive imagination. You know, you have an uncanny ability to smell trouble, and you have an equally uncanny ability to always come out on top. Julie is very gifted in her ability to get to the bottom of the most difficult cases and resolve them. Her investigative and intuitive skills are top notch. And her ability to control a courtroom demands attention and respect. In short, the two of you complement each other. I couldn't ask for a better team."

"Now who's trying to pull whose leg?"

"Betty was the one who clued me onto the fact the two of you had something going on, outside of work, that is. Up until she brought it up, it never entered my mind you two had that kind of history."

"Well, now that we have that out of the way, where do we go from here?"

"You mentioned that Julie was coming from my house, and a woman had tried to steal her briefcase."

"That's correct, sir."

"Then I suppose Julie must have told you about the envelope left at my house yesterday."

"Sir, I kinda forced it out of her. You see, I accused her of spying on me, and you were the one who put her up to it."

"Now that's about the craziest thing I've ever heard, AJ. Why would I want to spy on you?"

"Because you think I've gone to work for Higgins and the Core."

"Well, I must admit I've given that some thought, but I'm just not inclined to believe you'd do that. But I must also admit Higgins is a very shrewd and persuasive man. He even had me fooled for awhile," says Weathers.

"What do you mean, sir?"

"AJ? I'm about to tell you some things that may make you question my loyalty to this country, and your trust in me," he says with a very serious look on his face. "I've worked for Higgins for the past ten years."

"You? Impossible! Why?"

"You know my military career was in the intelligence sector."

"Yes sir, and from what I've heard, you were one of the best in the business."

"I'd like to think so, but be that as it may, there was a lot of intel we deciphered that was never acted upon, and innocent people died because of it. We had what I believed was solid intel on the locations of different terrorist leaders, terrorist groups, WMD's, but someone would either drop the ball and give our intel a low priority, or lose it in the system entirely."

"I personally watched a live feed of Osama bin Laden, as he was getting out of a truck near the Afghan border, taken by one of our remote controlled drones. We knew exactly where he was. We could have taken him out right then and there! But at the time, there were no standing orders to do so, and no one with the appropriate authority was available to act on it. And that was less than a month after 9/11! I was so mad I could have eaten nails."

"About a week after that episode, I got a call from one of Senator Higgins' aides. I met with Higgins for the first time across the street from the Lincoln Memorial, and we had a long talk. We met twice more before he told me about the Core and how we could handle some of the problems of our country, without worrying about a lot of red tape. All I needed to do was provide the intel he needed, and he would take care of the rest. At first, it sounded like it was too good to be true. But he made good on most of the information I gave him."

"When I told him I was retiring from the service, he said he could get me a high level intelligence position with the CIA. The pay was better, I'd be close to home, and I would have access to more sensitive information. Initially, things seemed to be

177

cruising along smoothly, but then we had a string of what appeared to be unfortunate accidents. We incurred losses where there shouldn't have been any, and certain government officials were getting caught up in the crossfire."

"After working for the CIA for almost two and a half years, I discovered these weren't simple unfortunate coincidences. They were being carefully orchestrated by Higgins and other key members of the Core. They were manipulating people's lives, intimidating or eliminating those who were impeding their control over the government and certain businesses dealing with the government. I couldn't believe I had been so gullible, blind to what Higgins and the Core were doing. I couldn't sleep, couldn't eat. I became irritable, and struck out at everyone, including Betty."

Weathers pauses a moment, then says, "I came home one night and found her crying. I had never seen her that way before. We sat down and had a long talk, and I realized I could no longer live that way. So, I made up my mind that I wanted out. That's also when I discovered, as an operative, there is no out, unless you want to find yourself in a pine box. That's when I told Higgins I had everything we had done together on disc, going all the way back to 2001."

"The good thing is, he believed me. And it's probably been the only thing keeping Betty and me alive all this time. I was able to bluff my way out of the CIA and into the Secret Service with minimal fuss. I wanted no part in feeding anymore information to Higgins or the Core. But even working for the Secret Service, Higgins saw that I could still provide information that would be useful to him."

"When I heard he was making a play for the Presidency, I decided it was time to figure out a way to take him down. That's where you and Julie come in. Julie is my star player. We need to try to take Higgins down politically and legally. But if we can't, that's where you and your expertise come into play."

"Now wait a minute," says AJ. "You're expecting me to take out Higgins? You can't be serious!"

"No, AJ, I'm not. But Senator Higgins is one cold hearted, calculating, power hungry, murdering, son of a bitch. While he's probably never been the one to actually pull the trigger, he's been responsible for hundreds of deaths around the country, possibly the greater part of the free world. We can't afford to have him as the President of the United States."

"So, tell me. Why do you have me protecting him?"

"As I've said from the beginning, Higgins asked for you specifically."

"How did he find out about me?" asks a perplexed AJ.

"I'm not really sure, but he seemed to have a fair amount of information on you, and none of it came through me. But frankly, I saw it working to our advantage."

"So, what's our next move?" asks AJ.

"We're just going to have to let this thing play out and see where it takes us. But we've also got to keep our eyes open."

"Now, what about the envelope that someone left at your house?"

"What about it?" asks Weathers.

"Are you going to let me help you with it?"

"Do I have a choice?"

"Not really, but I'd like to think you'd want my help," replies AJ.

"Do you know where it is?"

"Well, it should be in Julie's briefcase."

"And where exactly is her briefcase?"

"In the trunk of my car, along with my laptop," replies AJ. "I can get it, if you want me to."

"Why don't we wait until we know whether or not they're going to admit Julie?"

"Good point, sir."

"Besides, there's too much potential for someone to eavesdrop on our business."

About that time, AJ sees Julie being pushed down the hallway on a gurney. "Well, look who we have here!" says AJ with a big smile on his face. "It's about time you showed your smiling face down here. We were beginning to think you checked out without saying goodbye."

"Very funny. Can't you see I'm hurting here?" replies Julie grimacing from the jostling of the gurney as the orderly spins it around to back the head of it into the cubicle. The orderly is of

179

moderate height, thin, dark complexion and appears to be of East Indian descent.

"Sorry about that, Miss," the orderly apologizes, almost as though it were an afterthought. "The doctor should be down shortly, after he reviews your X-rays."

"When can I take this collar off? It's chaffing my chin."

"You're just going to have to wait until the doctor decides whether or not to remove it," replies the orderly as he walks away.

"Gee…Thanks for all your help," says Julie sarcastically.

"No problem, Miss," replies the orderly without looking back.

"I have a pet rock with better manners than that," mumbles Julie. Both AJ and Weathers smile and snicker at her comment. "I've had it with this place. I'm getting dressed. AJ? Hand me my clothes. They're on the tray underneath me."

AJ bends over and glances underneath the gurney, then says, "Julie? Are you sure you're on the same one they took you upstairs on?"

"What are you saying? You don't see my clothes under there?" Julie rolls to her right, exposing her bare backside to both AJ and Weathers. Weathers almost loses it and steps outside the cubicle.

"Julie? When did you get a tattoo?" asks AJ, barely able to keep from laughing out loud.

Suddenly, Julie realizes her predicament and quickly lays back on the gurney. "Damnit AJ. Are my clothes under there or not!" she snarls.

"Yes, they're under there, and that's where they're going to stay until the doc shows up. So just relax. It shouldn't be much longer. *I hope*," he says under his breath. "Can I get you anything?"

"Sure thing. How about my clothes?" she asks sarcastically.

"Sorry, no can do," he replies. "You're waiting for the doc to give you the all clear, then we can go home. Now, tell me about the tattoo."

"It's nothing really. Just a little butterfly, that's all. I'm not really sure why I did it," she replies blushing a bit.

"Well, I think it's cute," says AJ with a reassuring tone to his voice. "But I'm a little surprised I haven't noticed it before." AJ starts to ease out of the chair, slowly approaching her side.

"You've just been overwhelmed by my dazzling beauty, my luscious lips, my sparkling eyes, and perky breasts," she replies demurely, while gazing into AJ's eyes.

"Yeah, that's it. Or it might have been your bubbling personality..." He says as he's about to kiss her.

"Uh-huh," she replies with a smile as she starts to lift her head to meet his advance.

"Ahem! Pardon me for interrupting. I'm Dr. Payne. Ms. Robinson, right?" AJ stands up and backs away, allowing the doctor to come up next to Julie. The doctor pulls out a couple of the X-rays taken of Julie's neck and skull, holding them up to the light. "Well, Ms. Robinson, it seems that you were very, very lucky. Other than that nice little bump on your forehead, along with a few other bumps and bruises here and there, I don't see anything broken, and there doesn't appear to be any evidence of internal bleeding. Blood pressure, pulse, heart rate, color, respiration, hand/eye coordination all seem to be normal."

Dr. Payne pauses a moment, then says, "However, when your car slammed into that concrete pillar, practically every joint in your body hyper-extended. Muscles, tendons, and ligaments don't like that very much, and they're going to start telling you that pretty soon. I'm going to give you a shot to tide you over for now, and it's going to make you feel a little woozy. I'm also going to write a prescription for some muscle relaxers and something for pain management to take for the next few days."

"I'm assuming these gentlemen are here to take you home. I don't recommend driving or anything strenuous while you're taking them, at least until you get your sea legs back. Now, if you start getting headaches, seeing spots before your eyes, intense ringing in either or both ears, or anything else out of the ordinary, I want you either back here, or at least contact your doctor, right away. It could be anything from a minor concussion to a blood clot. I'm not trying to scare you, but it's important you don't ignore anything unusual. Okay?"

"Are you sure you don't want to keep her overnight, doc?" asks AJ.

"I would, actually. But we're already full, and I'm sure you've heard about the accident on the expressway. We're expecting several more patients just anytime now," he replies. "But it would be a good idea to spend the next couple of days in bed, and I'd alternate between cold packs and a heating pad on that neck."

"So, can I get this collar off me?" asks Julie.

"Certainly," says Dr. Payne.

"Oh, much better. Thank you," she replies while rubbing the back of her neck.

"Now, I hate to say it, but you should probably refrain from all forms of strenuous activity for at least a day or two," says Doctor Payne while looking at both Julie and AJ.

"You can get dressed now, and when you're ready, we'll have one of the orderlies get you to the door in a wheel chair."

"Nonsense. I can walk," says Julie.

"I'm sorry Ms. Robinson, but that's hospital policy. I hope you understand," says Dr. Payne.

"All right, just give me a couple of minutes, and I'll be ready. *Just so long as it isn't Gandhi,*" she replies under her breath.

"I beg your pardon?" asks Dr. Payne.

"Nothing…Nothing…I'll be ready in a minute."

"Very well. I'll have your prescription ready for you up front."

"Thank you."

"You're welcome," he replies as he walks toward the front desk.

Julie is staring at AJ, and she is gradually starting to look a little angry, when he finally says, "What?"

"Would you mind handing me my clothes, so I can get dressed, and we can get out of here?"

"Yes Ma'am!" AJ reaches underneath the gurney, pulls out a brown paper bag, and hands it to her.

"How about my shoes?"

AJ looks underneath again, "Ah! Here they are," smiling as he hands them to her.

"Thank you. Now, do you mind waiting outside while I get dressed?" AJ starts to say something, but he decides to keep it to himself. He steps out into the hallway, and draws the curtain behind him.

AJ spots an unattended wheelchair down the hallway, retrieves it, and slips it underneath the curtain. "Let me know when you're ready."

"Ready when you are," she replies. AJ opens the curtain and wheels Julie up to the front desk where she picks up her prescription, along with a copy of her bill.

"Wait here, and I'll get the car," says AJ as he rushes out the door to get the car.

Once by the door, Weathers leans over Julie's shoulder and says in a soft tone, "I had an interesting conversation with AJ, and it appears we may have gotten off on the wrong foot."

"How's that, sir?"

"We'll discuss it in the car."

"Okay," she replies, sounding a bit puzzled.

As AJ pulls up to the door, passenger side to the doorway. While Weathers wheels Julie out to the car, AJ rushes around to the passenger side to open the passenger door for them. When Julie stands up, she gets a little light headed before settling into the seat. "Are you okay?" asks AJ.

"I'm fine. I just got a little dizzy there for a moment. I'll be okay," she replies. He helps her with the seatbelt while Weathers settles in behind her.

Once back behind the wheel, he says, "Okay. Where should we go?"

"Well, if Julie is up to it, I think we should go to my place, and find out what's in the file and that disc."

"As long as I can prop my legs up and rest my head against something soft, I'm good to go," she replies.

"To Weathers' house it is, then," says AJ.

"Mr. Weathers, you said something about us getting off on the wrong foot. What did you mean by that?" asks Julie.

"It's a bit of a long story, but I'll try to give you the Readers' Digest version. I guess I should start out by saying that I've been working with Senator Higgins for some time." Weathers tells her about his dealings with Higgins over the years, and his determination in trying to take him and the Core down.

"When I learned you had joined the Secret Service, and wanted to relocate to Washington, I felt I had finally found who I needed to bring down Senator Higgins and the Core. But Julie, I want you to know, I was looking at this from the analytical side, nothing more."

"What are you trying to say?" asks Julie.

"I guess what I'm trying to say is, I never had the slightest idea you and AJ had any type of personal relationship. And you must admit, the first time you two saw each other in my office, things were a bit hostile."

"So, I'm sure you can understand my surprise when, AJ here, accused me of trying to use the two of you against each other. Nothing could be farther from the truth, I assure you. We have a formidable task, and the only way we have the slightest chance of succeeding, is by working together."

"I'm in," says AJ.

"Me, too," says Julie with a bit of reluctance in her tone.

"Good. Let's get to the house and find out what's in that envelope," says Weathers.

"Is there a pharmacy somewhere along the way?" asks Julie. "I think the shock of the accident is beginning to wear off. I'm starting to feel some pain in my back and neck."

"Are you sure you want to do this? Weathers and I can start going over the material, while you get some rest," says AJ.

"Not a chance. I'm in for the duration," replies Julie.

"AJ, turn right at the next intersection. There's a Walgreen's on the next corner," says Weathers.

"Sure thing."

"Julie? Give me your prescription, your Secret Service ID, and your insurance card. My neighbor is one of the pharmacists there. If he's on duty, I'm sure I can get this filled without you having to come inside," says Weathers. As Julie gives Weathers the prescription, and IDs, AJ turns into Walgreen's and parks near the front door. "If I'm lucky, this should only take a couple of minutes. Keep your fingers crossed."

"Good luck, sir," says AJ.

As Weathers enters the pharmacy, Julie asks, "Well, do you believe him?"

"About what? You mean not knowing that we had a thing going on five years ago?"

"Is that what you call it? A thing?" counters Julie with some resentment in her voice.

"Whoa now! Please Julie, let's not go through this again. It was painful enough the first time. We both made a mistake five years ago. You never told me how you felt, and you allowed the military dictate our lives. You walked out, not me." AJ looks away for a moment, then turns back and faces Julie again.

"But then, I didn't try to find out why, and I should have. That makes me just as guilty as you. I'm sorry, okay? So, maybe calling our relationship in London a thing is inappropriate, but it was not meant to diminish what we had. Julie, you made me feel so alive. I've never felt that way with anyone else, before or since. I mean that with all my heart. Julie, I love you."

"I love you, too, and I'm sorry for being so emotional right now. But it's not every day that I get shot at, total my supervisor's car, get pinched and prodded, then ferried back to my cubicle by an Indian who thinks he's the reincarnation of Dale Earnhardt!"

"Well, to answer your original question, yes, I believe he's telling the truth. He told me he's been working with Higgins for some time, beginning shortly after 9/11. He was sticking his neck out telling me that. But then he also told me a story about coming home and finding Betty crying. That's when he decided to move from the CIA to the Secret Service."

"And you buy that story?"

"Yes. Yes, I do. While you were upstairs interviewing Lisa, Mrs. Weathers and I talked for a while. She brought up the very same story. Weathers is a good man, so yes, I believe him."

"Well, I'm really curious to see what's in the envelope," says Julie.

"Me, too." replies AJ. "Look. Here he comes, but he's not smiling."

Weathers gets in the car and says, "Let's go."

"What happened?" asks AJ.

"Well, Ron is working today, but they're backed up, so it'll be an hour or so before they can fill it."

"Oh well, now what?" asks Julie.

"Not to worry. Ron said he'd have them delivered to the house. By the way, you don't want to lose these," he smiles and hands Julie her ID cards.

"Thanks," she replies.

Weathers' home
1320 hours local time

A few minutes later, AJ pulls up in front of the Weathers' home. Weathers opens the door for Julie, then both Weathers and AJ help her out of the car. Julie is really starting to stiffen up, grimacing with every move. "I really think we should have told the doc to get you a room for the night," says AJ.

"Nonsense! I'll be fine. Ow! Hey! Watch it!"

"Uh-huh…Sure you will," replies AJ sarcastically. "Stop," says AJ to Weathers. "Here, help me pick her up. I'll carry her up the steps."

"Are you sure about that?" asks Weathers.

"AJ, that's really not necessary, I'm fine," she says.

"Just relax, okay? I've got you," he replies, as he carries her up the steps to the front door. Weathers races ahead of him to open it.

"Betty? Lisa? Can we get a little help here?" shouts Weathers, as he's trying to clear a path for AJ.

"Robert? You're home early. What's all the fuss about?" asks Betty coming out of the kitchen. "Lisa and I were just finishing up the dishes from lunch. AJ! What happened to Julie? Is she all right? Put her down over there on the sofa."

AJ staggers to the sofa and eases Julie down onto it. "Thanks, Mrs. Weathers."

"Now tell me what happened," says Mrs. Weathers with concern in her voice.

As Julie tells Mrs. Weathers and Lisa about her ordeal, Weathers says, "Why don't you get the briefcase, and I'll start getting things set up in my office."

"I'll be right back," replies AJ, as he heads out the front door. Once down on the sidewalk, he casually glances down the street to see if any cars might be occupied or otherwise unusual, but sees nothing. Then while standing at the rear of the car, he looks up the street and notices a dark blue van with a man sitting on the passenger side, window down, elbow out, smoking a cigarette.

AJ opens the trunk, reaches under his windbreaker, and grasps his Beretta. Suddenly, he hears a door slam, and as he peeks around the trunk lid, he watches another man, dressed in a navy blue jumpsuit, and carrying a clipboard, walk down the steps, and gets in on the driver's side of the van. The passenger takes one last puff on his cigarette, then flicks it out the window as they pull away from the curb. As they pass by AJ, neither of them even look his way.

On the back of the van is a sign that says: *"Doug and Mike's Appliance Repair. We fix what your husband broke"*. AJ breathes a sigh of relief, holsters his weapon, picks up the briefcase, and heads back up the steps to Weathers' house.

As AJ walks through the living room toward the stairway leading upstairs, Julie says, "Where do you think you're going with that?"

"Weathers and I are going to work on the file and CD, of course."

"Not without me, you're not," she replies while trying to get up off the sofa.

"Julie, you need to lie down awhile and let that shot go to work."

"Tell me, how do propose to open my briefcase, if you don't know what the code is?"

"Julie, please. Give me a break here, will ya?"

"What was the agreement? We're all in this together? Well, either help me up those stairs, or let's set up shop down here."

"Why are you being so difficult?" asks AJ.

"The reason I'm in this condition is because of what's in that envelope, and I want to know why."

Weathers comes to the top of the stairs and says, "What's the holdup down there?"

"Julie won't give me the code to unlock her briefcase."

"Julie? What seems to be the problem?" asks Weathers.

"Robert? Julie? AJ? Have any of you had lunch yet?" asks Mrs. Weathers.

"Not right now, Betty," says Weathers.

"I'm fine," says AJ.

"Me, too," says Julie.

"Nonsense. Robert? I know you slipped out without eating anything, and I'll bet you haven't had anything all morning." Weathers sighs and shakes his head. "Julie? Since you were here around 9:30 this morning, and spent the last couple of hours in the emergency room, it's been a long time since breakfast." Julie nods her head. "And AJ? I bet you haven't had anything since early this morning either, so you and Robert march right into the kitchen and grab a bite to eat. There's lunchmeat, cheese, lettuce, and tomato in the fridge, along with the mayo and mustard. There's a pitcher of sweet tea along with another of lemonade I made for the boys. Soft drinks are in the door. There are some chips on the counter. Help yourself but don't make a mess. Julie, I'll bring you something. What do you have a taste for?"

"Mrs. Weathers, that's awfully nice of you, but I'm really not very hungry."

"Honey, that wasn't a question. If you want to go upstairs and help the boys do whatever it is you're trying to keep them from doing without you, you'll humor me and have something to eat."

Julie relents and says, "Yes ma'am. If you have some smoked ham and baby Swiss on wheat, along with a little lettuce, tomato, and mayo, would be nice."

"That's more like it," replies Mrs. Weathers. "Any chips?"

"No thank you," she says. "The sandwich will be more than enough, although I think I'd like to try the lemonade, if you don't mind."

"If you think you can sit up, you can eat right there," replies Mrs. Weathers. "I'll be right back with your sandwich and lemonade."

"Thank you, Mrs. Weathers."

"You're very welcome, child," replies Mrs. Weathers as she makes her way to the kitchen.

Lisa asks, "Is there anything I can do for you? I feel like a fifth wheel."

"Thank you, no I'm fine, really," replies Julie, grimacing as she tries to sit up. "Where are the boys? It's so quiet around here," she whispers.

"They've been playing their little hearts out all morning. They stopped long enough to eat, and then it was all over. Little David almost passed out face first in his plate!" she chuckles. "I had to carry him upstairs, while Mrs. Weathers guided Tim up the stairs and into bed like a zombie. He was out like a light, and David didn't even twitch when I laid him on the bed." Lisa's eyes are dancing, there's a smile on her face, and there is such life in her voice. "They can be such terrors sometimes, but when they're sound asleep, they look like little angels. I don't think I could live without them."

Julie can see Lisa is starting to feel better about herself, and her situation. She seems to be more at ease.

"Thank goodness for small favors," says Lisa. "Julie? Do you have any kids?"

That question really caught Julie off guard. "Me? No. I've never been married, and my life has been so hectic, I wouldn't have had the time."

"You have to make time for a family, or before you know it, your life will have passed you by. I know my life is a mess right now. I've lost my home, my husband, my clothes; I don't even have a job. But I have my health and my two boys. Somehow I know it'll all work out. I don't know how, but it will. I know it in my heart." Lisa pauses a moment, then asks, "Have you talked to AJ about having children?"

"Heavens no!" replies Julie. "We haven't seen each other in almost five years! I had no idea where he was, or if he was even interested in me anymore. Lisa, we're just starting to get to know each other all over again."

"Maybe so, but I've watched the two of you the times you've been here together, and I can tell you're right for each other. You even said so yourself this morning, remember?"

"Yes, I know what I said, but talking about children isn't on the menu right now," she replies. "I'd rather just take it one step at a time, okay? I just got him back, so I'd prefer not to spook him, if you know what I mean. I'll get around to it. Besides, I still have my career to think about."

"Okay, but I think you're selling AJ and yourself short."

"Let's talk about something else, okay?" says Julie.

"Here you go, Julie," says Mrs. Weathers, as she brings Julie her sandwich and drink on a serving tray. "I hope you don't mind that I toasted it for you."

"Oh, thank you, Mrs. Weathers, but you didn't have to do that."

"It's no problem, dear," says Mrs. Weathers. "Are you comfortable enough? I could get you a couple of extra pillows and a comforter if you wish."

"No thank you Mrs. Weathers. You're very kind. But as soon as they finish eating, we're going up to your husband's study and do a little research."

"Wouldn't you be better off staying down here and resting a bit?" asks Mrs. Weathers.

"I'll settle in on the love seat up there, and have the boys at my beck and call," she says jokingly.

"I bet you will," replies Mrs. Weathers. "But if they give you any static, just sing out. Lisa or I will be right on up."

"Thank you."

AJ and Weathers polish off their sandwiches in short order, but decide to give Julie a chance to finish hers before heading upstairs. "Any idea why those guys pulled such a stunt in front of witnesses?" asks AJ.

"Well, I can't say for sure, but I believe they anticipated Julie might wreck the car, and during the mayhem, retrieve the file," replies Weathers.

"If that's the case, then I'm starting to get really confused about all this. If someone in the Core planted the file in the first place, why are they going through so much trouble trying to get it back?"

"I have my suspicions, but I want to save them until we have a chance to look it over," replies Weathers.

"Sir, maybe it's none of my business, but where were you this morning? Julie said the two of you were meeting here to look over the file and disc, but then you blew her off. That's not like you."

"You're right, AJ," he replies. "I got a call from Higgins early this morning and said we needed to have a meeting."

"May I ask about what?"

"Well, it had a lot to do with you, and your little arsenal," replies Weathers.

"Oh, that," says AJ blushing a bit.

"That's a hell of a lot of firepower just to watch over a senator."

"You're saying that after the attempt on his life the other day, I overreacted a bit?"

"Did you bother tallying up what you told him you wanted? You have at least eighteen close support weapons, along with over 12,000 rounds of assorted ammunition, and not one, but two Barretts! Why didn't you ask him for a couple of Stingers while you were at it?"

"Well sir, I actually considered them, but I thought that would be a little over the top, wouldn't you?"

"You're kidding! Right?" asks Weathers in disbelief, but AJ is staring at Weathers with a serious look on his face. "AJ. You weren't really thinking of asking for Stingers, were you?"

AJ's stare slowly begins to turn into a grin, and he says, "No, sir. But I had you going there for a moment, didn't I?"

"You son of a bitch. Yes, I was beginning to believe you might have." Both of them have a good laugh.

"What about additional support? Did Higgins mention anything about getting some manpower?"

"Yes, he said that he's approached Secure-1 Executive Protection Services, Ltd., and they're supposed to be sending files on four men with extensive military training for you and the senator to review."

"That's good. Well, I'm ready to get started. What about you?" asks AJ.

"Julie?" shouts Weathers. "Are you about ready?"

"Whenever you are, sir," she yells back.

As Weathers and AJ start to lift her up on her feet, Julie immediately feels a little light-headed and says, "Whoa! When did the room start spinning?"

"Julie? Are you sure you're up for this?" asks AJ with concern in his voice.

"Oh sure. I guess that shot is finally starting to work. I'm certainly not feeling much in the way of pain right now," she replies with an exaggerated smile on her face.

"Julie? Julie," says Weathers trying to get her attention. "I think you'd be better off down here."

"Nonsense. I'm fine. Watch. Let me go, AJ. I'll show you," she says confidently. She starts to take a step and immediately gets weak in the knees.

"Take it easy there, Julie," says AJ. "Let's get you back on the sofa before you break something, like your neck."

"Okay, okay," she says as AJ helps her back down onto the sofa. "Maybe I do need a little help." Julie seems to be getting the giggles.

"Julie, I think you need to stay down here for now. Besides, when we get ready to leave, we'd have to help you back down the stairs, and you're probably going to be even more stove up than you are now. Plus, I think that shot has really done a number on you."

"But I want to help," she replies, and now it looks like she's about to cry. About that time, someone rings the doorbell.

"I'll bet that's your prescription," says AJ.

Mrs. Weathers answers the door. "Hi Ron. Thank you so much! Bye bye," says Mrs. Weathers waving to Ron as he rushes back to his car. She closes the door, turns and says, "He's such a nice man. Here you go Julie."

"Thanks Mrs. Weathers."

"Julie, please stay down here and rest for awhile," begs AJ. "Mr. Weathers and I will look this stuff over, and I promise if we find anything, we'll be happy to share it with you, okay?"

"Okay," she replies reluctantly. "I guess you're right."

"And if you're feeling better in a little while, we'll see about bringing you upstairs," he says reassuringly.

"You've got to promise me that if you find anything of significance, you'll come down and tell me about it," she says firmly.

"I promise," he replies. "I promise. Now lie down and let your body relax a bit, okay?"

"Okay," she replies as she forces a smile. "By the way, the code is 405."

"Thanks," says AJ as he turns and starts up the stairs. He stops and thinks about the significance of those numbers. *405. That's the month and day we first met at the hospital.* He turns, smiles at Julie, and she smiles back, knowing he's aware of the significance of those numbers, too.

"I'll get you a comforter," says Mrs. Weathers. Then she turns and points her finger at her husband and AJ whispering, "Now boys, I don't want to be hearing any noise from you two while you're up there doing whatever it is you need to do. Do you understand?"

"Yes Ma'am." they whisper in unison, and the two of them scurry up the stairs to Weathers' office.

"Is she always like that?" asks AJ.

"No, this is a new one on me," replies Weathers with a perplexed look on his face.

"You think it's a conspiracy?"

"Don't even go there," snarls Weathers. "Let's get to work on this file."

TLC: Chapter 28

AJ follows Weathers into his study, gently closing the door behind him. The last thing they need to do is wake up the boys sleeping across the hallway. As Weathers settles in behind his desk, AJ unlocks the briefcase, and hands Weathers the envelope. AJ pulls up a chair opposite from Weathers, and the two of them begin to pore over the contents of the envelope.

"Hmmm," says Weathers. "There appears to be more than one file here. Here, take that one and see if you can find anything interesting in there. I'll look over this one."

AJ opens the file, gives it a brief scan and says, "Sir, it appears that most of the names have been replaced with numbers, and from what I can see, they're all odd."

"If they're all odd numbers, it probably means they're members of the Core. I suspect the only real names we're going to find will either be contacts sympathetic to the Core or their targets."

"That sounds reasonable," replies AJ.

"Maybe there will be enough clues in these files that will help identify some of the members of the Core." Weathers pulls out a yellow legal pad and slides it over to AJ. "Write the numbers down as you go. Put a little something down about what they're doing, and maybe we'll find some correlation between the event and those involved. Hopefully, we'll get lucky."

"Good idea," replies AJ, then both of them settle down to read over the files. AJ periodically looks up glancing at Weathers. He seems to be reading very intensely, yet he has not written down a single number. AJ resumes his reading, making notes as he goes.

After almost an hour has gone by, AJ suddenly puts down the file, scans his notes, flips a few pages back in the file, checks his notes again, then exclaims, "Son of a bitch!"

"Keep your voice down! What?" asks a startled Weathers.

"This file has to be about Higgins!" he answers in disbelief.

"They're supposed to be about Higgins."

"Higgins and I had a lengthy conversation the other day, and I recall some of things he said," he replies.

"So?"

"Those incidents are right here in this file."

"Let me see that," says Weathers, as he reaches over the desk and takes the file from AJ. Weathers flips through a couple of pages, then glances at the file he's been reading, then just sits there for a moment staring at the wall.

"Mr. Weathers? Sir? Sir."

Weathers snaps out of it, and says, "You're right, son. This file is about time Higgins became a member of the Core, in May 1970." Weathers overlaps the two files then turns them around facing AJ and says, "For starters, the file I was reading was about my association with Higgins. If you look at the ID numbers, between the two files, they match. So, your assumption is correct."

"And when did you say you were first approached by Higgins?"

"Right after 9/11. Why do you ask?"

"When you and Higgins met, did he ever give you the song and dance about why he wants to take down the Core?"

"No," replies Weathers. "He approached me at the height of my frustration about not having the flexibility to take action against Bin Laden, Al Qaeda, and the Taliban. He capitalized on the fact the Core could bypass a lot of red tape and get things done. All he needed was intel. As our relationship grew, he told me some generalities about the Core. One that specifically comes to mind is you must be recommended and sponsored by an existing member of the Core. But, I don't recall much of anything else."

"Well, did he tell you much about the history of the Core? You know, their behind the scenes participation, like the Civil War, World War II, the Kennedys, that kind of stuff." Weathers seems to be drawing a blank, but then AJ asks, "What about Kent State?"

"Now that you mention it, yes I do remember him talking about the Kent State shooting. He seemed to know a lot about that incident, too," replies Weathers. "Why?"

"The day after the shootout on the expressway, I wanted to know why anyone wanted to kill him. He started telling me about the Core, and its effect on history. He got all choked up when he started talking about Kent State, because his niece was killed in that massacre."

"Well, I guess that would be a pretty good reason to know so much about it."

"Yeah? Well, according to this file, I don't think his niece, if he even had one, was anywhere near Kent State. Higgins orchestrated the whole thing," says AJ.

"What? You're not serious, are you?" asks Weathers in utter disbelief.

"You're right about prospective members being sponsored by existing members, but in Higgins' case, he happened to overhear two men having a rather heated discussion at the governor's ball in Las Vegas. It was shortly after Higgins had been elected to his state senator's post. One man, Andrew Carlson, was the CEO of a company that stood to make millions on a military contract, while the other was Senator Wooten, representing Nevada."

"Their discussion centered on yet another U.S. Senator who was spearheading a group blocking the bill that would approve the funding for that contract. After the two men separated, Higgins introduced himself to Senator Wooten, and the two of them became drinking buddies for the evening. While Senator Wooten was under the influence, Higgins casually inquired about the incident he had overheard earlier in the evening. The senator not only gave Higgins an earful about their argument, he also began telling him about the Core. Afterwards, Higgins did some research on the other senator, and presented a plan he believed would solve his and the Core's problem."

"Kent State," says Weathers.

"Kent State," replies AJ. "If you can't intimidate the man, you go after his family. In this case, the senator's daughter. Higgins offered to orchestrate the entire thing. He would arrange to have someone infiltrate a left wing, anti-war group on campus, and help incense them to demonstrate. He would also arrange the time and place of the demonstration, and even leak the information to the media. He would provide the means to identify the two girls, and the sniper to carry out the mission. Another infiltrator would be one of the first to fire into the crowd, and in the chaos, other guardsmen would also fire. He would provide all of this under one condition."

"He would become a member of the Core," says Weathers disgustingly

197

"Right," AJ replies.

"But if the Core had already been involved in eliminating other impediments prior to this one, what made this one so different?" asks Weathers.

"Think about it. John F. Kennedy was assassinated in '63, Robert Kennedy and Martin Luther King, Jr. in '68, and Ted almost got it in '69. Sooner or later, people start seeing a pattern, and this one was starting to look pretty obvious," says AJ.

"I see your point," replies Weathers. "But still, why didn't the Core threaten the senator about harming his daughter?"

"Because they didn't know she even existed," says AJ smugly.

"What do you mean?" asks Weathers.

"The senator was a widower and had never remarried. Years before he became a prominent figure in the Senate, his wife died during childbirth, although his daughter survived. The senator listed his wife's maiden name on the girl's birth certificate, and she was raised by his in-laws. Nevertheless, the senator was very close to his daughter."

"Higgins stumbled across this little tidbit and presented it to the Core. And yes, the Core wanted to use it to blackmail the senator into supporting the bill. But Higgins suggested it would make more of an impact on the senator if he were to find that nothing could be hidden from the Core. More importantly, no one was beyond its reach, plus they were willing to go to any length to achieve their goals."

"The Core was impressed with Higgins' ability to find such provocative and private information about the senator. They were also intrigued with his plan, and curious to see if he could carry it out."

"He is one heartless son of a bitch," says Weathers disgustingly, shaking his head.

"Wait a minute. There's more," says AJ. "After the Kent State incident, Higgins was brought into the Core, and given another task to perform. It seems other members of the Core took a very dim view of Senator Wooten and Mr. Carlson's outbursts at the governor's ball, along with the senator's divulgence of the Core to a near perfect stranger."

AJ continues, "To prove Kent State wasn't a fluke, Higgins was given the task of devising a way to eliminate both men, yet

198

make it appear to be an accident. He assured them it would not be a problem, and he would take care of them personally."

AJ adds, "Days after the bill passed, Senator Wooten and the Mr. Carlson chartered a plane out of Las Vegas to fly them up to Reno to celebrate. However, less than thirty minutes into the flight, radio communication was lost, and the plane disappeared from radar. The next day, the plane's wreckage was found half buried into the side of a mountain."

"One of the FAA investigators noted the altimeter was reading almost 1,500 feet higher than where the plane had struck the mountain. Had the plane been at the indicated altitude, it would have cleared the mountain with ease. While the investigator suspected someone might have tampered with the altimeter, there was no other evidence to support his theory. Since there was no "black box" on board to either prove or disprove this notion, and no other anomalies were readily apparent, the accident was listed as pilot error, and the case quickly closed."

"Higgins was a pilot for the CIA during the early 60's, so he was more than familiar with aircraft. It was a simple matter to adjust the altimeter to give a false reading, and since the pilot was flying purely by his instruments, it was easy to see how he flew into the side of the mountain. Higgins' position within the Core was now secure. As a bonus, members of the Core helped influence the Nevada governor's decision to appoint Higgins as Senator Wooten's replacement."

"Well, I guess you can't always tell a book by its cover, can you," says Weathers. "I knew he was capable of a lot of things, but I'd have never thought he was capable of murder on this scale or complexity. Have you found anything else of interest?"

"Not yet, I've just scratched the surface," replies AJ. "What about you?"

"No, most of what I've read so far is about Higgins and me, although it has confirmed some of my suspicions as to how he used the information I had passed on to him." Weathers thumbs through a few more pages of the file, then casts it off to the side, and starts looking at the other files in the folder. Suddenly there's a look of concern on his face. He picks back through a few files, then forward again. "Funny. There seems to be a file or two missing,"

"What do you mean, missing?" asks AJ. "How do you know some of the files are missing?"

"I'm going by dates," he replies. "There's a file missing shortly after Higgins became a member of the Core, then another one from about five years ago."

"That's weird," says AJ.

"Are you sure you don't have them over there somewhere?" asks Weathers.

"No sir, I've only got the one file."

"Then whoever sent me this package left them out deliberately."

"Maybe they implicate the person who sent you the package."

"I suppose that's possible," replies Weathers. "Look, it's been a pretty rough day for both you and Julie. Why don't we call it a day, so you can get her home and get some rest? I'm assuming you're going to take her to your place to keep an eye on her."

"Of course." says AJ. "But we haven't made much headway here, sir."

"It's nothing that won't keep for another day or two. Besides, we have the whole weekend to dissect this thing. And with a little luck, Julie will be well enough to help us. And don't forget, you've got to go back to work tomorrow, and you can't dare let on what you've learned here today."

"Don't remind me," says AJ. "I'm going to have a helluva time trying to wipe the look of disgust off my face while I'm around him."

"Well, I can tell you there are going to be a few surprises in store for you tomorrow. Hopefully some of them will help take the edge off a bit," replies Weathers.

"Are you sure you don't want me to stay?" asks AJ. "You know, I could take Julie to my place, and be back within the hour. I'd just want to…"

"Did you give your CO this kind of attitude when he assigned you a mission?" asks Weathers sternly, looking AJ right in the eye.

"No, sir," replies AJ reluctantly.

"I didn't think so," says Weathers. "Now get your ass down those stairs and take Julie home, so both of you can get some rest."

"Yes, sir," replies AJ with an obvious look of disappointment as he turns and starts toward the door.

Weathers walks up behind him, pats him on the shoulder, and says, "Look AJ, we're going to figure this thing out together, okay? It'll be all right. Besides, Julie needs you right now."

"Sir? She's probably down for the count."

"Boys? What's all the fuss about up there?" asks Betty as she stands at the base of the stairs.

"Nothing dear. AJ is on his way down to take Julie home for the evening," replies Weathers.

"Poor child," says Betty. "She fought that medicine for the longest time, but she's finally out like a light."

AJ turns to Weathers and says, "See? I told..."

"AJ?" growls Weathers.

"Okay, okay, I'm going, I'm going," he says while slowly walking down the stairs.

He leans over Julie and softly says, "Julie? Can you hear me?" Julie mumbles something incoherent, then snuggles a little deeper under the comforter. "Mr. Weathers, I think you're going to have to help me get her up, and down to the car."

"Not a problem, but what's going to happen when you get her back to your apartment?"

"I guess I'll cross that bridge when I come to it."

"I'll help you get her to the car," grumbles Weathers, "but you're on your own after that."

"I appreciate all the help I can get," says AJ as he picks her up, comforter and all. Weathers opens the door for him, then rushes down the steps ahead of him, opens the passenger door, then helps AJ load her into the car.

After belting her in place, AJ gently closes the door and says, "I feel guilty leaving you in the lurch like this. Are you sure you don't want me to come back and give you a hand?"

"Don't worry about a thing, other than keeping what you've learned here today to yourself. I must say I don't envy you tomorrow, but be on your best behavior. Besides, like I said, Higgins will have a few surprises for you tomorrow. Just get her home safe, and put her to bed. It's a good thing we're going into the weekend. It'll give her a chance to work on those sore muscles and joints."

"Yep, and she'll be stuck at my apartment, since her car is still at the office, so I won't have to worry about her trying to run around."

"Well, you better get a move on. Traffic is probably already starting to get heavy out there."

"I'm sure. Guess I'll call you tomorrow?"

"Sure thing, and I'll either call or email you if I find anything else."

"Thanks. Bye."

"Goodbye, AJ. Keep an eye peeled on your mirrors. You can't be too careful, you know."

"I hear ya. Later."

***

Meanwhile, at an undisclosed Washington area Army Munitions Depot, Senator Higgins and General Woolbright are watching the men load up the last of AJ's list of weapons and materiel into a Ryder hi-cube van.

"Well, General? Now that we've got AJ's little arsenal put together, do you think you have a safe place to keep it until tomorrow?" asks Higgins.

"Shouldn't be a problem, Bill," replies Woolbright. "What time should I have it delivered?"

"I'd prefer around 0900, 0930 at the latest. Do you think you could spare a couple of men to help AJ unload and set it up?"

"I'll take care of it," replies Woolbright. "Sorry this little shopping spree took so long, but AJ had a pretty unique list to fill. I'm sure Eberhardt and Keyes will be closed before we get there."

"I could tell we were running way behind schedule, so I called them while we were loading up at the DEA's armory. They're going to deliver it to the estate tomorrow around noon. It'll probably take that long for AJ and your men to get his stuff set up the way he wants it anyway."

"I wouldn't be the least bit surprised," replies Woolbright.

"He's going to need someone to build some racks to hold the weapons, tactical vests, and bandoliers, plus shelves and drawers for the magazines, grenades, and gas masks. I've got a couple of guys down at the Pentagon who are pretty good at putting things together like that. Want me to send them over, too?"

"Sure! I'd prefer to have someone we know and trust to do something like this. I'd hate for that kind of information to leak out."

"That won't be a problem with these men. They're already cleared to work in the Pentagon, so they know the drill about keeping things to themselves. I'll call their supervisor, and have him make the necessary arrangements."

"Works for me." replies Higgins. "I guess it's back to the ol' homestead then."

"Lieutenant?" says Woolbright. "Take us back to Higgins' estate."

TLC: Chapter 29
AJ's apartment building
1830 hours local time

The drive back to AJ's apartment was long, but thankfully, uneventful. He didn't see anyone attempting to follow them, so that was a good thing. Julie never woke up and hardly moved on the way back to his apartment.

He pulls into the loading zone in front of his apartment and tries to wake Julie. Her eyes open slowly, squinting against the harsh rays of the late afternoon sun, "Where are we?"

"We're back at my place. Think you can help me get you inside and to the elevator?"

"I think so," she replies. AJ gets out, walks around the car to the passenger side, and opens the door for her. Julie winces and groans a couple of times as she tries to reposition herself to help AJ get her out of the car. He helps her swing her legs onto the ground, then carefully holds her by her arms to help her out of the car. "Wow! That shot and those pills have really done a number on me. I can hardly stand."

"Steady, now," says AJ as he drapes her arm over his shoulder, walking side by side. "Let's get you into the building, okay? Keep your eyes forward. Don't look at the ground. Focus on the doors."

"I haven't felt this dizzy and out of whack since I rode the Crazy Teacup at the county fair!" she says. "I think I was ten at the time." Julie lets out a giggle.

"Come on, we're almost there. Just a little farther. You can do it. You can do it," he says as they approach the doors. Once inside the lobby, it's only a few more steps to the elevator. "Almost there." He presses the button for the fourth floor, the door closes, and the elevator makes a shudder as it starts upward.

"What was that?" shouts Julie, startled from the jolt.

"Nothing, just the elevator. We're almost there," he says softly, holding her close.

Finally, the elevator makes it to his floor, and again the elevator shudders to a stop. Julie goes limp, but he's able to slip one arm behind her legs to lift her up, and staggers toward the door of his apartment. Luckily, he still has his keys in his hands and is able to unlock the door.

Once inside, he gently brushes the door with his foot to close it, and carries her to bedroom. "Julie? Julie," he says softly. She mumbles something incoherent. "I'm going to lay you down on the bed, so I can undress you and get you under the covers, okay?" Julie nods her head.

AJ steadies her with one hand while he turns down the covers. He removes her blouse, but leaves her bra, then lays her down, gently works off her skirt, removes her shoes, and drapes the sheet and comforter over her. She rolls over on her side and snuggles under the covers. He stands over her for a minute, smiling, thinking about how beautiful she is, and how much he loves her, when he suddenly remembers he's parked in the loading zone. *"Shit!"* he says under his breath, and rushes downstairs to move his car.

***

Back in his apartment, he makes himself something to eat, and settles down in front of his computer. He checks his email, most of which is junk mail, then he starts scanning the news of the day. Although he's looking, nothing seems to be registering, that is until he sees a picture of a military vehicle that had been hit by an IED in Afghanistan. *"Damnit! I'm supposed to meet with Higgins' security supervisors tonight! I better call Brian and reschedule."* AJ pulls out his cell phone and starts to call, then says to himself, *"I can't do that. If I don't make that meeting tonight, I'll lose my credibility."* He thinks for a minute, then calls Agent Niles.

"Niles? It's AJ. Are you busy tonight?"

"No, why?" replies Niles.

"I need to ask you a favor."

"Sure. What do you need?"

"I have to go out to Higgins' estate tonight and meet with his security supervisors, but I need someone to stay here and keep an eye on Julie. The meds she's on knocked her out cold, but I just don't feel comfortable leaving her alone like that. Would you mind?"

"No problem."

"Great! I really appreciate it. See you in a bit."

"Any idea how long you might be out?"

"Well, it'll take me about 45 minutes to get there, and assuming that everyone shows up on time, the meeting should take about an hour, then the ride back. So, two and a half, three hours, maybe?"

"That'll work."

"So, you're cool with that?" asks AJ.

"Yeah, fine."

"Okay, see you in about an hour."

"Oh! AJ? What's the address?"

"5028 Forster, Apartment 418."

"Got it. See you in a bit."

"Okay, bye."

"AJ. AJ!" yells Niles.

"What?"

"Do you have cable?"

"Yes, I have cable."

"Any beer in the fridge?"

"No, sorry. No beer," replies AJ starting to sound a little put off by his questions.

"Got anything to snack on? Chips? Cookies? Crackers?"

"I think I have some microwave popcorn."

"That's okay. See you in about an hour."

"Is that it then?" asks AJ.

"Yes. Why?"

"Nothing. Never mind."

"Okay, bye," says Niles.

"Bye," says AJ, as he hits the "end" key. *"Give 'em an inch and they want a mile,"* he says to himself, shaking his head.

***

About an hour later, the buzzer goes off on the intercom. AJ gets up to answer it, "That you Niles?"

"Yes, sir."

"Come on up," says AJ as he presses the remote door release. A minute or two later Niles is knocking on his door. AJ opens

206

the door to find Niles standing there with a bag full of snacks and a six-pack of beer. "Moving in?" AJ asks sarcastically.

"No, sir," replies Niles. "I just thought I'd bring along a few things to drink and snack on while I watch the fights tonight. They're just about to start, too!" Niles makes a beeline to the TV, turns it on and starts flipping channels, and raising the volume at the same time.

"Hey!" says AJ in a harsh whisper. "Julie's asleep in the next room. Keep it down!"

"Sorry, I forgot," he replies while turning down the sound. "Would you mind putting the beer in the fridge?" Niles is already sitting on the edge of the couch, totally enveloped in the TV. "Say, is this high def? The picture looks fantastic!"

"Yeah, it's the new Samsung 55-inch 8000 series."

"Man, it's almost like you're right there! Fantastic! And you've got their new A/V 5.1 sub sat system, too! Wow! Way cool!"

"Niles? Keep it down, or else!" says AJ with a threatening look on his face. "If I come back and find that you've disturbed Julie in any way, there'll be a certain Secret Service Agent who will come up missing. Do make myself clear?"

"Crystal, sir. Crystal," says Niles looking more than a little embarrassed. "Sorry sir, but I really get into electronics and gizmos. Did I mention I'm a communications officer in the Army Reserves?"

"No, I don't think you did. How long were you in?" he asks. Niles is literally glued to the TV. AJ is beginning to get frustrated. "You know what? Never mind. Just keep it down to a mild roar and you'll be all right. Now I've shut the phone off in the bedroom, and here's the house phone. I'm not expecting any calls, but if it rings, go ahead and answer it. There's pen and paper on the end table for you if you need it. If you need anything else, just give me a call, okay? And if I run into any problems, I'll call you."

"Got it," says Niles while totally fixated on the screen. "Hope your meeting goes well."

"Me too," he replies. "I'll be back as quick as I can."

"Okay, later AJ," says Niles, as AJ heads out the door.

TLC: Chapter 30
Higgins' estate
2055 hours local time

The drive to Higgins' estate is relatively quick and painless, with AJ arriving a few minutes ahead of schedule. But as he pulls up to the front of the house, he spots a car that looks a bit familiar. Could this be the same Crown Vic he saw at Lisa's house? It's the same color, and it has government plates on it. AJ writes down the plate number and takes it in with him.

Just when he's about to call Weathers to verify the plate number, he's suddenly inundated by Higgins' supervisors standing in the hallway, raising hell about being dragged in for his meeting. AJ quickly takes control and gives everyone a piece of his mind in the process.

"Hey! Hey! Everybody into the break room, pipe down and take a seat!" The chatter turns to grumbling as everyone files into the break room. Once everyone has found a place to sit, he says, "Let me tell you guys something! All of you are supposed to be trained professionals, right? Your job here is to protect the life and property of Senator Higgins. Shouldn't be a big deal, should it?"

"You have a ten-foot wall surrounding the estate. You have a remote controlled gate to help keep out the riff raff and maintain the senator's privacy. You have cameras in key positions around the estate. And, from what I understand, there are at least five of you on duty 24/7, right?" The men have quieted down and are starting to listen to AJ.

"Then tell me how in the hell someone managed to sneak onto the property, sabotage the senator's limo, and get out again, all without being seen?" Some of the men are obviously a little embarrassed. "Tell me how they knew we were leaving here in my personal vehicle, when we were leaving, and what route we were taking?" There is dead silence. "Come on. Tell me." AJ pauses for a moment to allow them to reflect on what he's thrown at them.

208

"The senator has been paying your company a lot of money for services, that up until today, he hasn't been getting. That's changing right now. Everyone is going to start pulling their weight around here, or you can pack your things and go home."

"The senator and I damn near got killed the other day, because someone wasn't doing his job. I have a totaled, bullet riddled Hummer, and seven dead bodies in the morgue to prove it."

"Brian has copies of your policy and procedure manual for each of you." Brian starts handing out the pocket-sized manuals. "I suggest you read it and commit it to memory." Some of the men begin to mumble amongst themselves. "I expect you to become more observant, and either record or write down anything and everything you think is out of the ordinary."

"If you catch someone on the grounds who isn't supposed to be here, you will contact me immediately, and hold them until I get here to question them. There are no passes. There are no excuses. No one just falls over a ten-foot wall. It was intentional, trust me.

So, if someone's looking for a little excitement, they're going to get it. I'm putting all of you on notice. You'll be receiving a list of objectives and protocols I deem to be necessary, and will be in effect immediately. No exceptions."

AJ turns away and starts talking to Brian when another supervisor walks up behind AJ and says, "And just who died and made you king?" This guy stands about six foot five, obviously one of those weightlifter types, lots of muscle, massive hands, crew cut, overactive superiority complex, but a little short in the brain factory.

AJ slowly turns around to face this giant of a man, then looks up to him and asks, "Do you have a problem with these new guidelines?"

"Yeah, as a matter of fact, I do," he replies in a gruff tone. "Things have been going along pretty good up until now. I don't see why we should change a thing."

"What's your name?"

"My name's Anthony. Most of my friends call me Tony, but my professional name is Samson," he replies.

"What do you mean, professional name?"

"I'm a semi-pro wrestler. Maybe you've seen me on TV," he replies, obviously proud of his notoriety.

"No, can't say that I have, Anthony. I don't get much of a chance to watch TV. But when I do, it's usually the Discovery, Learning, History, or the Military Channels. Tell me, how long have you been a semi-pro wrestler?"

"About a year now, but I've been wrestling off and on since high school. I was in the top ten of the state, for my weight class, my senior year," he boasts.

"Did you spend any time in the military?"

"Me? I've never been in the military," he replies. "Why?"

"Well, it's obvious you don't like taking orders from your superiors. And being a Secret Service Agent, assigned by the President of the United States to protect Senator Higgins, makes me your superior."

"Oh yeah? Well, I don't think that you're superior to me," says Anthony. He starts to turn away from AJ, while simultaneously balling up his fist to take a swing at him. But AJ is anticipating him trying to fake him out. And just as Anthony turns and starts his swing, AJ plants a solid jab to the left side his abdomen. Anthony doubles up from the hit. AJ follows it up with a chop to the throat, then clasps his hands together, and slams Anthony between his shoulder blades, driving him to the floor. Once on the floor, AJ plants his left knee in the middle of Tony's back, just below the shoulder blades. Then he grabs Tony's right hand by the fingers, and bends them backward toward his forearm. Anthony is gagging and gasping for air. Seconds later, Anthony slaps the floor with his left hand, signifying his surrender. AJ releases his hand and backs away.

"Now, does anyone else have a problem with what we're trying to accomplish here?" There is total silence. "Very well. I'll be making my rounds daily, and I expect each of you to give me updates as to your progress. I want personnel files on everyone who works here, and I want them current. Since tomorrow is Friday, I'll give you until Monday noon to have them ready for me. Everyone who works here will have their firearms, baton, taser, and pepper spray certifications in their jacket by Monday, or they don't work here anymore. I will also review the files of any replacements. If their file isn't complete, don't bother bringing them to me. Is that clear?"

There's a half-hearted, "Yes, sir."

"What's that? I don't think I heard you!"

"*Yes, sir!*" bark the supervisors.

"That's more like it. Now, you know what needs to be done. I suggest you get started," snaps AJ.

AJ walks over to Anthony, who's still on his hands and knees, and extends his hand. "Are you okay?"

"I've never been hit like that before. It felt like you hit me with a ton of bricks. And you could have killed me with that karate chop to the throat!" he says while rubbing his throat and neck.

"Well, you could have knocked me into the next room if you had connected with that windmill swing of yours. And as far as my thrust to your neck, I deliberately pulled it so it would shock your wind pipe without crushing it," replies AJ as he helps Anthony to his feet.

"How'd you learn to do that?" he asks.

"Twenty years in the Marine Corps, Special Ops."

"Have you ever killed someone? I mean, hand to hand."

AJ looks down and says, "Yes."

"You don't act like you're proud of it," says Anthony.

"I've never enjoyed taking anyone's life. It's not something you should be proud of," says AJ, as he continues to look away from Anthony. "It's always been the last resort, when there are no other options available. If it's either kill or be killed, then you do what you have to do to survive, and hopefully your training will help see you through it."

"I thought that was what the military was all about. Killing, I mean," says Anthony.

"No, it's actually quite the opposite. Sure, the new guys fresh out of boot camp think they're ready to conquer the world, kick ass and take names. But once they're out on the battlefield, in the thick of it all, it's a whole different ball game. And when the shooting's over, and they're out there taking a body count, or see their buddies blown to smithereens, they're the first ones puking their guts out."

"I guess you're right," says Anthony. "I never thought about it that way."

"The military's primary goal is to help keep the peace. But you've got to be ready to fight at a moment's notice. There's an old saying that pretty much sums it up, and that is, freedom isn't free."

"Well, you won't have any more trouble out of me," says Anthony. "And if any of these other guys give you any static, just let me know, I'll take care of 'em, personally!"

"Thanks, Anthony," he replies smirking a bit.

"You can call me Tony."

"Okay, thanks, Tony." AJ turns, walks over to Brian and asks, "Who's in charge of security tonight?"

"Kenny is. Why?" asks Brian.

"There's a car parked out front that looks familiar, and I want to know if he knows who drove it, and where they are."

"Well, let's see if we can find out," says Brian. The two of them walk over to the center desk where Brian points to the third monitor and asks, "If it's out front, we should be able to see it on this screen. What kind of car is it?"

"It's a medium brown Crown Vic with government plates, and it's about 2 car lengths past the steps."

"Ed, swing the camera to the left of the front door and start zooming in," says Brian. Ed taps a button on the keyboard, then uses an attached joystick to turn and zoom the camera.

"Damnit!" yells AJ as he raps the desk with his fist.

"Where did you say the car was parked?" asks Brian.

"Right there," he says disgustingly, pointing at the place where the car should have been. You can still see the dew outline of where the car had been parked.

Ed asks, "You said it was a medium brown Crown Vic with government plates?"

"Yes," replies AJ.

"Well, whoever it was, they were here to see the senator."

"Are you sure about that?"

"Yes, sir, positive," Ed replies.

"How many were there?"

"Just one, sir."

"Do you know who it was?"

"No sir, but I've seen her here before," says Ed.

"You're sure about it being a woman?" asks AJ.

"Yes, sir."

"Can you access NCIC here?"

"What's that?" asks Ed.

"Never mind," replies AJ. "Tell me this. Can you give me a description?"

"Sure," says Ed.

"Well?"

"White female, about five foot five, five six, blonde hair, straight, about shoulder length, average weight and build, dark suit."

"Any idea how old?"

"Well, I didn't get a good look at her face, but I'd say, probably early to mid thirties, if I had to guess," he replies.

"Anything else you can remember? Was she wearing glasses, carrying a briefcase, anything?"

"No, sir. But if something else comes to mind, I'll write it down and give you a call."

"Good," says AJ, "and thank you."

"Anything I can do to help," he replies.

"Well Brian? I think I'm going to call it a night. Oh! Do you have the supervisors' files ready for me?"

"Yes I do," he replies. "They're in the office. I'll be right back."

"I'll walk with you," says AJ, and the two of them walk next door to the supervisor's office. With all the turmoil preceding the meeting, he hadn't noticed the new lock on the security room door.

AJ looks up to see if a camera has been installed to overlook the two security doors, when Brian says, "Keypads today, camera tomorrow, and the additional DVRs will be online the first of next week."

"Very good, Brian. I'm impressed," says AJ, patting Brian on the back.

"Thanks, but, I'm betting the senator's going to have a fit when he gets the bill!"

"You just worry about taking care of what I've asked you to do, and I'll take care of the senator. After all, we're all here trying to protect him, right?"

"The locksmith will be back tomorrow, so you can have him program your five digit access code into the system. He's also going to install another keypad lock on a hall closet up on the second floor. You wouldn't happen to know what that's all about do you?"

"Yes, I do," replies AJ. "I just hope it's big enough, and secure enough to handle what's going in there."

"Well, I know the locksmith will be installing a steel reinforced door and frame as well as the new lock. I also know all of the walls in this house are solid. Some walls are even supposed to be bulletproof."

"That *is* interesting." replies AJ.

"You're not going to tell me, are you," says Brian sounding a little disappointed.

"What's going in there? Let's just say we're going to have a small armory, and leave it at that for now, shall we?"

"That's not fair, you know," says Brian.

"Well, I'm not really sure what's going to be in there just yet, either. It'll be primarily fully automatic rifles, shotguns, and related ammo. Once I take inventory, I'll let you know. But I'll be the only one with the access code on that one. And if there's no camera anywhere near it, I want one added there, too."

"There's a camera on that floor already. It's about 30 feet away, but it has a zoom lens," Brian replies.

"Perfect."

"Are you going to talk to the senator about his visitor tonight?"

"No, it'll keep until tomorrow. Besides, it's late, I'm tired, and I've got to be back out here by 0800 hours. I'm calling it a night. How about you?"

"Yeah, I think I'll head home, too," replies Brian. "My shift starts at 0700, but then I've got four glorious days off."

"Must be nice," says AJ. "You married?"

"Used to be, but she couldn't deal with my condition," he replies while looking down toward his injured leg.

"Sorry to hear that," replies a saddened AJ.

"It's okay. I've been goin' out with this girl who's kinda' weird, Gothic lookin'. You know, pancake makeup, black clothes, fingernails, eyeliner, lipstick, and shit. She actually gets off on scars and stuff. She goes nuts when my leg starts shakin' and wants to jump my bones right then and there! Hell, the first time my leg started acting up, I thought she was literally gonna rape me!"

"Talk about extremes. Well, like they say, different strokes for different folks," replies AJ. "Well, goodnight Brian. See you tomorrow."

***

Meanwhile, back at AJ's apartment, it's approximately 2230 hours, and Agent Niles is wrapped up in the featured boxing match. The two previous bouts were mediocre at best. But this one has been one surprise after another. It's the eighth round and both boxers have kissed the mat at least once, and the referee almost called the fight due to one of the boxer's injuries. Both boxers are showing signs of sheer exhaustion, yet they continue to get in a good punch or jab now and again.

Niles is leaning forward, cradling a large bowl of chips, clutching a beer in his left hand, and the TV's remote in his right. Thoroughly engrossed in the fight, he's unaware of someone slowly and quietly unlocking the door.

Julie is awakened by an intense need to go to the bathroom. She can hear the faint, muffled sounds of the TV coming from the living room. At first, she tries to sit straight up in the bed, but between the sharp pain in her neck, and the effect of the drugs, she quickly changes her mind. She decides her best course of action is to roll on her side, ease her legs over the edge of the bed, and let gravity help her sit up.

Once she's upright, she pauses for a moment, allowing her head to clear, then slowly and cautiously tries to stand up. Again, her eyes dim from the loss of blood pressure. She waivers momentarily, but regains her balance, then slowly moves toward the bedroom door. As she opens the door, she props herself against the door frame to gain enough strength to make her way to the bathroom. Julie happens to notice a slow, widening beam

215

of light breaking around the entry door. Julie says, "AJ? Is that you?"

Niles thinks the TV has awakened Julie and hits the "mute" button on the remote. But as he starts to get up, he can see the dark figure of someone opening the door, and holding what appears to be a silenced pistol in their hand. Niles charges toward the door and yells out, "Julie! Hit the deck!" The assassin peeks around the door, raises the weapon and fires two rounds toward Niles. The first one misses him, hitting one of the cushions in the couch, sending dust, fabric, and stuffing exploding into the air. But the second round grazes his temple, and Niles crashes to the floor, sliding up against the door. The assassin is caught between the door and the doorframe and is furiously trying to force their way into the apartment. During all this commotion, Julie staggers to AJ's side of the bed and retrieves a pistol from the nightstand. She makes her way back to the doorway, steadies herself against the door frame, and fires two rounds into the door near head height of the intruder. Lucky for the assassin, it's a steel reinforced door, and while the rounds penetrate the apartment side of the door, they only dent the outside of it. The assassin panics and makes a hasty retreat.

Julie, still weak and groggy from her injuries and medication, staggers over to Niles and hits the "emergency" button on the alarm keypad. Then she grabs a clean dishtowel and sits down next to Niles. His breathing appears to be regular, but there is also a fair amount of blood on the floor by his head. She gently lifts his head into her lap and applies pressure to the wound to control the bleeding until the paramedics arrive.

TLC: Chapter 31
AJ's apartment building
2305 hours local time

In the distance, AJ can see all kinds of flashing lights, police and emergency vehicles in front of his apartment building. He steps up his pace and parks near the front of the building. Police and firefighters are everywhere. AJ flashes his ID to a couple of officers blocking the entrance of the building.

As he enters the lobby, the elevator opens, and two paramedics come out with Niles on a gurney, his head wrapped in bandages, and an IV in his arm. AJ calls out to Niles, but he doesn't respond. One of the paramedics asks, "Do you know this guy?"

"Special Agent Niles, Wesley Niles. Secret Service. How bad is he?" he asks.

"It's hard to say," says the paramedic. "Looks like the bullet just grazed the skull near his temple, but he's lost a fair amount of blood. We need to get him to the hospital right away."

"What about Julie?" he asks frantically.

"Oh, the girl? She's a little shook up, but she's okay," replies the paramedic. "The cops are questioning her upstairs."

"Here's my card," says AJ. "Call this number and tell them what hospital you're taking him to, and they'll get someone down there to take care of anything you need. Anything! Got it?"

"Yes, sir. I got it." replies the paramedic. "Hey! Clear the way! Coming through! Coming through!"

AJ enters the elevator and presses four. It seems to take forever for the elevator door to close. The elevator slowly but steadily starts its climb to the fourth floor. *"Come on, Damnit! Move! Move!"* he says under his breath. Finally the elevator comes to a stop on the fourth floor. A police officer attempts to block him from the scene. Again, AJ displays his ID, and the officer backs away. He calls out, "Julie! Julie!" as he works his way through the officers, detectives, and neighbors. Finally he sees her on the couch, wrapped in a blanket, talking to a detective. "Julie! Are you okay? What happened?"

"And who are you?" asks the detective in an arrogant tone.

"Special Agent Thomas Andrew Jackson and this is my apartment," he replies, again displaying his ID.

"Well, this is a crime scene in my jurisdiction. As soon as I'm finished taking her statement, you can talk to her," says the detective rather coldly, as he starts to ask Julie another question.

"Look detective. You're standing in my apartment, talking to my partner, who is also a Secret Service Agent, and the paramedics just hauled off another agent. Julie's already been through a lot today, is currently doped up on medication prescribed by a physician, and appears to be going into shock. I'm asking you to give me a minute so I can talk to Julie to satisfy my concerns as to her condition. Otherwise, I'll make a phone call, and turn this into a bigger cluster than you already have. Now what's it gonna be?"

The detective stares at AJ for a moment, then says, "All right, but I'm probably going to have to have her come down to the station and go through some mug shots for me."

"Detective…" says AJ, waiting for the detective to give his name.

"Morris. Detective Morris," he replies curtly.

"Well, Detective Morris, you evidently didn't hear what I just said about what she's already been through today. The doctor has restricted her to bed rest for the next couple of days."

"And Detective Morris?" says Julie, "I've already told you the only thing I saw was a dark figure pointing a gun from behind the door. He could have been anyone."

"You're sure about that, Ms. Robinson?" asks Detective Morris rather indignantly.

"Until I turned the kitchen light on, the only light in the area was coming from the TV and that table lamp over there, and it was on dim," she replies bluntly.

"And just so you know a little more about me, before I joined the Secret Service, I worked as an attorney for the Navy's Judge Advocate General's Office for five years, then jointly between JAG and NCIS for another five. If you want to find out what intimidation is all about, just keep up your current attitude."

One of the men from forensics is examining the bullet hole in the wall near the window. He shines his flashlight in the hole and can see the bullet. "Detective Morris? I think you ought to take a look at this," he says.

Detective Morris and AJ walk over to check out the bullet hole. Detective Morris says, "Okay, it's a bullet hole, so what? Dig it out, and let ballistics take a look at it."

"No. Look *at* the hole. It starts out small, like it's probably a 9mm or a .38, but it mushrooms out…a lot. I've never seen one expand that much that fast! The bullet looks like it has mushroomed more than twice its original size!"

That comment gets AJ's attention. There's only one bullet that expands to that extent in such a short distance, and that's the ammunition he uses. Hirtenberger. AJ's mind starts racing. *"Holy shit! I'll bet it's from the gun I loaned Higgins! He's trying to set me up! But why? I wonder if they've shot anyone else with it. And who will they use it on next?"* AJ tries to maintain his composure, but Julie can tell he's upset.

"AJ," Julie whimpers, "I'm feeling faint. Can you help me back to bed? I don't think I can make it on my own." AJ starts to put her arm behind his neck and over his shoulder, when Julie suddenly goes weak in the knees. AJ lifts her up in his arms and carries her to the bedroom. Once they round the corner, she whispers, "Try to get them out of here. We need to talk."

"Okay," he says under his breath. "Just give me a couple of minutes." He lays her on the bed, pulls the comforter over her, walks back to the door, turns out the light, then closes the door behind him.

"Detective Morris, we've both gotten off on the wrong foot here. But don't you have enough information to tide you over for the evening? Isn't there a chance we can finish this sometime tomorrow? I'm sure Julie will be feeling better by then."

"Yeah, you're probably right, and yes, I think we've got about as much as we can get tonight anyway," replies Detective Morris as the two of them are walking toward the door. "But I do have one thing puzzling me."

"What's that?" asks AJ.

"It appears the man who shot the other agent had a key to your apartment. Can you explain that to me?" as the detective points to the key still lodged in the doorknob. There is a small swatch of duct tape on the head of the key.

"Yes, I'm afraid I can," replies AJ. "If you'll follow me, I'll show you." AJ leads Detective Morris down the hall to the fire extinguisher cabinet. AJ leans the extinguisher to one side, revealing the faint sticky outline that matches the size of the duct tape on the key. "Somehow, he knew the key was here."

"How did the suspect know it was for your apartment?" asks the detective.

"Trial and error?" replies AJ.

"Why was he trying to kill you?" asks Detective Morris suspiciously.

"How do you know he was specifically planning to kill me?" asks AJ. "Maybe he was breaking into my place because the key fit my door. He had the gun handy just in case someone was in the apartment."

"Do you really expect me to buy that bullshit?" asks the detective.

"First off, you don't have a suspect. Second, you don't have a motive. And third, they didn't shoot me, they shot Niles, so how do you know the suspect was planning to shoot me?" counters AJ.

"All right, have it your way," says Detective Morris. "We'll call it off for the night, but if you find something, anything. I want you to give me a call, okay?"

"Sure thing, detective," replies AJ.

Detective Morris sticks his head in the apartment and says, "Okay, everybody. Pack it up and let's call it a night. Let these people get their rest. We'll see about getting a fresh start tomorrow." His team gathers up their gear, and slowly move toward the door, carefully stepping around or over the blood from Niles' head wound.

"Thanks detective," says AJ, shaking his hand. At the same time, AJ notices the bullet holes in the door are near chest level relative to his and Morris' height. "Is it all right for me to mop this up? You know, the longer it sits, the tackier it's going to get."

"Sure thing," replies Morris. "We already know whose blood it is. Funny thing though. We didn't find any shell casings."

"Excuse me?" says AJ.

"Yeah, shell casings. We're almost certain it's a 9mm, so being an automatic, we should have found shell casings."

"Maybe the gun ejected them out into the hallway, or they rolled under the doors for the elevator and fell down the shaft."

"Yeah, or maybe the tooth fairy picked them up," says Morris with a bit of sarcasm in his voice.

"Now that's a thought," says AJ rather flippantly. "Good night, Detective Morris."

"Good night, Agent Jackson."

AJ watches Morris and his team pile into the elevator, and once the doors close, he closes and bolts the door. He walks back to the bedroom, and gently knocks on the door.

"Come on in, AJ. I'm awake."

"Julie, are you sure you were aiming at his head when you fired?"

"Of course, I'm sure!" she says with some resentment. "And if that door hadn't been so solid, there'd have been a dead body to prove it. Why do you ask?"

"Well, the assassin was either a very short man, or a woman."

"And what makes you so sure of that?"

"Have a look," as he walks over and stands by the door. "See? If you hit where the suspect's head was, he had to be about five foot five." Then out of the corner of his eye, he spots a couple of strands of hair lodged in the doorjamb. They're long and blonde.

"What did you find?" she asks.

"Julie, I think our suspect is a woman. Look. These definitely aren't yours, and they're sure as hell not mine. Plus they're at the same height as your two shots."

"I wonder who it could be?" she asks.

"I'm willing to bet it's the same woman who tried to steal your briefcase."

"Well, that little bitch," she says with a bit of anger in her voice. "Just wait until I get my hands on her."

"Now hold on, Julie."

"Well, AJ? I have a question for you. What spooked you about the bullet they pulled out of the wall?"

"That bullet was probably manufactured by Hirtenberger of Austria. It was originally designed for their anti-terrorist response teams. They're lighter, faster, and more lethal than any other 9mm round currently on the market. They can expand up to 275% of size on impact."

"You seem to know a lot about that round," she says.

"I should, because it's the only ammo I use in my Berettas and MP5's. Do you remember me telling you about the gun I gave Higgins the day we were ambushed on the expressway, and how it came up missing afterward?"

"Yes."

"Well, I'm afraid someone just tried to kill you and Niles with it. If the cops find the gun, do the ballistics, and run the serial numbers, it's going to come back to me." AJ sighs and shakes his head. "And they're going to think I tried to kill the two of you. I'm screwed."

"Not so fast, Deputy Dawg," she says rather coyly, as she walks into the kitchen. Julie opens the lower drawer next to the refrigerator and pulls out a pistol, silencer first. "Does this look familiar?"

"The silencer isn't mine, but that looks like my Beretta," he replies. "How did you get your hands on it?" Julie hands him the gun. AJ ejects the magazine then clears the barrel to see how many rounds have been fired. It's missing four rounds.

"Well, Niles was charging toward the door when she shot him. When he collapsed, his momentum kept him moving enough to slide into the door, wedging the assailant between the door and the jamb. That would also probably explain why she was having such difficulty trying to force the door open, being a woman that is, and why both of my rounds are so low on the door when I returned fire."

Julie pauses a moment, then says, "Evidently, when I shot the door, it must have frightened her enough to drop the weapon and make her escape. When I rushed over to check on Niles' condition, and hit the panic button on the alarm, I noticed the gun just inside the door, next to Niles. I picked it up with a towel and hid it in the cabinet. I doubt we'll find any prints on it, but I knew you would want to have the gun checked out by our ballistic experts, and traced by our department. So rather than turn it over to the cops, I hid it, thank you very much."

"Julie? You're a gem. Yes! Thank you. Thank you very much!"

"By the way, AJ. You haven't shot anyone with this pistol before, have you? I mean, in the line of duty, of course," she asks.

"No, I haven't, so there's no ballistic map of it in anyone's file."

"That's a relief," she replies.

"Oh shit. I've got to call Weathers and tell him about Niles."

"Already done," she says. "While I was waiting for the cavalry to arrive, I called Weathers. I'm sure there are number of people on their way to the hospital, if they're not already there."

"You wouldn't happen to know where the shell casings are, do you?"

"No, I hadn't really thought about that, but they've got to be around here somewhere."

"Well, I'm going to clean up this mess in front of the door, then I'll look for the spent casings."

"If you find them, you should probably go ahead and give them to the police. If you don't, and they don't find any, they're going to suspect you're trying to hide something. Like you said, that's your ammunition of choice, and I'll bet you have more than a few boxes of the stuff lying around here. The last thing you need is having them go through your inventory and finding a match."

"You're right, of course."

"Look AJ. They don't have the gun, so they don't really have much to go on. That alone should give us enough time to find out who this woman is and tie her to the shooting."

"Well, I have a pretty good idea who she's working for," says AJ.

"Yeah? Who?"

"Higgins."

"Really? What makes you think that?"

"When I arrived at Higgins' estate tonight, there was a familiar looking Crown Vic parked in front of the house. But, by the time I had a chance to check it out, the car was gone. However, a security guard monitoring the cameras saw a woman, blonde, about five foot five, wearing a dark gray suit, come in and meet with Higgins. The guard never had an opportunity to see her face, and none of the cameras were being recorded. But

I'm betting it's the same woman who tried to snatch your briefcase."

"Now I'm starting to get confused. First we had someone break into Weathers' home and leave a file on Higgins. Then we had three men trying to kill me in front of the Homeland Security Complex in an attempt to retrieve the file. And now we have someone who just tried to kill Niles and me for the same file. Which ones are working for the Core?"

"Technically? None of them work directly for the Core. Here, think of it this way. All of the key members of the Core have their own operatives. I think the attack earlier today was designed to be a diversion. Their goal was to cause the accident. While our focus was split between saving you and trying to find out more about the men who shot at you, the female operative would steal your briefcase. Had she just taken the briefcase, instead of sitting there trying to open it, the plan might have succeeded. I'm pretty sure both attacks were made by operatives who either work directly for Higgins, or a member who's sympathetic to him."

AJ continues, "We also know someone within the Core provided us with the envelope containing files related to Higgins, along with a CD we haven't had a chance to look over yet."

"And what have you and Weathers discovered in those files?"

"Plenty, but I'll go into that in a minute," he replies. "You have one group within the Core who wants to either see Higgins dead, or at least out of the running for the Presidency. They'll use whatever means at their disposal to get it done. And then, of course, there's Higgins and his supporters, who know we have something on him, and they want it back, or at least destroyed, along with anyone who's seen it."

"Well, that's an interesting theory, I suppose, but I want to know what you and Weathers have discovered so far. Remember? You promised to tell me everything, and I'm going to hold you to it, so spill it."

"Okay, okay... So far we've found out that Higgins..." AJ proceeds to tell her about every detail of their discoveries that afternoon. Julie's eyes are dancing with excitement, like a child listening to a fairy tale for the first time, clinging to every word.

TLC: Chapter 32
AJ's apartment
Friday morning
June 17, 2011, 0600 hours local time

AJ wakes up and turns off the alarm clock before it awakens Julie. She's curled up in a semi-fetal position facing away from him, with her back barely brushing against his. He slowly slips from under the covers, and quietly closes the bedroom door behind him, stealing a final glimpse of Julie through the crack between the door and the frame.

He quietly makes his way down to the bathroom, taps the kidneys, then splashes a little water on his face. Staring into the mirror, he says to himself, "*I've got to get back into my morning routine now, or I never will.*" He gives himself a dirty look, then walks stealthily to the kitchen, and starts the coffee maker. By the time he polishes off a glass of juice and a bowl of cereal, his coffee is ready.

With mug in hand, he heads down the hall to the second bedroom, and begins his morning workout. Afterwards, he hops in the shower.

No sooner does he get his hair all lathered up with shampoo, he feels a gentle pair of hands caressing his body. Then Julie presses her body against his from behind, gently hugging him, and says in a very seductive tone, "Good morning."

AJ tilts his head under the showerhead to rinse off the shampoo, then slowly turns around, gazes into Julie's eyes, smiles, and says, "Good morning. I really didn't expect to see you up so early. I hope I didn't wake you."

"No, you didn't wake me, but I wish you had," she replies in a sultry voice.

"Julie, I have no idea what you have in mind, but I've really got to get ready for work," he says. "Both Higgins and Weathers will have my ass if I'm late. Plus, I've got to have my game face on around Higgins today, especially since I have a better idea of what kind of man he is. And I have a feeling what we discovered last night is just the tip of the iceberg of what he's done over the past forty years of being in the Core.

"Boy! Do you know how to spoil a mood."

225

"Look, I hate it as much as you, but you need to take it easy for next day or two anyway. Remember what the doctor said? Bed rest?"

"AJ? I'm feeling a lot better today. A little stiff and a bit sore in places, but overall, I'm fine."

"Tell you what. Just take it easy for the day, and if you're still feeling that way when I get back, we'll see what we can work out," he says with a smile.

"Work out. Hmmm. Now that could be interesting," she replies with a devilish grin.

"Julie? Stop it. Please. I've got to get ready for work."

"Okay, okay. But it's your loss, you know." The two of them take turns scrubbing each other down, then rinsing each other off.

As they're helping each other dry off, AJ says, "Now if that detective calls, tell him that we haven't found anything, and you don't have anything else to add to his investigation. Maybe he'll leave us alone for a while. And depending on what Higgins has planned for the day, I'll try to stop by and see how Niles is doing, too."

"That would be nice. I'm sure he'd appreciate that."

"Now, if you don't mind, I still have a few things to do before I start getting dressed."

"No problem. I'll see you in the kitchen."

After shaving and brushing his teeth, he goes back to the bedroom, and gets dressed. Walking into the kitchen he says, "You know? I just realized you're pretty much stuck here for the day. No wheels."

"Oh, I'm sure I'll manage. By the way, what was the name of that pizza place? I still have a craving for a good pizza."

"Well, I hope the guy who showed up the other day isn't their only delivery guy, otherwise we'll probably have to go there to pick it up."

"I'll order it this time, talk to the manager, and see if I can get everything straightened out. Now what was the name of the place?"

"What else? Chicago Style Pizza! Now, I really have to go."

"Okay. Go ahead. Don't let me hold you up," says Julie sounding frustrated and upset.

"Please don't be mad at me," he begs.

"I'm not, really. It's just not fair, that's all."

"I know, I hate it is as much as you do. Should I have maintenance come up and repair the wall, and see about replacing the door? Or should I wait and have it done next week?"

"Well, I suppose you should probably call them and make them aware of the repairs that need to be done. But I'd also tell them you want them to take care of it sometime next week. I think I'll take your advice and get some rest today."

"That's my girl. Call me if you need anything, okay?"

"I will."

"Now, how do I look?"

"Good enough to eat!" she replies with a teasing smile on her face. "I know, I know, it's off to work you go."

"Later, dear," he says as he leans forward and tries to give her a peck on the cheek.

"Hey! You're not getting off that easy," she says as she wraps both arms around his neck, pulling him down to her and gives him a long passionate kiss.

"Well, that part still works. I'll see you this afternoon."

Julie walks him to the door and stands in the doorway until the elevator arrives. As he enters the elevator, he turns to her and waves goodbye. Once the elevator doors close, her smile turns to sadness, as she closes the door.

Julie starts to pour herself a cup of coffee when she is startled by the doorbell. She remains silent for several seconds and the doorbell rings again. Finally, she says, "Who's there?"

"Maintenance, miss," replies the voice from the other side of the door.

"I didn't know my boyfriend had called you already," she says as she tries to tiptoe toward the bedroom to get AJ's pistol from the nightstand, puts on a robe, and grabs her cell phone.

"Well, miss. As far as I know, he didn't, but the police called the office and told them about the incident last night," says the voice. "And, miss? There's nothing on the lease that mentions Mr. Jackson has a roommate."

"Just hang on a minute, I'll be right with you," she says while calling AJ.

AJ has just gotten out of the elevator when his phone rings. "Julie, wha…"

227

"There's a guy standing at the door claiming to be from maintenance!" she whispers.

"I'll be right there!" he replies while sprinting up the stairs. He stops halfway between the third and fourth floors, pulls out his Beretta, then quietly proceeds to the fourth floor. Once reaching the floor, he can see the man standing in front of the door, dressed in a gray jumpsuit with the word "MAINTENANCE" across the back at shoulder level. He's in his fifties, a bit overweight, balding, but otherwise unassuming. AJ decides to holster his weapon, and casually walks up behind him and says, "Good morning."

"Holy shit! Wuh-Wuh-Where did you come from?" says the man, obviously startled by his presence.

"I just took the trash downstairs. I'm AJ, Thomas Andrew Jackson. This is my apartment," he says while reaching out to shake the man's hand. "Can I help you with something?" Hearing AJ's voice, Julie opens the door, while hiding the pistol behind her.

"I'm ah, Harry, Harry Petrovsky. I'm the maintenance supervisor of the building. You see, ah, I got this notice from the office that there had been ah-ah-an incident up here, and they wanted me to fill out a report on the ah-ah-damages," he says acting and sounding a bit nervous.

"Well, for starters, I think we're going to need a new entry door," as AJ points to the two dents in the door.

"I don't think I've ever seen anything like that before," he says while running his fingers over the dents. "This is a tr-triple wuh-walled, foam ca-core, st-steel reinforced da-door. It would take something like a ba-bullet to do that kind of da-damage."

"Well Harry," says AJ, "That's exactly what you're looking at."

"Now, who-who-who would do a th-th-thing like th-th-that?" he asks.

"I'm afraid I did," says Julie sheepishly. "But only after someone tried to break in and shot Niles first."

"Sa-Sa-Someone got sh-sh-shot?" he stutters.

"Yes, Agent Niles was wounded, and I'm afraid one of the cushions from my couch, along with the outside wall were damaged as well."

Harry's face goes pale and says, "I tha-tha-think I need to sit down sa-sa-somewhere. Do you ma-ma-mind if I ca-ca-come in? I'm not fa-fa-feelin' too goo-goo-good."

Julie steps behind the door, still hiding AJ's pistol out of Harry's sight and says, "Please come in and sit down. There's a stool by the bar, or you can sit on the couch. Would you like something to drink? Water? Coffee?"

"Wa-Wa-Water would be fa-fa-fine. Tha-Tha-Thank you," he replies. Julie goes into the kitchen to fix Harry a glass of water, and hides the pistol in a drawer near the refrigerator.

"Here you go Mr. Petrovsky," she says, handing him the glass of water.

"Th-Th-Thank you, mi-mi-miss," he says.

"My name is Julie, Julie Robinson."

"Mr. Petrovsky? Are you okay? Should I call the paramedics?" asks AJ.

"Na-Na-No. I'll be alright in a mi-mi-minute or ta-ta-two," he replies, trying to catch his breath. "I-I-I hate vi-vi-violence. Wuh-Wuh-When I lived in Ra-Ra-Russia, muh-muh-my family li-li-lived in fa-fa-fear eh-eh-everyday. Pe-Pe-People were be-be-being sh-sh-shot or taken away all the ti-ti-time. Muh-Muh-Many of them wa-wa-were not re-re-really cre-cre-criminals. Th-Th-They were ja-ja-just sta-sta-starving. Th-Th-They wuh-wuh-were hun-hun-hungry. Ba-Ba-But there wuh-wuh-was no foo-foo-food." Harry reaches into his jumpsuit and pulls out an inhaler. His hand is trembling as he raises it to his mouth, and takes two deep breaths.

"Harry, let me call the paramedics," says Julie sympathetically.

"No. No. I'm feh-feh-feeling better now. Ja-Ja-Just give me a fa-fa-few min-min-minutes. I-I-I'll be-be-be okay," he replies, shaking his head.

"Well, if you're okay, I've got to go to work. I'm late already. If you have any questions, Julie should be able to answer them for you. If not, I'm just a phone call away."

"Th-Th-Thanks Mr. AJ. I-I-I'll just ch-ch-check out a few th-th-things here, and I-I-I'll be on my wuh-wuh-way," he says.

As AJ starts walking toward the door, he motions Julie to follow him. Standing at the door, he says, "He seems harmless enough, doesn't he?" Julie nods her head in agreement. "Give me a call when he gets through with whatever it is he wants to check out. Then try to get some rest, okay?"

"Okay, and thanks for coming to my rescue. I feel so foolish."

"Well, you can never be too careful, you know," he says. "But I've really got to get going."

"Go on, I'll be fine."

"Walk with me to the elevator?" asks AJ.

"Sure, why not?" Julie replies. "Mr. Petrovsky? I'll be right back."

"Ta-Ta-Take your time," he replies.

The two of them stand next to the elevator gazing into each other's eyes, waiting for the elevator to come up. Finally the elevator arrives, and AJ leans over to kiss her one more time. Just before their lips touch, Julie says, "I love you, AJ."

"I love you, too," he replies, just before he kisses her. Julie feels as though she could walk on air. AJ enters the elevator, presses the button for the first floor, all the while, staring at Julie until the doors close.

Julie goes back into the apartment, closing the door behind her. "Feeling any better Mr. Petrovsky?" she asks, but he doesn't answer, and he's nowhere to be seen. "Mr. Petrovsky?" She looks behind the counter to see if maybe he had passed out and fallen while attempting to get up, but he's not there either. "Mr. Petrovsky?" She calls out again, as she walks slowly down the hall, peeking into the first bedroom, then the next. Still, no sign of him. Then she notices the bathroom door is almost closed, the light is on, and she can hear the sound of running water.

*** *

AJ is still smiling from his thoughts of Julie when suddenly, the elevator shudders to a stop on the third floor. As the doors open, a little old man pushes a cart with miscellaneous tools on it into the elevator. "Going down?" he asks.

"Yes, sir," replies AJ.

"Oh, what the hell. Down, up, down, up," he sighs. "Seems like I spend half my day on this damn thing." The doors close, the elevator shudders again, and they continue their descent to the first floor.

"Looks like you and Harry are off to a busy start this morning."

"Yeah, Mrs. Morgenstern, in 320, roused me out of bed this morning. Stopped up her toilet again," he says shaking his head. "I wish I knew what in the hell she keeps puttin' in that damn thing." AJ is grinning and shaking his head. "And she told me about some kind of commotion on the fourth floor late last night. Said it sounded like a shootout or somethin'. Probably just someone had their TV turned up too loud. I suppose I better go up there and check it out after I find out what's wrong with Mrs. Lieberman's garbage disposal." The old man pauses for a moment, then looks up at AJ and asks, "Who's Harry?"

"Your partner? Harry? He's already up there checking out my apartment, right now."

"Partner?" he exclaims. "Mister? I've been the only maintenance man in this building for the last twenty years!"

"Stop the elevator!" yells AJ.

"What's wrong?"

"Just stop it! Stop it!" The old man tries to stop the elevator, but it's already passing the second floor. "Don't you have an override key?" AJ asks frantically.

"No, I lost that thing years ago. But as soon as we hit bottom, we'll be going up again."

"I can't wait that long!" The elevator finally gets to the first floor, and as the doors start to open, AJ yells, "Call 911 and tell them we have an intruder in apartment 418! See if there's a Detective Morris on duty!" He bolts out of the elevator and heads for the stairs again.

"Who?" asks the old man as he sticks his head out of the elevator.

"Never mind! Just get 'em down here!"

"He must think I have a cell phone or somethin'," he says under his breath, as he presses the emergency stop button and starts pulling his cart out of the elevator. He stops, cups his hand, holds it next to his ear and says, *"Hello? Anybody there?"* Then he looks at his hand, shakes his head, and says to himself, *"Young people these days. Always assumin'."*

***

Julie is standing in front of the bathroom door, trying to peek inside without opening it any farther, but sees nothing. Again she calls out, "Mr. Petrovsky? Are you all right?"

But there is no response. Fearing he might need some immediate medical attention, she starts to push on the door when suddenly the door flies open, and Harry zaps her with a stun gun to the abdomen. She drops to the floor like a stone, unconscious.

"Oops? See what happens when you forget to knock?" he says to himself while standing over her. He pockets the stun gun and pulls out a pair of latex gloves from his waist pocket. Once he has them on, he kneels down next to her, and secures her hands and feet with zip ties. He then leans over her, and picks her up with one arm behind her knees, the other under her arms. *"I'm getting too old for this shit,"* he says to himself as he struggles to lift her, then turns around and lays her in the bathtub, as it slowly fills with water.

A splash of water to her face startles her to consciousness. Realizing her predicament, she starts to panic, but Harry obviously has control of the situation. She starts to scream, but Harry places his hand over her mouth, then pushes her under the water. After holding her there for several seconds, he pulls her up and says, "Look lady, we can do this the easy way, or the hard way. I don't have a problem with either."

"What do you want?' she asks, gasping for breath and struggling against her restraints.

"You know? I like that in a woman. Straight to the point," he says with an evil smile. "But you know what else? I hate it when a woman starts acting coy with me," and he pushes her under again, this time holding her down longer than before. When he finally brings her to the surface, she's gasping and coughing up water. "Somehow I get the feeling you ain't no fish. So I think you might want to tell me what I want to know, before I decide to confirm my suspicions."

"Well, if I had to guess, I'd say you're looking for a certain file," she says, breathing deep and fast.

"Ohhh, you're good! You're really good! But I still don't think you fully understand the gravity of the situation," he says as he starts to push under for a third time.

Suddenly, he feels the cold steel barrel of AJ's Beretta butted up against his temple.

"Actually, I don't think *you* understand the gravity of the situation," says AJ in a slow but deliberate tone. "Now, lift her out of the water, and set her down over there."

"I don't know if I can lift her out of the water," he says, grunting as he tries to get his arms under her. "I think I twisted my back getting her in here."

AJ cocks the hammer and says, "No problem. I'll just cap you and get her out myself."

"Wait a minute! Wait a minute! I think I got her!" he says, straining and grunting as he lifts her dripping body from the tub.

AJ slowly backs into the doorway, gun firmly aimed at Harry's forehead, allowing him just enough room to maneuver. "Now sit her down on the toilet, gently, then step backwards into the tub, hands behind your head, fingers interlaced."

"But AJ, I might fall."

"Do it now, or the last thing you're going to see is the muzzle flash from my gun." AJ says in a more agitated tone.

"You wouldn't shoot an unarmed man, now would you?" he asks coyly.

"If you're one of the Core's operatives, your entire body's a weapon, just like mine." Harry remains motionless. "Harry? I don't make a habit of repeating myself."

"Okay, I'm goin', I'm goin'," he says, while placing his hands behind his head, and stepping into the half filled tub.

AJ turns his attention to Julie, who is shivering from being cold and wet, sobbing softly. He pulls out his pocketknife, and with a single stroke, cuts each tie. "I'm so sorry for leaving you here alone with him," he says softly and affectionately as he wraps her in a large bath towel. "I guess I should have expected something like this."

"How could you have known?" she asks, as she looks up to him with tears in her eyes. "He had me fooled, too."

Both hear the water slosh in the tub as Harry shuffles his feet. "Don't move!" barks AJ, pointing his pistol at Harry.

"I hate it when my feet get wet. Reminds me of when I was workin' down at the docks. What a miserable fuckin' job that was."

"Harry? Put a cork in it and save it for the cops."

Harry starts to smile, then asks, "You called the cops?"

AJ turns away from Harry, focusing on Julie and says, "No, the real maintenance man called the cops. I ran into him on the lower level when he got on the elevator."

Harry's smile suddenly turns to fear. With AJ's attention focused on Julie, Harry leaps out of the tub, slams AJ into Julie, and makes a dash down the hall.

AJ struggles to his feet and yells, "Harry! Stop! Or I'll shoot!"

But Harry continues to scramble toward the living room, and dives for his toolbox. He opens it and pulls out a suppressed MAC-10, rolls onto his back, and fires a sweeping burst toward the bathroom, unleashing its entire magazine.

AJ wraps himself around Julie to protect her. Luckily for AJ and Julie, the MAC-10 is terribly inaccurate, and except for a few bullet holes here and there, along with all the tile shards and drywall dust, neither of them are hit. When the shooting stops, AJ peeks around the corner to see Harry struggling to unjamb the weapon. AJ says to Julie, "Stay here," and marches down the hall, wading through the cloud of dust hanging in the air toward Harry. "Drop it Harry! You haven't killed anybody yet, but you're really starting to piss me off!" Yet Harry continues to fight with the weapon. AJ is now standing at Harry's feet, pistol aimed at his head, and says, "Harry, I've already told you I'm not in the habit of repeating myself. Put down the weapon or you're a dead man."

Harry stops, looks up at AJ and says, "It was a piece of shit anyway," and tosses it aside. "I guess today, just ain't my day," he says with a sigh of frustration.

"Okay, roll over on your stomach, put your hands behind your back, and cross them."

"You've got to be fuckin' kiddin'!" he says emphatically. "I can't. I'm too big."

"Well, do the best you can," he says while planting his knee in the middle of Harry's back. AJ reaches into Harry's toolbox and pulls out a few zip ties. He ends up wrapping each wrist with a zip tie, and adding a third one to tie them together, then cinches them down.

"Hey! Not so tight! You'll cut off my circulation!"

"Once the cops get here, they'll probably put you in real cuffs anyway, so just relax, okay?"

"Have I gotta stay down like this?" AJ ignores him. "You know? Your carpet smells like it's got mold in it. I'm allergic to mold."

"Harry? I'm willing to bet you're a lot more allergic to lead."

"Come on AJ," he begs. "Let me sit up, okay? Like you said, I ain't killed nobody yet."

"Oh, all right. You can roll over and sit up, but I want you to answer a few questions for me."

"I don't know, AJ."

"Harry, I haven't Mirandized you yet, so anything you say is inadmissible as evidence anyway."

"Well, since you put it that way."

"Why are you here?"

"Like I said, I'm here to get an estimate."

"Harry? I don't have time for bullshit. Now, why are you here?"

"Okay. I was sent to get a fuckin' file."

"Who sent you?"

"You know I can't tell you that."

"Well, you either have to be working for Higgins, or one of his supporters."

"Maybe, maybe not."

"You know? Someone tried to break in here last night and shot a Secret Service Agent in the process. And now, here you are. You just tried to drown Julie, and shot up my apartment. I think there's a good chance they'll pin both attempts on you. Do you think the Core will come to your rescue, especially since I caught you red-handed like this?" AJ pauses a moment to let that comment sink in. "I wouldn't count on it. You'll be going away for a long time."

"One never can tell."

"Harry? Is that even you're real name?"

"It'll do for now."

"You seem to be pretty calm about all this."

"Let's just say I know a little more about what's goin' on than you do," Harry says with a wicked smile.

About that time, two men show up at the door with guns drawn. "Police! Nobody move!" One of the men points to AJ and says, "Show me your hands! Identify yourself!"

"Jackson, Thomas A., Secret Service. ID number Sierra, Sierra 55191. This man entered my apartment under false pretenses, attempted to drown my girlfriend and shot up my apartment," he says pointing at Harry.

"Put down your weapon and show me your ID." AJ starts to reach into his coat for his ID. "Carefully! No sudden moves." says the detective.

AJ slowly withdraws his ID and shows it to the detective. "You guys got here pretty quick. But I don't recall hearing any sirens."

"Dispatch told us to run Code Two, lights, no siren. They said this was the second break-in attempt at your apartment."

"Yeah, Detective Morris took the call last night," says AJ.

Both men lower their weapons and enter AJ's apartment. "So, you think he's the same guy who tried to break in last night?"

"Could be," replies AJ.

"Well, I'm assuming you'll be pressing charges, then," says the detective.

AJ looks around at his apartment, then says, "What do *you* think?"

"Okay, we'll take it from here," says one of the detectives as both men help lift Harry to his feet. One of the detectives picks up Harry's toolbox, then starts towards the door, following Harry and the other detective.

"Aren't you going to read him his rights?"

"You're Secret Service. Haven't you done that already?"

"No, I didn't arrest him. I merely detained him."

"Well, that'll keep until we get him to the station."

"How can I get in touch with you? What's your name?" asks AJ.

"I'm Detective Wilson and he's Johnson."

"Don't you want to take our statements?" asks AJ.

"No, we'll just use what Detective Morris and his team got last night. I'm sure that will be sufficient. It's a pretty open and shut case. But we'll call if we need you for anything," says Detective Wilson while standing in front of the elevator.

"Well, I'm sure the Secret Service will want to talk to him."

The elevator arrives, and out comes the real maintenance man, dragging his cart behind him. Once the old man and his cart are clear, the two detectives and Harry get on the elevator.

"No problem, just make an appointment," replies Detective Wilson as he presses the button for the first floor.

"Will do," says AJ as the elevator doors close.

"What in the hell happened up here?" says the old man.

"I'm afraid it's going to need a new door, along with some tile and plaster work, and a fresh coat of paint," says AJ apologetically. "And thanks for calling the cops for me."

"I didn't call the cops. I don't have a cell phone, and by the time I got Mrs. Lieberman to answer the damn door, I had completely forgotten about it."

"Well, I wonder who called the cops?" asks a perplexed AJ.

"What cops?" asks the old man.

"The two men who just took Harry away."

"Those two guys? They're not cops. The three of them drove up here in the same car about thirty minutes ago, parked back there in the alley. I saw 'em when I got back from the hardware store."

"Why didn't you tell me?" asks AJ.

"Ya didn't ask."

"What were they driving?"

"Some big, brown, four door sedan. Maybe a Ford, Mercury, or a Lincoln. At my age, they all start to look alike."

"Watch Julie for me, will ya?" says AJ as he breaks and runs down the stairs to the first floor, then out the back exit, hoping to catch a glimpse of the car. Nothing. He runs to the front of the building, looking up and down the street. Still nothing. "Shit!" he yells out loud, while trying to catch his breath.

About that time his phone rings. He looks at the display and sees that it's Higgins. *Oh shit. I've stepped in it now."* he says to himself.

He opens the phone to answer the call when Higgins says, "Is this how you show your gratitude for giving you a day off? It's a quarter after eight! Where the hell are you?"

"My apologies, sir. But I've had a series of situations catch me off guard this morning."

"Nothing serious, I hope," says Higgins sarcastically.

"No sir. I think I've got it under control," he says while trying to catch his breath.

"Then I expect to see you within the hour." With that, the line goes dead.

"Yes…sir," he says to the dead line. AJ mouths a few colorful words and starts walking back to the building.

Back at his apartment, he finds the old man pouring himself a cup of coffee, and Julie is nowhere in sight.

"I'm sorry, but I don't think I caught your name," says AJ.

"That's because ya never asked fer it," says the old man.

"Well?"

"It damn sure ain't Harry!" the old man says with a smile and a little laugh.

"I really don't have time for games, so if you don't mind."

"My name's Patrick. Patrick O'Malley."

"Do you mind if I call you Patrick?"

"I like that better than 'hey you'!" he says with a laugh. "Yes, Patrick or Paddy is fine. You must be Mr. Jackson, our resident Secret Service Agent."

"Please Patrick, call me AJ. Most everybody does."

"Okay, AJ it is."

"Where's Julie?"

"I think she's in the bedroom, packing." He leans over close to AJ, cups his hand by his mouth, and half whispers, "I think all this excitement has probably been a little too much for her. She seems a bit high strung."

"Actually, she's been through a lot in the last 24 hours. Yesterday, three men shot at her and caused her to have an accident, totaled her boss' car. From there, she got pinched, poked and prodded at the hospital, before they finally turned her loose. Then around 2230 hours last night, someone tried to break into the apartment, and shot another agent in the process. And just now, a man posing as *you,* zapped her with a stun gun, then tried to drown her in the bathtub. And finally, the guy shoots up my apartment!"

"Sounds like she's the kind of woman ya don't want to be standing next to in the middle of a thunder storm," says Patrick.

"Huh?"

"I think the poor girl's snake bit! You know…bad luck? And by the sounds of it, she's spreadin' it around!"

"Sorry?"

"While she's the focus of the calamity, somebody else, or their property, is taking a beatin', too!" AJ's standing there with a dumbfounded look on his face. "It's as plain as that look on your face! She totals her boss' car, another agent gets shot, and look at this place! I'm tellin' ya! The lassie is bad news! Wake up and smell your coffee!" He stops his ranting momentarily, sniffs it, then takes a sip. He savors it for a moment, spits it out in the sink, then says in a calm tone, "This is shit, by the way. I don't suppose you have any Connemara, Twelve Year Old, Peated, Single Malt hiding in your cupboard. It might help take the edge off."

"What's that?"

"Oh, laddie," he says closing his eyes and smiling. "Truly, nectar of the gods! Fine, fine Irish whiskey, made the way Mother Nature intended."

"I think I might have some Jack Daniels in the upper cabinet, next to the fridge."

"I'd just as soon drink camel piss," he snarls, as he turns and dumps the rest of the coffee down the sink. "Never mind."

"How long is it going to take to fix it?"

"Oh, AJ. I don't know. Changing out the door, swapping over the hardware, shouldn't take more than an hour, maybe two. The bullet hole, now that's a different can of worms. Ya gotta clean it, mud it, let it dry, then sand it. Then, ya have to mud it again, let it dry, sand it, and prime it. If it looks good, then ya can paint it. That'll take a couple of days."

As Patrick stares down the hall toward the bathroom, he says, "But the bathroom and the hallway? Geez! You've got bullet holes, busted tile, and drywall all over the place! And I'm probably going to have to tear out part of the wall to see if any of the wires got nicked or cut. Now that's out of my league. It's fortunate the dividing walls between apartments are solid concrete, or ya might've had the makings of a lawsuit on your

239

hands. Luckily, having been in the business as long as I have, I've got a few connections. Ya got renters insurance?"

"Yes, but I'm not sure if they'll cover something like this."

"Just let me take care of them for ya, okay?"

"Back to the original question. How long?"

"Probably a week to ten days, give or take a day or two."

"A week?"

"Come on AJ. Look at this place! Even after I get everything put back together, the outside wall over there, the entire hallway, including the ceiling, and the bathroom, all of it will have to be repainted. And I don't know if I'll be able to find a replacement tile to match what was originally in the bathroom. I'll be bustin' me hump to get it done in a week!"

"Well, I guess you better get started." AJ looks at his watch and says, "Holy shit! I've got to get out of here! Julie? Julie?" AJ rushes to the bedroom door and knocks. "Julie? Are you decent?"

"Give me another minute, and we can go," she says.

"We? Go where?" he asks.

"You can drop me off near the office on your way out to Higgins' place. I'll pick up my car, head to my place, and start unpacking."

"But Julie, the doc said..."

Julie flings open the bedroom door, cuts him off and says, "Well, I sure as hell won't be getting any peace and quiet around here, now will I! And I don't have a bed to sleep on at my own apartment yet. Got a better idea?"

"How about a motel?" he asks meekly.

"Excuse me," says Patrick. "Might I make a suggestion?"

"What!" says both AJ and Julie in unison.

"Apartment 416 is both vacant and furnished. Now it may not fit your tastes, exactly, but it is convenient and available."

AJ looks at Julie and says, "What do you think?" Julie's thinking while drumming her fingers on the door. "How bad can it be?" AJ looks over to Patrick and asks, "Is it clean?"

"Spotless."

"Julie? What do you say? It'll just be for a few days. And you know I need to keep an eye on all my hardware or take it with me. Have you any idea how much of a pain in the ass that would be?" AJ looks over to Patrick again and says, "We'll still be able to keep this apartment secure, right?"

"Absolutely." Patrick replies.

"Julie, please?"

Julie relents and says, "Oh, all right."

"Thank you, Julie. Thank you, Patrick." He looks at his watch again and says, "I'm gonna' be dead meat if I don't get out of here right now."

"Then I guess you better go," Julie says reluctantly. AJ reaches over to Julie, pulls her to him, and gives her a deep, long, passionate kiss.

"Think that will hold you until I get back this evening?" he asks with a smile.

"I suppose," she replies, acting a little coy. "Yes, yes, I'll be fine. Now go, before I change my mind."

"Love you," he says, rushing to the elevator.

"Love you, too." she replies, then turns to talk to Patrick. "Now, tell me about 416."

"You see, it's my sister's apartment, and she's…"

TLC: Chapter 33

"I was beginning to think you guys were gonna leave me hangin' up there," says Harry. "Of all the luck."

"You were supposed to wait until AJ left for work, question the girl, get the file, eliminate her, then leave," says Wilson. "What happened up there?"

"I was standin' in the stairwell, out of sight, waitin' for him to go to work. I heard him get on the elevator, and that's when I made my move. I rang the doorbell and waited, then rang it again. But the little bitch was suspicious of me from the get go, and called AJ for help. While I was talkin' to her through the door, AJ came up the stairs and slipped up behind me. Boy! Did he scare the shit outta' me! Anyways, I shifted into my stutterin' routine, and did a pretty good job of convincin' 'em I was harmless."

"So what happened after that?" asks Johnson.

"AJ ran into the real maintenance supervisor on the elevator, and busted me before I could get her to tell me where the file was."

"Well, that sucks," says Wilson.

"Not only that, but he says the cops are comin', and I figured you guys would be monitorin' his cell phone and get me outta' there before the real cops showed up."

"But he never made the call," says Johnson.

"I know. He said he told the real maintenance man to make the call. That's when I panicked and tried to off 'em with that piece of shit MAC-10 you guys gave me. The damn thing dumped the whole twenty rounds, and then wouldn't let me release the magazine. I'm lyin' there like a sittin' duck. He coulda' shot me right then and there!"

"Why didn't he?" asks Wilson.

"Beats me. After he tied my hands, he started askin' me questions, bullshit stuff, know what I mean?"

"What did you tell him?" asks Johnson with some concern in his voice.

"What? Are you fuckin' kiddin'? I didn't tell him nuthin'. But he thinks I'm workin' for some guy named Higgins. Do you believe that shit?"

"Perfect," says Wilson.

"Come on guys, when are you gonna get these fuckin' ties off my wrists? My hands are startin' to go numb."

"This looks like a good place," says Wilson, as he pulls into an alley between a couple of old abandoned buildings. Both Wilson and Johnson get out of the car. Johnson opens the back door, helps Harry out, then leads him to the front of the car.

"Hey! What are you doin'? So I didn't get the fuckin' file. I didn't tell 'em nuthin'. I swear!" Johnson pulls out his pistol, and slowly screws on its silencer.

"I believe you Harry, but we can't afford to have you changing your mind," says Wilson. "Goodbye."

"Wait a minute! Wait! Give me another chance! I know I can get that file!" pleads Harry.

Wilson nods his head toward Johnson, and he puts a round in the back of Harry's head. Both men get back in the car and leave Harry's body in the alley.

Heading back to Washington, Wilson says, "You know? AJ, the Secret Service, and the cops are going to be scratching their heads on this one."

"Yeah, you've got to hand it to McCarthy having us pick up a thug with no military record, and a rap sheet a mile long," replies Johnson. "It's a shame Harry didn't get the file though."

"Yeah, McCarthy's not going to be too happy about that," says Wilson with a sigh.

"You better pull out the MAC before you ditch the tool box. We don't want it to fall into some gangbanger's hands."

"Sure thing," says Johnson, as he reaches into the back seat and grabs the toolbox. "Oh shit."

"What?"

"It's not here!"

It's almost 0920 hours when AJ finally pulls up to Higgins' estate. While AJ is talking on the intercom to have the gate opened, a Ryder hi-cube van pulls up behind him. AJ can see two men in military fatigues in the vehicle. As the gate opens, AJ proceeds toward the mansion, and the truck is right on his bumper. AJ calls security.

"Security, Jamison."

"Brian, this is AJ. Are you expecting a van this morning?"

"Are you referring to the one following directly behind you?"

"Roger that."

"Yes, sir. I believe that is the package you ordered through the senator, sir."

"Who gave you confirmation?"

"The senator notified the night shift that your package would be arriving by Ryder truck this morning. And that was followed up by the Army's dispatcher at 0830, advising us of an ETA between 0915 and 0930 hours, sir."

"Roger that. Brian, as a safety measure, I'd prefer to have at least two or three of your men standing by, just inside the front door, if you please."

"Copy that. I already have three security personnel, armed, and on their way, sir."

"Very good, Brian. Now you're thinking."

"Thank you, sir. See you at the front door."

"Roger that." AJ comes to a stop about three car lengths past the front door, allowing ample room for the van to stop and unload in front of it. AJ walks to the driver's side of the van, and introduces himself. "Good morning, Sergeant. Jackson, Thomas A., Secret Service."

"Good morning, Agent Jackson. I'm Sergeant Carter, Franklin D. and Private Chandler, Robert E. Compliments of General Woolbright and Senator Higgins. Private Chandler has the manifest, sir."

"Well, let's have a look see," says AJ, as the three of them walk to the back of the van. While Private Chandler unlocks the padlock and raises the rollup door, AJ's eyes seem to light up as he takes a few moments to scan the manifest. "Okay. Let's get started. We should have six Benelli M3's."

"Check," says Chandler.

"Six H&K MP5's, with suppressors, spotlights, pulse lasers, night sights, and collapsible stocks."

"Stand by one," as Chandler opens a dove gray painted wooden crate labeled 'Manufactured by Heckler & Koch, Austria'. "Check."

"Six Steyr AUG's."

"Check."

"And two Barrett M82A3 .50 caliber semi-automatic rifles with Leupold auto ranging scopes."

"Stand by one," he says while opening both long, graphite-colored hard cases, each holding one of the rifles, broken down. "Check."

Brian walks up as Chandler and Carter are moving some of the crates around to speed up the inventory process. "Looks like Christmas came early this year!"

"Hi Brian," says AJ. "Can you do me a favor and check in the rest of this equipment? I really need to let the Senator know I'm here."

"No problem, AJ. Do what you need to do."

"Thanks. If I'm still out of pocket by the time you've completed checking in the equipment, will you see that it gets hauled up to the second floor?"

"Not to worry. I've got you covered."

"Now all I've got to do is figure out how I'm going to organize this little armory in a bare closet."

"Agent Jackson? The general advised me to inform you he has assigned two men to assist you in outfitting your armory, sir," says Sergeant Carter. "I believe it'll be Sergeant Wallace, and Corporal Davenport. They should be here within the hour."

"Well, I'll have to be sure to thank General Woolbright for his foresight and consideration." Reluctantly, AJ leaves Brian and heads down the hall to see Senator Higgins.

As AJ enters the library, he finds the Senator staring out the window, nursing a large mug of coffee. "Senator Higgins? I want to apologize for not being here on time. But considering the circumstances, it couldn't be helped."

"I'm all ears, AJ," replies Higgins while continuing to gaze out the window.

AJ pauses for a moment, collecting his thoughts, plus being careful to hide his true feelings.

"Well sir, it actually started last night. While I was having a meeting with your security supervisors, someone tried to break into my apartment, and shot a Secret Service Agent in the process."

"How badly was she hurt?' he asks.

"Agent Wesley Niles was shot near his left temple. The last time I saw him, he was unconscious, and strapped to a gurney. I haven't had a chance to check on him since then."

"Sorry, I assumed it had been a female partner. I was with Weathers yesterday when you called about the accident."

"Well, Agent Robinson was there as well. She was able to repel the intruder, although she never actually saw who it was."

"So, I take it they were not able to actually get into your apartment."

"No sir. That didn't happen until this morning."

"What?" asks a surprised Higgins. He turns toward AJ and says, "Someone tried to break in again?"

"No sir, they were a little more subtle than that."

"I'm sorry, I don't quite understand."

"Well, a man posed as the maintenance supervisor of the building and wanted to look over the damage to the apartment from the night before. After spending a few minutes with the guy, I felt comfortable in leaving Agent Robinson alone with him. However, I happened to run into the real maintenance supervisor in the elevator and managed to capture the imposter."

"That's amazing! You really are a one man army."

"Not exactly sir. You see, shortly after I caught him, two men posing as detectives arrived and took him away."

"You said, posing?"

"Yes, sir. They weren't real cops. They all managed to escape before I realized who they were."

"That's a shame, coming up empty handed like that," he says shaking his head.

"Well, I wouldn't say that, sir," he replies.

"Oh?"

"Well, I have reason to believe the intruder last night was a woman, and I'm pretty sure we've crossed paths before."

"Really! What brings you to that conclusion?"

"After Agent Robinson's accident yesterday, a woman tried to steal her briefcase. And last night, Agent Robinson fired two rounds at head height of the intruder. The placement of those rounds put the intruder's height about the average height of a woman."

"Very interesting."

"But there is something else bothering me about the incident."

"And what would that be?"

"The intruder had the Beretta I gave you when we were attacked on the expressway."

"How do you know that?"

"Because when Agent Robinson returned fire, the intruder dropped it."

"Unbelievable! I wonder how she got her hands on your gun?"

"Senator. Do you remember what you did with that pistol after the shooting?"

"I thought I had given it back to you."

"No sir."

"Hmmm. Then I must have left it on the seat somewhere. I really don't remember," says Higgins, as he turns back to the window.

"Well, it's not that important," says AJ.

"So, you think the two attempts on your apartment are related?"

"Wouldn't you, sir?"

"Any idea what they were looking for?"

"I think so, but I won't know for sure until I catch one of them."

"Well, you have definitely had your hands full for the last twenty-four hours, so I guess I can't fault you for being a little late this morning. So, please accept my apology, AJ."

"There's no apology necessary, sir."

"AJ? I insist."

"Very well, sir. Apology accepted."

"After you get your armory squared away, why don't you take the rest of the afternoon off and check on your friend?"

"Sir, you are my first priority, and there's still a lot that needs to be done."

"I don't have any plans to leave the estate today, so I'll be fine. The sooner you get that armory set up, the sooner you can check on Agent Niles."

"Thank you, sir."

***

AJ's timing couldn't have been more perfect. Brian, Carter, and Chandler have already gotten all of the equipment to the second floor, and the general's outfitters have already started taking measurements for fabricating the cabinets and racks for his armory.

Everything seems to be going smoothly until George, the head butler, comes up to the second floor.

"AJ? The Senator has asked me to inform you that you and these young men are invited downstairs to have lunch with him."

"Thank you, George, but we're on a tight schedule, and we need to get this done before the end of the day. Please offer our apologies to the Senator."

"AJ, the Senator was afraid you might say something like that, so he also told me to tell you this is not a request."

"Well, if that's the case, please inform the Senator we'll be down as soon as we secure everything in the armory. It should only take us a few minutes."

"Very well, sir. I shall inform the Senator."

"Okay fellas, you heard the man," says AJ. "Let's get everything put away and grab some lunch."

And what a spread it is! To one side of the dining room, is a large buffet table. On one tray, there are a half dozen types of breads, while on another are all manners of cold cuts. On yet another, there are a variety of cheeses. Another tray is brimming with fresh veggies. And finally, there is a larger tray with a wide array of fresh fruit.

At the opposite end of the table are all manner of soft drinks, juices, and water, all in a bed of crushed ice. A tray full of ice filled glasses sits next to the bottled drinks.

As the men start loading up their plates, Senator Higgins walks up to each of the men, introduces himself, and shakes their hand. After he makes the rounds, he prepares his own plate. He waits for the men to take their seats, then stands at the head of the table and says, "Gentlemen, thank you all for coming out today, and helping Agent Jackson here, set up his little armory. I hope I don't have to remind you that any and everything you see and do here remains strictly confidential. Are we clear on that?"

All of the men nod their heads and say, "Yes, sir."

"Good. Now, before we dig in, are there any practicing Jews, Muslims, or Atheists here?" he asks smiling. Everyone shakes their head. "Very well. Let us say grace. Father in heaven, thank you for this beautiful day and allowing us to bathe in your light of life. Thank you for the opportunity to live in a country where any man has the freedom to pursue his dreams and goals without concern of his beliefs, his color, or religion. Bless this food we about to receive in your Son's holy name. And forgive us of our sins against our fellow man. Amen."

"Amen," say the men in unison.

"Okay, fellas. Eat up!" says Higgins.

Just as everyone is about to chow down, Brian rushes into the dining room and says, "Senator? They're here." In the background, the sound of an 18-wheeler can be heard rumbling up the drive.

AJ asks, "Who? What?"

"A little surprise," says Higgins with a big smile on his face.

All of them make it to the front door in time to see a massive shadow pass by the entrance, and the rumble of the diesel engine can be felt permeating the doors, windows, and walls.

One of the outfitters yells out, "Holy shit! What in the hell is that?"

Higgins flings open the door and all that can seen are the huge gold letters against the British Racing Green side of the enclosed semi trailer that read: Eberhardt & Keyes Coachbuilders, Ltd., New York, New York.

249

Once the rig comes to a stop, two men hop out of the cab on the passenger side of the truck. Both men are wearing spotless white jumpsuits, with one of them carrying a clipboard.

"Good morning, gentlemen! My name is Edward Keyes, III," he says in a distinctly British accent. "I'm looking for a Senator William Henry Higgins."

Higgins steps forward and says proudly, "That would be me."

"Good morning, sir. We have a delivery for you, and another for you to review."

"You don't say," replies a smiling Higgins.

"Yes, sir. We were working on the second vehicle when you called and cancelled your factory pick up yesterday. And since you asked us to deliver the first vehicle to your home, we felt it appropriate to put a couple of extra people on the second vehicle, to see if we could complete it and deliver it at the same time. While it is still far from complete, I thought we'd bring it along anyway."

"Enough with the labor pains, show me the baby!" exclaims Higgins.

"Very well, sir." Edward turns to the other man who's standing near the back of the trailer and yells, "Okay Peter, open her up!"

Peter starts manipulating various hydraulic levers, which open, lower, and extend the rear of the trailer, turning it into a ramp. Edward disappears around to the far side of the trailer, and they hear what sounds like cargo doors opening and being secured to the side of the trailer.

Then, out of the silence is heard, "VROOM! VROOM!" followed by a calmer, yet erratic rumble. Slowly, but steadily, Edward starts backing the black, stretched Hummer H2 out of the trailer. Peter is standing off to the driver's side, at the end of the ramp, guiding him down.

As the Hummer exits the trailer, Brian says, "It really must be Christmas!"

Once off the ramp, Edward parks the vehicle at the base of the steps of the front door. Immediately, everyone rushes down the steps for a closer look at this finely chiseled work of mechanical art.

Edward gets out of the vehicle and hands Higgins a leather wrapped binder containing legal papers and a description of the work performed on the vehicle. Edward opens the driver's side passenger door and begins to explain the amenities of the vehicle. "Senator Higgins, while this vehicle has essentially the same mechanicals as Mr. Jackson's vehicle, there are a number of unique amenities. Some of the more notable ones include the 60-inch stretch, four individual reclining, massaging, and climate controlled seats, two facing forward, two facing back, four 19-inch, wide screen LCD monitors that fold down on either side of the two custom floor mounted consoles. All four monitors have access to satellite TV and Internet services. Also, inside each console is a wireless keyboard and mouse, so the monitors can be used as a computer display. We also moved the sunroof from the front to the passenger compartment and added the privacy wall."

"On the mechanical side, we reduced the compression on the engine slightly, and added a supercharger. Total output is well over 600 horsepower and over 600 pounds feet of torque. We also swapped the standard automatic for the heavier duty Allison transmission, which gives you an extra gear, and higher fluid and torque capacity.

The roof, sides, and firewall have seven layers of Kevlar, and the floor has over nine layers, plus a series of 1½-inch ceramic armor plates underneath both the front and rear passenger compartments. All glass is the latest in polycarbonate technology. Both Fuel Safe tanks are wrapped in several layers of Kevlar as well.

The tires have a foam core, and can be run flat for up to 50 miles at speeds up to 45 miles per hour over virtually any terrain. This vehicle is equipped with a GPS transponder that will allow you to track it anywhere in the country. You'll also find a disc in the binder that will allow you to program your own computer to access this service."

Suddenly, Jeffrey, the detailer, pops up out of nowhere and cries out, "Let me see! Let me see! Holy shit! The *Man* has one bitchin' SUV!"

AJ says, "Mr. Keyes, this is Jeffrey Samuels. He's the senator's detailer, one of the best I've ever seen."

"Pleased to meet you Jeffrey," says Edward, as he shakes Jeffrey's hand. "Now, if you'll be so kind as to introduce yourself to Peter, over there, he'll tell you all about the paint and interior materials of the vehicle, along with their proper care."

"Yes, sir, and thank you!" says Jeffrey beaming. He's happier than a kid in a candy store.

"Mr. Jackson, I'm assuming you'll be doing the driving," says Edward.

"Yes, for now," he replies half-heartedly, as he thinks about the Hummer he owned for such a short time.

"Well, for the most part, everything up front is pretty much the same as yours. Obviously, the turning radius is going to be a bit wider, and you'll need to take a few extra precautions when backing up. And while this one is a little bigger and heavier than yours, it doesn't give much away in the power category."

"What do you mean mine?" asks AJ. "Mine's totaled, collecting dust in a junkyard somewhere."

"Really?" says Edward in a questioning tone. He looks over to Higgins and says, "He doesn't know?" Higgins just shrugs his shoulders.

"Know what?" asks AJ with a perplexing look on his face.

"Go ahead," says Higgins nodding his head to Edward. "You're the one who let the cat out of the bag."

"Peter!" Edward calls out. "Bring out the other one!" Peter motions Jeffrey to go up the far side of the trailer, while he trots up the near side, opens a side door near the nose of the trailer, then climbs up inside.

"What other one?" asks AJ.

"Well," begins Higgins, "after I ah, talked with Edward here, about how your Hummer saved our collective asses, and then heard about how your insurance company was dicking you around, I kinda talked them into buying back your Hummer, for research purposes of course, in exchange for building one for me and replacing yours."

"Senator, I don't know what to say," says a shocked AJ.

"A simple thank you would be a good start, don't you think?"

"Thank you, sir. I can't believe you did that for me. You shouldn't have."

"AJ, if it hadn't been for you and your Hummer, I wouldn't be standing here right now. I owe you my life, and I believe in paying my debts."

"Sir, I was doing my job."

"And I'm showing my appreciation."

About that time, AJ's Hummer comes to life. VROOM! VROOM! This time, you can see the walls of the trailer vibrating from the pulses of the engine and its exhaust. Edward walks over to AJ and says,

"Your vehicle is not quite complete. We're in the process of transferring all salvageable components from your original Hummer. We had also planned to swap your engine into this one, but we had to send it back to World Products. One of the heads had a bullet lodged in it."

"This engine has a larger supercharger with a built-in air to liquid intercooler, plus a larger throttle body and injectors. We've added the Allison transmission, and upgraded the exhaust system. It's now 3 inches from the header pipes, through the cats, to the Flowmaster mufflers, then out the back. This one makes over 700 horsepower, and the torque number peaks at more than 650 pounds feet. It's an absolute beast!"

Even though the Hummer is idling, while moving within the trailer, it sounds like rolling thunder. The hair rises on the back of AJ's neck, and he can't hide his excitement.

Finally, the Hummer's nose peaks out from inside the trailer. The body is a deep charcoal gray metallic. The bumpers, brush guard, luggage rack, step rails, and other trim are all matte black. The centers of the Centerline forged aluminum wheels have a charcoal gray anodized finish, while the lips are polished. They're shod with Goodyear Wrangler dual-purpose tires. Auxiliary lights are mounted in the brush guard, and on the roof rack. These lights, manufactured by Hella, appear black when off, adding to the already sinister look of the Hummer.

"First off, I should tell you, we didn't have a yellow Hummer in stock. Since GM is dropping the entire Hummer Line, new H2's are hard to come by. Since Senator Higgins claimed the black one for himself, the only other colors we had under construction were white, red, and charcoal gray. Senator Higgins made the selection."

"You can rest easy, Edward. He made the right choice. It's very impressive."

"As I mentioned earlier, we're scavenging all we can from your damaged Hummer, such as the scanners, seats and monitors, computer, etc. There are a few items that haven't been installed or fully functional yet. But it was so close to being done, well, I thought it would be a nice surprise."

"Edward, it's perfect. Thank you."

"In the meantime, we'll continue working on the interior and the electronics. We're about a week to ten days from completion, followed by a thorough shakedown. Once the vehicle passes our inspection, we'll contact you to schedule a time for delivery, unless of course you'd like to pick it up at our facility. That's completely up to you."

Edward hands AJ his business card and continues, "Once you take delivery, drive it for a couple of weeks, and make notes of anything that's not working properly, or doesn't meet your expectations. When you're ready, give us a call and we'll make arrangements to pick it up at your convenience, provide you with a loaner, and take care of any niggles you find. Any questions?"

About that time, Jeffrey lowers the passenger window, grinning from ear to ear, and says, "AJ, this is the baddest ride I've ever been in. When the motor's runnin', it feels like it's alive! Chicks are gonna dig this!"

"That's enough Jeffrey," says AJ, starting to feel a little embarrassed. "Come on out."

"Give me a minute, okay?"

"Why? What's the matter?" asks AJ.

"Because…" He waves for AJ to come closer, then whispers, "I'm sporting a woody!"

"Oh! Okay. Take your time," he says, smiling and shaking his head.

"What's the matter? Is everything all right?" asks Edward.

"Everything's fine. He's just a little excited," replies AJ, cracking a smile.

Finally, Jeffrey is able to regain his composure, rushes over to Higgins and says, "Senator Higgins! These about the wildest rides I've ever seen. They've got stuff on them I've never even heard of. Wait'll I tell the brothers about this. No one's gonna believe my boss has the bitchinest set of wheels in Washington!"

"Now Jeffrey," says Higgins, "You know you can't disclose anything about this to anyone. Remember? You signed a confidentiality agreement strictly forbidding you to talk about this very thing."

"Damn! The one thing I can really relate to, and I can't breathe a word about it," he says with an obvious look of disappointment on his face. "I understand, sir. My lips are sealed."

"But at least you'll get to work on the bitchinest set of wheels in Washington," says AJ with a grin.

"That's true," he replies, forcing a smile.

Edward walks up to Higgins and says, "I hope everything is satisfactory for you, sir."

"Quite satisfactory, Edward, quite," he replies.

"Well, sir, if you have no additional questions, we'll load up Mr. Jackson's vehicle and be on our way." Edward turns to AJ and reaches out to shake his hand. "It was a pleasure meeting you, Mr. Jackson, and I look forward to seeing you again very soon."

"The pleasure was all mine, Edward. And please call me AJ."

"Thank you, AJ. I sincerely hope this one fares better than the last."

"You and me both! I'll be in touch."

"Good day, gentlemen," says Edward as he starts walking back to the truck. "Peter! Load up!" With those words, the driver fires up the semi, and billows of black smoke leap from the twin stacks as the engine roars to life. Peter drives AJ's Hummer back into the trailer, checks the ramp and doors to make sure they're secure, then climbs up into the cab, waving as they leave the grounds.

"Okay. Party's over. Let's polish off lunch and get back to work. We've got an armory to finish!" barks AJ.

Sergeant Carter steps up to AJ and says, "Sir, if you have no further need or our services, Private Chandler and I need to get back to base."

"Very well, Sergeant. I appreciate the help. You're dismissed."

"Thank you, sir." With that, both Chandler and Carter get back into the van and follow the semi to the gate.

As the rest of them start walking back into the house, Brian says to AJ as he pats him on the back, "Man, if this is your idea of fun, I've got to start hangin' out with you more often!"

"I wouldn't make it a habit of standing too close, if I were you. I've had a fair amount of lead thrown my way, too, you know."

Brian stops dead in his tracks and says, "Oh yeah, I forgot about that." Brian thinks for a moment, then rushes to catch up to AJ and says, "Well, maybe you could give me a two minute warning before the fireworks start."

"Come on," AJ says with a smile. "We've both got plenty of work to do."

"I know, I know," replies Brian while shaking his head.

"Jeffrey!" yells AJ. "Do you think you can find a place to park that thing, somewhere out of the way?"

"How about my place?"

"The Senator would probably send me out on a search and destroy mission if you were to take it off the grounds, don't you think?"

"I was just foolin' around, AJ," says Jeffrey as he opens the driver's door of Higgins' new limo.

"I'm not," AJ replies, without looking back. It's a shame, too, because the look on Jeffrey's face is that of complete and utter shock.

Jeffrey's hands are shaking as he reaches for the ignition key to start the vehicle while saying to himself, *"Man, it's gettin' to where you don't know if someone is jivin' with you or not!"*

AJ's apartment
1230 hours local time

Patrick has covered the living room furniture and floor with drop cloths in an effort to capture most of the dust and debris from his demolition of the bullet riddled bathroom wall, along with the repairs on the hallway walls and ceiling.

Julie is in the process of transferring food from AJ's refrigerator to the one in apartment 416, when Detective Morris knocks on the open door. "What in the hell is going on? Seems to be a little overkill here for a single bullet hole in a wall."

"Well," says Julie, "AJ's a bit of a perfectionist. After looking at the apartment in the daylight, he decided he wanted to have the whole apartment repainted."

About that time, Patrick pops out of the bathroom and says, "It's a good thing I started tearing that wall out," when he's startled by the detective's presence. "Aye! Ya' didn't mention we had company."

"Hi. I'm Detective Morris. I was just saying to Ms. Robinson here, this seems to be overdoing it a bit for just one bullet hole."

"Oh laddie! Ya must be blind or somethin'. Just look down this hallway! There's got to be closer to twenty! With that comment, Julie rolls her eyes, and shakes her head.

"Now, I know for a fact this didn't happen last night. Ms. Robinson, would you mind telling me what's going on here?"

"It's kind of a long story."

"That's okay, I'm not going anywhere."

"Well, it all started when a man, who called himself Harry..." and Julie proceeds to tell him the story.

After listening to Julie's detailed explanation, he asks, "Would you mind telling me why you didn't call us? We are the police, and this is our jurisdiction, you know."

"Detective? You're absolutely right, but I recall you telling us you'd be back this morning. So we decided to wait until you got here. We didn't want to spoil your morning donut break."

"Now Ms. Robinson, that's not very funny. I don't take my donut break until sometime after lunch, even later when I'm on nights." He pauses for a moment, then continues. "Let's cut the crap, okay? I know you and AJ are Secret Service agents, and you're probably used to doing things your way. But I have a job to do, too. So, we can either work this out together as a team, or we can waste each other's time by getting our bosses involved, creating more red tape and hard feelings between our departments."

"Okay, follow me," says Julie, leading him to the second bedroom and to AJ's computer. "We have direct access to NCIC, and I've been doing a little investigating of my own since this morning's little incident."

"Have you found anything?"

"Actually, more than I thought I would," she replies, while making a few keystrokes. Suddenly, Harry's mug shot and rap sheet pop up on the screen.

"Hey! I know that guy!" says Morris.

"Really?"

"Yeah, he's small time. I've busted him a couple of times myself. He has a history of B&E's, and assault. He's also been involved with collecting protection money, cracking heads, and busting kneecaps for some of the small time hoods in the area. What's he got to do with this?"

"He was the one who assaulted me and shot up the place."

"Not a chance. This is way out of his league."

"Patrick? Could you come here for a moment?" she asks.

"Anything for you, deary," he replies.

"Do you recognize this man?" she asks.

"That's the bastard who made a mess of this place, and he was one of three men I saw in the alleyway this morning."

"Are you sure about that?" asks Morris.

"As sure as I'm standing here, detective." he replies. "Are you challenging my integrity, son?"

"No sir. I wouldn't do such a thing. My apologies," says Morris.

"Thank you, Patrick," says Julie.

"Well lassie, if you have no objections, I'm going to grab myself a bite to eat. Can I get you anything?"

"No thanks, I'll be fine. Besides, I have company," she says flippantly.

"If you change your mind, just press #102 on the intercom. Okay?"

"Thank you, Patrick."

"Back in a bit," he says as he leaves the apartment.

"So, what about the other two men? The ones posing as detectives."

"Nothing, so far, but I'm really not surprised."

"But you said you found more than you thought you would. I don't understand."

"Detective, I was surprised to find Harry's information online. The people we're up against don't have mug shots or rap sheets on NCIC, or anywhere else for that matter. They don't exist."

"Are you telling me they're ghosts?" he asks sarcastically.

"In a manner of speaking, yes, I suppose you could say that. Tell me. Were you ever in the military?"

"Yeah, six years in the Army, First Battalion, 35th Armored Division why?"

"Any kind of security clearance?" she asks.

"Level Two."

"Well, I can't tell you much, but even what I do tell you, you can't tell anyone else about it."

"About what?"

"First, I need your word that you won't divulge anything I'm about to tell you," she says.

"Now, Ms. Robinson…"

"Do you want to help solve this case or not?"

"Of course I do, but you're asking me to withhold information from my own department. You know, I could take you downtown, and…"

"And after my boss gets through reaming your boss, and his boss a new asshole, your ass would be sitting behind a desk for the rest of your career. That is, if you're lucky enough to even have a job after he gets through with them."

"Are you threatening me?"

"Detective? Yes or no."

Morris pauses for a moment. He finally relents and says, "You must have been a damn good attorney."

"Still am," she says with a smile. "You still haven't answered the question."

"Yes ma'am," he sighs. "I'm in." About that time Morris' phone rings. "Detective Morris….Really? Where? Have you called the coroner yet? I'm not far away. Tell 'em I'll be there in five minutes. And tell 'em not to touch anything! Got it?" Morris ends the call.

"Somebody died?" asks Julie.

"Yeah, and I think it's Harry. Are you up for a quick trip down the street?"

"Sure. Just let me find my keys so I can lock up." Julie grabs her purse, cell phone, and keys, then takes the elevator down with Detective Morris.

***

Less than two miles from AJ's apartment, Julie and Detective Morris arrive at the scene. There are two uniformed officers, along with three people from forensics, another detective, and two men from the coroner's office. Detective Morris flashes his badge to the officers, and the two of them walk up the alley to Harry's body.

His body is lying on its left side, facing away from them. His hands are still secured behind his back. Julie looks away for a moment as they approach the body.

Once they get to where they can see his face, Morris asks, "Is that him?"

Julie forces herself to look at him, and says, "Yes, that's him." She's apparently not feeling well by the look on her face.

"Ms. Robinson, you can wait in the car if you want. I'll only be a minute or so, then I'll take you back."

She says, "Thanks," turns, and stumbles into Detective Morris.

"Do you think you can make it back to the car?" he asks.

"Yes," she sighs, "I'll be fine," as she starts walking back to the car.

"Who's the skirt?" asks the other detective.

"Just a possible witness, that's all," Morris replies.

"To this?" asks the detective.

"No. There was a burglary in her apartment building, and the suspect matches his description," replies Morris.

"Looks like Harry got in with the wrong crowd this time," says the detective.

"Think it was a mob hit?" asks Morris.

"Nah, he was standing when he was shot," says the coroner.

"A mob hit usually has the victim on their knees. See? The bullet entered at the base of the skull, angling upward, rather than near the crown going down. Also, there's very little evidence of powder burns, meaning there was either some distance between him and the shooter, or a silencer was used. My money's on a silencer. Best I can tell, he's been dead a few hours, three, maybe four at the most, meaning he was shot in broad daylight. Somebody would have heard the gunshot."

"Find anything on him? ID, money, anything?" asks Morris.

"Haven't searched him yet, but the first thing that caught my eye is the fact that he's wearing latex gloves, and his hands are tied behind his back."

"Maybe he got caught being somewhere he wasn't supposed to be," says the other detective.

"I suppose that's possible," replies the coroner. "But it appears he gave up without a struggle. There's no visible evidence of bruising to his hands or face."

"So, I wonder why they shot him?" asks the detective.

"Wait a minute. I think I've found something," says the coroner, as he pulls out a folded piece of paper from the inside pocket of Harry's jumpsuit.

"Let me see," says Morris as he grabs the paper from the coroner. He opens it, glances at it for a moment, then folds it back up, and sticks it in his pocket.

"Well, what did it say?" asks the other detective.

"Grocery list," replies Morris.

"You're shittin' me!" says the other detective.

"Now, why would I do a thing like that? Here! You want it?"

"No, no, never mind."

"Guys? There's something in his left pocket. It feels like it might be a gun. Jason, help me roll him on his back."

"Wouldn't it be easier if we freed his hands first?" asks Jason, the coroner's intern.

"Good point, Jason," replies the coroner. "Want to do the honors? Just cut the one between the wrists."

"Got it," says Jason.

"Okay, easy does it," says the coroner as they roll Harry onto his back. He reaches into Harry's pocket and pulls out the stun gun he used on Julie. "Bag this for me, and tag it as coming from his left front pocket."

"Forensics, do you have anything?" asks Morris.

"We've got a single spent 9mm shell casing, Winchester, recent manufacture. We have a partial footprint in some wet paper refuse near the body that seems to be recent, and a partial tread mark down there near the entrance. Looks like a police spec Goodyear."

"Well, it looks like you have everything under control here, so I think I'll take the lady back to her apartment before she passes out from this heat. And you better hurry up and get him tagged and bagged before he starts stinking up the place."

"Yeah, rigor mortis is already starting to set in," says the coroner.

"Let's load him up and get out of here. I've already gotten another call. We've got a jumper on 15th Street."

"I guess he couldn't wait for the elevator," says the other detective sarcastically.

"Well, you know what they say, it's not the fall that gets ya, it's the sudden stop," says the coroner.

Detective Morris gives the coroner one of his business cards and says, "Call me if you find anything else out of the ordinary with this guy, will ya'?"

"Sure thing, detective," he replies.

As Detective Morris starts walking back to the car, he casually reaches into his pocket to pull out his car keys, but they're not there. He starts to check his other pockets, but as he walks out of the alley, he can see Julie sitting in the car, reading a newspaper, and the car's running. He gets in the car and sees his keys in the ignition and says, "I know I turned the car off, locked it, and pocketed the keys."

Without looking up from her reading, Julie says, "Yes, yes you did."

"Then how in the…"

"You were the one who told me to wait in the car. I knew it was locked, and since it's pretty warm out there, it wouldn't make any sense to stand next to or sit in a hot car, so I borrowed your keys."

"But how…"

"Ask me no questions, I'll tell you no lies," she replies while continuing to read the newspaper.

"So, I guess that means your little episode at the body was just an act."

"Oh, that? That was nothing. While working with NCIS, I once worked a crash site in Virginia where an FA-18 pilot undershot his carrier landing. The only recognizable body parts were his organs, and they were all over what was left of the cockpit." Detective Morris feels a bit queasy from her graphic description. "But, to answer your question, yes, that was just an act. I didn't want to get involved in playing twenty questions." She pauses a moment, then continues, "So, did they find anything?"

"Well, they've determined it wasn't a mob hit."

"That's pretty obvious. He was shot standing up."

"Am I the only one who didn't know that?"

"Sorry. Anything else?"

"Yeah. They found a stun gun and this," he says, handing her the piece of paper the coroner had found in Harry's jumpsuit. Julie carefully opens it and sees that someone has handwritten AJ's address.

"How many people have touched this without protection?"

"Well, the coroner was wearing gloves, so I guess you, me, and Harry, along with whoever wrote the note. Why?"

"If there's another set of prints on here besides ours, we may have finally gotten a break on who's behind this."

"Okay. Where do we go from here?"

"Have you ever been to FBI headquarters?" she asks.

"No, can't say that I have."

"Well, there's a first time for everything. I just wish I had an opportunity to clean up a bit and put on some make up."

"Ms. Robinson? You look just fine."

"Then let's go!"

Higgins' estate
1530 hours local time

The rest of afternoon seems to run smoothly for AJ. The general's outfitters complete the armory, and help AJ store the arms, then load some of the magazines and bandoliers with ammo. Finally, AJ stands at the door, looks things over and says, "Fellas? You've done an outstanding job. It's about as perfect as it can get, especially starting something like this from scratch."

"Thank you, sir. It was our pleasure. And it certainly felt good to get out of the Pentagon for a day. Anytime you need something, just give us a call," replies Sergeant Wallace. "But I've got to tell you, this is quite a unique arsenal you have here. When we first started laying things out, I could understand the shotguns, the submachine guns, even the smoke and tear gas grenades. But the stun grenades, night vision, gas masks, and the Barretts? I thought to myself, *"He must be expecting some pretty serious trouble somewhere down the road."* Then it all came together when the Hummers showed up. You and the senator were the ones attacked on the expressway! Son of a bitch! My hat's off to you, sir."

AJ is more than a little embarrassed by his notoriety. "I don't know what to say, other than I was just doing my job, Sergeant."

"I gather you were in the military."

"Twenty years in the Marines, Special Ops."

"Stripes or bars?"

"Are you kiddin'? Stripes, of course. Never ask another man to do something you're not willing to do yourself," replies AJ. "I just never saw myself as officer material."

"You're my kind of man, sir."

"Look guys, you've had a long day, and I appreciate everything you've done. And please be sure to thank the general for me. I owe him one."

"Will do, AJ. Have a good one. Like I said, if you need anything, give us a call, okay?"

"You got it, Sergeant. Now get out of here."

Both Sergeant Wallace and Corporal Davenport snap to attention and salute AJ.

"Now, you know that you don't salute a civilian, even an old war dog like me."

"Begging your pardon sir, but other than General Woolbright, I can't think of very many officers worthy of the compliment, sir. It's men like you who get things done."

With that comment, AJ also snaps to, and returns the salute. As the men gather up their tools, AJ keys up the house radio and says, "AJ to Jamison, AJ to Jamison."

"Jamison, go ahead," replies Brian.

"If you want to check out the armory, now would be the time to do it."

"Copy that. I'll be right up."

"And if you should run across George, you might want to let him know housekeeping needs to make a pass up here. There's wood chips and dust all over the place."

"Copy that. I'll let him know."

A few minutes later, Brian is standing next to AJ looking over the armory and says, "Do you think you're really going to need to use this stuff? I mean, you've got enough hardware here to hold off an entire company!"

"I admit I might have gone a bit overboard, but if the need arises, we should have the necessary firepower to repel virtually any threat."

"I'd say."

"By the way, are any of your men into guns? I mean, like a gunsmith, armorer, something like that."

"Well, there are a few of them who are on the company's combat shooting team. A couple of them are pretty good, too. I know one of them loads his own ammo, even has a few custom made handguns. What are you thinking?"

"A couple of things, actually. First, I need someone to go through each of these weapons and make sure they all work as they should."

"Including the Barretts?" asks Brian excitedly.

"No, I'll take care of them myself," replies AJ.

"You know, AJ? You're just no fun at all."

"Well, you could offer to help me," he replies.

"Okay. Could I help you with the Barretts, AJ?"

"I'll sleep on it."

265

"Gee, thanks. What else?"

"Well, Higgins was supposed to have four men come in from Secure-1 Executive Protection Services to be his personal bodyguards, but so far, no one's shown up. I'd like to have a few guys I can trust as backups, just in case something goes wrong. I'd prefer them to have some military training if possible, preferably with a background in Special Ops, SEAL, Rangers, or Delta."

"I could talk to this guy I have in mind, as well as ask the other supervisors to see if they have any recommendations."

"I'd really appreciate it, and I've made up my mind."

"About what?"

"You helping me with the Barretts."

"Well?"

"Well, I'm going to need a gun bearer."

"A what?"

"A gun bearer. You know, someone to carry the guns. Those things are heavy!"

"No shit! Twenty-eight pounds, and that doesn't include the scope or the carrying case."

"Yeah, forty pounds would probably be a safe bet," says AJ, straight faced. "Oh! And let's not forget the ammo. Can't test fire the rifles without ammo."

"And where do you plan on doing that?"

"Well, we can't afford to do it here, but I know of a place where we can do it without raising too much attention."

"And just where would that be?"

"Quantico, of course," replies AJ smiling. I still have friends down there, and I'm sure they'd even let you on base, if I ask them to."

"Gee! Thanks for the vote of confidence." says Brian sarcastically.

"Come on Brian. Even though my day started out in the toilet, at least the rest of it has been pretty outstanding. Wouldn't you agree?"

Suddenly, AJ realizes he hasn't spoken to or heard from Julie all day. "Hang on a minute. I need to check on Julie." He tries the apartment first, but there's no answer. "Funny, she doesn't

266

answer. I'll try her cell phone. Maybe she's still moving things from one apartment to the next."

Julie's phone goes to voice mail on the first ring, "This is Julie Robinson. I'm not available right now. Please leave your name, number, the time you called, and a brief message. I'll get back to you as soon as possible. Please wait for the beep." BEEP!

"Julie, it's me. Where are you? I just tried the apartment and now this. Unless I hear from you in the next few minutes, I'm heading home. Please call me ASAP. Bye."

"Something wrong?" asks Brian.

"Julie's not answering the house phone or her cell phone. That's not like her. She can't go anywhere, no wheels."

"There's always a cab or public transportation."

"True, but she'd have called me if she were going out. I've gotta go." AJ closes the door to the armory, gives it a good tug to verify it's secure. While taking the stairs down to the first floor, AJ says to Brian, "I want a recorder on that camera running all weekend, and I want someone to check that door every hour on the hour. Got it?"

"I'll tell my staff to start right away, and I'll put it in the log for the next shift."

"Good, by the way, aren't you here a little late this afternoon? I thought shift change was at 1500 hours."

"It is, but Kenny's running a little late. Today is his daughter's birthday, and I said I'd cover for him until he gets here."

"Isn't that going to mess up your company's scheduling policy? Especially since Kenny's on a different shift from you?"

"Well, we take care of these situations outside of company policy. Kenny will cover for me one day next week."

"You know, Brian. I'm starting to warm up to you. I think we're going to get along just fine."

"I hope so. It's bad enough you want to use me as your gun bearer. Next thing you know, you'll probably want me to hold the targets, too!"

"You know? That's not a bad idea. Moving targets…What a concept!"

"AJ?" says Brian, giving him a dirty look.

"Don't worry Brian, I'm only kidding."

"I know."

267

"Would you mind telling Higgins that I've gone to check on Julie, and I'll give him a call sometime in the morning to let him know when I'll be coming out."

"Sure thing, AJ. Have a great weekend."

"You, too, Brian," he says, while getting into the Crown Vic. He sits there for a moment, thinking about the Hummer, then says to himself, *"Yes!"*

On the way back to his apartment, AJ calls the apartment and Julie's cell phone several times. He's really starting to get worried, when suddenly his phone rings, and it's Julie. "Where in the hell have you been? I've been trying to call you for the past half hour!"

"I'm sorry AJ, but Detective Morris and I have been at FBI headquarters for the past couple of hours, and we had to turn our phones off while we were in there."

"What were you doing at the FBI, and why is Detective Morris with you?"

"It's a long story, but the short side of it is somebody killed Harry, and we found something else."

"What?"

"AJ, you and I both know our phones may be compromised. I'll tell you when we get back to the apartment. Okay? By the way, have you talked to Niles today?"

"No, I've been busy all day. I was going to check on him on the way back, but when you didn't answer your phone, I, I panicked. I was afraid something had happened to you, and I wasn't there to protect you."

"That's so sweet, AJ. But I'm okay. Why don't you go ahead and stop by to see how he's doing. Detective Morris will stay with me until you get home."

"Niles will have to wait. I'll be back at the apartment in about 10 minutes."

"Okay, but we're still a good thirty to forty-five minutes out."

"No problem. Say! Did you remember to order that pizza?"

"No, and I don't have that number with me either," she replies.

"Maybe we'll go out to eat tomorrow night and check out their menu," he adds.

"You mean sit down at a table with real plates and eating utensils like normal people?"

"What's wrong with paper plates and plastic ones? When we're done, all we have to do is drop them in the trash. No muss, no fuss," he replies.

"Would you mind picking up something on the way home? I'd do it, but I left my purse in the apartment."

"Sounds like a plan. Wendy's or Burger King?" asks AJ.

"Wendy's."

"Beef or chicken?"

"Chicken."

"Fried or grilled?"

"Grilled, with lettuce, tomato, and honey mustard. No onions."

"Fries and a Coke?"

"Coke's okay, but I'd prefer a baked potato."

"What about Morris?"

She looks over to Morris and says, "AJ wants to know if you want anything."

"Same as yours will be fine," replies Morris.

"Double it, AJ," she says.

"Okay, see you back at the apartment. I'll put 'em in the oven to keep 'em warm."

"Low, AJ. Make sure the oven is on Low!"

"Okay. I got it. Low."

"See you soon. Bye."

"Bye, Julie."

"What was all that about? The *"Low"* part, I mean," asks Morris.

"It's an inside joke, nothing really," she replies.

"Uh-huh," says Morris.

TLC: Chapter 37
Higgins' estate
1730 hours local time

Senator McCarthy has come out to visit with Higgins at his estate
to discuss the upcoming banquet and to see his new limo.
Higgins meets McCarthy at the base of the steps, shakes his hand,
then starts leading him to the garage area.

"Come this way, Joshua. You gotta see this! This is gonna
knock your socks off."

"What, Bill?"

"My new limo!"

"Gee, Bill. If you've seen one Lincoln, you've seen 'em, all!"
he says rounding the corner, coming face to face with the
Higgins' new Hummer. "Wow! This thing's huge! When did
you get it?"

"This afternoon. Had it delivered right here to the estate by
one of the owners of the company!"

"Impressive! Who built it?"

"Eberhardt and Keyes, Ltd. out of New York. It's the same
outfit that built AJ's Hummer."

"Well, how does it feel to own a tank? Probably has all the
accoutrements and ride of one, too," he says smugly. Higgins
opens the driver's side passenger door and says, "Get in."

McCarthy starts to get in, but stops once he takes a look
inside. "Whoa!"

"Go on, get in," says Higgins.

"Nice. Very nice!" he says touching the leather seats and
feeling the plushness of the carpet under his feet.

"If it wasn't for AJ's Hummer, you and I probably wouldn't
be having this conversation right now. That damn thing of his
took a pounding and kept on running! The coachbuilder said
there were almost a hundred bullet holes in it, all of it military
grade, full metal jacket, and not one of them got past their armor.
In fact, with the exception of some sheet metal and minor frame
damage caused by him ramming that van head on, and broad
siding the suburban, it was still drivable! You couldn't have
done that in the Lincoln. We'd have been sitting ducks!"

"You're probably right, Bill. But a limo needs to have more than just survivability, leather seats and plush carpeting."

"Oh, you haven't seen anything yet," says Higgins, grinning ear to ear. "The seats recline, have built-in heating and cooling, plus massage. There's built-in Internet and satellite TV access for both front and rear facing seats, air ride suspension, and God only knows what else. They had to give me a damn manual to tell me about all this thing has and does."

"Oh! And talk about bullet proof, this thing has Kevlar everywhere, bulletproof glass, and those new ceramic armor plates mounted underneath to protect me against grenades, roadside bombs, and mines. It's pretty damn close to being a tank!"

"Well, since you put it that way, I might have to get one of these, too. But I think I'll have mine painted silver, like my DBS." McCarthy pauses a moment, then changes the subject. "Let's talk about the party. You know there are going to be five assassins." Joshua reaches into his briefcase and pulls out a thick manila envelope.

"Why didn't you tell me you recovered the file from Robinson and Weathers?" asks Higgins.

"We haven't yet. No, these are the personnel files on the five assassins. I'd get them to AJ as soon as possible, so he can prepare his team to apprehend them before they can get to you."

"Now where's the sport in that?" scoffs Higgins. "That's like shooting fish in a barrel. It's not the catch of your prey, but the hunt! And the fact that you, too are subject to being the prey, makes it all the more exciting. Exhilarating! Gets the heart pumping!" he says while beating his chest. "Makes you feel alive! Besides, even if one of them should succeed in their task, we have the antidote, right?"

"Of course," replies Joshua. "You can't be President if you're dead, now can you? Besides, if they were to kill you, then I'd be next in line for the Presidency, and they'd be planning a TLC for me. Thanks, but no thanks."

"What makes you think they're not already?"

"For starters, they don't know I'm going to be your running mate, just yet. After all, I was the one who presided over the meeting selecting the assassins for your upcoming TLC. I'm sure

271

our pairing will come as quite a shock to a number of the members of the Core."

"And that's why we'll be taking out their best operatives the night of the party," says Higgins. "Afterwards, they'll all be running scared. I'll bet at least half of those who aren't already with us, will come crawling, begging to let them stay on. And the rest will either be taking early retirement, or extended leaves out of the country."

"Or a last ditch, full bore frontal assault," says McCarthy.

"I doubt it, but even if they do, AJ and our people will take care of them. He's put together quite a little arsenal of his own, with my help, of course. According to General Woolbright, a team of six combat trained men could easily take on a small army with the hardware AJ has on hand."

"So, after a little over two hundred and thirty years, we're really going to wipe out the Core," says McCarthy.

"No, Joshua. But we are going to do a major house cleaning. We're going to get everyone working on the same page. We're going to end the bickering and the backstabbing, and all the other bullshit that's infected the Core over the past one hundred years. We're going to make it something a man can be proud to be a part of. Together, you and I are going to make history!"

"Okay, okay. Save your speech for the podium. We still have a lot of things to do between now and the Fourth of July. First off, I think we should make the announcement a little more low key."

"What do you mean, low key?" asks Higgins sounding more than a little offended.

"I think we should keep it invitation only, but Jesus, Bill. It's July! Not only that, it's the Fourth of July! It's a celebration of freedom and our independence. Even a three-piece suit is going to get pretty warm. And instead of having your party at the Watergate Hotel, why not have it here, on your estate? I'm sure AJ would feel a bit more comfortable here. Your house is already set up with security, and your kitchen is certainly up to the task of taking care of three hundred or so guests. And even if they can't, you can have it catered just as easily here as there."

McCarthy continues, "It'll be easier for AJ and his team to watch our backs here, and the overall atmosphere will make it that much more personal. You certainly have the room for it, both inside and out. And let's not announce it as a retirement party. After all, it's going to be the Fourth of July! Make it a surprise! You could have a live orchestra or ensemble in the grand ballroom for the more mature set, and a live band or DJ out back near the lake for the up and comings. We could make our announcements over dinner, then have a spectacular fireworks display on the lake. You'll spend less money, and still get the same effect. Better! I'll bet. It'll be perfect!"

"Well, since you put it that way," Higgins thinks about it for a moment, then says, "You're right. I like it. The only downside is parking. There's no way I'm going to allow anyone to ruin my landscaping."

"You can make arrangements with a business or retail store nearby. They're going to be closed for the holiday anyway. You can hire a valet service to shuttle the cars back and forth when the guests come in, then bus them out when they're ready to leave."

"You've got room to park about twenty to thirty cars for certain dignitaries, right? Make it a first come first served basis. That'll make more people inclined to show up early or at least on time. And more importantly, it'll make anyone's attempt to escape all the more difficult."

"Okay, I must admit that it makes a lot of sense. Besides, I haven't had a party out here since I got the place. It could be fun. I'll have my secretary get started on the invitations first thing in the morning. We're going to be cutting it pretty close."

"You'll see. This will work out for the best," says Joshua, as he starts to put the file back in his briefcase.

"Hold on a minute, Joshua. Maybe I should have a look at those files. One really can't be too careful."

"I couldn't agree more," replies Joshua with an evil grin.

TLC: Chapter 38
AJ's apartment
1800 hours local time

AJ arrives at the apartment, and opens the door to see practically everything draped in dull white drop cloths. *"Well, this certainly looks inviting,"* he says to himself sarcastically, as he sets down the cardboard tray of soft drinks, and slides bag of burgers and potatoes into the oven, setting the temp on low. He stores the soft drinks in the refrigerator.

Looking down the hallway, he can see where Patrick has begun mending the bullet holes on either side of the hallway, although he hasn't touched the ones on the ceiling yet. He can also see a fairly large hole in the dividing wall between the bathroom and hallway, where Patrick must have been working on the wiring. *"Hmmm. So much for privacy."*

Looking into both bedrooms, he finds everything clean and in proper order. *"Thank goodness Julie closed these doors, or everything would be covered in dust!"* AJ goes back to the hallway and stares at the living room, then carefully pulls back the drop cloth from the couch, coffee, and end tables, then gently sets the lamps back on the end tables. He folds up the drop cloth and lays it next to the outside wall, out of the way.

Next, he lifts the drop cloth from the TV and stereo equipment, again folding it, and laying it on top of the other one. Then he turns to pull the drop cloth off the chair, near the TV, and bumps into something underneath it. He gently taps it with his foot a couple of times, and initially can't figure out what it is. Suddenly he remembers. *"It's gotta be Harry's MAC-10."* Sure enough, underneath the drop cloth, he finds the gun lying up against the chair, right where Harry had tossed it.

Just as AJ is about to pick it up with his handkerchief, there's a gentle knock at the door. He hastily covers it back up and gets up to answer the door. But as he gets close to the door, he hears the telltale sign of someone trying to unlock it. He steps off to the hinge side of the door and draws his weapon. Once unlocked, the door begins to open slowly. AJ tries to catch a glimpse of who it might be by peeking in the gap between the door and jamb, but all he can see is a dark mass. As the person clears the door, AJ slams the door closed behind him, steps in front of it, blocking their escape.

"My God son!" yells a startled Patrick. "Ya scared the hell out of me!"

"Well, you did a pretty good job of scaring me, too, you know," says AJ while taking a deep breath and holstering his weapon.

"You were going to shoot me?"

"Patrick, I had no idea it was you. But considering what's happened here the last couple of days, I don't think you can blame me for being a little edgy."

"I suppose not, me boy," he says, trying to catch his breath. "I don't suppose the offer still stands on a drink of that whiskey you have in the cupboard."

"What? I thought you said you'd rather drink…"

"I know what I said, but that was before you scared the life out of me. Just a shot to calm me nerves."

"Straight up, or over ice?" asks AJ.

"Neat, if ya please."

AJ reaches into the cabinet, pulls out a couple of highball glasses, and sets them on the counter. Then he digs in the cabinet and comes out with the bottle of Jack Daniels. He pours about two fingers worth into the first glass, when Patrick says, "A little more, if you don't mind." AJ gives him a suspicious look, but then continues to pour until he says, "Fine son. That's good." He hands Patrick his glass, then pours one for himself. The two of them retire to the living room, with AJ sitting in the chair next to Harry's gun.

"Do you mind if I ask you what brought you up here this late in the afternoon?"

"Not at all, laddie. I just came to check on the walls, to see how the spackling was coming along. Some of the holes were pretty deep, and I wanted to make sure I didn't put too much in. Sometimes the stuff will shrink or crack, and that just means it'll take that much longer to repair."

"I see you had to knock out a fair amount of the bathroom wall."

"Aye, the conduit that supplies the wires to the switches got hit and pulled free of the junction box. I've got a buddy of mine coming out tomorrow to have a look at it. We may have to take out the one side completely and replace the conduit. That alone might take the better part of the day to repair."

"I can see this is really going to put a dent in my pocketbook," AJ sighs and shakes his head.

"Don't you worry, laddie. I've got it all under control."

"Somehow, that sounds a whole lot like 'trust me', and we all know what happens when someone says that."

"Ye of little faith, me boy," says Patrick.

"Well, it's your show for now, so I'll leave you to it."

"That's the spirit!" With that comment, Patrick holds up his glass and says, "Here's to a long and happy life."

AJ reprises, "To a long and happy life." Then, both men look each other in the eye, turn up their glasses, and polish off their drinks with a single gulp.

"Ahhhh," they say in unison.

"Laddie, may I have another?"

"Patrick? It's your funeral," replies AJ, as he takes his glass to the kitchen for a refill.

"Nonsense. I've polished off an entire bottle of Mother's Milk at a single sitting, and I'm still here to tell the tale."

"I'm sure that's exactly what it is. A tale."

"Sonny, if I were a wee bit younger, I'd make you eat those words."

"Patrick? When you drink, are you normally a lover or a fighter?"

"In my younger days, I had no problem bedding down the lasses."

"That's not what I meant, Patrick. When most people drink to the point of being drunk, some love everybody, while others want to fight everybody. Which category do you fall into?"

"First off, AJ, I'm a long ways from being drunk. But secondly, and even more important, a wise man knows his limitations."

"Interesting choice of words, but you still haven't answered my question, exactly."

"Well son, I'm way too old to be fightin' a young pup the likes of you, drunk or sober."

"Good answer. The same as last time?" AJ asks as he starts to pour him a refill.

"If you would be so kind," replies Patrick.

"No problem. Here ya go."

AJ raises his glass and says, "My turn."

"Be my guest," says Patrick.

"To those who have gone before us. Semper Fi."

"Semper Fi." says Patrick, and the two of them gulp down their drinks again.

Just as AJ starts to sit down, he hears someone at the door again. He glances at his watch, then reaches under his jacket, resting his hand on his Beretta. Patrick starts to move, but AJ motions for him to stay still. Patrick's eyes are as big as saucers and are fixed on the opening door.

AJ? Are you in here?" asks Julie as she enters the door, followed by Detective Morris.

"Yes, I'm here. Patrick and I were just having a drink. Care to join us?"

"Not really. Other than a bag of chips and a Coke at FBI headquarters, I haven't had anything to eat all day. I'm starved!"

"Well, the food is in the oven, and the drinks are in the fridge. Help yourself."

"I guess I better check on the walls and see if I can give them another coat. Then I'll be on me way," says Patrick. "Thanks for the drink."

"My pleasure. And I apologize for scaring you like I did."

"No need, laddie. Like you said, things have been a little crazy around here the past couple of days. I don't blame you for being a little skittish."

"Thanks, Patrick."

"But before the weeks out, I am going to introduce you and your taste buds to one of the finest Irish Whiskeys money can buy. One taste and you'll swear you've had a taste of heaven."

"I look forward to it," says AJ. "Go ahead and do what you gotta do. Detective Morris, Julie, and I have some things to discuss."

"I shouldn't be but a minute or two, then I'll get out of your hair for the rest of the evening." Patrick gets up, sets his glass on the counter, then turns on the hallway light, inspecting his repairs as he proceeds down the hall.

AJ walks into the kitchen, and joins Julie and the detective. The three of them wolf down their sandwiches and potatoes, while waiting for Patrick to leave.

"What's the story about making sure the oven was on low?" asks Morris. "Ms. Robinson wouldn't clue me in."

"We had ordered a pizza, and I put it in the oven to keep it warm. Somehow or another, the oven was too hot, and the box began to smoke and triggered the smoke alarm."

"I can see how that could put a damper on things," replies Morris smirking a bit.

"Okay, laddie. She's all set for the night. I'm assumin' you and Julie will be stayin' next door until we get all this straightened out," says Patrick heading for the door.

"Well, I don't know. I haven't had a chance to talk to Julie about that. I overheard you mention that it's your sister's apartment."

"Aye, I was tellin' Julie, my sister, Maggie is vacationing in Ireland for a bit. She's not due back for another month or so. I'm sure she won't mind. All I ask is that you leave it the way you found it."

"Now, you're sure about that, Patrick?" asks AJ.

"Absolutely." he replies.

"Julie? What do you think?" asks AJ.

"In case you haven't noticed, I've already moved most of the food from the fridge, as well as most of the dry goods over there already. I was working on the clothes when Detective Morris showed up."

"Well then, Patrick. I guess that's a yes."

"Wonderful!" he says. "Just in case you decide to sleep in tomorrow, since it's Saturday, we won't start anything until sometime after 10."

"Sounds fine. But we may be going out tomorrow. That's one of the things I need to discuss with Julie. So, we'll just have to see how the day goes, okay?"

Patrick nods his head in agreement.

"Good evening, Patrick," says AJ.

"Good evening to you, too, AJ, Julie, Detective," replies Patrick as he walks out the door.

"Nice man, but I was beginning to think he was never going to leave," says AJ.

"He's just lonely, AJ. His wife died a couple of years ago, after a long, drawn out battle with cancer. Did you know he actually owns the building? And with his sister gone, about the only thing he hears all day is someone complaining about something."

"Okay, let's talk about what you found out, and then I'll tell you about my day."

"Well, for starters, Detective Morris showed up to see if we had come up with anything that might be useful in his investigation, and found Patrick and myself trying to repair the apartment."

"And I'm still a bit pissed off about you not reporting the second break-in this morning," interjects Morris.

"First off," replies AJ sounding a bit surly, "it wasn't a break-in, and secondly…"

"AJ, save it," says Julie sounding rather abrupt. "In the midst of our conversation, Detective Morris got a call about a homicide down the street, and the description seemed to match Harry. Turns out, it was, and in the course of searching the body, the coroner found a piece of paper that Detective Morris was able to get his hands on before anyone else could read it."

"And?" asks AJ.

"It was this address, handwritten on a piece of paper," she replies. "That's why we went to FBI headquarters, to see if we could pull up any prints, and maybe get a handwriting analysis done."

"Did they find anything?"

"Oh yeah," replies Julie.

"Was it Higgins?"

"No, it seems we have another heavy hitter in the game."

"Wait a minute," says AJ. "How much have you told Morris about what's going on? You know this is a matter of national security."

"AJ, Detective Morris is former military. He understands."

"Julie, so far, I've had to deal with at least ten men who were former military, and all of them were trying to kill me or the senator."

"I thought you looked familiar," says Morris. "You're the guy who killed those seven terrorists on the expressway earlier this week!"

"Actually, I only took care of six. The senator shot the last one."

"You said ten. What about the other three?"

"Guys! Focus!" shouts Julie.

"Sorry," says Morris.

"To answer your question AJ, I haven't told him much. I put in a call to Weathers, but all I got was his voice mail. He's evidently at the hospital with Niles."

"Well, who's this new heavy hitter?"

"He's another senator. Joshua Abrams McCarthy."

"What's his story?"

"He's in his mid to late forties, tall, good looking, comes from a long line of politicians. He's in his second term in the Senate. Married into money. Big money."

"His wife is very well known in the world of finance, business acquisitions, that kind of thing. She also runs one the largest law firms in the country."

"Joshua has a thing for exotic cars. He supposedly has a collection worth a few million dollars. He also likes to play the field, as far as women go. The paparazzi have caught him with a number of women, many of them models, over the past couple of years, but his wife seems to be rather complacent about the whole thing."

"Either that or giving him enough rope to hang himself," says AJ. "Do you think he's working with Higgins?"

"It's hard to say," replies Julie. "All of the other operatives have been former military, but Harry has no military background at all."

"What's his M.O.?" asks AJ.

Morris pipes in, "Mostly small time stuff, B&E's, assault, muscle for some of the local small time hoods."

"So, how did Harry die?"

"A bullet to the back of the head, near the base of the skull," she says. "His hands were still tied behind his back, and he was still wearing those latex gloves."

"Well, it definitely wasn't a mob hit," he replies.

"Am I the only one who didn't know that?"

"Morris, how long have you been a detective?"

"Five years."

"And you've never worked a homicide involving a mob hit before?"

"No, I've primarily worked B&E's, robberies, and occasionally vice. Remember, that's why I was here last night."

"Can't either of you guys stay on track here?" screams Julie.

"Julie, calm down, will ya? You got PMS or somethin'?"

"Don't go there, AJ. I'm warning you. Besides, what do you know about PMS?"

"I've read Cosmo."

"And just what is that supposed to mean?"

"Now look who's gotten off track," counters AJ.

"AJ? Sometimes, you're impossible."

"Okay," says AJ. "Where are we? We've had an attempted break-in resulting in an agent getting shot. Next, we have a man posing as the maintenance man, who attempts to drown you…"

"You forgot to mention that part," says Morris with a stern look on his face.

"No, I didn't," Julie shrugs her shoulders. "You just weren't paying attention."

"Then shoots up the apartment, gets picked up by a pair of phony cops, murdered, and found with a note, handwritten by a U.S. Senator, with my address on it."

"Yep. That about covers it," says Julie.

"What?" says Morris. "Am I the only one here who hasn't got a clue as to what this is all about?"

"I understand perfectly," replies Julie.

"Me, too." says AJ. "So, I guess the answer to your question is…yes."

"Look," says Morris in a pleading tone, "I'm the one who came up with the handwritten note that gives you the name and another piece of this puzzle you're working on. Don't you think I deserve some answers?"

"Maybe, but that's not a decision we can make. Like I said, this is a matter of national security," says AJ. "It'll have to come from higher up, and that's not up for discussion. You can file a complaint through your department if you want. But I can guarantee you, the only thing it will do is create more headaches for you."

Morris sighs and throws his hands up in frustration, while sliding back on the couch. AJ continues in a more sympathetic tone, "Give us the weekend. We'll talk to our boss, and see what he says. He's a pretty reasonable guy to work with, although he doesn't respond well to any type of bullying. We'll tell him how you've helped us, and with a little luck, we'll be able to fill you in by Monday. Deal?"

"Do I have a choice?"

"What do you think?" says AJ.

"Okay, Monday it is, then," he replies, as he starts walking toward the door. "Oh by the way, here's my card. If you talk to your boss over the weekend and he gives the okay, feel free to call me."

"If something happens, we'll let you know. Take it easy and have a good weekend."

"You, too," says Morris. "Talk to you Monday."

"Goodbye detective," says AJ as he closes the door. "Finally! Peace at last," he says, as if a heavy load had been lifted from his shoulders.

"What do you say we grab a few clothes, go over to 416, take a long, soaking bath, and relax a bit?" asks Julie with a devilish smile on her face.

"That sounds like a plan, but I have to do something first," he says walking back to the second bedroom.

"What's that?"

"Those phony cops forgot to pick up Harry's MAC-10 when they grabbed him and his toolbox," he says, as he comes back to the living room with a large plastic bag, and one of his assault bags. "Maybe there's a serial number or some latent prints on it somewhere." He whips the drop cloth away from the side of the chair, revealing the weapon, just as he had found it earlier. He places his opened pocketknife in the trigger guard, carefully lifting it, then eases it into the plastic bag. He seals the bag, then places it inside the assault bag.

"I wonder how they missed it?" asks Julie.

"Harry tossed it to the side when I cornered him, and it must have been partially hidden by the chair when the two of them helped Harry off the floor. And I guess Patrick just didn't see it when he was laying out the drop cloths."

"Now what?" she asks.

"We'll set the alarm, and lock up the place for the night. Next, we'll enjoy a long, relaxing bath, then snuggle up under some fresh, clean sheets together…"

"I knew there was something I forgot to tell you," she says, blushing a bit.

"What?" he asks with a puzzled look on his face.

"Maggie is an old maid."

"So? What does that have to do with snuggling under the covers together?"

"Twin beds."

"You're kidding," he says in disbelief.

"AJ? I wish I were. Believe me. By the way, do we have plans for tomorrow?"

"Yes, we do," he says with a smile. "First, we'll need to drop Harry's gun off at the FBI and have them run a full battery of tests on it and see if there's any history to it."

"I don't see that as being critical, but go on."

"Then we're going out to Higgins estate to introduce you to Senator Higgins, and a little surprise! Actually, it's not quite so little."

"And what might that be?"

"Well, if I told you, it wouldn't be a surprise, now would it?"

"I suppose not. You know it's going to be a little difficult looking him straight in the eye without trying to put it out."

"I know, but it'll be worth it. Trust me!"

TLC: Chapter 39

Ms. O'Malley's apartment
Saturday morning
June 18, 2011, 0700 hours local time

Morning breaks, and AJ begins to stir. As he slowly opens his eyes, the first things that come into focus are the pink walls, and the frilly, flowered, multi-colored drapes hanging over the windows. *"Oh shit! Where am I?"* Then he remembers he's in Ms. O'Malley's apartment, next door. *"Oh God! Thank you! Thank you!"* Still trying to get his sea legs, he steps out into the hallway, with the intent of going to the bathroom, but finds himself standing in the living room instead. *"What tha…?"* Ms. O'Malley's apartment is a mirror image of his. *"This is going to take some getting used to,"* he says shaking his head. *"Thank God I didn't have to go to the can in the middle of the night."*

As he wanders down the hall to the bathroom, he notices a number of Ms. O'Malley's family pictures along both sides. Many of them are from the 50's and 60's. One in particular catches his eye. It's a picture of a much younger Patrick, decked out in his dress Army uniform, with a young lady standing on either side of him, arm in arm. The one on his right is wearing a wedding gown and holding a bouquet of flowers in her right hand. The one on his left is wearing a somewhat plainer and darker gown, holding a smaller bouquet in her left hand. AJ feels a bit of emotion coming over him. He rubs his eyes, turns away, and continues down the hall to the bathroom. After he taps the kidneys, he stands before the mirror, staring at himself, lost in thought.

Julie slips up behind him, wraps her arms around him, and says with a song in her voice, "Good morning! I slept like a rock last night. How about you?"

"Like the rock slept on me. You mind turning the volume down a notch or two? Like a whisper?"

"This doesn't sound like the AJ I know. What's wrong?"

"Strange room, strange bed, soft mattress. I don't think I drifted off to sleep until sometime around 0300 or so. I feel like my back's out of whack or something. Legs are stiff, too. Maybe we should just rough it and move back into my place."

"No way, Jose. Once they start sanding on the walls and ceiling, there'll be dust hanging in the air for hours. It'll be in our clothes, our food, everywhere. You can go if you want, but I'm staying right here.

"Okay, you win. I'll figure something out. Maybe I'd be better off sleeping on the floor."

"I don't think it's going to take anything that drastic, but yes, we'll figure something out. Now tell me. When do you want to get the show on the road?"

"First things first. I'd like to get something in my belly before I start planning out the rest of the day. Besides, I'm still trying to wake up.

"Do you want me to make breakfast? I make a pretty mean ham and cheese omelet," she says proudly.

"Sure, why not. I've been carrying you all week."

"Hey! That was a little below the belt, don't you think?"

"Julie, you're right. I'm sorry. I'm just a bit cranky today. I'm a pain in the ass when I don't feel good."

"You know? I'm the one who shouldn't be feeling well. After all, I'm the one who slammed into that column at the office, got zapped with a stun gun, and a swimming lesson in the tub."

"Yeah, but at least you have those fun pills to take the edge off. I don't."

"AJ? For your information, I haven't taken any of those fun pills since yesterday morning. Would you like one? How about two? I'll get them for you if you'd like."

"You know what? I think I'll just take a couple of Advils and lay in the tub for a little while. The hot water should help my muscles relax, and I'll be good to go."

"Are you sure about that?"

"Yeah, I'm sure." AJ leans over and turns on the hot water to start his bath.

"So that's it?" she asks with some resentment in her voice. "What?"

"We've been apart for almost five years, yet after being back together for less than five days, we've already stopped talking to each other." Tears are welling up in her eyes, as she turns to walk away.

"Whoa, whoa, whoa," he says while gently grabbing her arms, and pulling her back to him. "I haven't stopped talking to you. I'm just tired, and stiff as hell from that damn soft bed. Honest."

"You're not just saying that, are you?" she asks while trying to fight back the tears.

"Look Julie. I love you from the bottom of my heart. That's the truth. But we've both had a rough week, and that bed in there didn't help matters one little bit, and to wake up in a strange room with pink walls and frou-frou drapes? Come on. There's only so much a guy like me can handle in a week."

"Well, since you put it that way…" She turns around in his arms, facing him, smiles, and says, "I guess I can forgive you this time. But don't think you're going to be able to make a habit of this." Catching him completely off guard, she gives him a light punch to the stomach.

"Hey! What did you do that for?" he asks rubbing his stomach. "That hurt, you know."

"I'd start your bath, if I were you," she says, walking down the hallway. "Breakfast will be ready in twenty minutes, and counting."

"You know? Those biscuits you like take twenty-four minutes to bake, and you haven't even turned the oven on yet."

"We're having wheat toast!"

"But what if I said I wanted biscuits?" he asks.

"I'd have to say, tough!" she yells back.

"Oh…Okay, I guess."

"What did you say?"

"Nothing. Never mind," he yells back. *"Somehow, I get the feeling today is going to be a pretty interesting day,"* he says to himself, as he eases into the hot steaming water.

The hot bath and Advils do the trick for AJ. Plus, Julie's ham and cheese omelets are perfect. Even the coffee tastes great. The two of them take their turn in the bathroom without a hitch, and within the hour, they're ready to start the day.

Walking to the elevator, Julie says, "Okay. What's the surprise?"

"Patience, my dear. Patience."

"AJ? You're making me crazy with this," she says in a frustrated tone, while entering the elevator.

286

"Well, the sooner we start moving on down the road, the sooner you're going to find out," he says as he pushes the button for the lobby.

"Can we pick up my car on the way? We're not going to be that far from the office. We can be in and out in five minutes."

"Sorry, but that's not on the program for this morning," he replies, as the doors open on the main floor.

"I could have you arrested for kidnapping. You do know that, don't you?"

"That's going to be pretty hard to prove, especially since you have a loaded Sig 226 in your purse. In fact, I could probably turn it around on you and claim you were kidnapping me."

"Fat chance."

"Julie? It's Saturday. Will you just try to relax and enjoy the day? It's going to be fun," he says as the two of them walk out to his car. "Okay?"

"If it isn't, do I get a refund?"

"Will you just get in the car? Please?"

"Okay, okay," she says reluctantly.

"First stop? FBI. Second stop? Disneyland!"

Julie does a double take at AJ and says, "What?"

"Never mind. Just hang on." he says, as he speeds out of the parking lot toward FBI headquarters.

After they drop off the MAC-10 at FBI headquarters, they head out toward Higgins' estate. AJ takes out his phone and calls Higgins, but gets his voice mail. "Good morning, sir. It's 0945 hours, and I wanted to let you know Julie and I are on the way out. We should get there within the next twenty to thirty minutes. I'm calling security as an alternate. Bye." He ends the call, then calls security.

"Security. State your name and business."

"Hi. This is AJ, who's this?"

"Hi, AJ! It's Tony. How are you this morning?"

"Fine, and you?"

"Same here, AJ," says Tony. "I hear we have an armory up on the second floor. We've been keeping an eye on it for you. And we see the boss got a decked out Hummer! Sweet! All the guys are drooling over it!"

"Well, I hope they haven't gotten any of it on the paint. Jeffrey will have a fit!"

"No sir, just kiddin'," says Tony, chuckling a bit.

"I know. Say, do you know where Higgins is? I just tried his cell phone, and all I got was his voice mail."

"He probably can't hear it. He and a handful of guys are down at the shooting range warming up. The senator thought you and he were going to pair up."

"Oh shit! That's right. Tony, can you send someone down there to tell him I'm on my way. I'll get there as quick as I can, okay?"

"Sure thing, AJ. I'm sure he'll be glad to hear it."

"And would you ask George to take the Remington down there for me? I'd appreciate it."

"No problem AJ. Consider it done.".

"Thanks, Tony."

"See you in a few." AJ ends the call.

"It seems like the surprise is on you," says Julie.

"I'm afraid so. I'm sorry Julie, but Higgins mentioned it to me a while back, and with all the things that have gone on this week, I forgot about it. I'm sorry."

"Okay, so where does that leave me?"

"Well, I guess you can take the car and go over to Weathers house if you want. I'm sure he's already digging into that file and CD."

"That sounds like a good idea, but what about you? How will you get home?"

"Well, you could pick me up later in the day, or I could catch a cab, meet you at Weathers' place, then we could stop by the office and pick up your car."

"Now that sounds like a good idea," she replies.

"There's something else I need to tell you. Higgins has done something completely out of character."

"He did? What was that?"

"He went to bat for me and got my Hummer replaced."

"He did what?"

"Yep. I can't believe it myself. He was so impressed with how mine performed that day on the expressway, he ordered one for himself, and talked the coach builder into buying mine back, and replacing it."

"I just find that so hard to believe," she replies.

"Me too. I saw it, touched it, and I still can't believe it."

"And it's at Higgins' estate?"

"No, the company that's building it brought it out to show me when they delivered his new limo. They're still in the process of transferring bits and pieces from the other one."

"One question."

"Yeah? What's that?"

"Is this one yellow, too?"

"No, thank goodness. It's charcoal gray. It's pretty unassuming, actually."

"I'll bet it is," she says while trying not to giggle.

AJ takes out his phone and calls security again.

"Hi AJ," says Tony.

"Yeah, it's me again. Would you mind asking one of your men to meet me at the gate? I've got Julie with me, and I'm going to let her take the car."

"Sure AJ. No problem. What's your ETA?"

"Oh, about five maybe ten minutes."

"I'll have someone there before you arrive."

"Thanks, Tony."

"No problem, AJ."

"See you in a few."

"What was all that about?" asks Julie.

"This way, you don't have to come inside the estate. The place will really blow your mind. Once you see it, you're going to want the ten cent tour, and let me tell you, ten cents wouldn't begin to cover it. The place is huge. It's got sixteen bedrooms, eighteen bathrooms, a grand ballroom, an indoor swimming pool, a library, a formal dining room, and a commercial kitchen. There are fountains and gardens all over the place. You could easily spend the day there."

"I get the picture, AJ. Calm down."

"I guess what I'm trying to tell you is, I'd like to show you around the place, or at least have George give you a tour. The place is both impressive and beautiful."

"I'll be it is. Maybe next time, okay?"

"Let's plan on next weekend. What do you say?"

"That sounds good to me, AJ," she says with somewhat of a forced smile.

"Okay, here we are," he says, pulling up to the gate. Tony's waiting for him in the golf cart. "Do you know how to get to Weathers' place from here?" he asks.

"Yeah, I'm sure I can find it," she replies. "Go down there and show 'em how it's done."

"I will. Julie?"

"Yes?"

"Please be careful," he says. "The past couple of days have been unnerving for me. I was afraid I might lose you. They were probably the worst days of my life. Please, keep me posted."

"I will," she says in an appreciative way. "Love you."

"Love you, too," he replies, as he gives her a kiss on the cheek. They wave to each other as she drives away.

AJ rushes through the gate and hops on the golf cart with Tony. "Is this the express bus to the shooting range?"

"Yes, sir! And the party's already started," he says as he starts driving back to the house.

"What do you mean, party?"

"The senator usually has about six or eight people over, once or twice a month for skeet shooting. They talk a little, shoot a little, drink a little…"

"Wait a minute. You said drink? It's not even noon yet, and you say they're shooting and drinking?"

"Yeah, most of the time, things are pretty cool, but every once in a while, someone drinks too much and does something stupid. Just before you came to work here, the guy who used to operate the trap machine stepped out of the bunker to take a leak. Everybody was supposed to have their guns cleared, house rules. Some yahoo picked up a gun from the rack and pointed it at him. It turned out the damn thing was loaded, and the poor guy took a shot to the legs. Luckily, it was a target load of #9's, but it took the doctors almost an hour to pick out all the shot."

"Pull up to the house for a minute, will ya?"

"What for? George has your shotgun already down there."

"Just do it," he says with anger in his voice.

"Whatever you say, AJ," replies a concerned Tony. Tony pulls up to the front of the house and stops. As AJ bails out of the cart and bounds up the steps to the front door, Tony asks, "Do you want me to wait for you?"

"No thanks, I'll walk."

Walking down the hall, AJ passes one of the security guards. "Good morning, AJ," says the guard with a smile.

"No, it isn't," he replies in almost what sounds like a growl.

The guard is taken aback by the tone of his comment. "Have I done something wrong, sir?" he asks.

"Not yet," he says, as he passes the young man. "Do yourself a favor and stay away from the shooting range for the next twenty minutes or so."

The young man stops dead in his tracks, then turns toward AJ and says, "May I ask why, sir?"

"No, you can't," he replies without breaking step or looking back.

"Yes, sir," replies the visibly shaken security guard.

AJ takes the elevator to the second floor, and walks over to the armory. Standing between the camera and the keypad to prevent anyone from seeing his access code, he opens the door, goes inside, then closes the door behind him.

The room is pretty snug, considering all the cabinets, shelves, and hardware in there. He unlocks the padlock that secures a cable run through the trigger guards of the Benelli M3's, and takes one of them. He then reinserts the cable and locks it again. He performs a cursory inspection, checks the action, bolt, and firing pin. Everything appears to be working properly. He opens a couple of drawers before his finds the one holding the five-round boxes of 12-gauge ammo. He loads seven rounds of 00-buckshot into the feed tube, pulls the bolt back, loads one into the barrel, then adds the eighth round. He drops the two remaining rounds into his left jacket pocket. Ready to leave, AJ opens the door to find Tony standing there waiting for him.

"AJ? Sorry man, but I've got to ask you. What are you up to?"

"Nothing. Just a little target practice."

"Well, I can't say that I've ever shot skeet before, but I don't think that shotgun, or the ammo you have stored in there, is designed for it."

"Really?" says AJ as he lays the shotgun on his right shoulder. "Let's find out." AJ starts walking toward the elevator, and Tony steps in front of him again. AJ stops, stares at the floor a moment, then looks up at Tony and says, "What?"

"You're not going to do something foolish are you? Like shoot somebody or somethin'?" asks Tony looking more than a little concerned.

"Tell me something Tony," says AJ sounding very disgusted. "What's more foolish than mixing guns and alcohol?"

"AJ, I know I can't stop you or nothin', but please think about this before you kill anybody. Those are some pretty important people down there."

"Tony? What makes you think I'm going to kill anybody?"

"A loaded shotgun, and looks that could kill without one?"

"This?" says AJ, as he points at himself. "I've just got my game face on, that's all." AJ presses the button for the elevator, and as the doors start to open, both AJ and Tony start in. "Look, Tony. There are certain rules that I live by, and there are no deviations from those rules. Rule number one. A man is always responsible for his actions. Always. It doesn't matter if he's drunk or sober. The copout that he was drunk and didn't know what he was doing, is exactly that, a copout. If a man drinks, he knows his judgment and reflexes become impaired. So if a guy gets drunk, then hurts himself or someone else, he knew what he was doing, before he did it. Rule number two. I enforce rule number one."

"Somehow, I think everyone down there is going to be in for a big surprise," says Tony sighing and rolling his eyes.

"Come on, Tony. It's going to be fun!" AJ's eyes are dancing.

"I think that's going to depend on whose point of view you're looking from."

As the door opens on the main floor, the two of them start walking down the hall toward the shooting range. "Just don't say anything about the shotgun, okay?"

"AJ? I'm not saying nothin' about nothin'!"

"Good!" says AJ with a wicked smile on his face. "Oh! And I'd try to stay out of the line of fire, if I were you."

"Line of fire?" Tony stops so fast, you'd think he stepped into a puddle of super glue. "Oh shit! You *are* going to kill somebody! Tell you what, AJ. I think I'll take a rain check on this little party, and wait for the next one."

"That's up to you, but if the senator wants me to team up with him for a little skeet competition, this will be the last party where alcohol is served."

"Here, take my radio," says Tony. "I'll pick up another one back in the office. Holler if you need anything."

"Thanks. I'll do that." As Tony turns and starts to head back to the office, AJ stops, turns and says to Tony, "You *do* have the paramedics on speed dial, right?" Tony just shakes his head and keeps on walking. AJ continues down the path toward the shooting range.

Gunshots and laughter can be heard in the distance. AJ is starting to get angry again. He shifts the shotgun from his shoulder to a more ready position with both hands holding the shotgun across his chest.

Rounding the corner, he sees five men, wearing the obligatory hunting garb, each standing in one of the firing positions. Higgins is standing in the far right position. Two other men, dressed in similar clothing, are standing next to a portable bar, each holding a highball glass, while three other men, casually dressed, and obviously bodyguards for one or more of Higgins' guests, are standing off to the side, under a large oak tree. So far, none of them have seen AJ yet. He decides to prop the Benelli against a tree, out of sight from the range.

As luck would have it, George is tending bar. AJ casually walks up to him and asks, "How many of the guests are drinking alcohol?"

"Well, the two men standing right over there are. The one on the left is having Jack with Coke, and the man next to him is having a screwdriver. From left to right on the line, the first man is on his third beer. The guy next to him is clean, as is the next guy. They never drink when they shoot."

George continues, "The one standing next to Senator Higgins is working on a Bloody Mary, his third, and the senator is faking them out with ginger ale over ice."

AJ says, "Tony was telling me that before I started to work here, one of the senator's guests shot the trap operator. Is he here?"

"Yes, he's the one drinking the Bloody Mary. You know? He really can't hold his liquor. He hasn't hit a single clay this round. Not one. And once he gets three or four drinks under his belt, his common sense takes a vacation, if you know what I mean."

"No, no I don't. Care to enlighten me?"

"The guy gets belligerent, verbally abusive, and downright mean. Two of those guys over there are his. I understand they're constantly trying to keep him out of trouble. Hardly any of the nightspots around D.C. will even let him in anymore. The guy's a walking time bomb."

"Who is he? What does he do?"

"His name is Chad, Chad Oliver. His family is rich, old money. But he's also made his own fortune playing the stock market. He's been accused of being involved with some insider trading, but they've never proven it. Fancies himself being a big game hunter or something. But word is, he's never been out on a hunt in his life. He'd probably get lost the moment he passed the city limits. His idea of roughing it would be having to make his own drink."

"That bad, huh?"

"Just wait. This round is almost over. I'll bet he comes over and orders another drink. Watch."

Sure enough, at the end of the round, Chad meanders over to the bar and says, "Hey asshole! Give me another fuckin' Bloody Mary! And put some booze in it this time! I swear that last one was a fuckin' virgin!" Chad is finding it difficult to stand, and is leaning against the bar to help steady himself.

AJ is standing there, watching Chad, and his temper is rising. Just as AJ's about to say something, Higgins walks up to him and says, "I guess you forgot about our little game today."

"I'm afraid so, sir. I've had a lot of things on my mind this week, and it just kind of fell to the wayside."

"Don't worry, AJ. All is forgiven. George even brought your shotgun down for you."

"Sir, I hate to rain on your parade, especially since you've done so much for me. But I have one unbreakable rule."

"And what's that?"

"I don't drink and play with guns. And I don't hang around with people who do."

"AJ, those are pretty strong words."

Chad turns to face them and says in his drunken stupor, "What kind of pussy won't drink and shoot?" Chad's two bodyguards have pricked up their ears and are watching the situation.

"You're lookin' at him," says AJ.

"Is that a fact? I'll bet you a thousand dollars I can outshoot you just like this."

"Senator, did you hear that?" asks AJ.

"Yes, I did AJ, but you don't want to take advantage of the poor boy. He's not himself when he drinks."

"So, you know how he gets when he drinks."

"AJ, what are you implying?" asks Higgins, sensing some impending doom.

AJ is staring at Chad with a wicked smile on his face and says, "I've only been standing here a few minutes, but so far, the only thing I've seen you hit is air."

"I'm not doing that bad. I've hit a few of them," he says smugly, looking away.

"Anybody keeping score?" asks AJ. The man drinking the screwdriver tries to hide the score sheet. AJ walks over to him and says, "Mind if I take a look at that?" The man reluctantly hands it to him. "Hmm…Tell me. Are you a computer expert?"

"Well, no. I'm in banking," he replies smugly. "Why?"

"I was just wondering whether you were keeping score or working on a new binary computer program."

He looks away, embarrassed by AJ's comment. "I have no idea what you're talking about," says the banker.

AJ holds up the score sheet for everyone to see. "Well, I'll explain it to you. If you notice the scores of Charlie, Roger, Vince, and Bill, there are a lot of ones, along with a few zeroes mixed in here and there. But if you look at Chad's score here, he has a perfect row of…*zeros*!" A couple of the guys are snickering behind Chad's back, as AJ continues to taunt him. "I don't know about the rest of you *gentlemen*, but it's pretty obvious to me that Chad here, can't hit the broad side of a barn!"

Chad's bodyguards are starting to approach AJ from behind. Chad's face turns beet red, incensed by AJ's comments, and as rage overcomes him, he yells, "I'll show you!" He starts to raise his shotgun to shoot AJ, but AJ deflects the barrel away from his body, just before Chad squeezes the trigger. The gun goes off, and the blast lands just inches away from the feet of his approaching bodyguards!

In the blink of an eye, AJ sweeps Chad's feet out from under him, while simultaneously snatching the gun from his hands. For a moment or two, Chad appears to levitate, perfectly parallel to the ground. After landing flat on his back, AJ twirls the shotgun in his hands, drops to one knee, and thrusts the butt to less than an inch from Chad's face. AJ pauses for a moment, allowing Chad to evaluate his situation. The bodyguards start to advance on AJ again. While still facing Chad, AJ lowers the shotgun toward the bodyguards and says, "I think there's still another round in here, and I can assure you, I'm not drunk." Both men stop dead in their tracks.

"AJ!" yells Higgins. "That's enough! I have half a mind to fire you."

AJ stands, breaks the action, and ejects both shells; one fired, one live. Both guards breathe a sigh of relief. AJ then walks

296

over to Higgins, hands him the shotgun, stares into his eyes, and snarls, "And what about the other half?"

"Go back to the house and wait for me in the library."

"Is that an order, sir?"

"You can call it anything you want!"

"Yes, sir," snaps AJ, as he turns and starts walking back to the house. He stops by the tree, picks up the Benelli, then continues on.

While Chad's bodyguards help Chad back to his feet, Vince walks up to Senator Higgins, and says, "Bill? Charlie and I have decided we're going to call it a day. I think we've all had enough excitement this weekend."

"Come on guys, the show's over." Higgins forces a smile while trying to smooth things out. "The day's still young. AJ was just letting off a little steam, that's all."

"Actually, Charlie and I agree with AJ. It's not a good idea to mix guns with alcohol. People have a tendency to get careless, and someone eventually gets hurt, or killed," he says, as he looks over in Chad's direction.

"What are you lookin' at?" snarls Chad. Vincent turns away without a response.

"And for future reference, don't bother inviting either of us if you're going to be serving alcohol on the range. It's stuff like this that gives the sport a bad name."

"Faggots!" yells Chad.

After Vincent's remarks, everyone starts packing up and heading for home. As Chad starts to leave, he staggers up to Higgins sneering, "You better put a leash on your boy, before something happens to him."

"Son, you better hope you don't piss him off any worse than you already have, because he'll turn you and your boys into sushi faster than you can say Japanese Take Out."

"We'll just have to see about that." Chad turns to his men and growls, "Come on! Let's get outta here."

AJ walks down the hallway to the elevator, returns to the second floor, and places the shotgun and extra shells back in their proper places. He decides to leave the shotgun loaded, although he ejects the round from the chamber, as a safety precaution. As he opens the door to leave, he finds Tony standing there once again. This time he has a big smile on his face. "Man! That was awesome!"

"What was?"

"Taking Chad down like that! Man, that was so cool. I couldn't keep up with your hands!"

"I thought you went back to security."

"I did!" he exclaims. "We watched the whole thing on the cameras. The whole thing's on video!"

"You're kidding," AJ says disbelievingly.

"Nope. Everything. I wish we could have gotten the audio, though. I bet you had some pretty cool things to say." AJ is blushing. "But I've got to ask you something."

"What's that?" asks AJ.

"Why did you take the shotgun down there if you weren't going to use it?"

"That's a very good question, Tony." He smiles, secures the door to the armory, then starts walking toward the elevator, with Tony in tow. The door closes and they start to descend to the first floor.

"Aren't you gonna' tell me?" he asks.

"Nope. You figure it out."

"Damnit, AJ. That's not fair."

"Just think about it for awhile. I've got a meeting with the senator. But, I'll look you up before I leave."

"Promise?"

AJ holds up two fingers in the fashion of the Boy Scouts salute and says, "Scout's honor."

"Okay," Tony replies sounding disappointed. As both of them leave the elevator, Tony heads back to security, while AJ walks toward the library.

When AJ enters the library, he finds Higgins already standing in front of one of the large picture windows overlooking the gardens, holding a glass of Jack Daniels over ice.

"Close the doors, and have a seat," he says in an authoritative tone while gazing out the window. AJ does as he asks, and sits down.

Higgins continues, "You know? On the Fourth of July, we're going to have one hell of a party here. Music, food, celebrities, fireworks, and I'm going to announce my intention to run for the office of President of the United States." Higgins pauses a moment, turns and slowly starts walking toward his desk and AJ. "Do you have any idea how much it costs to run a campaign of this magnitude?"

"No sir, I…"

"Millions!" he yells. "Millions! And we're coming out of the gate behind a lot of power hitters already shaking hands and kissing babies. Do you have *any* idea as to what you just did out there?" AJ is biting his tongue.

"The Olivers have their fingers in everything. Banking, finance, the stock market, international trade, oil… Everything. Chad's father and I go way back, before that little shit was even born." Higgins stares at a framed black and white photo near the corner of his desk. It's a picture of Simon and Higgins, standing shoulder to shoulder, while they were Thailand. "Back then, Simon, Chad's dad, and I flew together out of Thailand, over Laos, Cambodia, and Vietnam. We were fresh out of school, and we both had the flying bug."

"The CIA was paying us good money to see the Orient from the air, along with dodging the occasional pot shots and triple-A the Commies threw at us every now and then. But we were young and bulletproof. At least we felt like we were. Unfortunately, some of our flying buddies weren't so lucky."

"All of us had something going on the side, too, a hobby so to speak. Some of us ran guns, drugs, people, etc. But not Simon. His head was in numbers."

"Some of us had our own oriental wives over there. We'd have one of the men dress up in uniform and pass him off as a preacher," he said with a smile as those memories began to fill his eyes. "Then we'd go through the motions of getting married. We saw it as a way of minimizing our exposure to some of the diseases they had over there. Some of that shit was pretty nasty."

"But Simon looked at it from a different perspective. He decided to set up a brothel, complete with a restaurant, a strip club, a barbershop and a clinic. There was always a nurse or doctor on the premises. Before a girl could work there, she'd have to get checked out. And once she was cleared, she was allowed a limited number of regulars, all of them military. The girls were put on salary and lived there 24/7. They also had the option of working in the restaurant, strip club, or barbershop."

"Even the men had to be checked out before they could hook up with one of the girls, and proper protection was a must. If any of the girls got caught letting the guys mess with them without protection, they were gone. And any guys trying to force the girls to do them without using protection were barred from the place."

"He'd occasionally arrange fashion shows for the girls, so they'd always look nice. He had stuff flown in from places like Fredrick's of Hollywood, to really nice things from Paris and Japan. His place wasn't cheap, but at least the guys knew they weren't going to be taking anything home, plus they could get a good meal and a haircut."

"Even with all the things he was doing for the girls, he was making money hand over fist. And if you think about it, his side job was probably the safest, and made the most sense. Plus the guy got laid every night!"

AJ says, "That's all fine and good sir, but I don't see…"

"AJ, the Olivers are one of the key players in my election bid. With their help and influence across the country, we've got a fighting chance of not only getting the Democratic nomination, but winning this election. While I might have a chance without them, I'd certainly feel better knowing I had them in my corner. Son, I want you to apologize to Chad."

"What? Sir, that's just not going to happen! First of all, I'm not your son. Secondly, you must be out of your mind. He just tried to shoot me! He's a loose cannon! Tony tells me he shot one of the staff not that long ago, and George says he's been banned from practically every nightclub in Washington. As far as I'm concerned I just did you and him a favor!"

"How do you figure?"

"For starters, he just found out that not everybody is going to back down, just because he's an Oliver. He also found out his bodyguards aren't always going to be able to protect him."

"Anything else?"

"Yeah! He can't shoot for shit!"

"Now AJ, I'll admit he's still got a lot to learn about the real world, but…"

"Senator, don't bother asking me again, because I'm not changing my mind. I don't care if you threaten to fire me, take the Hummer, or anything else. I don't have much that I can call my own. I'm a simple man, really. But I have a strong sense of what I feel to be right and wrong. And from that, I've established some basic principles that I try to live by, day by day. It's those principles that kept me alive all those years in the Marine Corps, and I'm not about to compromise them now. Not for you or anybody else."

"Well, I guess that's it then," sighs Higgins, as he turns toward the window again.

"Should I call Weathers, or do you want to do it?" asks AJ.

"What for?" asks Higgins.

"I thought you just fired me," replies AJ.

"No, I can't do that."

"But you just said…"

"AJ, I know what I just said," he says while still gazing out the window. "No, I think I need to nip this in the bud and talk to Simon."

"Is there anything else, sir?" asks AJ.

"As a matter of fact, yes, there is. I got a call from Secure-1 Executive Protection Services today. They had some sort of glitch in their office and the files of the bodyguards were never sent."

"So, are they on their way?" asks AJ.

"They're going to send them along with the bodyguards early next week."

"Any specific day or time?"

"No, the person who normally takes care of their travel arrangements has been off the past few days, but should be back on Monday."

"You said the party's going to be here, on the Fourth, right?"

"Yes, we'll be using a valet service recommended by the security company, and arrangements have been made with a local retailer to rent their parking lot for the evening. There's a service drive that's normally kept locked that we'll use to keep the traffic moving in one direction. You'll need to have guards posted at both gates. You'll also need to order a couple of portable guardhouses for them as well, just in case we have foul weather."

301

"As for entertainment, I've hired the university's stringed ensemble to play in the grand ball room, but I haven't decided what I want to do about music for the younger people and the fireworks display."

"May I make a suggestion?" asks AJ.

"Certainly."

"Your detailer, Jeffrey is a DJ. On the weekends, he works at a club called Sal's Place, downtown. I haven't seen him work, but if he can handle music as well as he details cars, I don't think you could go wrong using him. He's even got a stage name. Doo Whopp."

"Do what?" asks Higgins.

"No sir. Doo Whopp," AJ says. "I'll bet he'd jump at the chance to do something like this for you, and I'm sure his price would be more than reasonable."

"Doo Whopp." Higgins sighs and shakes his head. "Where on earth do the kids get these names?"

"What do you say, sir?"

"Fine, fine."

"Do you want to tell him, or should I?"

"Be my guest, AJ. I have more important things on my mind right now. I need to contact the caterers again, call the landscaping service…" Higgins' voice tapers off as he continues to gaze out the window.

"Well, if there's nothing else."

"No, no, go ahead. Enjoy your weekend. We'll start fresh on Monday."

"Very well, sir. See you Monday."

"0800. Don't be late."

"I won't sir. Good day, Senator."

"Good bye, AJ." As AJ opens the door to leave the library, Higgins says, "Close the door behind you, if you don't mind. I'd like a little privacy right now."

"Yes, sir," he replies, and closes the door behind him. AJ starts down the hall on his way to the garage, when he remembers that he promised Tony an explanation. "AJ to Central. AJ to Central."

"Central, go ahead AJ."

"Is Tony available?"

302

"Charlie One is walking the grounds, sir."

"How's that?" asks AJ.

"Charlie One to AJ. Charlie One to AJ."

"This is AJ, go ahead Charlie One."

"Meet me at the north garage."

"Roger that Tony, I mean Charlie One," says AJ smiling and shaking his head, as he starts walking toward the garage.

"Charlie One, clear."

AJ meets up with Tony at the garage, which is also where Higgins' new Hummer is parked.

"AJ?" says Tony. "This thing's impressive as hell!"

"Have you sat in it?" asks AJ.

"Are you kidding? Hell no! I'd never do anything like that without someone's permission. Besides, I think the thing's locked and the alarm's on."

AJ walks over to Jeffrey's office, turns on the light, and checks the keyboard. Sure enough, the keys are hanging there. Walking back to the Hummer, he disarms the alarm, causing the horn to honk and the lights to flash momentarily. "Go ahead. Get in."

"Wow! This thing's a little tight for a guy like me," he says. "But this thing is loaded! I've never seen anything like this before, except maybe in a magazine or somethin'. Computer... GPS...DVD."

AJ inserts the key into the ignition and starts it. The engine roars to life. VROOM! It catches Tony completely off guard. "Holy shit AJ! Is this thing alive or what?"

"Funny. Jeffrey said the same thing the other day. Hmm. I wonder if Jeffrey did a little fiddling around here." AJ reaches up and presses one of the Home Link buttons, and sure enough, the garage door starts to open. AJ smiles and says, "Will you look at that." AJ moves the shifter into Drive, and just barely touches the throttle, and the tires chirp in protest. AJ looks over to Tony, and he's all smiles.

"Maybe we can go cruisin' one day. What do you say?" asks Tony.

"Let's hold off until I get my Hummer, okay?"

"Sounds like a plan. Tell me, AJ. Since you have no wheels, how are you gettin' home?"

"Would you mind calling me a cab?"

"I have a better idea. I just happen to have a cousin who runs a limo service. I'll see if he can pick you up. Where are you going?"

"1539 Adams Street."

"I'll give him a call and see if he's got something available."

Sure enough, less than a half hour later, Tony's cousin shows up in a stretched white Lincoln Town Car. At first, AJ feels a little weird getting in back, rather than driving, but after settling into the comfortable and plush leather seat, those feelings quickly disappear.

As AJ's limo passes through the gates, he doesn't notice the car parked across the street. Inside it are Chad and his two bodyguards.

"I want somebody to keep an eye on him, and find out who is head of security today," says Chad.

"What have you got on your mind, Mr. Oliver?" asks Vinny, one of his bodyguards.

"I want that son of a bitch dead! Nobody touches me like that. Nobody!" he yells at the top of his lungs. "Nobody!"

"But boss, he's Secret Service! We could get in a lot of trouble killin' him," whines the other bodyguard, named Marko.

"Do you think I give a fuck about what you think? I told you I want him dead! What part of dead don't you understand?"

"What about the head of security? What do you want to do with him?"

"Higgins was telling me they've upgraded their security cameras and have recorders on everything. There are at least two cameras down by the range. I want the tapes from those recorders."

"I don't know boss," says Vinny. "That sounds like it could get a little sticky."

"What is it with you guys? Are both of you turning soft on me or something?"

"No boss! It's nothin' like that. It's just we've never tangled with the feds before, you know."

"You know what? Pull up to the gate. Do it now!"

"But Mr. Oliver, we just left there."

"Are you fuckin' deaf? Listen to what I'm saying. Pull up to the gate...*right fuckin' now!*"

"Yes sir, Mr. Oliver," cowers Marko. He pulls up to the gate, and presses the call button on the keypad.

"Hi Mr. Oliver. Did you forget something?"

"Yes, I think I left my sunglasses down at the range."

"I could have one of the guards try to find them for you and drop them in the mail."

"They're actually kind of sentimental to me, a gift from my mother, just before she passed away. I made a special trip back just to pick them up. I hope you understand."

"Very well. I'll have the supervisor meet you at the steps and escort you down to the range."

"Thank you."

"I didn't know your mother was dead." says Marko.

"She's not, you idiot!"

"But what about the sunglasses?" he asks.

"When was the last time you saw me wearing sunglasses?"

"But boss. I don't understand."

"Just shut up and drive, will ya'?"

Tony is standing in front of the house when Chad's limo pulls up to the curb. Chad lowers his window and says, "I just came back to get my sunglasses. I think I left them down at the range."

"Mr. Oliver? One of my men just walked down there and found nothing, and I had another one of my guys review some of the video taken this morning down at the range. None of it showed you wearing sunglasses."

"What's your name?" asks Chad.

"Most of my friends call me Tony, but it's Anthony to you."

"Who's the supervisor here, Anthony?"

"I am, Mr. Oliver."

"Well, Anthony, I'd like to buy those tapes taken down at the range this morning. Tell me. How much are they worth to you?"

"They're not mine to give, Mr. Oliver. But if the senator says you can have a copy, I would imagine whatever the cost of the disc is, plus a small fee for the copying charge."

Chad pulls out a wad of one hundred dollar bills, and starts folding them, one at a time, then places them on the lip of the window. "I don't think you understand, Anthony. I want the

305

originals. How much are they worth to you?" he asks with a wicked smile on his face.

Tony flips the bills back into his face and says, "They're certainly not worth losing my job over. I'd suggest you leave while you can. And by the way, you're on candid camera right now," he says, while pointing to the camera behind him.

"You're going to regret this Anthony!" he yells.

"Oh. And Mr. Oliver? I've been recording this conversation, too," he says, pulling a compact digital recorder from his shirt pocket. "Have a good day."

"Get us out of here! Go! Go!" Marko speeds around the loop and heads back to the gate. "That son of a bitch! I'll show him who's smarter."

"What are we going to do Mr. Oliver?"

"I haven't decided yet, but for now, I want to find out everything there is to know about AJ and our new friend Anthony."

"Boss, I think I've seen Anthony before," says Vinny.

"Yeah? Where?"

"On TV, except his name isn't Anthony, it's Samson."

"Samson? Like in the Bible Samson? Are you saying he's an actor?"

"No, wrestling. I'm pretty sure I've seen him on one of the local cable channels. He's not bad either."

"Boys, I think you just gave me an idea."

TLC: Chapter 41

AJ is enjoying his leisurely ride in the back of the limo. And the smile on his face seems to indicate all of his troubles are behind him, at least for now. It's the weekend, and the only thing on his schedule is to catch up with Julie and see if they're making any progress on the file and CD. AJ gives her a call. "Hi Julie, how are you and Weathers doing on the files?"

"We haven't touched the files yet. I've only been here about thirty minutes. Traffic was a pain in the butt getting over here. We've been going over what the two of you discovered while I was sedated."

"Has he done anymore research on the files since Thursday?"

"Not really. He's been pretty much tied up at work, and once he gets home, Betty and Lisa have had some pretty intense honey-do's for him to take care of."

"Have you talked to him about Detective Morris yet?"

"No, I thought I'd wait on that until you got here. How long do you think Higgins' party is going to last?"

"It's already over. I was a real party pooper."

"Okay. What did you do?" she asks curiously.

"Let's just say I rained on their parade. You know? I seem to recall someone telling me that one or both of our phones have been compromised. I'll tell you all about it when I get there."

"I can hardly wait. Hurry up!" she says excitedly.

"I'm on my way. See you in a few."

***

A short time later, AJ arrives at Weathers' home. The three of them go up to Weathers' study and talk about yesterday's events, and what they should do with Detective Morris. After much discussion back and forth, Weathers says, "Here's what I'm willing to do. I'll go online tomorrow and see what I can dig up on Detective Morris, and from there, see what his background was with the military."

"He mentioned he spent six years in the First Battalion, 35th Armored Division, and had a Level Two security clearance," says Julie.

"Well, that helps narrow the field a bit," he replies. "I don't suppose he gave you his rank, any campaigns he participated in, or the name of his commanding officer, did he?"

"No, sir. Sorry," she says, sounding disappointed.

"No need to be, Julie," he replies in a comforting tone. "I'm sure I'll find everything I need with the information you gave me."

"Come to think of it, he also said he's been a detective for five years."

"Now see? You just added another piece to the puzzle. Every little bit helps." Julie forces a smile.

"So, AJ, I hear you have a new Hummer!" says Weathers smirking. "I even heard it's supposed to be, I believe Julie said you used the term...unassuming?"

"Well, this one's charcoal gray, and most of the trim is matte black, so it shouldn't stand out in the crowd quite as much as the yellow one."

"Just keep in mind that it's your personal vehicle. You have a company car for work. Besides, I doubt Higgins would be inclined to replace it a second time," he says with a serious look on his face. "Have I made myself clear on that?"

"Yes, sir...No, sir...I mean, I don't plan on using it for work, sir," he replies feeling embarrassed.

Finally, Weathers can't hold it in anymore, and bursts out laughing. Julie is in tears, howling with laughter.

"What?" asks AJ in total confusion.

Weathers tries to catch his breath, while saying, "You should have seen the look on your face when I told you not to use it for work!" Weathers bursts out laughing again.

"Okay guys, are we going to spend the afternoon making fun of me, or are we going to get down to business?"

Julie and Weathers start to calm down for a moment, look at each other, then both burst out laughing again. "Guys, I think I'm going to try to find Lisa and the kids. I know they'll appreciate me," he says, with some resentment in his voice.

"Oh, AJ," Julie says in an attempt to settle him down. "We don't mean anything by it, but the expression on your face. It was priceless!" Instantly, both of them start laughing again.

"Okay. That's it. I'm outta here." he bellows, and storms out of Weathers' study and down the stairs.

Mrs. Weathers catches him at the base of the stairs and asks, "What's wrong AJ? Why are you so upset?"

"It's nothing Mrs. Weathers," he replies. He stops and ponders that remark, allowing it all to sink in. Then he smiles and says, "It really is nothing. You know? It's been a rough week for all of us, and I guess I let it get to me. I apologize for being so stupid."

"AJ, you were just caught up in the moment. And now that you've taken the time to reflect on it, you see it's nothing to worry about."

"Thank you, Mrs. Weathers."

"I didn't do anything. You did it all by yourself," she replies in a comforting tone. "Why don't you join Lisa, the boys, and me in the kitchen? We're making chocolate chip cookies. Do you like chocolate chip cookies?"

"Love 'em, Mrs. Weathers. Love 'em." The rest of the afternoon is relatively quiet, with AJ spending most of it with Mrs. Weathers, Lisa, and the kids.

***

A short time later, Julie ventures downstairs attracted by the aroma of fresh baked cookies that had made its way up to Weathers' study. As she's about to enter the kitchen, she sees AJ playing with the boys, smiling and having a good time. Lisa is standing off to the side watching them. Lisa turns and catches Julie staring at AJ and the boys. It's obvious Julie can see AJ is relaxed playing with them. When Julie looks up, she realizes Lisa has caught her in the act. Lisa just smiles, then turns back to watching AJ and the boys.

Julie enters the kitchen and asks, "Has someone been baking cookies?"

"I did! I did!" the boys yell simultaneously.

AJ looks up and smiles at Julie as she leans over to pick up little David. Julie says with a look of surprise on her face, "It looks like you got about as much on you as you baked!"

309

"Uh-uhh!" says David. "Timmy did it!" All of them start to laugh. "Timmy got me *all* dirty!"

"Did not!" says Tim.

"Did too!"

"Did not!"

"Okay boys," says Lisa. "That's enough. Now go up to your room and play with your toys, okay?"

"But mommy! I want to play with AJ!" says Tim.

"Me, too!" yells David.

"Now boys, you've been playing with Uncle AJ for over an hour. It's big people time now," says Lisa.

"But Mommy! No upstairs!" cries David.

"Yes, Mommy! No upstairs!" cries Tim.

"Boys? You know what? You haven't had your afternoon nap, have you? I think it's sleepy time, don't you?"

"No, Mommy!" cries David. "Play! Play!"

"No, Mommy! No nite nite!" cries Tim.

"Mrs. Weathers? Will you help me get the boys up to bed?" she asks, as she picks up David. Both boys are crying now. "They really do need their nap."

"I'll help you, Lisa," says Julie.

"I don't mind," says Mrs. Weathers, as she starts to get up from her chair.

"Please, Mrs. Weathers, I want to do it. You've helped Lisa with the boys all week."

"Thank you, child," she replies.

Julie starts to pick up Tim, when Lisa says, "Here, take David. I'll take Tim." David is already starting to get sleepy. His eyes have that glazed over look to them. Julie looks over to AJ, smiles, then she and Lisa take the boys up to their room.

Before they reach the top of the stairs, David goes limp, sound asleep. Once in their room, Julie carefully lays David in his bed, as Lisa lays Tim in his. While Tim is trying his best to stay awake, he's fighting a losing battle. In less than a minute, he's out like a light.

"Wow! That was fast," whispers Julie.

"Yeah, they're kind of like a light switch. They run, and run, and run. But then when they stop, it's all over," says Lisa while gazing at the boys. Lisa motions to Julie to follow her out of the room, then gently closes the door behind them.

"You're right," whispers Julie, "They do look like little angels when they're asleep."

"I saw how you looked at AJ while he was playing with the boys. Now do you believe me?"

"Yes, but I don't know if I'm ready to have any kids just yet. He hasn't even proposed to me!"

"Well, just don't wait too long. The opportunity will pass you by before you know it. AJ's a good man, Julie, and he loves you. I can see it in his eyes, just as much as I see it in yours. And you know? You're both adults. And I bet you consider yourself an independent woman, don't you."

"Of course. I'm not afraid to stand toe to toe with any man," she scoffs.

"Then instead of you waiting for AJ to ask you to marry him, why don't you ask him to marry you? You know, put the monkey on his back."

"Lisa, that sounds like a dare," she says, giving her the eye.

"Call it what you wish, but I'm telling you, you and AJ are meant for each other."

"Tell me, Lisa, what's the latest with you and Sean? Any landmark decisions?"

"Yes. I thought about it all day Thursday and Friday. I called him last night, and told him he needed to make a decision."

"Lisa? I thought we had an agreement that *you* needed to make a decision," says Julie, fearing Lisa was having second thoughts.

"I asked him whether he wanted to have the boys on the first and third weekends or the second and fourth weekends?"

"Wow!" says a surprised Julie.

"I told him I wouldn't embarrass him in court over his infidelity, provided he agreed to pay reasonable child support and alimony. We'd discuss numbers once I picked out an attorney."

"No need. You've got one. Me!" says Julie proudly.

"Thank you, Julie. And I told him I hoped he didn't need anything out of the house, because it was gone. I'll bet he's still scratching his head on that one," she says with a degree of satisfaction. "I told him I expected a check within the week, and gave him the Weathers' address."

"You go girl! I'm so proud of you," says Julie beaming.

"But Julie, I've got to find a job, and a place to live. Plus, I need to find a place that can take care of the boys while I'm at work."

Lisa continues, "Mr. and Mrs. Weathers have been really wonderful, especially since AJ more or less dumped us on them. Please don't get me wrong. I appreciate everything AJ has done for me, too. But it's time I started making my own way."

"What did you have in mind?" asks Julie.

"Honestly? I have no idea. I don't even have a car."

"Can you type?"

"Yes. Why?"

"Have you ever done any secretarial work; filing, receptionist, that kind of thing?"

"Yes, but it's been a while. What are you thinking?"

"Hang on a minute. I have an idea," says Julie as she walks over to Weathers study and knocks on his door. "Mr. Weathers? May we come in?"

"Of course, Julie."

As Julie and Lisa walk into his office, she says, "Lisa needs a job."

"Well now, that's a very admirable thing and all, but how can I help?"

"For starters, we need a computer."

"Okay," he replies, sounding a bit confused.

"Lisa can type, and she's had some secretarial experience. I seem to recall you can take the Civil Service Exam online."

"All right," he says, still trying to figure out what's on Julie's mind.

"After she passes the exam, do you think we could get her a job in the secretarial pool at work?"

"Let's get Lisa set up to take the test first. While she's doing that, you and I can check the postings for any open positions and see where that takes us. I'll also give Martha a call to see if she's aware of anything open or about to."

"I don't know," says Lisa with a look of concern. "It's been years since I took a test. What if I fail?"

"Lisa, you're not going to fail," replies Julie confidently. "You'll be fine. And once you get on, you'll have a decent job, with a good salary, healthcare, retirement, even a daycare allowance. They'll even help you find a good one in your neighborhood. You'll be back on your feet in no time."

"But I have to pass first, right?"

"Lisa, what kind of grades did you make in school?" asks Julie.

"Mostly A's, but I did get a B in Phys Ed a couple of times."

"How can anyone make a B in Phys Ed?" asks Weathers.

"My coach was a lesbian, and I wasn't."

"Oh! Okay, sorry I asked," says an embarrassed Weathers. Lisa just smiles.

As Weathers gets up from his chair, he says, "Here Lisa, have a seat, and I'll help get you set up. Just follow the directions, fill out the application, use our address as your mailing address. You can also use Julie, AJ, and me as references. Then take the exam. I think it takes about an hour or so. Once you get done with that, feel free to print out any information you need by clicking that button, right there. And you're done."

"I guess it seems simple enough," she says. "After I finish taking the test, then what?"

"Come downstairs and join us." he replies. "I'm sure we'll find something to do."

"Okay. Look out world. Here I come!" says Lisa with excitement in her voice.

Lisa fills out all the necessary forms and takes the test online. The whole thing takes less than two hours to complete. When she comes back downstairs, it's obvious to everyone she's starting to feel better about herself.

The rest of the afternoon is relatively quiet, especially since the boys are sleeping. AJ and Julie stay for dinner, then leave shortly afterward.

***

Once back at Ms. O'Malley's apartment, AJ and Julie settle down and enjoy a bottle of wine, while listening to music playing softly in the background

313

As they're getting ready to go to bed, AJ flips on the bedroom light and is surprised to find the twin beds pushed together. "Hey! What's this?" he asks.

Julie walks up behind him, wraps her arms around him, and says softly, "I called Patrick this morning to check on the progress of the apartment, and I mentioned you thought the mattress was too soft. I didn't mention anything about pushing the beds together, though."

He sits down on the bed, and it appears to be much firmer than the night before. He stands up, lifts the mattress, and finds a sheet of plywood between the mattress and box springs. "How'd this get here?" he asks with a perplexed look on his face.

"I guess that was his idea of firming up the mattress."

"Well, I think it helped," he says, lying down on the mattress and flouncing around a couple of times. "A lot!" He hops off the bed, walks over to her, looks into her eyes, and says, "Thank you, thank you very much." He leans over, clutches her head in his hands, and gives her a soft, longing, kiss.

"You're, you're welcome," she says, seemingly star struck by his gentleness.

As both of them start to undress AJ asks, "Shower or bath?"

"Oh, I don't know," says Julie. "What do you feel like?"

Creeping up on her, he says, "I...feel...like...a shower!" He grabs her, and she squeals. Then he picks her up, throws her over his shoulder, and carries her down the hall to the bathroom.

She cries out, "What in the hell are you doing? Put me down. Put me down!"

Needless to say, Julie and AJ end up doing more than just taking a shower!

TLC: Chapter 42

Ms. O'Malley's apartment
Sunday morning
June 19, 2011, 1005 hours local time

After having a roller coaster of a week, plus Saturday night's bathroom and bedroom antics, both of them are exhausted. Sunday is its polar opposite.

AJ awakens to a light tapping on the hallway door. He yawns, stretches his arms, then tries to focus on his watch. *"10:05! Holy shit! Where'd the time go?"* He jumps out of bed, puts on a pair of boxers and grabs a T-shirt on his way to the door. He looks through the peephole and sees Patrick. He unlocks the door slowly, and whispers, "Keep it down. Julie's still asleep."

Patrick nods his head, and quietly slips inside, gently closing the door behind him. AJ tiptoes back to the bedroom, closes the door, then tiptoes back to the kitchen. Patrick is already digging in the cupboard.

"What are you doing?" asks AJ.

"I'm lookin' for me bottle."

"What bottle?"

"Me Connemara, ya twit! What have you done with it?"

"I haven't got a clue what you're talking about," he replies scratching his head and rubbing his eyes. "Remember? You and Julie were the ones moving things from my apartment to this one."

"Son? Ya haven't made any coffee yet? Whatcha been doin' all this time? Sleepin' the day away?"

"As a matter of fact? Yes. Yes, I have, thank you very much."

"Well, I guess that board underneath the mattress did the trick!" he says with a twinkle in his eye.

"Yes it did, and I thank you," replies AJ. "So, tell me. What's on your mind this morning?"

"Well, laddie, I have some good news, and some not so good news," he says while setting up the coffee pot.

"Okay, what's the bad news?"

"Let's talk about the good news first, if ya don't mind. Okay?"

"Sure, fine, whatever," AJ says with a yawn.

"The muddin' and sandin' are comin' along just fine. I should be able to prime and paint the hallway tomorrow or the next day."

"That is good news, Patrick. What about the bathroom?"

"Aye. Now that's the bad news," he says sadly.

"What's wrong?"

"Remember I was tellin' ya it might be a wee bit difficult to find a matching tile fer it?"

"Yes."

"Well, accordin' to the owner of the hardware store, that tile hasn't been made in over ten years. Worse, the company that made it has long since gone out of business."

"So, what does that mean, Patrick?"

"What that means, AJ me boy, is we're gonna have to tear out all of the old tile, and replace the lot of it. That means we're gonna have to pull the sink and the toilet, too."

"I'm sorry, Patrick. I really am. So what does that do to your timeline?"

"Oh, laddie! That's gonna throw us back another week, easy!"

"That's putting us pretty close to the Fourth, isn't it."

"With the Fourth being on a Monday, it might set us back a few more days."

"Why am I not surprised," sighs AJ, shaking his head. "Well, it is what it is. In for a penny, in for a pound. Isn't that how the saying goes, Patrick?"

"Aye, laddie. It does."

"So, tell me, Patrick. What does that bottle look like?"

TLC: Chapter 43
Higgins' estate
Monday morning
June 20, 2011, 0800 hours local time

AJ pulls up to the gate of Higgins' Estate, and before he can get his window down to press the button on the intercom, the gate begins to open. *"I wonder who's minding the store this morning?"* AJ says to himself. About that time, his phone rings. He looks at the number. It's security.

"AJ here, who's this?"

"It's Tony, AJ."

"You mind telling me why the gate started to open before I had a chance to identify myself?"

"Your tag number is in our database, so rather than have you goin' to the trouble of stoppin' and identifying yourself…"

"And what if someone had stolen my car, or was holding me hostage? Now the son of a bitch is inside your perimeter. You just lost your first line of defense."

"Sorry, I hadn't thought about that," he says apologetically.

"Look, Tony. I know you mean well. But this isn't about courtesy or convenience. It's about security. Protecting the senator, okay?"

"I gotcha, AJ. It won't happen again."

As the gates close behind him, a white van slows to a crawl as it drives past the gate. Vinny squeezes off a few pictures of the back of AJ's car.

"Did you get his tag number?" asks Marko.

"Yeah, I got it," Vinny replies. "Let's get outta here." The van picks up speed and continues down the road.

AJ pulls up to the front of the house, and notices the senator's new limo isn't parked out front where it should be. *"Now what?"* he asks himself. Heading up the steps, Tony opens the door to meet him.

"I'm really sorry AJ. I don't know what I was thinkin'. You're trying to make things better, and all I'm doin' is makin' 'em worse."

"Tony? What are you beating yourself up for? It was an honest mistake. If things were less volatile, what you did might have been acceptable."

"Yeah?"

"But you've got to keep in mind someone is trying to kill the senator. Your job is to protect him. Consider everyone who pulls up to that gate as a potential threat. Remember that."

"I will. I promise," says Tony. "Oh…AJ?"

"Yes?"

"Remember that Oliver fella, Chad, from the weekend?"

"How could I forget?"

"Well, shortly after you left, he came back and tried to buy the tapes from me."

"What tapes?"

"You know…The tapes. All of the cameras are being recorded now. There are two of them down by the range. He wanted to buy them."

"And what happened?"

"I told him they weren't for sale, plus he was bein' recorded tryin' to bribe me."

"Really?"

"Yeah. He was layin' hundred dollar bills on the lip of the window, and I just flipped 'em back in his face."

"Very good, Tony."

"Not only that, but I've started keepin' this little digital audio recorder with me, and even got his bribe on here. Boy! Did that piss him off!" says Tony as he lets out a chuckle.

"I'll bet it did! Good job, Tony. I hope you put all that in your report. And I'd recommend transferring the recording to one of the computers for future reference, just in case he decides to try something else."

"Report's already done AJ, and I'll make the transfer right away."

"Keep up the good work, Tony," he replies, smiling with approval. "By the way, do you know what's going on with the senator?"

"Oh yeah. He wants to see you in the library."

"Is anything wrong? Is he sick or something?"

"No. He seemed okay to me."

"Well, I guess I better find the senator and see what's on the agenda for today."

"See ya around, AJ."

"Later, Tony."

AJ walks down the hall to the library and finds Higgins standing in front of his favorite window.

Higgins says, "You know? It never ceases to amaze me how beautiful this view is. The trees, the gardens, the fountains…Do you have a nice view at your place, AJ?"

"Honestly, I can't say that I've noticed. It's usually late when I get home, and all I want to do is just sit down and relax."

"Do you have a house, condo, or an apartment?"

"Apartment, sir."

"You know, you're just pissin' that money away, don't you?"

"Yes sir, but being in the Secret Service, especially someone like me, well, I could be transferred at any time. Owning a house or a condo would just complicate things."

"You have a point there, AJ." Higgins pauses a moment, then says, "But you might look at it from a different perspective. If they know you own a house or a condo, they might decide to transfer someone else instead of you."

"That's a good point, sir. I'll have to give that some thought."

Higgins turns around, walks over, and sits down at his desk. "I guess you're wondering what we're going to do today."

"Yes sir. Since the limo isn't out front, I gather we're not going to Washington today."

"That's a very good assumption, AJ. As a matter of fact, we're probably not going to be visiting Washington until after the Fourth of July."

"You haven't received any more death threats or anything like that, have you?"

"No, no, no. Nothing like that. But this party is going to require my personal attention for the next several days. It's going to be a stellar event."

"I've called a temp service, and they're sending over a dozen young ladies to start addressing invitations, and making phone calls for me. We'll be setting them up in the sitting room on the second floor above me here. I've got AT&T bringing out a dozen cellular phones, and Office Depot is supposed to deliver a dozen HP laptops and printers before noon. Hallmark is supposed to be dropping off five hundred blank invitations that were originally ordered for someone's anniversary party last year. Would you believe their monogram just happened to be WHH?"

"Imagine that," says AJ. "Sounds like you couldn't have done any better if you had planned it."

"Yeah. I was able to buy them for twenty-five cents each. I'm just not too crazy about the color, though," he says, pondering his decision.

"What color are they, Senator?"

"They're a pale blue linen. I was hoping for parchment."

"Sir, I'm sure the blue will be fine. After all, blue is masculine, remember?"

"Yes, you're right, of course. Yes. Blue will be fine." Higgins' mind seems to be somewhere else.

"Senator? Are you all right?"

"Yes, I'm fine. I've just got a lot on my mind right now."

"I can appreciate that, sir. Me too." AJ hesitates for a moment, then says, "Sir, do you mind if I ask you a question?"

"No, go right ahead, AJ."

"Did you have an opportunity to speak with Mr. Oliver about his son's actions over the weekend?"

"Yes, and I have to tell you, he was more than a little unhappy about you manhandling him the way you did. But after thinking about it, he felt it was probably the best thing that could've happened to him. I wouldn't give it another thought, AJ."

"So, he's still going to help back your campaign bid for the Presidency?"

"Yes, AJ. Everything's fine, just fine."

"Well, I'm glad to hear that, sir. It was bothering me all weekend."

"Like I said AJ, I wouldn't give it another thought." Higgins rises from his chair, walks back to the picture window, then says, "You know? Since we won't be going anywhere for the next few days, why don't you go down to security and check on all this new gear you've ordered, and make sure it's all hooked up and working the way it should."

"I was just thinking the same thing, sir. I'll get right to it."

"AJ?"

"Yes, Senator?"

"On your way out, would you mind closing the doors for me? I'd like to be alone for awhile, if you don't mind."

"Not at all, Senator. I guess I'll see you sometime later on during the day, sir?" AJ hesitates a moment, waiting for Higgins to answer, but he says nothing. AJ closes the doors.

As AJ walks down the hall, his phone rings. It's Weathers. "Good morning Mr. Weathers. How was the rest of your weekend?"

"Fine, AJ. Are you in a position where you can talk?"

"If you mean, am I away from Higgins? Yes sir, but remember, Julie seems to think one or both of our phones have been compromised."

"Great!" he says, sounding frustrated. "Where are you?"

"I'm at Higgins estate, why?"

"His phones are supposed to be secure, right?"

"Yes, sir."

"Good. Call me from one of his landlines. We need to talk."

"Yes, sir. Give me a minute, and I'll call you back."

"Okay. Bye."

AJ hurries down to the security supervisor's office, knocks on the door, punches in his security code, and enters the room. Sitting at the desk, he calls Weathers.

"Weathers," he says.

"Yes, sir, it's me," replies AJ.

"Why didn't you tell me you had a run in with Chad Oliver at Higgins' estate? Do you have any idea who he is?" he exclaims.

"I was going to, sir, but you and Julie were having too much fun ribbing me about the Hummer."

"Oh, that's right. But that's beside the point. AJ, Chad's a very dangerous man. He's crazy! Actually, he's worse than crazy. Tell me. How much do you know about him?"

"Well, I know he can't shoot for shit after he has a couple of drinks under his belt."

"Very funny. Seriously, how much do you know about him?"

"According to Tony and George, he shot one of Higgins' employees a couple of months ago, and he's been banned from practically every nightclub in and around Washington."

"That's right. But do you know why?" he asks.

"I would think it's because he's a short tempered, rich kid with an attitude, who hasn't grown up yet."

"AJ, he's thirty-two years old. I'm pretty sure that establishes him as an adult, at least in the legal sense. While it's true he's either started, or at least been a part of, fights in a number of clubs, he's also suspected of beating a man into a coma!"

Weathers continues, "Chad made a pass at a guy's girlfriend, and the guy got a little huffy. Chad and his bodyguards were asked to leave, but they waited for the couple in the parking lot."

"Chad's bodyguards allegedly held his girlfriend and made her watch as Chad beat the guy with a pipe. Afterwards, he slapped her around a bit, kidnapped and raped her, then kicked her out of the car in the middle of nowhere. He was arrested and jailed, although his father and Higgins arranged for his bail. There were even a handful of witnesses, but before the case ever made it to trial, the witnesses either recanted their testimony or disappeared."

"What about the girl?"

"She had a nervous breakdown, and was checked into an institution."

"So you're saying he got away with it."

"I'm afraid so. AJ, the word crazy really isn't appropriate. But when Chad sets his mind on something, he doesn't let up. All I can say is watch your back."

"Thanks for the warning, sir. But the senator says he spoke to his father over the weekend, and he said everything is under control."

"AJ. Are you going to believe Higgins or me? Think about it."

"You're right, of course. I will. I promise. And I appreciate the info."

"Now I've got more bad news for you," says Weathers.

"This is beginning to sound like a typical Monday. Now what?" asks AJ.

I started checking out that CD today."

"And?"

322

"It's a combination of files, photos, audio, and video, and while Higgins is in a couple of shots, it's mostly about someone else. Senator Joshua Abrams McCarthy."

"How's that for a curve ball? Now I wonder what he's got to do with all this?"

"Well, by the way the disc started, I thought it was some sort of surveillance recording. This guy has a dance card Hugh Hefner would envy. I'm not just talking about pics you'd see in People or those rags like the National Enquirer, I'm talking about hardcore, bedroom acrobatics!"

"Then there's audio of some conversations about what appears to be some under the table business deals, copies of contracts, overseas accounts, all kinds of stuff. I haven't gone through the entire disc yet, but it's beginning to look like Higgins and McCarthy have been working together for some time. In fact, McCarthy might be Higgins' running mate for Vice President."

"Then that would help explain the handwritten note found on Harry's body, now wouldn't it?" AJ ponders the situation for a moment, then asks, "Sir, do you know if McCarthy's a member of the Core? And what about Oliver? I wonder if he's part of it, too?"

"AJ? I think you're starting to get paranoid again. Simon Oliver is a millionaire several times over. While I can't say I know that much about him, I doubt he has any involvement, or even any interest in the Core."

"Did you know that Oliver and Higgins both flew for the CIA back in the 60's?"

"I knew that Higgins did, but I didn't know about Oliver. Are you sure about that?"

"Yes, sir. Higgins told me. But I'd suggest checking it out, though."

"I'll handle that personally," says Weathers.

"The senator was telling me about some businesses that Oliver was running over there, outside of the CIA. But considering his knowledge of what Oliver was doing, I think there's more to it than just admiring the man. I think the two of them might have been partners. Maybe they still are."

"Tell you what I'll do, AJ. Up until now, I've deliberately tried to keep my distance from the Core, but considering everything that's going on, I'm going to stick my neck out and talk to a couple of people, and see if I can help you get a handle on this."

"Thank you, sir."

"I hope you realize that once I start asking questions, there's a distinct possibility I could become a target. I want you to promise, if anything happens to me, you'll make sure Betty is taken care of."

"Sir, I really don't think…"

"AJ, I want your word, and I want it now," he says with an authoritative tone.

"Yes, sir. You have my word."

"Now, tell me. What are you and Higgins going to be doing today?"

"I'm on my way to check on house security. Oh shit!"

"What?"

"I forgot to tell you that Higgins is having a party here on the Fourth of July! It's also going to be the time he plans to publicly announce his plans to run for President."

"Do you mind telling me when you found this out?"

"Saturday, sir. He kind of mixed it in there while he was reaming me a new asshole for assaulting Chad."

"That's only two weeks away! How does he expect to get his invitations out in time?" asks Weathers.

"He's already hired a temp service, arranged for computers, printers, invitations, phones, the works. Those invitations will go out in the afternoon mail."

"Sounds like a man on a mission," replies Weathers. "What's the latest on additional bodyguards? Weren't you supposed to have gotten some files last week?"

"Higgins says there was a screw up on their end, and the files weren't sent. But both the men and their files will be here in the next couple of days."

"Sounds rather convenient, doesn't it? It's going to be a little difficult to check somebody out if he's already infiltrated your ranks."

"Yeah, I think it stinks, too. I guess we could schedule a pool party, and see how many of them have surgically removed tattoos." says AJ sarcastically.

"As Betty would say, pray for the best, but prepare for the worst."

"Yeah, Mrs. Weathers said that very phrase the day I brought Julie out to talk to Lisa."

"You don't say." Weathers pauses for a moment. "She's a good woman…probably better than I deserve."

"Sir? Don't talk like that! She loves you very much. She believes in you, too!"

"That's what I mean, son." You can hear the hurt in his voice. "I haven't been the husband she deserves."

"Sir. Knock that shit off!" barks AJ. "Your wife loves you. And she knows you love her. In her mind, that's all that matters." Suddenly, there's nothing but silence. AJ waits several seconds, then says, "Sir? Are you still there?"

A few more seconds pass, then Weathers says in a very calm, but firm voice, "Son? If anyone else dared raise their voice to me like that, I'd have them up for insubordination. I'm going to give you a pass…this time."

"Thank you."

"But I wouldn't make a habit out of it, if I were you. Next time, you might not be so lucky." His voice is now more authoritative.

"Yes, sir. I understand."

"Now, get on about your business, and we'll talk more later," says Weathers in a more normal tone.

"Yes, sir."

"And AJ?"

"Sir?"

"Thank you."

"You're wel…" click, "come," says AJ to a dead line. As AJ hangs up the phone, there's a knock at the door. "Who is it?"

"It's Tony. Can I come in?"

"Sure, Tony. Hang on a sec, and I'll get the door for you." AJ gets up, and opens the door. "What's up?"

"The senator just got a call from that bodyguard company. I guess they're flying in tomorrow."

"Any idea what time?"

"Sometime around 11am, I think."

"Well, I guess I need to call Brian and see if he still wants to make that trip out to Quantico."

"What trip?"

"Brian's offered to help me test fire the Barretts, and the closest place to do that is the range at Quantico. I want to make sure they work properly before I put them into service."

"Can I go? I've never fired anything like that before."

"Who's the supervisor tomorrow morning?"

"Me, I'm afraid," sounding more than a little depressed.

"Tony, your responsibilities lie right here tomorrow," says AJ patting him on the back. "Are the new bodyguards taking a cab from the airport, or do we have to pick them up?"

"The senator wants me to pick them up."

"Well, maybe the senator will let you use his Hummer. What better way to impress the hired help than to pick them up in a hopped up, stretched out, bulletproof SUV!"

"Yeah!" says Tony all excited. "Do you really think the senator would let me drive it?"

"Well, I can't speak for the senator, but I personally think it would be a great idea. We need to put some miles on it anyway. After all, the thing's been here since Friday and hasn't left the estate. I'll try to put in a good word for you. How's that?"

"Thanks AJ. I'd appreciate it."

"No problem, Tony. By the way, you wouldn't happen to know how I could get in touch with Brian, do you?"

"Yeah, sure. Pull out the drawer in the middle of the desk, and you'll find a sheet of paper taped to it. 'H' is for home, 'C' is for cell, and 'P' is for pager."

"Yep. There it is." As he picks up the phone and starts dialing one of Brian's numbers, he says, "Anything else, Tony?"

"No, I think that about covers it."

"Okay, I'll see you later. Good luck tomorrow."

"Thanks, AJ. Later."

"Hello, Brian? This is AJ. You wanna meet me here at the estate tomorrow and do a little shooting?"

TLC: Chapter 44
Gold's Gym
Monday afternoon
June 20, 2011, 1630 hours local time

After work, Tony goes to the local gym for a workout. His meeting with Higgins didn't exactly go as planned. Higgins wants him to pick up the bodyguards at the airport, but he wants him to take the Lincoln instead of the Hummer. Tony is really bummed by the whole thing. While he's changing clothes in the locker room, one of Chad's bodyguards comes in. At first, Tony is on the defensive, looking to see if either Chad or the other bodyguard might be somewhere around.

"What are you doing here?" Tony asks in a threatening tone.

"I like to watch wrestling, and when I seen ya over at Higgins' place, I said to myself, *"I know this guy! He's Samson!"* I'm right, ain't I," he says.

"Could be. Why?"

"I'd like to shake your hand!"

"What for? What's this about?" asks Tony suspiciously.

"My boss is an asshole, plain and simple. What you and AJ did to him the other day, well, he deserved that and more. A lot more."

"If you feel that way about him, why don't you quit?"

"I can't. I owe him money. A lot of money."

"So what does that have to do with me?"

"Nothin'. I just came down here to work out, same as you."

"Funny, I don't remember seeing you work out here before."

"Yeah, I usually come out in the mornin's. The boss spends most of the night out on the town, so he sleeps in during the day. Kinda reminds me of a vampire, if you know what I mean," he says smiling. "Look, Samson, I mean Tony. Can I call you Tony?"

"Depends on where this conversation is going."

"I'd really like to get your autograph."

"Are you serious?" asks Tony.

"Serious as a heart attack!" he replies.

"What's your name?"

"My name's Vinny, Vinny Morelli."

327

"Nice to meet ya, Vinny," says Tony, as the two of them shake hands. Tony's hand literally swallows Vinny's.

Tony and Vinny spend the next hour working out on the various exercise machines, and eventually, a little friendly competition starts. Tony sets up his barbell with two hundred pounds, with Vinny spotting him. Tony does a quick set of ten reps. Vinny says, "I can do that."

Tony says, "Go ahead, I'll spot you." Vinny lies down on the bench and does a quick set of ten, just like Tony.

"Good job." says Tony. He pulls the safeties from the shaft, walks over to the rack and picks up two twenty-five pound weights, adding one to each side, then reinstalls the safeties.

"Watch this!" Tony lies down on the bench, wipes his hands with the rosin bag, and grabs the shaft. He adjusts his grip, then with a mighty grunt, he lifts the barbell from the rack, and does ten reps again, although at a somewhat slower pace. Vinny helps Tony guide the barbell back onto the rack. "Thanks, Vinny."

"Don't look now," says Vinny, "but I think you have an admirer," he says with a smile.

Tony sits up, faces Vinny and whispers, "Who? Where?"

"There's a tall, busty, blonde over there in pink sweats that hasn't taken her eyes off you since you started liftin' weights."

"Really?"

"Yep! She's rubbin' her thighs together, when she watches you move. I'll bet her motor's runnin' in overdrive!"

"Think you can handle two-fifty?" asks Tony.

"Yeah, sure," Vinny replies flippantly.

"Okay. Be careful," warns Tony.

"Don't worry about it. I'll be fine," says Vinny.

Tony stands behind him and helps Vinny clear the barbell from the rack. Tony tries to steal a glance at the girl, but she catches him, and their eyes immediately lock onto each other. She smiles and blushes. This gal is built like a brick outhouse, and every brick's in place. Suddenly, Tony hears, "Four-r-r." You can see the muscles in Vinny's arms starting to quiver from the stress they're going through. "Fi-i-ive." Now the muscles and tendons in Vinny's neck are standing out, and his face is starting to turn red. "S-s-six…Tony…Help me!"

Tony reaches out and grabs the barbell just as Vinny's arms collapse from the strain, barely preventing the barbell from crushing his chest. Tony lifts the barbell, and sets it safely back in the rack.

"Wow! That was close!" exclaims Tony.

"You're tellin' me!" replies Vinny while gasping for breath. "That thing coulda' killed me!"

"Well, that's what you had me for," says Tony.

Vinny takes a quick glance at the blonde, then turns to Tony and says, "You know? You're a hero to that babe, now. I betcha you could get into her pants, and she'd help ya!"

"Nah, I couldn't do that."

"Whaddayamean you can't do that? You're not gay or nothin', are ya'? You been takin' them steroids and got a little… you know."

"No, it's nothing like that. I just don't jump into things that easy. I want to get to know the person before I go jumpin' into bed with 'em. After all, I have a reputation to uphold. I'm Samson!"

"So, you're the romantic type, the knight in shinin' armor, 'eh?"

"Yeah, I guess you could say that."

"Well that makes you a hero and a gentleman! You're gonna have that babe eatin' out of your hand in no time!" Both Tony and Vinny look over to the blonde and smile.

"I'm gonna take a shower," says Tony.

"Right behind you!" replies Vinny.

About twenty minutes later, the two of them come out of the locker room. Tony is looking for the blonde but doesn't see her anywhere. He walks over to the desk and asks the receptionist, "Do you remember seeing a tall, blonde lady, in pink sweats, a little while ago?"

"You mean Marilyn?" asks the receptionist.

"Yeah, that's her," says Tony, faking it.

"She just walked out the door. You might still be able to catch her in the parking lot."

"Gee! Thanks!" he says rushing out the door. At first he doesn't see her, but then he hears an engine barely turning over, but refusing to start. As he starts walking toward the noise, he can't believe his luck. It's Marilyn.

"Having troubles, miss?"

"It's Marilyn, Marilyn Monro. Like the actress, but without the 'e' at the end. I made it up myself," she says.

"What seems to be the problem?"

"It won't start. It acts like it wants to, but it just won't," she says, sounding a bit upset. "Do you think you can fix it for me?"

"I don't know, but I'll have a look at it." Tony pops the hood, checks out the belts, the battery, and cables. "Turn it over for me, will ya'?"

The engine starts turning over slowly, then Tony wiggles a cable on the battery, and the engine fires right up.

"Wow! You're my hero!" She jumps out of the car, rushes up to Tony and gives him a great big kiss.

"Gee! Thanks lady! I mean, thanks Marilyn, ah, Miss Monro," he says nervously.

"No, it's Marilyn to you, Tony," she says in a sultry voice.

"You know my name?"

"I asked the lady at the desk while you were getting cleaned up. She says you're a wrestler, too! I love a man who works out."

"Miss Monro, I mean, Marilyn, your battery cable is loose. It's a simple fix. A pair of pliers should do it. I'd do it for ya, but I don't have any with me."

"I think I have a pair at home. Think it'll get me home okay?"

"Yeah, it should, but I'd fix it right away. You never know when or where it'll work loose again."

"Okay," she pauses a moment, then says. "Tony?"

"Yes?"

"Would you like to take me out sometime and buy me a drink?"

"Sure!" he replies. "Would tomorrow night be too soon?"

"No, tomorrow would be fine," she says with a smile. "Here's my phone number. Call me anytime." She gets back in her car, waves at Tony, then drives away.

Vinny comes walking up to him, and says, "What was all that about?"

"Her battery cable was loose, and I fixed it."

"Anything else?"

"I think we have a date for tomorrow night."

"That's great!" says Vinny. "Want to meet me here around 10 tomorrow morning and pump up?"

"Actually I wanted to go with AJ out to Quantico tomorrow morning. But Senator Higgins wants me out at the airport by 11, so I'll probably be leaving about that time."

"Well, maybe we'll run into each other again sometime. Nice workin' out with ya."

"Yeah, same here, Vinny. See ya."

As Vinny watches Tony get into his car and drive off, he calls Chad. "Hi boss. Marilyn and I made contact. They've got a date for tomorrow night."

"Did he say where?" asks Chad.

"No, but I just found out that Tony's gonna be leaving around ten tomorrow morning, heading out to the airport. And AJ will be going out to Quantico about the same time. If we're lucky, and Tony leaves first, we might be able to off both of them tomorrow before lunch!"

"We'll have to figure out a way to have Marilyn stall Tony long enough so we can plant a bomb, then she can activate it when she gets out of the car."

"What'll we do with AJ?"

"His Crown Vic isn't bulletproof. We'll catch him out on the expressway, and mimic the attack he was in last week. You and Marco pick out a driver, get yourself some black fatigues and AK47's. If anyone is close enough to see you, they'll think the same group of terrorists did it."

"But boss? What if somethin' goes wrong?"

"Don't worry about it. I'll be around to make sure you guys don't screw it up."

331

TLC: Chapter 45

Higgins' estate
Tuesday morning
June 21, 2011, 0945 hours local time

Brian is late, and AJ is already pacing up and down the driveway
in front of Higgins' mansion. He and one of the security guards
have already brought down the two Barretts and loaded them into
the trunk of the Crown Vic. He's also preloaded five ten-round
magazines with 700 grain FMJ's, storing them in a small assault
bag, stowed with the Barretts. He even remembered to pack an
extra pair of ear muffs and safety glasses for Brian. Considering
the Barretts take up most of the room in the trunk, AJ dropped his
jump bag on the floor behind his seat. In it, are his ear muffs and
glasses, along with his H&K MP5 and a half dozen mags.

Tony comes out of the house, walks over to AJ, and says,
"You know? I'd give my left nut to go with you and Brian to
Quantico."

"Well, I wish he'd hurry up and get here. I'd like to get on
down the road."

"Speaking of that very thing, I need to get on the road myself.
Are you going to bring back some targets for me to drool over?"
asks Tony.

"If there's anything left of them, sure. What are you going to
do with them? Hang 'em on the wall or something?"

"Maybe. What kind of targets will you be shooting at?"

"To line up the sights, we'll be shooting paper; first at one
hundred yards, then three hundred, and five hundred yards. If we
have any ammo left, or if we can borrow some, we'll move over
to another range that has armored targets. Some of the targets are
out around a thousand yards, but they have a few moving targets
in the one hundred and three hundred yard range. We'll see how
well we can judge speed and distance there."

"Stop it, AJ. You're killin' me!"

"But the fun stuff is where you get to shoot at soft targets."

"Soft targets?"

"Yeah, we'll stop somewhere on the way down to Quantico
and pick up a few melons of different sizes and shapes. They
have jigs laid out on one of the ranges that will allow us to place

melons, or other soft material, in the head and torso positions. That way you'll get an idea as to what happens to a body when they get hit by one of these babies," he says while showing Tony one of the .50 caliber rounds.

"Jesus Christ! How could anyone survive after getting hit by one of those?"

"I doubt anyone could. Between bullet weight, diameter, impact and muzzle velocity, the average body would probably shut down instantly. Of course, a torso or headshot would be an immediate fatal wound. You'd probably never even know what hit you."

"That's it. I'm outta here. I hope you and Brian have a great time without me!" he says sarcastically. "See you when I get back from my joy ride."

"Be careful out there. Just because you're driving what's supposed to be a bulletproof car, doesn't mean you are." yells AJ.

As Tony starts to drive off, he flips AJ the bird.

"For three bucks, I could fix that for ya'."

Tony stops, looks back at AJ, and says, "Why three bucks?"

"That's how much one of these rounds cost."

"Bite me!" yells Tony as he drives away.

***

After Tony clears the gate, he starts fiddling with the radio, trying to find a station more to his liking. He's unaware of the white Ford van following him a few car lengths back. In it, are Vinny, Marko, and Ricki.

Ricki Valentine is a recent wash out from the law enforcement training academy. While he passed the physical, aptitude, driving, and marksmanship tests, his mental abilities were found to be lacking. He didn't wash out because he wasn't smart. Ricki had been a near straight A student in school. No, Ricki's problem was he couldn't function under pressure.

"Don't get too close to him, Ricki. He might recognize us," says Vinny.

"Vinny, you're sitting in the shadows. No one can see you. Just relax. I know what I'm doin'. I learned this in drivin' school," he replies "How far up the road is Marilyn?"

333

"Shouldn't be far. You can't miss her. She's drivin' a pearl white Seville, and she's wearing a white hat, blouse, and skirt, with matching heels. Man, would I like to get a hold of that!"

"Vinny? Stop talkin' like that. You know she's my sister."

"You're just jealous, because she *is* your sister. I bet you'd take her out, too, if you had the chance." says Vinny with a hearty laugh.

"Nah, she's not my type."

"Whaddayamean she's not your type? Are you gay or somethin'?"

"You know, Vinny?" says Ricki. "That comment of yours is getting pretty stale. I'm beginning to wonder if you might be gay or somethin'!"

Vinny eases up next to Ricki, pulls out a stiletto, sticks it up against his neck, and says in a guttural tone, "You little shit. If you weren't drivin', I'd slit you open from neck to nuts. You know that? Just shut up and drive. All right?"

"Whatever you say, Vinny. Just calm down and put that knife away, okay?"

***

Tony notices that traffic is slowing down, and the cars in the outside lane are trying to merge into the inside lane. As he gets closer, he can see a woman standing next to her car. It's Marilyn, and she's gorgeous in that white outfit. He pulls up behind her and turns on the emergency flashers. Then he gets out of the car, walks up to her and asks, "What happened? Did it die on you again?"

"I'm afraid so, and I need to get to the airport." Tony can see she's pretty upset. "Damn car. I hate you! I hate you!" she cries as she kicks one of the tires. "Now look what I've done! I've ruined my shoe!" And the tears start to flow.

"There, there Marilyn," he says holding her in his arms. "Everything is going to be okay. It must be your lucky day, because I'm on my way to the airport, too. I'll be happy to give you a lift. But first we need to get your car out of the road. You steer, I'll push." Tony spots the van behind him and yells out. "Hey you! Give me a hand here!"

"Vinny! He wants me to help him! What should I do?"

"Go and help him! While you and Tony are pushin' the car out of the way, Marko will hide the bomb under the car. Just take your time, okay?"

"I'm scared," says Ricki.

"Just get out there and help him, damnit!" yells Vinny.

"Okay, okay."

***

Brian is cursing up a storm! Traffic is all but stalled, and he's less than a mile from Higgins estate. "Damnit!" He cries out. *"I better call AJ, or he's going to have a fit!"* he says to himself. He pulls out his phone and makes the call. "AJ? Brian."

"Where the hell are you? You're late, you know."

"I'm sorry man, but it's the traffic. It's gotta be some sort of gaper's block. Wait a minute. Holy shit! You should see this babe! She's a real looker! Dressed up all in white!"

"You know, you could save the blow-by-blow description, Brian."

"Uh-oh, you're really not going to believe this."

"What?"

"Tony's pulled up behind her, and trying to give her a hand."

"Bullshit!"

Finally, traffic starts moving again after they pass by Marilyn and Tony. Unfortunately, Brian doesn't see Marko slipping out the back of the van.

"Okay, traffic is moving again," says Brian. "I should be there in less than five minutes."

"You better be, or I'm leaving here without you."

***

Tony is already trying to push the car by himself, as Ricki runs up to give him a hand. Meanwhile, Marko slips out the back of the van, eases up the passenger side, then ducks down behind the limo. Marko then crawls down the passenger side of the limo, and places the bomb next to the gas tank. The bomb is held in place by a powerful magnet. Once the bomb is secured, Marko

335

flips a switch to activate the bomb. He crawls back to the rear of the limo, then rushes back to rear of the van.

Tony and Ricki finally get the car out of the road. Tony shakes Ricki's hand and thanks him for the help, then escorts Marilyn to the limo. Tony starts to walk her to the back, but she says with a smile, "I'd rather ride in front with you, if you don't mind."

"I'd like that, Marilyn," he replies with a smile. As he opens the door for her, he asks, "By the way, are you flying out, or meeting someone?"

"Meeting someone," she says. "My mother."

Tony walks back around to the driver's side, gets in, turns off the flashers, and drives away. "What are you going to do when you get there?" he asks.

"I can rent a limo, I suppose."

"I'd like to help you if I could, but I've got some guys I have to pick up. Between them and their luggage, there probably won't be much room left."

"It's not a problem. You're helping me right now. If it weren't for you, I would still be stuck on the side of the road, and my mother would be wondering what happened to me." She starts to cry again.

"Oh Marilyn," he says in a sympathetic tone, "It'll be all right. We'll be there before you know it."

Marilyn takes off her hat, then slides over next to Tony, and rests her head on his shoulder. "You're a nice man, Tony. You know? I think you're the first guy, since grade school, who hasn't tried to take advantage of me."

"What do you mean, Marilyn?"

"You know, touch me, pinch me, stuff like that."

"You mean, harassment type stuff?"

"I guess you could call it that. Yeah."

"Well, the next time someone does anything like that to you, just let me know. I'll kick their ass!"

"That's about the nicest thing anyone has ever said to me, Tony. You know? You're my knight in shining armor."
Marilyn reaches up and gives him a kiss on the cheek, then rests her head back on his shoulder. Tony is so happy he could burst!

Ricki has turned around and is heading back to Higgins estate to intercept AJ.

"Man I'd like to be around when that thing goes off! KA-BOOM!" yells Marko.

"That reminds me. Send a text message to Marilyn reminding her to push the button as soon she gets out of the car," says Vinny to Marko. "I just hope she's got brains enough not to let Tony see the message."

"How much time is there from the time she pushes the button and the bomb goes off?" asks Ricki.

"Ten minutes," says Vinny.

"Is that enough time? I mean once she hits the button, there's no stopping it, right?"

"That's right, Ricki."

"Well, what happens if she presses the button, and then Tony gets caught up in traffic at the terminal?" he asks.

"Then the feds are gonna think they're under attack!" says Marko cracking a smile.

"Yeah! 9/11 all over again!" says Vinny, chuckling.

"Hey guys. That's not funny. The whole country will shut down again. You want to be responsible for that?"

"What are you talkin' about? We didn't set the bomb. Your sister will be the one responsible," says Marko.

"No! You're not going to pin that on Marilyn!"

"Shut up, Ricki. Just shut up and drive! Nuthin's happened yet. It's pure speculation on our part. Ain't no point in worryin' about nothin' until somethin' happens. Got it? I just hope AJ hasn't left the estate yet."

About that time, Vinny's phone rings. It's Chad. "Hi boss."

"Hi boss, my ass! Where the fuck are you guys? You're supposed to be parked down the street from Higgins' place, waitin' for AJ to come out!"

"But boss! We just got through puttin' the package in Tony's limo. We're on our way there now! Honest!"

"Well, hurry your ass up, cause I'm not waitin' here forever! Got it?"

"Yes boss. Step on it, Ricki. The boss is pissed!"

"I'm goin'! I'm goin'!"

Brian comes flying down the driveway, screeching to a halt just behind AJ's car. AJ doesn't even flinch. He walks up to Brian's car door, points to his watch and says tersely, "You're late! That makes me late! And I'm never late! Let's go!"

"Hey! Good morning to you, too!" says Brian sarcastically.

"You got everything?" asks AJ.

Brian pats himself down and says, "Head, shoulders, chest, arms, hands, legs, feet...Yep. I'm covered."

"Smart ass. Get in the car!"

"Look AJ, I'm sorry about being late. But I couldn't help it. There was a gaper's block at least a half-mile long back there. I'm serious!"

AJ is ignoring him as he's whipping down the drive.

"If you don't believe me, call Tony. He'll tell you."

Just before he reaches the gate, he nails the brakes.

"You're telling me that Tony stopped to help some beautiful woman stuck on the side of the road."

"Yep. Actually she was still in the road. That's why he stopped to help her."

"Call him."

"What?"

"Call him. I want to talk to him. If what you're telling me is the truth, I'll apologize. In fact, I'll even let you shoot first. How's that?"

"You swear?"

"Hell no I won't swear! But I'll give you my word. If you're tellin' me the truth, you can shoot first."

"Deal." Brian dials Tony's number. "Hello, Tony? It's Brian. AJ wants to talk to you. Hang on." Brian hands AJ his phone.

"Hey, Tony. How are you doing? That's good. Look, Tony. Brian says he saw you stop to help some lady in distress on the side of the road. Is that right? Uh-huh, right, okay, okay, okay. Be careful, now. Okay, bye."

"Well?"

"Brian?"

"Yes?"

"Tony says you're full of shit." AJ passes through the gate, out onto the road, and starts heading out to I-95.

"No he didn't. You just don't want to let me shoot first. Damnit! You made the deal! Not me! AJ! I expect you to honor the deal! I won fair and square! AJ! Talk to me, damnit!"

***

After dealing with stop and go traffic for about a half hour, AJ and Brian are finally cruising down I-95. Things have calmed down between them, and they're trading war stories on the way out to Quantico. Neither of them is paying attention to the van slowly gaining on them. AJ is driving in the outside lane, as the van advances on them on the inside lane.

Without warning, the van performs a PIT maneuver, effectively causing AJ to lose control of his vehicle. The rear wheels of the AJ's car have lost traction, and the van is now pushing the car down the road sideways, with AJ's door pinned against the van. AJ whips out his Beretta and snaps off three quick rounds into the windshield of the van. Ricki slams on the brakes, allowing AJ a moment to regain some control of the car. AJ floors the accelerator, launching them across the median, and into oncoming traffic. AJ just misses an oncoming car on the inside lane, but a semi clips the passenger side quarter panel near the bumper, spinning the car like a ground bound Frisbee. As the car spins off the road, one of the tires digs into the ground, causing the car to flip on its top.

The men in the van lose sight of AJ's car as the semi locks up its brakes, creating clouds of blue-gray smoke boiling from the squealing tires. After the semi clears the point of impact, all that can be seen is a cloud of dust where AJ's car left the road and continued into the trees.

Vinny yells, "Turn around! Turn around! Let's go! Let's go!" Ricki spots a place a few hundred yards down the road where they might be able to cross over. He accelerates down the road to the spot where he wants to cross.

***

339

Finally, AJ's car comes to a stop. Luckily, both AJ and Brian were wearing their seatbelts. "Holy shit!" says Brian. "What in the hell just happened?"

"Somebody just tried to kill us, and damn near succeeded!" he replies. Through the dust, AJ can see the driver of the van looking toward them, then accelerates down the road. "Get out of the car!"

"What?"

"Get out of the car. *Now!* They're coming back!"

"You're shittin' me!" yells Brian.

"Think you can cover me while I put together one of the Barretts?" asks AJ as he crawls out the window. "I just hope they're still in one piece!"

"What do you mean?" he says while watching AJ slide out. Out of the corner of his eye, he can see something hanging down at the back of the car. It's the twisted trunk lid, dangling from the driver's side hinge. "Great!" he says, sarcastically.

After AJ clears the window, he gets up on his hands and knees and looks back inside at Brian. "Will you stop hanging around and give me a hand?"

AJ spots both hard cases just a few feet away from the car. Both of them seem to be intact. He opens the case closest to him and sees that the rifle appears to be okay. While moving over to the second case, he can see Brian still fighting with his seatbelt, rocking the car, and cursing up a storm.

AJ gets to his feet, walks over to the passenger side of the car, jerks on the door a couple of times, and finally works it free. Then he reaches into his pocket, pulls out his knife, and says with an evil smile on his face, "Here! Let me give you a hand!"

AJ severs the belt at the anchor point, causing the belt to race across Brian's legs, through the buckle, then across his chest, freeing Brian before he can say, "Wait!"

As AJ turns away and rushes back to check on the second Barrett, he says, "You're welcome."

***

340

Ricki starts to turn off the road, but spots a small ditch at the bottom the median.

"What's the problem?" yells Vinny.

"I don't know if we can make it across. We might get stuck," says Ricki.

"No we won't. Just gun it! We've got to finish them off before they have a chance to get away!"

The median is rough, and just before he drops the front wheels into the ditch, he guns it, causing the front tires to barely skip over it. But he loses momentum, and sure enough, the rear wheels drop into the ditch. They're stuck.

***

While AJ starts to assemble one of the Barretts, Brian staggers out of the car, rubbing the side of his head. "Somebody get the name on that truck?"

"For a moment there, I thought it had ours! Would you mind grabbing my bag out of the back seat? In it, you'll find my MP5 and six mags. You have used an MP5 before, haven't you?"

"Yes, I have, but what do you plan to use, your Beretta?"

"No...This!" he says, as he picks up the fully assembled Barrett, complete with bipod and scope. "There was another bag in the trunk with magazines for the Barretts. See if you can find it for me."

As Brian looks around for the second bag, he says, "You know, there's a strong possibility that scope is out of whack. We took two pretty solid hits, plus the rollover."

"I know, but these scopes are specifically designed to take a lot of punishment. And since it was locked inside a foam filled case, I'm willing to take a chance it won't be too far out of alignment to hit that van down there."

"Where?" asks Brian as he hands the bag to AJ.

"Down there, in the median. He appears to be stuck. I've been watching him rock back and forth ever since I cut you loose."

"You're sure they're the ones who tried to ram us?"

"What do you mean *tried*?"

341

"I just don't want to be shooting up some innocent bystanders or some do-gooders trying to help us out."

"Tell you what. Why don't you run on down there and ask them?"

About that time, the truck driver who hit them comes running back to see if he can help them.

"Hey fellas, I just called 911, and they're supposed to have…" He stops mid sentence when he sees Brian taking a position behind a tree near the road, holding the MP5 at the ready. "What the hell are you guys up to?" Then he looks over to AJ and sees him inserting a magazine into the Barrett. "What the fuck is that?"

"Sir? Can you see that van down there?" asks AJ.

"Yeah, sure," says the truck driver.

"Did you see what happened to us before we jumped the median and crossed your path?"

"I damn sure did! Those mutherfuckers in that van down there rammed you guys, and…"

"Thank you, sir," says AJ. "See? I told you!"

"Okay, now what?" asks Brian sarcastically.

"Stand by one," he says while adjusting the range finder on the scope. "Hey! This is one of the new ones with the laser range finder! Cool!" AJ pulls the bolt back to charge the barrel, then looks at the truck driver and says, "You might want to stand back about twenty feet or so. This thing's a little loud."

"Sure thing mister," says the truck driver as he backs away. "By the way, what's the range to that van?" he asks.

"According to the range finder, it's about four hundred and fifty yards."

"That's a little over a quarter of a mile! Will that thing reach that far?"

"Are you kidding? There are Marine snipers in Iraq and Afghanistan taking out targets over a mile away with these rifles."

"Bullshit!" says the truck driver.

"Ah, Brian?" says AJ.

"What!"

342

"While you're not exactly in the line of fire, you *are* ahead of the muzzle of this thing. You might want to consider finding a safer position."

"Yeah, right!" he says scrambling to get behind AJ.

"Who are you guys, anyway?" asks the truck driver.

"He's Secret Service, and I'm a security supervisor," replies Brian.

"Is this the government's idea of handling road rage?"

"Fellas?" says AJ. "You might want to try to find a little cover. Two men just jumped out of the van armed with AK-47's." Suddenly, they can hear bullets whizzing through the trees!

"Get down!" yells Brian, as he pushes the truck driver to the ground.

"Hold your ears and open your mouth!" yells AJ, as he takes aim at one of the gunmen.

"What did he say?" asks the truck driver.

"One away!" BA-ROOMM!!

A ten-foot semi-circular patch of grass is instantly blown flat in front of the rifle, as the ground shakes. Down range, the round pierces the magazine of Vinny's AK-47, then hits him square in the chest, lifting him off his feet, then laying him flat on his back. The bullet continues, unabated, until it hits the side of the embankment less than twenty feet behind the van. The round kicks up a cloud of dust and debris over ten feet high.

Marko stops dead in his tracks after witnessing Vinny getting shot. Realizing his obvious exposure, Marko decides to turn tail and run back to the van.

AJ follows him back to the van through the scope. Marko opens the back door, but just before he climbs in, he fires another burst toward AJ and Brian.

AJ yells out, "Two away!" BA-ROOMM!!

This time, the round rips through the left quarter of the van, about three feet above the floor. It catches Marko just underneath the left armpit, bursting through his chest and out the other side. Again, the round kicks up a cloud of debris on the far side of the van. AJ continues to peer through the scope until he sees Marko tumble out of the van.

Ricki is obviously in a panic. He's racing the engine near its breaking point, and the rear tires are going up in smoke! AJ stands up, walks over to Brian, holds out his right hand, and says, "Give me the gun."

"Why? What are you going to do?" he asks.

"I'm going to try to take him alive, if he'll let me."

"Why don't you just shoot him and get it over with? He's an operative, you know."

"No, I don't think he is. In fact I don't even think he's ex-military. He could have gone on the offensive with the others, or tried to slip away, while the others attacked us." AJ thinks for a moment. "I'm betting he's young, inexperienced, and right now, scared shitless."

"So, go down there and get him."

"I'll appear more intimidating if I'm carrying a machine gun, rather than walking up to him, brandishing a pistol."

"Well, just think how much more intimidating you'd be walking down there carrying the Barrett!" he replies sarcastically.

"Do you want to go down there and get him, or shall I?" asks AJ firmly.

"Please! Be my guest!"

"Then give me my gun."

"Okay, okay, here," he says while holding up the MP5.

"Tell you what. If you want, you can watch both of us through the scope on the Barrett. There are still eight rounds left, including one in the barrel. Safety's on, but I'd prefer you keep your finger away from the trigger, okay?"

"No problem," says Brian.

AJ starts walking down toward the van along the outside of the highway. Considering the distance and the heat of the day, it's going to take him a few minutes to get there.

***

While AJ heads toward the van, Brian decides to call Tony. "Hey Tony, it's Brian. You're never going to guess what just happened to us."

"Yeah?" says Tony, "Well, you're not going to believe what happened to me!"

344

"Tony, I already know about the girl. I was caught up in that gaper's block when you were helping her out."

"But I bet you didn't know I drove her to the airport."

"No way. Really? From where I was, she looked like a real knockout."

"Yeah. She's beautiful, and on top of that, I think she likes me."

"Now Tony, don't be getting your hopes up. Girls who look like that don't normally hook up with guys like you and me. No offense."

"She called me her knight in shining armor. And she said I was the first guy who hadn't tried to take advantage of her. Brian, I think I'm in love."

"Whoa there, big guy. Take it easy. I've heard of love at first sight and all, but please. Give me a break here. Do you even know her name?"

"Yeah. Her name is Marilyn, Marilyn Monro. It sounds just like the actress, but she spells it without the 'e'. I even have her card with her phone number on it. I got that from her yesterday."

"Yesterday? You mean today wasn't the first day you saw her?"

"No, I met her at the gym where I work out. I saw one of Chad's guys there, too."

"What?"

"Yeah, he told me that he hated working for Chad, but he couldn't get away, because he owes him a lot of money. He said he liked the fact that AJ and I embarrassed him over the weekend, and he wanted my autograph."

"Wait a minute. What happened over the weekend?"

"Higgins had one of his shooting parties, and Chad got drunk. AJ embarrassed him, and then Chad tried to shoot him. But AJ put him on the ground and took his gun away from him."

"So where do you fit in all of this?"

"After AJ left, Chad came back and tried to bribe me into giving him the tapes from the cameras down by the range. But I wouldn't give 'em to him."

"So, why are you out at the airport?"

"Higgins sent me out here to pick up the bodyguards from Secure-1."

345

"Have you picked them up yet?"

"Yeah. We're on our way back, but there's some kind of acc…" Suddenly, the line goes dead.

"Tony? Tony!"

***

At first, Ricki doesn't notice AJ coming toward him. He's too busy trying to rock the van out of the ditch, plus there's still sporadic traffic coming up the road. AJ pulls out his phone and puts in a call to the Secret Service.

"Central? This is Thomas Andrew Jackson, ID 55191. We have a situation out here on I-95 about five miles north of the Quantico exit. My car's been totaled, and we've taken fire from two suspects. Both are down, and I'm approaching a third. According to the truck driver who hit us, he's called 911, so law enforcement and emergency units should be on the way. You might want to confirm that for me."

"Are you aware of any civilian casualties?" asks the operator.

"No, but I'm willing to bet there are a few people who need to stop and check their drawers, me included. The truck driver is a little shook up, and I'm certain his semi has sustained some damage."

"We'll get a team airborne immediately, and alert Quantico of your situation."

"I'd ask them if they wouldn't mind sending up a couple of armed Super Cobras, or Hueys to keep the media birds away."

"That sounds like a good idea. How can they identify you?"

"Hopefully, we'll be the ones still standing."

"Agent Jackson, you mention, we. Who are the others?"

"Brian Jamison was riding in the car with me. He's a security supervisor on Senator Higgins' payroll. And the truck driver. Both of them should be standing near the car. It's on the northbound side of the highway in the trees. You should see fresh skid marks from the semi that is now parked on the northbound side, which is in close proximity to my car. They should also see a white Ford panel van stuck in the median, facing east, about five hundred yards south of the semi. And

346

right now, they should be able to see two bodies near the van, as well."

"Copy that, Agent Jackson. Are you aware of any other suspects in the area?"

"Only the one I'm approaching at this time. I think I can take him alive, at least that's my plan."

"Agent Jackson, are you sure you don't want to wait for backup?"

"Negative, Central. I'm almost on top of him now."

"Just be careful, Agent Jackson. We'll alert law enforcement and emergency services of your location and situation."

"Roger that, Jackson, out," and he terminates the call.

Finally, the engine throws a rod from all the abuse, and the engine coughs and sputters to a stop. AJ can see Ricki banging on the steering wheel in a fit of anger, fear, and frustration. He looks like he's barely in his twenties.

AJ decides it's time to cross over to the median, and proceeds to upset a couple of drivers, who promptly honk their horns as he attempts to cross in front of them. This causes Ricki to look up in AJ's direction.

The sight of AJ carrying a submachine gun only adds to his distress. He attempts to start the van again, but the engine is locked up. Ricki is starting to feel like a wild animal trapped in a cage. *What can I do? Where can I go?* Adrenalin is pumping through his veins, and it feels like his heart is about to jump out of his chest.

Then AJ calls out. "You in the van! Show me your hands! Do it now!"

Ricki snaps back into reality, looks out his window, and sees AJ standing about fifty feet away, with his MP5 pointed in his direction.

As AJ slowly continues walking toward the van, he says in a calmer tone, "Show me your hands. Prove to me you're unarmed, and I'll lower my weapon. I don't want to hurt you."

Brian can clearly see both AJ and the driver through the scope. The young man raises his hands, and AJ lowers his weapon.

"Now, with your left hand, open the door slowly. Then come out with your hands behind your head, fingers interlaced." Ricki follows AJ's commands. Once Ricki is out of the van, AJ says,

347

"Turn around and face the van. Keep your hands behind your head. Everything's going to be all right."

As Ricki turns to face the van, AJ starts walking toward him. Out of the blue, AJ hears a bullet whiz by his head, immediately followed by the sound of a gunshot fired from behind him, off to his right.

Suddenly, there's a splash of blood on the side of the van where Ricki's head had been. The shot startles the truck driver and Brian, too! Both look across the road to see a black Lincoln parked on the side of the road, almost perfectly parallel to them with its trunk open. A man is standing on the far side of the car with what appears to be a bolt action high powered rifle, equipped with a bipod and scope.

"Where'd he come from?" yells Brian.

"Beats me! He wasn't there a moment ago!" replies the truck driver.

As AJ starts to run toward the van, a second bullet whizzes by, just inches from his head. He instinctively dives for the deck and crawls the rest of the way to the van.

Brian is frantically struggling to move the Barrett around to where he can get a shot at the man behind the Lincoln. While the sniper fires another round at AJ, Brian gets the Barrett pointed in the right direction. He lies down next to it, and tries to get the sniper in his sights. Heat waves are rising off the pavement, plus cars and trucks are still moving in both directions, making it almost impossible to get off a shot. Brian yells out, "Hey you! What's your name?"

"My name's Ted!" he yells back. "You gonna shoot that guy or not?"

"I can't without a spotter. I might hit an oncoming car or truck! I need your help!"

"What can I do?"

"Stand close to the road, so you can see traffic coming from both directions. When it looks like the road is going to be clear for a few seconds, give me a signal so I can shoot!"

"You want me to stand in front of that thing? Are you fuckin' crazy?"

"Once that guy takes out AJ, he's going to start shooting at us! What's it going to be?"

"Since you put it that way…" Ted uses the trees for cover, getting as close to the road as he dares.

Brian is starting to sweat, and it's collecting in his eyebrows. He has the shooter in his sights, safety is off, finger barely resting on the trigger, waiting for Ted's signal.

The sniper fires yet another round at AJ. *"Damnit! Give me a signal, will ya?"* Brian says under his breath, while trying to control his breathing. Then out of the corner of his eye, Brian sees Ted wave, and he fires. BA-ROOMM! In the heat of the moment, Brian jerks the trigger, causing the muzzle to shift a hair to the right, missing the sniper, but blowing out the rear door glass on both sides of the car, catching the sniper completely by surprise. The sniper swings around and takes aim at Brian. He fires. POW! Luckily the round goes over Brian's head.

"Now you've done it!" yells Ted.

The sniper ducks behind the Lincoln to reload. Through the scope, Brian can see the back door open for a few seconds, then close again. *"I've got you now!"* he says to himself. "Ted!"

"Shoot! Damnit! Shoot!" screams Ted.

BA-ROOMM!! This time, Brian is in control, squeezing the trigger slowly, but firmly. The round center punches the back door, and the seat cushion literally explodes as the projectile passes through the passenger compartment. The interior is instantly filled with dust and debris. The round rips through the door on the other side, flinging it open, almost tearing it from its hinges.

"Holy shit! Did you see that?" screams Ted. "It looks like a bomb went off inside the car!" The interior appears as though it might be on fire, but it's just dust mixed with smoke rolling out of the window and door openings.

Since the sniper seems to be focused on Brian and Ted for the moment, AJ seizes the opportunity to start running up the center of the median to close the gap between him and the sniper. He also notices there's no traffic coming toward him anymore. Evidently the police have finally arrived and are beginning to hold up traffic. There's still some traffic on Brian's side of the road, however.

Brian doesn't see any movement around the car, so he's beginning to think he might have hit the sniper with that last

349

round. But the sniper has positioned himself next to the front wheel, using it and the engine block as protection from the Barrett.

Now that the sniper has reloaded, he leans out and away from the car, to see if he can find AJ. He has little trouble spotting him scrambling up the median. Still using the wheel to protect his torso, the sniper gets into a prone position, and extends the bipod to help stabilize the rifle for the next shot.

Brian spots the bipod in front of the wheel and can now see the barrel protruding past the bumper. Brian aims just above the rim of the wheel, knowing the round will probably hit the top of the engine block. He's not sure if the round will pass through it or not, but he's counting on it making one hell of a noise. Once again, he calls out, "Ted?" No response. "Ted!" He's nowhere to be seen. "Damnit Ted!" he yells. "Where the hell are you?" Ted has run back to the cab of his semi.

AJ is unaware of the sniper drawing a bead on him as he continues his run up the median. Brian is waiting for an opening in traffic long enough to take his shot. A drop of sweat is dangling from his brow over his right eye, quivering as though it could fall any second. Brian's breathing is very shallow, trying to minimize any movement of the rifle. *"Come on…Come on…"* His finger is slowly putting pressure on the trigger. *"Come on… Come on…"* BA-ROOMM! The round hits just above the rim, as he planned. The tire explodes, and the car drops due to the sudden loss of pressure. Almost simultaneously, the round hits the top of the engine block, turning metal and plastic into tiny bits of deadly shrapnel. It also ruptures the high-pressure fuel line, spraying the top of the hot engine with fuel. The hot, vaporized fuel ignites almost immediately, blowing the hood completely off car.

Like a wild turkey answering a mating call, the sniper unexpectedly pops up. Even AJ is caught by surprise. But Brian is ready. *"Gotcha!"* BA-ROOMM!! The round hits the sniper square in the chest, tossing him down the embankment. AJ looks over to Brian, and Brian says to himself, *"You're welcome."*

TLC: Chapter 47

Exhausted, AJ slows to a walk as he approaches the Lincoln. Flames are dancing about four to five feet above the motor from the burning gasoline. As Brian steps out from the tree line to survey the damage, two helicopters can be heard in the distance. Ted comes out of hiding, walks up to Brian and says, "Holy shit! That's about the damnedest thing I ever saw!"

"Well, you've never served in the military, have you."

"Nah. Look at me," says Ted. "I'm too fat, too short. Even when they had that lottery thing, with the draft? You know, Vietnam? My number was high enough that I never got called." Ted shakes his head. "Good thing, too."

"Why's that?"

"I hate boats! I throw up just standin' on one at the docks!"

"Motion sickness," says Brian. "They have wrist bands and pills for that."

"Tried 'em. Tried 'em all. Nothin' works for me. Flyin's the same way." About that time, two Marine Super Cobras fly over them near treetop level.

"Well, at least you can drive wherever you want to go," he says, while patting Ted on the back. "By the way, thanks for helping me out there. If it hadn't been for you, I might have shot a car or a truck, or that guy could have shot the lot of us."

"Sorry I chickened out on ya, but the noise! What is that thing? A cannon or somethin'?"

"Actually, it uses a .50 caliber Browning Machine Gun round. It's called the Barrett M82A3 Precision Sniper Rifle."

"Was that other fella, AJ, blowin' smoke when he said they're snipers hitting targets over a mile away?"

"No, in fact, there are some documented kills up to a mile and a half away."

"Kills? As in people?" asks Ted, starting to feel a little queasy.

"Terrorists, Ted, terrorists."

Ted starts to gag and runs back into the trees.

AJ crosses the road near the Lincoln as the first Secret Service helicopter lands about a hundred feet behind it. The rotor wash fans the flames from the engine compartment, spreading heat,

351

smoke, and dust toward AJ. He raises his arm to block the heat from his face as he walks past the front of the car.

Approaching the crest of the embankment, he first spots the rifle, then about fifteen feet down the embankment, the body; face down and motionless in the tall grass.

There's a massive exit wound, almost perfectly centered, just below his shoulder blades. Amazingly, there isn't much blood immediately around the wound, especially considering the round probably took out his heart and both lungs. But as he gets closer to the body, he notices the tall grass, surrounding the body, is covered with a reddish black mist. It's blood and tissue.

Two men come rushing down the hill, with one yelling, "Don't touch that body! Secret Service!"

Still staring at the body, AJ reaches into his pocket and pulls out his ID.

"Agent Morgan," he says, identifying himself. "Did you do this?"

"I'm Agent Jackson. No, but I shot two out of three down there," he says while pointing to the van. "Brian Jamison made this shot from across the road over there," as he points toward the opposite side of the road.

"Do you know who he is?" asks Agent Morgan.

"No, I was about to roll him over until you told me not to. Anybody got any gloves?" The man standing behind Agent Morgan hands him a pair. "Thanks."

"That's one hell of a hole! But I don't see much in the way of blood," says Agent Morgan.

"That's because it was turned into a mist," says AJ. "Look around you, Agent Morgan. It's everywhere. You're standing in it."

"Holy shit! I've never seen a shotgun blast do that before!"

"That's because it wasn't a shotgun blast. This wound was caused by a 700grain, .50 caliber, full metal jacket projectile, traveling over 2,850 feet per second. That's a little over a mile in two seconds."

"What kind of gun fires a round like that?"

"They're usually fired from a Browning Heavy Machine Gun, but in this case, a Barrett."

"What's a Barrett? And what are you doing with one out here on the highway, Agent Jackson?"

"It's a long story, Agent Morgan. You see? I've been assigned to protect Senator Higgins. Brian Jamison, over there, is one of his security supervisors and…" AJ tells him the story of how he and Jamison were on their way to Quantico to test fire the rifles, when they were attacked.

"Well," says Agent Morgan, "Let's see who we have here." AJ reaches across the sniper's back, and Morgan positions himself near his hips.

AJ says, "On three…One…Two…Three!" Both men grunt as they roll the lifeless body onto its back.

"Oh shit," says AJ, completely surprised by who it is.

"Do you know this guy?" asks Morgan.

"Oh yeah. I know him."

"Well, who is he?"

"Chad Oliver." AJ stands up, and stares at the body for a moment. After peeling off the gloves, he drops them on the body, then turns and starts trudging up the hill.

"Is that it?" asks Agent Morgan as the two Super Cobras fly directly overhead.

As AJ continues to make his way up the hill he replies, "No, but I wish it were. Tell your men to pull the plates off this car and that van."

"And why's that?"

"We don't want the media to back track the vehicles to Oliver. He's high profile, Agent Morgan. No names to the press, no info whatsoever."

"That's a tall order Agent Jackson," says Morgan tersely. "Under whose authority?"

"Mine, for now, but how high would you like it?" replies AJ in a calm, almost detached tone. "I can probably have the President, or his Chief of Staff call you within the hour, if you wish."

"That won't be necessary, sir," replies Morgan nervously. "Agent Marks!"

"Sir!" replies Agent Marks.

"Pull the plates on the Lincoln and the van."

"Yes, sir!"

353

"Anything else, Agent Jackson?" asks Morgan.

"I'd have both vehicles towed to our impound yard for further investigation."

"I agree, Agent Jackson. I'll get them rolling as soon as possible."

"Everyone here is a John Doe until you hear otherwise. Understand?"

"Sounds like this goes pretty high up, sir."

"Yes, it does. Take your pics and get 'em bagged as quick as you can. The last thing we need is a bunch of dead bodies showing up on CNN."

"Yes sir."

"And when you get a chance, call up Quantico and see if they'll hold the bodies for us, at least for now."

"I'll get right on it, sir."

AJ pulls out his phone and calls Weathers. "Sir? Remember that little conversation we had about me watching my back?"

"So you've already heard about the airport," says Weathers.

"Airport? What about the airport? Oh. You're talking about the bodyguards flying in from Secure-1. Yeah, I know all about that. Higgins sent Tony out to…"

"AJ? Tony's dead. And so are the bodyguards, along with at least another thirty or forty innocent people. The last tally on the injured was over fifty."

"What? What in the hell happened?"

"It's too early to tell, AJ, but it looks like somebody planted a bomb in the limo. Tony had already picked up the bodyguards, and was on his way back when…"

"When what, sir?"

"There was a minor fender bender near one of the exits, and traffic was at a standstill. Tony was stalled next to a gasoline truck that was almost empty. In this heat, the tank must have been saturated with fumes, and when the bomb went off," Weathers pauses a moment, then says, "Damnit AJ. There's a sixty-foot crater where the return lanes used to be!"

"Wait a minute, sir. How do they know it was Higgins' limo?"

"Since 9/11, all the major airports have cameras everywhere, and everything's recorded. Someone just happened to be

354

monitoring the camera in that area and witnessed the explosion, at least until it knocked out that camera, along with five others in the area. People felt the shock wave inside the terminal building!"

"Holy shit!"

"TSA was able to back up the tape and ID the license plate. At least none of them knew what hit them, God rest their souls." Weathers pauses again to collect his thoughts. "The FBI, Homeland Security, BATF, NSA, the FAA, all of them are already out there digging, probing, and poking around. They suspect it was an act of terrorism, so they've closed the airport."

"Chad Oliver," says AJ.

"What?" asks Weathers disbelievingly.

"Chad Oliver. He was behind it."

"Look AJ, I know I told you that Chad was crazy, but this?"

"Sir, I wasn't calling you about the airport, or the bodyguards."

"You weren't?"

"No sir. Chad just tried to kill Jamison and me while we were on our way out to Quantico."

"By himself? No, that doesn't sound like Chad, AJ."

"You're right about Chad not acting alone, sir. Three men, and I'm betting two of them were his personal bodyguards, rammed us, then tried to kill us. I was able to neutralize two of them, and tried to capture the third. Almost had him, too, but Chad shot him. Damn near shot me, too, but Brian took him out, just before he got me."

"Who's Brian, and how do you know it was Chad?"

"Brian Jamison is one of Higgins' security supervisors, and I just ID'd Chad's body."

"Now hang on a minute, AJ. Why would Chad want to kill Higgins' bodyguards? That just doesn't make any sense. I thought he only had a beef with you."

"That's what I thought until I had a conversation with Tony yesterday. It seems Chad came back to the estate after I left and tried to bribe Tony into giving him the tapes from the cameras down by the range. Tony refused, plus he told Chad he was being recorded in his bribe attempt. I guess that made Tony a target, too."

"Well, that certainly gives us a motive, but I'm not sure how we're going to prove it. There are still a lot of loose ends, like how and when did they plant the bomb, and how was it set off. No, this isn't going to be very cut and dry, I'm afraid."

"We'll get it all sorted out, sir. Don't worry." AJ pauses a moment. "By the way, does Higgins know about Tony and the bodyguards yet?"

"I haven't called him, but if he watches CNN, I'll bet he suspects."

"Ah, sir?"

"Yes, AJ?"

"I'm going to need another car."

TLC: Chapter 48

After all of their statements and pictures are taken, AJ and Brian, along with their hardware, hitch a ride in one of the helicopters back to the Homeland Security Complex. Brian doesn't say a word the entire trip. Upon their arrival, AJ takes Brian down to meet with Weathers for a debriefing.

Brian seems to be nervous and uneasy. While AJ brings Weathers up to speed on the morning's incident, Brian hardly says a word. He either nods his head in agreement with AJ, or occasionally throws in a comment. After talking with Weathers for almost an hour, Brian asks to use the bathroom, and excuses himself.

"Something's wrong with him," says AJ with a concerned look on his face. "This morning, he was cutting up and carrying on. Now? I just don't know, but it seems like he's hiding something."

"Well, AJ. Considering everything the two of you have been through this morning, I'm more surprised by your behavior. The way you've explained the initial attack, almost getting T-boned by a semi, taking out two armed suspects, being pinned down by Chad. Your description of those events is as though you were more like an observer rather than a participant." Weathers pauses a moment, then adds, "Brian shot and killed a man today. It was obviously done in self defense, but he took a life."

"I understand all that, sir. But he's ex-military. He was okay up until we got on the chopper. He's not comfortable here."

"Well, AJ?" says Weathers, smiling, "I can't say that I'm very comfortable here either. And I work here."

"Come on, sir. You know what I'm talking about. He could be an operative." AJ pauses a moment then says, "After I shot Chad's bodyguards, I told Brian that I wanted to take the driver alive, and he called him an operative. Maybe he's one of Higgins' men, or maybe someone else's."

"Tell you what. I'll see about getting a couple of prints off him, and maybe do a background check through our database, see what turns up. How's that?"

"And I'll scan everything in his file, including his military ID, and Social and send it to you in an email as soon as I get back to the estate."

"That'll help."

Brian finally comes back to the office. "Brian? Are you okay?" asks AJ.

"Not really. All the excitement, the heat and all. Plus I never liked choppers much, especially since Iraq. The locals were constantly taking pot shots at us."

"I thought you said you were in the motor pool."

"I was, but whenever we were headin' out for R and R, or our trucks broke down, especially if it was a hot spot, we'd sometimes take a chopper."

"Well, Brian and I really need to get back to the estate," says AJ. "I still haven't talked to Higgins yet. Dreading it, really."

"Yeah, you couldn't pay me to be in your shoes right about now," says Weathers. "I don't envy you at all. Just keep in mind you didn't have a choice in the matter. You didn't go looking for Chad. He came out gunning for you."

"Well, I'm not too inclined to think Higgins is going take it very well," surmises AJ. "Especially since Simon's son killed Tony and his bodyguards. I have a feeling there will be some very heated discussions about all this."

"Now AJ, we can't prove Chad was responsible for Tony's death."

"What do you want!" AJ exclaims near the top of his lungs. "Who else would do something like that? The Core? Jesus Christ!"

"AJ? Mr. Weathers?" Brian says in a subdued tone. "I think I need to tell you something."

"Go ahead. Speak up, son," says Weathers in a sympathetic tone.

"While AJ was walking down the highway to try to take the last subject alive, I called Tony. I had mentioned to AJ earlier I had seen him stop to help a woman stalled on the side of the road. She was quite a looker, too. Traffic was pretty much stalled in both directions because of her."

"Okay, but what does that have to do with anything?" asks Weathers.

"Tony told me that after he got her car off the road, he gave the woman a lift to the airport. He also mentioned he had seen her the day before at the gym where he works out."

"So, he had met the woman before. So what?" says AJ.

"Up until yesterday, Tony had never seen her at the gym before. But what was even more suspicious, one of Chad's bodyguards was there, too. In fact, the guy approached him, and the two of them had a rather lengthy conversation about Chad."

"Go on," says Weathers seeming intrigued.

"I think the woman was a diversion to allow Chad's goons to plant a bomb in the car while Tony was helping the woman. And I think the woman was the one who activated the bomb after she got out of the car."

"Makes sense. But how are we going to find this woman?" asks Weathers.

"Well, for starters, the woman was wearing white; hat, blouse, skirt, and shoes. She's blonde and built better than a Hollywood Bimbo. Yes!" says Brian excitedly.

"What?" asks AJ with a perplexed look on his face.

"Marilyn, Marilyn Monro. Just like the actress, but without the 'e'."

"What are you talking about?" asks AJ. "Are you saying this woman's name is Marilyn Monro? Come on! Give me a break!"

"Look, AJ. That's what Tony said her name was. He said she even gave him a business card with her name and number on it."

"Well, it definitely sounds like something worth looking into," says Weathers. "I'll turn it over to a couple of the interns and see if they can find anything on her."

Weathers adds, "With all the cameras around the airport, odds are she was recorded. Since we know what time the bomb went off, it should be a simple matter of backing up the tapes between the time of the explosion and the time the bodyguards' flight arrived. She shouldn't be that hard to spot. Maybe we'll get lucky and get a face to go with the description."

"Maybe," says AJ smugly.

"What else did you talk about while you had him on the phone?" asks Weathers.

"Not much sir. He said he had just picked up the bodyguards and was on his way back when they got caught up in a traffic jam. That's when the phone went dead." Martha calls in on the intercom. "Mr. Weathers? Forensics is on line one for you."

Weathers presses a button on the intercom. "Thank you, Martha." He puts the call on speakerphone and says, "Weathers."

"Paul Bennett, Forensics. Agent Jackson said we should give you a call if we found anything."

"Agent Jackson is here with me. Any luck?"

"I believe so, sir," he replies. "We found cellular phones on each of the victims, and in the process of checking them out, we found one of them had sent a text message, shortly before the incident."

"And?"

"The message reads: Don't forget to press the button when you leave the car."

"Was there a name attached to the text message?" asks Weathers.

"No name, sir. But the memory slot for that number had the initials M M."

"Marilyn Monro," says Weathers under his breath.

"Excuse me, sir?" asks Bennett.

"Nothing. It's not important. Anything else?"

"Most of the calls seem to be going to or coming from a Chad Oliver."

"As soon as you get a printout of the names related to calls made to and from those phones, I want a copy of it on my desk before the ink dries."

"Yes, sir, Mr. Weathers."

"Thank you for the information, and please keep me posted on anything else of interest."

"Will do, sir."

"Good bye." Weathers ends the call.

"Well fellas," smiles Weathers, "I think we have a solid lead between Chad and the bombing at the airport. Now all we need to do is find Marilyn Monro."

"I'll head out to the airport as soon as I drop Brian off at Higgins' estate."

"Not so fast AJ. You're not the only agent under my supervision. I'll get it handled. Your primary job is still protecting the Senator."

"But sir!"

"No buts, AJ."

"I still need a car, sir," he says frustratingly.

"Here," says Weathers, while throwing him a set of keys. "Take mine."

"Thank you, sir."

Weathers points his finger at him and says, "Now AJ? This one's brand new. Not a scratch or a nick. I want it back the same way. Are we clear on that?"

"Yes, sir. Got it!"

"Now, get out of here and get back to work!"

AJ snaps to and says, "Yes, sir!" Looking over to Brian, he says, "Time to go, Brian."

"I'm right behind you."

As the two of them get into the elevator, Brian asks, "You mentioned something about the Core. What is that?"

"Brian? That's on a need to know basis, and right now, you don't need to know," says AJ.

"Gee, thanks," replies Brian with a look of disappointment on his face.

Suddenly, AJ's phone rings. It's Higgins. "Yes sir, Senator. I was…"

"I need you back at the estate. Something terrible just happened! A bomb went off at the airport, and I haven't been able to get in touch with Tony."

"Yes, sir. I'm aware of that. Brian and I are leaving Weathers' office right now. We should be there within the hour, sir."

"Brian's with you?"

"Yes, sir."

"What are you doing down there?" he asks.

"It's a long story, sir. I'll bring you up to speed when we get back to the estate."

"Bring him along. This is going to affect him, too."

"We're on our way."

361

TLC: Chapter 49

As AJ and Brian pull up to the gate, AJ presses the button for the intercom.

"State your name and business," says the voice over the intercom.

"Agent Thomas Andrew Jackson, Secret Service. Who's this?"

"Agent Jackson, the senator is expecting you. Opening the gate now. Standby."

"Did you recognize that voice?" asks AJ.

"Can't say that I did," replies Brian.

"Think your security company sent out a new supervisor to replace Tony already?"

"It's possible, but I have no idea who."

"Well, I guess we're about to find out."

When AJ pulls up to the front of the house, they see a man in plain clothes and dark sunglasses. He's standing near the base of the steps, with an MP5 suspended from his shoulder.

"That's different," says Brian with a look of concern.

AJ walks up to him and says, "Agent Thomas Andrew Jackson, Secret Service. Who are you?"

"You're expected, Agent Jackson," says the bodyguard, coldly, looking straight ahead. "The senator will brief you in the library."

"How many of you are there?" asks AJ.

The bodyguard slowly turns his head toward him and says, "Agent Jackson, the senator will brief you on everything you need to know."

AJ stares at the bodyguard for several seconds, then, with Brian in tow, walks up the steps to the front door, where George meets them.

"Brian," says AJ, "I guess you better check on security, while I talk to the senator, okay?"

"On my way. That guy was kinda' spooky, wasn't he?" comments Brian.

"Yeah. My guess is he's probably one of the senator's operatives."

"What?" asks Brian.

"Never mind. Just go." Brian heads toward security.

"Who are these guys, and where did they come from?" asks AJ, while he and George walk down the hall to the library.

"I don't know. Some of them came by car, and a couple of others were dropped off by helicopter."

"How many are there?" asks AJ.

"Four, maybe five, I think. They haven't been here long. Twenty, maybe thirty minutes at the most."

"What about hardware? Did any of them bring any black bags with them?"

"All of them, AJ," George replies looking worried. "What's going on? I heard something about a bomb going off near the airport."

The two of them come to a halt in front of the closed doors of the library. "I'll tell you all about it after I talk to the senator, okay?"

"All right," says George as he turns away and starts walking back down the hall. But just as AJ is about to knock on the door, George stops, turns around and says, "AJ?"

"What, George?"

"I'm glad you're back," he says, forcing a smile.

"It'll be okay, George."

AJ knocks on the door. "Come in," says Higgins in an authoritative tone. Higgins is standing near his desk talking to another man dressed in a similar manner as the one standing guard at the front door. "AJ? I want you to meet Alpha One."

"Excuse me, sir? What's with the call sign stuff?"

"As you may surmise, Alpha One, here, is one of my operatives. Assassins, I think you called them. You don't need to know his real name."

Alpha One stands about six feet, two hundred pounds, brown hair, muscular, but trim build. All in all, quite similar to AJ. Everything, but the dark sunglasses, that is.

"How many, sir?" asks AJ.

"Four for now, and they're all Alphas."

"Chain of command?"

"Alpha One is in direct control of his team. He'll take orders from you, provided they don't countermand any of mine. At that point, mine prevail."

"How will I know which one is which, sir?" asks AJ.

"The only one you need to talk to is Alpha One," he says curtly. "Look AJ, these men are going to be roaming the grounds, as well as in and around the house. Anyone caught on the grounds who is not wearing a uniform, or carrying proper identification, will be taken into custody or shot. The Core has gone too far this time!"

"So, you think the bomb was planted by the Core?"

"Don't be ridiculous! Of course it was the Core!" barks Higgins. "Who else would have done it?"

"Chad Oliver, sir."

"What are you talking about? Why would Chad want to kill me?"

"You weren't the target, Senator," says AJ bluntly. "Tony was his intended victim, as was I."

"Why? Were you out at the airport with Tony?"

"No sir. Brian and I were on I-95 heading toward Quantico, when three of Chad's men tried to kill us. Damn near did it, too."

"I don't understand. Why would Chad want to kill Tony, and how do you know the three men worked for Chad?"

"Chad came back to the estate after I left Saturday and tried to buy the tapes from the cameras down by the range. Tony refused and told him he was being recorded while attempting to bribe him."

"Cut to the chase, AJ. How do you know the three guys who tried to kill you worked for Chad, and how do you know Chad was involved?"

"Because all of them are dead, sir."

"Well, if they're all dead…"

"That includes Chad, sir. He tried to kill both Brian and me. We didn't know it was him until after he had already been shot, not that it would have made any difference, sir."

Higgins looks over to Alpha One and says, "Leave us." Alpha One heads toward the door, without saying a word. Once he's left the room, Higgins starts, "What in the hell happened out there?" Higgins walks over to the bar and starts to make himself a Jack Daniels over ice.

"We're still trying to put all the pieces together, but as of right now, it looks like Chad baited Tony with a woman in distress on

364

the highway, about a mile down the road from here. While Tony was helping the woman, one of Chad's men planted a bomb in the limo. Tony gave the woman a lift to the airport, and somehow she activated the bomb after she exited the vehicle, probably with some sort of remote control."

"How much of this can you prove?" he asks while pouring his drink.

"Brian was caught in the gaper's block associated with the broken down car. He saw Tony get out and assist her. I spoke with Tony briefly by phone, and he confirmed the stop."

"That still doesn't prove anything, AJ," he says gruffly, while walking back to his desk.

"I'm not done, Senator," he replies in a firm tone. "While we were dealing with the three men in the van, Brian called Tony a second time, and found out he had taken the woman to the airport, where he dropped her off and picked up your men. He mentioned being stuck in traffic, when suddenly the line went dead. As best we can tell, that's the time the bomb went off."

"Okay, we still don't know there's any tie to Chad."

"Sir! After I had neutralized Vinny and Marko, Chad's bodyguards, I'm sure you remember them from the weekend," he says sarcastically, "I attempted to capture the third one. Just as I was about to take him into custody, Chad shot and killed him, then he tried to kill me. If Brian hadn't been there, he might have succeeded. I owe him my life."

"Are you saying Brian shot Chad?"

"Yes, sir. Brian was also taking fire from Chad. There were no other options, sir."

"Well, well, well. I must agree Chad was evidently obsessed with trying to kill you, but I still don't see the tie-in with Chad killing Tony and my bodyguards," Higgins says smugly.

"Forensics found cell phones on each of the bodies. One of them had sent a text message shortly before the bomb went off. It said something to the effect of: don't forget to press the button when you leave the car."

"So?" Higgins asks while taking a sip of his drink.

"The message was sent to the woman Tony had picked up on the side of the road," replies AJ.

"You're sure of that," says the senator glaring at AJ.

AJ hesitates for a moment, knowing he hasn't been able to verify it, then says, "Yes, sir. We are."

"Anything else to help prove this woman had something to do with Chad and Tony?"

"Yes, sir. Tony told Brian by phone, just before the bomb went off, he had first contact with this woman yesterday, at the gym where he works out. He was also approached by Vinny while working out at the gym. Tony had never seen either of them at the gym prior to that day."

"I must admit that would be pretty hard to blame on coincidence," he says with a sigh. "I guess I overreacted a bit, didn't I."

"Senator? Under the circumstances, I'd have probably made the same call. But sir, your problems are probably still far from over."

"Why's that, AJ?"

"Simon Oliver, sir?"

"What about him?" asks Higgins, while walking back to the bar.

"Sir, his son is dead. Men under your employ are responsible for his death."

"AJ? You and Brian removed a cancer," he says while preparing himself another drink. "The truth is, Chad had been nothing but trouble from the time his hormones became active. Booze, drugs, hookers. The boy couldn't keep his mouth shut, or his tool in his pants. He's lucky some streetwalker hadn't cut it off."

"Wait a minute! Are we talking about the same Chad you almost took my head off over the other day?"

"Like I said, AJ. I haven't been myself lately. Remember, I was with you last week when those seven men attacked us on the freeway. Plus, I've been dancing with Simon through Chad for the past few months, trying to sew up his backing my campaign, and I didn't need you mucking it up for me."

Higgins pauses for a moment and rattles the ice in his glass, then takes another sip. "After I talked to Simon about your altercation with Chad over the weekend, I discovered their relationship had been strained for some time. Chad had been in and out of rehab so many times, they kept a room reserved for

366

him. The boy was a ticking time bomb. He finally went off today."

"You know, the FAA, BATF, FBI, and Homeland Security have closed the airport because they think the bombing was a terrorist attack. The whole country is back on high alert. Chad's twisted ideas of getting revenge has paralyzed the entire country. How do you propose we fix that?"

"First of all, where are the bodies?"

"I had them taken out to Quantico listed as John Does."

"And the vehicles?"

"I had the license plates removed and towed to the agency's impound yard, awaiting further investigation."

"Good. Do you think any news groups were able to get in close enough to get a plate number or a good shot of the bodies?"

"No sir. When I called in the situation, our office called Quantico, and requested a couple of Super Cobras be dispatched to keep them away from the perimeter."

AJ continues, "Quantico contacted the media birds and told them a training exercise was underway, and it would be in their best interest to avoid the area."

"And they bought that?"

"Tell me, sir. What would you do if you were being circled by a couple of helicopters loaded with Hellfire missiles, rockets, and a minigun?"

"Okay, here's what we'll do…"

Later that afternoon, Brian, AJ, and a couple of the security guards are sitting in the break room, when CNN breaks into their normal programming. "We interrupt this program to bring you a special announcement by the Director of Homeland Security. Please stand by."

Seconds later, the Director of Homeland Security takes the podium. "Ladies and gentlemen. The Department of Homeland Security, the Federal Bureau of Investigation, the Bureau of Alcohol, Tobacco, Firearms, and Explosives, the Transportation Security Administration, the National Security Agency, along with the FAA, and local law enforcement and emergency agencies, have made significant progress regarding the terrorist attack at Ronald Reagan Washington National Airport earlier today."

"It has been determined that a small, radical right wing group, based here in the United States, attempted to take out the terminal building. This group, with no known ties to any foreign or international terrorist group, was attempting to implicate either al-Qaeda or the Taliban as the terrorists in this attack."

"A bomb, made of similar materials commonly used by those foreign terrorist groups, was placed on a fuel delivery truck. For reasons unknown to us, possibly to refuel, the truck was in the process of leaving the airport, when it was caught in a traffic jam, near the terminal building. The bomb's explosive power was enhanced by the vapors trapped within the fuel tank causing heavy casualties and loss of life."

"What's the latest estimate?" cries out one of the reporters.

"We're still checking with area hospitals, but our latest tally is approximately forty known dead, and seventy-three confirmed casualties, many of them critical. Our hearts go out to those families."

He pauses a moment, clears his throat, then continues. "Security cameras located at the airport, showed a suspicious vehicle near this fuel truck earlier in the day. A description of the suspect vehicle was dispatched to area agencies, and was soon spotted on I-95 leaving the Washington area, traveling at a high rate of speed. While attempting to effect their capture, the terrorists were involved in a traffic accident near Quantico. A shootout ensued leading to a number of casualties."

"How many terrorists were there?" asks one of the journalists.

"Our reports indicate there were four terrorists," he replies.

"How many were casualties?" yells another.

"Our reports indicate four casualties."

"How many dead?" cries out another.

Again, the director pauses. "Ladies and gentleman, after due consideration from all agencies involved, we will be reopening Ronald Reagan Washington National Airport within the next twenty-four hours. All other airports have been given the go ahead to resume normal flight activity, and we are returning to Threat Level Yellow. This meeting is over. Good day." The director then leaves the podium, while journalists and photographers try to get his attention.

"Well. That was certainly neat and tidy," says Brian in a sarcastic tone.

"Look," says AJ. "We all know that it wasn't a terrorist attack. And we know there are no other terrorists out there to worry about. Chad was the ringleader of this little group, and he's dead. You ought to know, you shot him."

"Don't remind me," Brian says, curtly.

"It was pointless to have the entire country paralyzed over Chad's obsession of trying to get even with Tony and me. End of story."

"Not quite, AJ. What about the girl?" asks Brian.

"You mean Marilyn?"

"Yes, Marilyn."

"Well, I don't think she'll be talking to anyone," replies AJ.

"How do you know?"

"I got a call from Weathers a little while ago. Two cameras focused on the arrivals side of the terminal showed a woman, matching Marilyn's description, getting out of a black limo, then moments later, getting into a Yellow Cab.

"Okay."

"Our investigations department contacted the cab company to find out where Marilyn was dropped off. Turns out, the cabbie had called in just before the explosion, saying he had picked up a fare, but was stuck behind a fuel truck in the return lane. That was the last transmission received from that cab."

"Well, that sucks."

"As far as Higgins knows, Chad only had the two bodyguards. Forensics has confirmed the two men I shot were Vinny and Marko. We're not sure how the third guy came into play. His name was Ricki Valentine. He was a recent law enforcement trainee, but washed out on his psych eval. Under normal circumstances the guy was fine, but when the pressure was on, he folded."

"Yeah, he nailed your ass pretty good with that PIT maneuver, didn't he," chides Brian.

"And get this, he had a sister by the name of Rosa. The two of them lived together. About two years ago, she had her name changed to Marilyn Monro, just like the actress, but without the 'e'."

"I guess that pretty much closes the book on this one," sighs Brian.

"Not entirely," says AJ. "We need to confirm whether she's dead or alive."

"What's that supposed to mean?"

"Someone is going to have to go down to the morgue and identify the body."

"What are you looking at me for?"

"According to the information we have, other than Ricki, Marilyn had no next of kin. And since you're the only one of us who's seen her, you're it."

"You're kidding, right?"

"I'm afraid not. If she's dead, then it's over. If she's not, then we have someone on the outside who could blow the lid off this thing."

"Are you saying that if she's not dead, we're going to kill her?"

"Absolutely not. But we will need to put her into protective custody for awhile, at least until after Higgins' Fourth of July party."

"And if she's alive, on what grounds will you be holding her?"

"Brian? According to Marko's text message about pushing the button as you leave the car? That makes her an accessory."

370

"Okay, I'll agree with that," he says. "But, do I really have to go to the morgue?"

"What are you afraid of? They're all dead. That's why it's called the morgue." AJ pauses a moment to let his comments sink in, then continues. "Look Brian. If you'd prefer, you can go around to the different hospitals and look over people who are in a lot of pain and agony. Most of them will be burned, some beyond recognition. You know what gasoline does to people. Think about it. Which makes more sense? The morgue or the hospital?"

"You're probably right, of course," he replies with a sad look on his face. "But if I don't find her there, I'll still have to go to the hospitals."

"Tell you what. Let's give it until tomorrow. Hopefully, most of the bodies will have some form of ID with them. All that information gets keyed into the NCIC database anyway. Let's just hope her name shows up, that's all, dead or alive. Then we'll figure out what the next step will be."

"Thanks for understanding, AJ," says Brian. "I still see Terry's face every time I go to sleep. I should have stopped him." You can see the emotion starting to build by the expression on his face.

"Brian, when you're time's up, it's up. There's nothing any of us can do to stop it. Even if you had been able to save him that day, what about the next day, or the day after that? I believe our lot in life is to do the best we can with what we've got. The Man upstairs has a plan for all of us. And for the most part, we're just along for the ride. A very wise woman once told me: No one knows what tomorrow's going to bring. One can hope for joy and happiness, but it could just as easily be sorrow, pain, and misery. We pray for the best, but prepare for the worst."

"Those are some pretty profound words. Who told you that? Your Mom?"

"No. Mrs. Betty Weathers."

Considering how the week started out with a bang, the rest of the week pretty much slipped by like a whisper. Higgins operatives disappeared as quickly as they had arrived and were only conspicuous by their absence.

With Chad and his thugs out of the picture, AJ can concentrate on preparing for Higgins' Fourth of July Bash. Higgins relented in allowing AJ to bring in four Secret Service Agents, plus another to man a mobile command post.

While the doctors have released Agent Wesley Niles from their care, he has not been authorized to return to active security duty. He's been going stir crazy sitting at home, and considering his past experience in communications with the military, AJ cleared it with his doctors and Weathers for him to run the mobile communications unit.

Agents Julie Robinson, Steven Anderson, Michael Rollins, and David Lawson will assist AJ in keeping an eye on Senators Higgins and McCarthy. Weathers will tag along as an active observer.

All of them spend the next few days studying the layout of the grounds and the house. Brian gives them a tour of the security center and shows them a detailed map of where the cameras are located on the grounds, as well as their field of view. AJ assigns each of them an access code for the armory, along with a list of its contents.

All of them are overwhelmed by the size and beauty of the house and the gardens. George takes particular pleasure in showing Julie around. He also takes the time to speak very highly of AJ, telling of his dealings with Higgins and the confrontation with Chad at the shooting range. Julie is truly captivated with George, and the two of them get along splendidly.

Higgins is an excellent host. Lunch is served promptly at noon, and healthy snacks, such as fruit and granola bars are available in the dining room throughout the day. Water, fruit juice, and soft drinks are kept chilled in a bed of ice just outside the kitchen.

Higgins spends part of Saturday afternoon talking about how he plans to introduce himself and Senator McCarthy as running mate. Carpenters and electricians are running all over the place trying to get the platforms, lighting, microphones, and speakers set up in just the right places. Even the pyro-technicians are in on some of the meetings. Three small barges have been anchored on the lake for the fireworks display, and with a little luck, it will be synched to Doo Whopp's DJ equipment.

Higgins found a fly in the ointment when the catering company delivered over three hundred pounds of Maine Lobster Tails, only to discover the kitchen's commercial freezer was far too small to handle the load.

Luckily a truck with a twenty-four foot freezer box was quickly located and delivered to the estate. A companion refrigerated truck, of the same size, was also rented. Both were parked near the access door to the kitchen. An additional bonus was the fact that both units could be operated from a 240-volt electrical system.

Then the lawn care crew showed up the same time the rental company arrived with the tables and chairs that were to be set out on the grounds. AJ and Rollins had to threaten the people from the rental company with incarceration before they would allow the lawn care crew to do their job. But once this skirmish was resolved, everything else started falling into place.

TLC: Chapter 52
Higgins' Estate
Sunday evening
July 3, 2011, 2130 hours

The night before the party, AJ, Julie, and Weathers are sitting out on the veranda, overlooking the gardens and the lake. The moon is full, and there's hardly a cloud in the sky. Stars are twinkling all over. There's a slight breeze coming off the lake, cooling things off just right.

"Some people have all the luck," says Weathers looking out toward the lake.

"Yep, I was about to say the same thing," replies AJ while reaching up and stretching his arms. "Thank God I don't have to pay for all this stuff. You know I heard those lobster tails cost the senator over seven thousand dollars! And between the wine and champagne, that's another ten!"

"AJ? You haven't even scratched the surface. You have the hors d'oeuvres, salads, vegetables, potatoes, three varieties I'm told, prime rib, for those who don't care for seafood, and let's not forget dessert. Oh! And we also have the chef and his four assistants, the stewards, and the clean up staff. I think it will average about two hundred dollars per person, and he has either verbal or written commitments for at least three hundred and fifty people."

"You're talking about seventy thousand dollars for this party?" asks AJ.

"No, I didn't say that."

"You just said it was going to cost about seventy thousand..."

"Just to feed them, AJ," says Weathers. "That doesn't include the rentals, the carpenters, electricians, construction materials, etc. The fireworks display is costing him another fifteen thousand, give or take. The stringed ensemble? He's donating five thousand dollars to the school to go toward musical instruments and other equipment; tax deductible, of course. Then there's the valet service and the three buses to shuttle the carhops from the parking lot, and the guests back to their cars when the party's over. That's another five thousand dollars. The tables, chairs, podium, lights, PA system, Jeffrey..."

"You mean Doo Whopp," corrects AJ.

"Doo Whopp, the freezer and refrigerator trucks, invitations, temp service, postage, computers, phones, ad infinitum. He'll be lucky if he can keep this little shindig under a half mil."

"Oh my God!" shrieks Julie.

"And would you believe the owner of the parking lot wanted five thousand dollars, stating that he'd need to cover any potential losses related to vandalism or theft," says Weathers shaking his head.

"Sounds like highway robbery to me," replies AJ.

"I'm sure Higgins has a trick or two up his sleeve and will get around to payback," says Weathers.

"Do you think we're ready?" asks AJ.

"I must admit I feel better having the party here than at the Watergate Hotel like he planned. Since we know the attack is supposed to be covert, meaning it should be up close and personal, we shouldn't be worried about long-range targets. Besides, there's nothing close around here with any elevation to speak of. While someone could hide in the tree line on either side of the property, they'd be shooting into the crowd." Weathers pauses a moment while he looks out over the property. "No, I don't they'd try anything like that. Too risky."

"I still feel like we're missing something. I can't quite put my finger on it."

"AJ, no one can ever cover all the bases. Sometimes it's so obvious you want to kick yourself for missing it. Others are so obscure, or the odds are so outrageous, you wonder why anyone would even consider taking the risk. It's a crapshoot, always has been, always will be. Someone's always trying to build a better mousetrap."

"Speaking of mousetraps," he calls Niles on the com link. "AJ to Mobile One. AJ to Mobile One."

"Go ahead for Mobile One."

"How many cameras have you been able to tag with your new toy?"

"Not as many as I would have liked. So far, I have most of the grounds covered, along with both gates. But I only have four interior cameras working. I'm getting some kind of interference,

375

looks like sixty cycle stuff. Maybe some bad RF units. It's too early to tell."

"Roger that."

"What are you and Niles up to?" asks Weathers with a perplexed look on his face.

"While Wesley was laid up in the hospital, I loaned him my laptop and wireless card. He found an electronics warehouse that has these wireless radio frequency thingamajigs that tap into the video feeds on the security cameras. Depending on distance and terrain, they have a range up to a thousand feet. Rollins and Anderson spent part of the day plugging these things in, and now we have our own personal feed off some of the cameras. That way, if we should lose Higgins' security room, we still have some eyes around the place."

"Radio frequency thingamajigs, you say," says Weathers smiling, and Julie starts to giggle.

"Look sir, my electronics nomenclature only goes so far. You ought to be happy I remembered radio frequency."

"I'll keep that in mind. Oh! Did I tell you Lisa aced the Civil Service Exam? She has an interview on the eleventh."

"That's wonderful!" says Julie.

"She's got to be walking on air," says AJ.

"Yes, she is. When I left the house, she was still humming, singing, and carrying on." Weathers pauses, then groans as he hauls himself out of the chair. "Well, I don't know about the rest of you chickens, but this old rooster's headin' to the hen house."

"We're right behind you, Mr. Weathers," says AJ. "AJ to all units. AJ to all units. Let's pack it up for the night. Showtime's at 2000 hours tomorrow. Guests will start arriving around 1830 hours. I want everybody ready to rock and roll at 1700 hours. We'll stage by Mobile One. Copy?"

"Mobile One, message received and understood."

"Rollins and Anderson, message received and understood."

"Lawson, sir. Message received and understood."

Julie looks up to AJ, smiles and says, "Agent Robinson, message received and understood."

"Mr. Weathers, sir? How about you?" asks AJ.

"Don't look at me, I'm JAFO," says Weathers, without looking back.

376

"JAFO? What the hell is that?"

Weathers stops, turns around and says, "You're not much of a movie buff, are you?"

"I've watched a few movies in my time. Why?"

"Do you remember a movie called 'Blue Thunder' with Roy Scheider, Malcolm McDowell, Warren Oates, and Daniel Stern made back in the 80's? Scheider was a chopper pilot for the Los Angeles Police Department, and the military wanted him to test a new type of helicopter. It had all kinds of high tech gear on it, but the thing that bothered Scheider's character, was the fact that it had a Gatling gun on it."

"Yeah, I think I remember that movie, but what does that have to do with JAFO?"

"Daniel Stern's character was fresh out of the academy and wanted to fly. But since he wasn't a pilot, the option for him was to be an observer." Weathers is smiling, waiting for the light to come on for AJ.

"Observer…JAFO…JAFO…" he pauses for a moment.

"I got it!" In unison, the two of them say, "Just another fucking observer!" Then all three of them have a good laugh.

"Good night, Julie, AJ," says Weathers as he walks away.

"Good night, sir," says AJ. "See you tomorrow."

TLC: Chapter 53
AJ's Apartment
Monday afternoon
July 4, 2011, 1600 hours

AJ is pacing the floor, waiting for Julie to get out of the bathroom.

"Julie? It's time to roll. We've got exactly one hour to get to Higgins' place."

"Keep your shirt on, I'm almost done," she tells him through the bathroom door. "Do you have everything?"

"Of course I have everything! I'm the one ready to go. You're the one holding up the parade!"

"How about your black bag?" she asks.

"Yep! Already in the car, ready to go."

"Well?" she says, as she opens the door. "So am I."

"Julie!" he says looking totally stunned. "You look like you just walked off the cover of Business Week, Vogue, or Working Woman!"

"Stop it," she says nervously. "You've seen me in this outfit before."

"Really? When?"

"Oh, AJ. You're getting in way over your head," giving him the evil eye. "That isn't funny. Not funny at all!"

"Is that the same suit you wore to that party at the American Embassy in London, where I made a near perfect ass of myself?"

"It's not your fault you had more citations and campaign ribbons than the general, AJ."

"You know, what really ticked me off, was he didn't even know we had a presence in Afghanistan. Where had he been hiding? The moon? It's guys like him that made me proud to be a noncom. At least I knew what the hell was going on."

"You're telling me that's why you turned down two Battlefield Commissions? Because you didn't want to be like him? Look at Weathers!"

"That's apples and oranges. Weathers was in intelligence. It was his job to know what was going on," he replies, somewhat arrogantly. "You know the main reason I turned down that commission. I needed to be on the ground, with my team. I

378

needed to make sure they did everything they were supposed to do, and in turn, do my absolute best to get them back home, preferably alive and in one piece."

"But AJ, you're not a Marine anymore. You're Thomas Andrew Jackson, Secret Service. You're the man of my dreams, the man of my life. I love you AJ, with all my heart."

"Most of what you say is true, and I love you, too. But Julie, once a Marine, always a Marine. Semper Fi."

"I know what you mean. I just meant you're not wearing that uniform anymore."

"Julie, it's not about the uniform, but the man inside it. That part never leaves."

"Come on, you don't want to be late." It's obvious Julie is a little disappointed in their conversation, but AJ is focused on the job waiting for them at Higgins' estate.

***

By the time Julie and AJ arrive, everyone else is already gathered around the mobile communications van. Wesley is testing and fitting everyone's com-link. "Okay! Everyone has fresh batteries, which means everyone should be good to go for a minimum of twelve hours, give or take an hour. I've personally tweaked each and every unit to make sure they're all working at optimum efficiency."

"What did you say?" ask Rollins. "I think my com-link is dead. I couldn't hear a word you said."

"That's because I wasn't talking to you on it."

"Oh. Sorry. Never mind." says Rollins, making a funny face.

"Seriously, people. Once you get at least fifty feet away from the van, try your com-link. If it doesn't work, bring it back, and I'll replace it. Okay? Great! AJ? It's all yours," says Niles.

"Okay! Today's the big day. There's going to be music, celebrities, dignitaries, fireworks, and five assassins going after Senator Higgins."

Everyone starts looking at each other and mumbling their concern. "Yep, I know what you're thinking. This isn't going to be easy. According to our intel, this is supposed to be covert,

379

meaning no guns, no full frontal assault. It could come from a handshake or a pat on the back."

"So, what are we looking for?" asks Rollins.

"We're going to be looking for a lot of things. First off, clean cut, masculine, military types. In other words, guys who don't look like they belong in a suit."

"But AJ. The other dignitaries, and even some of the celebrities, are going to have bodyguards. Some of them will be former military," says Anderson with concern in his voice.

"True, but they won't be seeking out the senator. They'll be focused on trying to protect their employers. No, the men we'll be looking for will be like sharks sniffing out their prey. They'll be working through the crowd, looking for the right time to strike. It'll be difficult trying to find them at ground level, so a couple of us will have to try to stay above them, while the rest of you stay close enough to respond."

AJ continues. "The good news is that both the house and grounds have a number of cameras scattered about. Thanks to Rollins and Anderson, our mobile unit is able to monitor some of these cameras directly. There is also direct communication between house security and Mobile One, and while security has access to our com-link, they've been advised only to use it in an emergency."

"It'll be fairly easy to keep an eye on Higgins and McCarthy while they're on the grounds. Almost any spot on the veranda will give you an excellent view of the grounds below. Once inside the ballroom, overhead observation will be more difficult. There are only two places you can observe from above, and that's from the balconies on either side of the ballroom. That'll make us easy to spot, and could put us in jeopardy as well. So, if we're working inside, we'll take turns working both sides of the ballroom, random intervals, okay?" Everyone nods their head.

"Mr. Weathers? I'd like you to pair up with Agent Robinson. Anderson? Pair up with Lawson. Rollins, you're with me. Let's go to work. Good hunting, and watch your backs."

***

AJ and Rollins check out the doors of the rooms on the second floor, making sure all of them are locked. Niles is still fiddling with some of the feeds from the in-house cameras trying to get a better signal, but it appears to be a lost cause. Julie and Weathers are casually walking around on the main floor and out to the veranda. Anderson and Lawson are out walking the grounds near the lake.

At 1800 hours, Niles calls out on the com-link, "Mobile One to all personnel. Mobile One to all personnel. Be advised the floodgates are open. Repeat. The floodgates are open."

"Wait a minute. I thought guests weren't supposed to arrive before 1830 hours," says Rollins.

"They aren't," replies AJ, obviously disappointed by the change. "AJ to Mobile One. AJ to Mobile One. What happened? Why are they admitting guests a half hour ahead of time?"

"Mobile One. From what I can see from the video feed, traffic is already starting to back up, creating a major traffic hazard. I can barely make out some flashing lights farther down the road. Probably a fender bender."

"Well, I just hope the valets are ready for the onslaught." says AJ.

"Copy that," replies Niles.

***

Luckily, the valets are ready, and with the exception of a few malcontents, everything seems to be going smoothly. The valets are literally dancing between cars, opening doors, assisting their occupants from their vehicles, and directing them toward the steps up to the grand entrance.

It's a virtual Who's Who of everyone of importance in both government and business in and around Washington. The paparazzi are having a field day, and reporters from the major networks are clamoring to get "exclusives" from celebrities and key government officials.

Once inside, the guests are greeted by stewards offering wine and champagne, while others are carrying trays with all manners of exotic and unusual hors d'ocuvres. The ballroom is spectacular with its ornate architecture, perfectly lit artwork, and antique chandeliers. Even the ceilings are covered with beautifully detailed murals.

The stringed ensemble continues their warm up, as the guests begin to arrive. Just below the veranda, which overlooks the gardens and the lake on the backside of the house, Doo Whopp is busily setting up and testing his equipment, totally oblivious as to what is going on around him.

Doo Whopp is bent over a box of CD's when AJ eases up behind him and taps him on the shoulder. Do Whopp bolts upright and spins around to see who had almost made him jump out of his skin. "Holy shit man! Don't *ever* do that again!"

"Jeffrey? I mean Doo Whopp, you look like you just saw a ghost!"

"Very funny, very funny," he replies. "You almost gave me a heart attack!"

"Sorry about that. Do you have everything under control here?"

"Yeah, I'm just about ready to jam some tunes, man. Look, AJ. I want to thank you for puttin' the word on the senator about me and my side gig. I really appreciate it."

"My pleasure. Besides, you might even pick up a few more gigs by playing here tonight. There'll be a lot of money floating around here. You could be playing some very ritzy gigs before you know it! You might even have your own limo and chauffeur pretty soon, along with a bunch of young honeys vying for your attention."

"Yeah, right," he says smugly. "I'll just be happy spinning music and taking care of business."

"Well, I need to get back to work. I just wanted to wish you good luck."

"Thanks, AJ. You too!"

"Later," says AJ as he meanders back into the crowd.

***

Higgins is standing in front of his favorite picture window staring out toward the gardens. McCarthy is nursing a glass of wine,

382

sitting in one of the high backed leather chairs near Higgins' desk, looking as though he's bored out of his mind.

Higgins says, "You know? Here we are, on the threshold of making history."

"How's that?" asks McCarthy seemingly preoccupied with his wine glass, holding it up to the fading sunlight. "You and I will be the first members of the Core seeking the highest offices of the United States. And we're going to win. Not only the nomination, but also the election! I know it! I can feel it in my bones!"

"Glad to hear it," replies McCarthy rather flippantly. "I'd hate to know we did all this for just shits and giggles. Would you believe that Michelle wouldn't even come to the party with me? She said she had a headache."

"Well, crowds of people, loud music, and fireworks aren't exactly the recipe for curing a headache, Joshua."

"No, but she's been avoiding me a lot lately. She's been very aloof, like she's plotting something."

"You have to admit that you haven't exactly been focused on any sort of family life for some time. How many women have you been seeing over the past six months?"

"Only three: Elizabeth, Jennifer, and Yvette. Sorry, better make that four. Tatyana. My God! The legs on that girl? Mmm-Mmm!"

"How long have you been seeing her?"

"Since last week. She's part of the Russian dance troupe playing in New York. This girl can fold herself up in so many different ways…I had no idea the human body could do things like that. Unbelievable!"

"Hold your horses, Joshua. It's time to focus on business, okay? Looks like our guests are already arriving. What do you say we go out and mingle a little?"

"Sure beats staring at these four walls. Let's go."

Showtime!

One of Higgins security team calls out on their radio frequency. "Security Central to Mobile One. Security Central to Mobile One."

"Go ahead for Mobile One," answers Niles.

"Black Jack One and Two are on the move, heading toward the ball room."

"Copy that." With that, Niles calls out on their com-link. "Mobile One to all units, Mobile one to all units. Black Jack One and Two are mobile, moving toward the ball room."

"AJ to Mobile One. Do you have a visual?"

"Negative, AJ. Sorry."

"Copy that. AJ to Weathers. AJ to Weathers."

"Go ahead for Weathers."

"Rollins and I are splitting up and going to the balconies. I'd like you and Robinson to hang close to Black Jack One and Two."

"Roger that, AJ. Moving in to intercept."

"Copy that," says AJ. "AJ to Lawson. AJ to Lawson."

"Go ahead for Lawson."

"I want you and Anderson to move in closer to the house."

Suddenly, Anderson hears a faint, crackling sound behind them. "Standby one. Suspect in the tree line, approximately twenty yards from my location," says Anderson in a loud whisper. "Going to check it out."

"Lawson, watch his six." says AJ.

"Copy that, AJ. I'm on it," replies Lawson. Both men proceed along the tree line with guns drawn.

"AJ to Mobile One. AJ to Mobile One. Do you have a visual on Lawson and Anderson?"

"Roger that, but I don't have a visual on their target. It's evidently in the trees and out of range."

"Copy that. Continue to monitor their progress."

"Roger that." A minute or so later, Anderson finds his suspect. It's a fawn.

"Anderson to Mobile One, Anderson to Mobile One."

"Go ahead for Mobile One."

"Advise all units, false alarm. Repeat, false alarm. Advancing toward the gardens."

"Copy that, Anderson," says Niles.

"All other units copy Anderson's traffic?"

"Rollins and AJ copy direct."

"Weathers and Robinson copy direct."

***

Higgins and McCarthy mingle with different dignitaries and government officials for almost a half hour in the ballroom. Then McCarthy casually nudges Higgins, motioning him to follow.

"What are you doing?" asks Higgins in a disgruntled tone. "Do you have any idea who I was talking to back there?"

"Yeah, some stuffed shirt with one foot on a banana peel, and the other in the grave. Follow me. I just found some fresh meat!"

"What are you talking about?"

"Stop asking questions, and just come on." McCarthy is on the heels of a very beautiful young woman. She's blonde, stands about five foot nine in three inch heels, really nice shape, and her hips are rocking just so!

"Damn it Joshua," says Higgins in a hushed but firm tone as he tries to stop McCarthy. "Can't you think with something above your waist for just a little while?"

"Sure! Just not right now, that's all," he replies with a devilish smile.

"Come back here Joshua. We need to be talking to…"

Joshua ignores Higgins and follows the young lady out to the veranda, then down the steps to the gardens. Higgins stares at him angrily for a moment, but finally throws up his hands in frustration and follows behind him.

Once the young lady reaches the bottom of the steps, she's greeted by a handsome young man. Joshua spots her wedding ring. It's a rock! Four, maybe five carats, easy. Joshua nods and raises his glass to both of them as he walks by. They return the gesture.

When Higgins catches up to McCarthy, he says, "Well that was a pretty good recovery, considering you could have made a complete *ass* of yourself at *my* expense! We're looking for votes, endorsements, donations, and lots of it! The last thing we need is to have your picture plastered on the front page of the Washington Post with your hand up the skirt of a newlywed."

"You're just jealous because I spotted her first."

"Bullshit! I have enough to worry about without thinking about a dame."

McCarthy stops and says, "Wait a minute. I've known you for what, twelve years? And I've never once seen you with a woman. Not once. Why is that?"

Higgins takes a step closer to McCarthy and says, "I don't have to explain my personal life to you or anybody else." He starts to turn and walk away, but turns back to McCarthy and adds, "You know? Your sex drive more than compensates for any of my short comings, so why don't we just leave it at that?"

"Bill? Are you gay?" he asks rather flippantly.

Higgins gets right up in his face and growls in a low, guttural tone, "If we weren't standing in front of over a hundred people right now, people I've paid good money to be here, I'd cut your heart out and feed it to the fish. Actually, I think I'd start with your balls, then your heart!"

"Now Bill. Is that any way to be talking to your running mate?"

"You know? It's not too late for me to change my mind about that."

***

Having positioned himself near the center of the veranda, overlooking the mob of people in the garden, AJ spots a man who seems to be stalking Senator Higgins. AJ alerts Rollins through his com-link, and the two of them start working their way toward the Senator and the suspect.

Both Rollins and AJ try to stay outside of the suspect's field of view as they approach him from behind. AJ manages to get within arm's length of the suspect, when he notices the man slipping something onto his finger. Just as the assassin is about to strike, AJ grabs his arm, as Rollins jabs his pistol into the assassin's left kidney. The two of them shuffle the assassin off to a room adjacent to the ballroom, away from the senators and the other guests.

"Hey! What's going on?" shouts Higgins, as he and McCarthy watch AJ and Rollins walk away with the assassin.

"Wow! That was close." says a surprised McCarthy, as he starts to take a sip of his drink.

"Gentlemen," says Weathers, "We need to get you back to the library right away."

"But Bob, we're just getting started. What just happened?"

"One of the Core's assassins was about arm's length from you," says Weathers as he starts making a path through the crowd.

"Look, Bob. AJ's got everything under control," says Higgins, while walking up the steps to the veranda.

***

Once in the room, away from the other guests, AJ and Rollins attempt to remove the ring from the assassin's finger.

"What's your name? Who are you working for?" asks AJ gruffly, but the assassin remains silent.

Suddenly, the assassin manages to break free of Rollins' grasp, shoves AJ away, and pulls a pistol from a holster in the small of his back. Rollins charges the assassin in an attempt to knock him off balance, but not before the assassin fires off a round, striking Rollins in the left shoulder. Instinctively, AJ gets off two rounds, centered in the assassin's chest.

The assassin's arms fall to his side, dropping the pistol. He stands motionless for a few seconds, with a blank stare, then falls forward like a freshly felled tree, slamming to the floor with a resounding thud.

Upon hearing the gunshots, panic erupts. People are screaming and running in all directions!

"Let's get to the library! Now! Now!" shouts Weathers leading Higgins and McCarthy, with Julie covering the rear. Both Weathers and Julie have their guns drawn and at the ready.

AJ rushes over to Rollins who's cursing under his breath, "Two tours in Iraq, and not a scratch. No! I have to get shot in the States, at a party, and no combat pay!"

"Are you all right?" asks AJ with concern in his voice.

"Hell no! I'm not all right! The son of a bitch shot me, and it hurts like hell! I think he shattered my collarbone, too!" replies Rollins, obviously in a lot of pain. "Is he dead?"

AJ looks over to the assassin and can see a dark pool of blood starting to ooze around his neck and shoulder. There's no visual evidence of respiration or pulse. His eyes are open and fixed. "Yeah, but don't worry about him. Just hang in there. I'll get the medics in here right away." AJ barks over the com-link, "Mobile One? Mobile One. Rollins has been shot. Get the medics in here now. We're in the sitting room just off to the left of the ballroom. We've got a stiff in here, too."

"Well, I figured something was going on in there," says Niles. "People are piling out of there like rats from a sinking ship! What about Black Jack One and Two?"

"Weathers and Robinson should have them secured in the library any moment now."

***

About that time, McCarthy cries out, "Why don't you take us out to the chopper and fly us out of here?"

Julie says flatly, "That's a medevac unit, and one of our people needs it more than you!"

"Is that a fact?" yells McCarthy. "I'm a U.S. Senator, and my safety is more important than one of your men."

"Rollins was shot protecting your sorry ass!" yells Julie. "Now get in the library. You'll be safe in there."

***

"Mobile One to AJ. Medics are coming in through the kitchen, less traffic that way. Once they get him on the stretcher and stable, we can get him out with the chopper.

"Good idea, Niles. Now you're thinking. See? I told you'd be okay under pressure."

388

"Thanks. How bad is Rollins?"

"It could be a lot worse. The round hit above his vest and looks like it might have shattered his left collarbone. He's going to be down for a while, but I think he'll be okay. Radio the chopper and tell them to spool it up. I want them ready to dust off as soon as they get Rollins onboard."

"Copy that!"

"Thanks Niles. Okay, the medics are here. I'm off to join Weathers and Robinson."

"House Security to AJ! Security to AJ!" crackles over the com-link.

"Go ahead for AJ."

"We have two intruders moving around on the second floor with guns drawn."

"Where on the second floor? Who is this?" asks AJ.

"They're in the west wing, directly over the library. You called me Kung Fooey, sir," he replies timidly.

"Who told you that?" asks AJ.

"Jamison, sir."

"Sorry about that. I really didn't mean anything by it," says AJ sounding a bit embarrassed.

"It's okay, sir. I had it coming."

"What's your real name?"

"Brandon, sir. Brandon Lee," he replies. "My dad was a Bruce Lee fan, and he named me after Bruce's son."

"Okay Brandon, what are they doing up there?"

"Well, it looks like they're going to try to make a frontal assault on the library. They just pulled a large bag out of the closet, and it looks like it's got a couple of assault vests, two M4's, and…Uh-oh."

"What?"

"One of them spotted the camera. They just took it out."

"Great!" says AJ sarcastically, shaking his head.

"Did you know that Jamison was working tonight?" asks Brandon.

"No, why?"

"Because he's coming down the hallway toward security. He's keying in." Brandon inadvertently continues to hold the transmit key down. "Hi Brian. What are you doing here? I

389

thought you had the night off. Hey! What tha'." The radio goes silent.

"Brandon? Brandon!" yells AJ. "Mobile One! Mobile One! Have Lawson and Anderson converge on Higgins' security room *now*! Hold Jamison for questioning. Don't shoot unless it's absolutely necessary. We have to regain control of the security office. Otherwise, they'll be able to watch our every move."

"You think Jamison is one of the assassins?" asks Niles. "How do we know Brandon isn't one of them, and Brian's onto him?"

"We don't. Mobile One, have you been monitoring the airwaves for any unusual chatter?"

"Roger that. But I haven't picked up on anything so far. Mobile One to Anderson and Lawson. Move in on the security office. Use extreme caution. Be on the lookout for Brian Jamison. He's considered armed and dangerous. Hold him for questioning. Termination is authorized, but only as a last resort."

"Delay that termination order!" barks Weathers. "I want him alive."

"Weathers! Weathers! Have you been monitoring the chatter?" asks AJ.

"Roger that, AJ. Robinson and I have Blackjack One and Two secured in the library. How do you want to handle the two men on the second floor?"

"Are you up to giving me a hand with that detail?"

"Roger that, but don't you think we're a little outgunned? They've got assault rifles, and all we've got are handguns," replies Weathers with some concern in his voice.

"Not to worry, we have both the element of surprise, and my little black bag."

"I hope you're right, on both counts. Either way, we're about to find out. I assume you'll be going up the ballroom side. I'll come up from the far end of the wing. Maybe we can catch them in a crossfire."

"Do you think it's wise to leave Robinson alone to protect Blackjack One and Two?" asks AJ.

"You've already taken out one assassin. We have another in security, and the two upstairs. That only leaves one more assassin. I think Robinson can take care of herself, don't you?"

"Just be aware that all of the rooms are locked on the second floor, so you're not going to find much cover up there. I'd try to stay on the library side of the hallway. That way they'll have to step out into the hallway to see you."

"Good idea."

"Let me know when you get into position, then we'll move in on them together, okay?"

"Copy that," replies Weathers. "See you on the second floor."

AJ stops by a small closet next to the stairway, unlocks it, pulls out his black bag, and rests it on the table by the door. He pulls out his H&K MP5 and its suppressor. He screws on the suppressor, and checks to make sure that both the spotlight and laser are working properly. Reaching back into the bag, he grabs three 40-round mags, placing two in his jacket pocket, then slams the last one into the receiver. He releases the bolt, placing a round in the chamber. He also grabs a concussion grenade, stowing it in another pocket. Then he zips up the bag, puts it back in the closet, and locks the door again. Now, AJ begins making his way up the stairway.

***

Meanwhile, back in the library, "Did you hear what that little bitch said to me?" asks McCarthy.

"You're lucky that's all she did! She's the one your men shot at the other week."

"Well, when this is over, I want her fired! Nobody talks to me that way!"

"While we're on that subject, what was all that bullshit about while we were down below the veranda?" Higgins starts walking toward McCarthy with an angry look on his face. "Do you really think I'm gay?"

"Of course not, Bill. I was just making conversation, that's all."

"Well, that's not the type of conversation you should make out in public, especially tonight!"

"Point taken," says McCarthy. "But tell me, why haven't I seen you with any women?"

"I had a wife, two actually, although the first one wasn't actually legal. It was more or less for show."

"Care to enlighten me on that, Bill?" asks McCarthy looking a little confused.

"While I flew for the CIA out of Thailand, I had a wife of convenience. We faked the marriage. In fact, most of us did. Oh, the girls thought they were married, but we weren't. She wasn't real happy when I left her there, either. But I don't think she could have coped with the American way of life, and she'd have probably held me back politically, too. I couldn't have that."

"Any kids?" asks McCarthy.

"By Ling-Ling? Nah. I was feeding her birth control pills. I told her they were vitamins. Thank goodness she couldn't read English."

"Okay, so you loved her and you left her. Then what?"

"Then there was Ellen. Fiery redhead. God she was gorgeous! The first time I laid eyes on her, I knew. I knew she was the one."

"Well, what happened?"

"We dated awhile, then I started my law practice, got married, bought a house, and had a son."

"I didn't know you had any kids," says McCarthy.

Higgins looks up at McCarthy, and it's a look that would make any man quiver. "The birth was complicated. Something happened and Ellen began to hemorrhage. They had to perform an emergency hysterectomy to save her life. Both she and the boy lived, but the hysterectomy really messed her up. Those things screw up their hormones something fierce."

"Before the surgery, our sex life was perfect, but after…" Higgins shakes his head in disgust. "Nothing helped. Hormone therapy, this shot, that shot, counseling…nothing."

"Then one day, I came home and the house was almost empty; furniture, her clothes, the kid's clothes, everything. She left a note saying she was going home to her parents, and I shouldn't follow her."

"What did you do?" asks McCarthy.

***

As AJ begins his ascent up the stairway to the second floor, he's looking and listening for any telltale signs of movement. Suddenly, he hears the dull thumping sound of footsteps coming toward him, and considering the erratic rhythm of the footfalls, he knows it has to be more than one person.

He moves to the inside of the turn of the stairway to take

393

advantage of the wall as cover. He can see the faint shadows of two people coming down the steps, getting closer and closer.

Just as he releases the safety on his MP5, he hears the giggle of a young woman, and decides to hide the MP5 between him and the wall.

As the young couple round the corner, AJ says casually, "How are you this evening?"

They're both startled by his presence and his question. The young man replies with a crackle in his voice, "Fine, and you?"

"I'm with the Secret Service, and I need to know why you were up there."

"Well, ah, we were just looking around. We didn't mean anything by it," replies the visibly shaken young man.

"I need to see your invitation."

"I, ah, we don't have one. We came with her father. He's known Senator Higgins for years and is a major contributor to his campaign," replies the young man, nervously.

"I'm still not satisfied with what you were doing upstairs," says AJ sternly.

"We just wanted to be alone, you know?" says the young lady, almost in tears. "Please don't tell my father, please?"

"While you were on the second floor, did you see or hear anyone else?"

"Yes, sir. Less than fifteen minutes ago, there were two men checking the doors in the hallway," replies the young man.

"Are you sure there were only two?"

"Yes sir, but they didn't see us," says the young man.

"How's that?"

"Because we were already in one of the bedrooms when they checked the doors," replies the young man as his girlfriend begins to blush.

"How is that possible? All of the doors were locked. I checked them myself, less than an hour ago."

The young man cracks a smile and pulls out a couple of key blanks and says, "Well, they're not much of a lock."

"Okay," replies AJ with a smirk. "You're going to find that almost everyone has left the party. If you don't see your father out front, you're probably going to have to call him and find out where he is."

"What's going on? Where did everybody go?"

"Someone just tried to assassinate the Senator."

"Holy shit! Did anybody get hurt?"

"One of my agents was wounded in the process of subduing the suspect." The young man notices the machine gun AJ is trying to hide. His eyes bug out, his jaw drops, and as he takes a step back, he starts to stumble over the step behind him. "Whoa there, young man. It's all right. There's nothing for you to worry about, but I'd go on downstairs and try to find her father right away. This party's not over yet."

"Whatever you say, sir. Goodbye. Come on Linda! Let's get out of here!" says the young man, literally dragging his girlfriend down the stairway.

As AJ starts up the stairs again, he hears Weathers whispering on the com-link. "AJ? AJ! Where the hell are you?"

"I'll be at the top of the stairs in a minute. I ran into a young couple coming down the stairs."

"You can fraternize with the guests later," says Weathers in a loud whisper.

"At least they confirmed we only have two suspects on this floor to deal with."

"Maybe, but that means we still have an assassin unaccounted for."

"Are you at the top of the stairs?" asks AJ.

"Roger that. I'm in the stairwell, and from what I can see, the hallway's clear."

"Can you tell whether the doors are open or closed where our suspects are supposed to be?" asks AJ as he settles into position. AJ peeks around the corner and sees Weathers on the opposite end of the hallway.

"Looks like they're open," replies Weathers.

"Well, let's hope they're preoccupied enough to let us get the drop on them before they catch us in the open."

"Ready when you are," replies Weathers.

"Remember, stay close to the wall, okay? Now if they come out, hit the deck, and I'll take care of them."

Weathers nods his head and replies, "Roger that."

"Let's go," says AJ as the two of them begin advancing toward the open doors. AJ is almost to the doors when one of the assassins steps out into the hallway and spots Weathers trying to cross over to the near side.

AJ yells, "Down!" As Weathers drops to the floor, AJ squeezes off two rounds from his silenced MP5. Both rounds find their mark in the back of the assassin's head, but not before the assassin squeezes the trigger on his M4, firing wildly in Weathers' direction in full auto mode. Weathers curls up in the corner as the rounds fly all around him. One of them grazes his left calf about midway between his ankle and knee. He flinches in pain, but luckily the wound isn't serious.

***

Suddenly Higgins and McCarthy hear muffled machinegun fire.

"Now what?" asks Higgins.

"Sounds like gunfire!" yells McCarthy.

***

Without warning, the second assassin cuts loose with a full auto burst from his M4, sending AJ to the floor, and away from the entrance. Bullets, plaster, and dust fill the air in the hallway.

AJ calls out to Weathers, "Are you okay?"

"Yeah, looks like just a flesh wound. I'll live. What do we do now?"

At that moment, the second assassin fires a short burst about three feet above the floor near Weathers, then another burst near AJ, slicing through the wall, sounding like a swarm of angry hornets.

AJ pulls out the concussion grenade and shows it to Weathers. Then he waves his arm motioning Weathers to crawl back to the stairwell for cover.

Once he sees that Weathers is out of harm's way, AJ eases up close to the doorway, pulls the pin, and rolls the canister into the room. The grenade explodes before the assassin can duck for cover, knocking him off his feet.

***

396

"Holy shit!" yells McCarthy, as both of them look up at the ceiling. "Are they bombing the place?" The shockwave from the blast shakes the entire west wing. Dust falls from the ceiling in the library, rocking the chandeliers, and even jarring a few books off the shelves!

After a few seconds of silence, Higgins says, "Whatever it was, I guess it's over."

"I wonder what happened?" asks McCarthy while waving at the floating dust.

"I'm sure we'll find out in a few minutes," replies Higgins.

Higgins walks over to the wet bar and pours himself a shot of Jack Daniels over ice, then says to McCarthy, "I feel like having a drink. What can I get you?"

"I'll have the same, thank you," McCarthy replies.

***

As AJ enters the room through the thick cloud of smoke and dust, he sees the assassin having a difficult time trying to get to his feet, clearly shaken up and disoriented from the blast of the grenade.

It's obvious AJ has the upper hand, but the assassin struggles to raise his rifle.

AJ says, "Lower your weapon. It's over. I don't want to hurt you." But the assassin does not comply. "Look. It doesn't have to end this way." Yet the assassin continues to raise his rifle. AJ has no choice. His laser paints a dot between the assassin's eyes, then he fires. The assassin goes limp.

AJ shoulders his weapon, then walks over and squats down next to the assassin's body. He checks for a pulse, but there is none. He takes the assassin's pistol, and slips it into his waistband in the small of his back. He pockets the magazines, then shoulders the assassin's rifle. As he rises and turns to face the doorway, he sees Weathers standing there, staring at him and the dead assassin. AJ walks past Weathers, drops to one knee by the dead assassin in the hallway. Again, he checks for a pulse. Nothing. He pockets his pistol and magazines, picks up his rifle, shoulders it, then stands back up.

397

Without a word, he starts walking toward the stairwell when Weathers asks, "Son, are you all right?"

AJ stops cold, drops his head down, sighs, then says, "No, I'm not." He slowly turns around to face Weathers, and says, "I just killed two young men who probably had no idea why they were here. Both of them were probably in their early to mid twenties, given the same song and dance they gave David."

"AJ, I saw you trying to warn him. He knew you had the drop on him, but he wouldn't put it down. You had no choice."

"In his eyes, neither did he," says a saddened AJ. There's a moment of silence, then he bolts upright and says, "Something's not right here."

"What do you mean?" asks a puzzled Weathers.

"Look at this. These guys are wearing dark clothing, bulletproof assault vests, ski masks, carrying pistols and machine guns, but no silencers. If this were an operation behind enemy lines, this might be considered covert, but not here. I'd call this…" AJ pauses a moment, then it hits him. "Shit!"

"What?" asks Weathers.

"A diversion. We've been had!"

AJ bolts down the stairway. At the base of the stairwell, he removes the magazines from the assault rifles and drops them in a trash can. He hides the M4's in the shadow underneath the stairwell. Next, he slowly cracks the door open just enough to see down the hallway. He can see the doors to the library are closed, and Julie is standing across from them, occasionally glancing toward the ceiling. Everything appears to be normal.

AJ opens the door a little wider and whispers, "Julie…Julie!" Startled, she turns toward AJ. He then motions for her to join him in the stairwell.

"What in the hell happened up there? It sounded like World War Three had started! Are you okay? Where's Weathers?"

"We had two assassins with machine guns up there, but they've been neutralized. Weathers took a round in the leg, but I don't think it's serious. And I'm okay, I guess."

"So, why did you leave Weathers?"

"Something just doesn't feel right. Our intel said the attempt on Higgins was supposed to be covert, not a full bore frontal assault. I think the two men upstairs were a diversion to pull us off Higgins and McCarthy. I expected to find the doors flung open, and you…" He pauses for a moment, then asks, "Well, have you heard anything?"

"From the library? No, I haven't."

"Weathers? Weathers! Can you hear me?" asks AJ, trying to reach him on his com-link.

"Yes, I hear you. Is Julie okay? And what did you mean by a diversion?"

"Julie's fine, and from the outside, everything appears normal. I don't get it."

"Get what?" asks Weathers.

"I think the two guys up there were just a diversion to pull us off Higgins and McCarthy, so the real assassins could get to them. Now, I don't know what to think." He pauses for a moment, then asks, "Are you coming down?"

"No, AJ. I'm starting to feel a little lightheaded. I think I'm going to sit the rest of this show on the sidelines. After all, I'm not used to getting shot, much less shot at."

"I didn't think you were bleeding that badly. Do you need me back up there?"

"No, son. It's not that. I'm just feeling a little faint, that's all. I think the adrenalin rush from all this excitement has gotten the better of me."

"Well, at least try to get back into the stairwell until we can get the paramedics up to you." He pauses a moment then says, "AJ to Mobile One."

"Already have medics on the way, AJ," replies Niles. "They should be there any minute."

"Thanks, Niles." AJ peeks out the door again to make sure the area is clear, then the two of them exit the stairwell.

***

Since the battle seems to have ended on the second floor, Higgins says, "Once this is over, we can start rebuilding the Core. Together, we can weed out the dead wood, and bring in some new blood. We'll need to protect some of the members of course, such as General Woolbright and a few others. We'll be a shoo-in for President and Vice President."

McCarthy walks over to the bar to pick up his drink, smiles, and pats Higgins on the back. Higgins feels the needle prick him. He backs away from McCarthy in total surprise. "What in the hell are you doing?" Higgins presses a button on a hidden transmitter on his belt.

***

Suddenly, both Julie and AJ hear a beeping sound. "What's that?" asks Julie.

"Higgins. Something's wrong." Julie draws her Sig, and AJ shifts his MP5 into position. "Are you up for this?" asks AJ.

"It's not like either of us have much of a choice now, does it?"

"Stay behind that wall until I tell you it's safe to come out."

"No way Jose. We're doing this together."

"We don't have time to debate this, so I'll break left, you break right. There's a large desk and chair near the door. It should give you some cover if someone starts shooting."

"What about you?"

"Me? Haven't you noticed? I'm practically bulletproof!"

Julie presses her hand against his chest and can tell he's wearing his vest. "Well, you know, you're not the only crack shot around here. And your head's not exactly bulletproof either," she scoffs.

"That's true, but at least you're on my side. On three."

***

McCarthy smiles and says, "I suggest you have a seat and let the poison do its work. You know, when I first arrived on the Hill, I truly admired you and the work you were doing. And after being inducted into the Core, I was honored to work with you and be an active participant in steering America's history."

"But Bill, your goals and ideals have become dated, much like you. It's time to have someone younger, smarter, and more aggressive take the lead. I've lived in your shadow long enough."

Without warning, AJ and Julie burst into the library and find McCarthy standing next to Higgins. AJ takes aim at McCarthy and barks, "Back away from him and raise your hands so I can see them!" As McCarthy raises his hands, AJ can see a stainless Walther PPK in his right hand.

Just as AJ is about to order him to drop it, a female voice says, "AJ, I think *you* should drop your weapon." It's Michelle, and she's holding a similar Walther to Julie's head.

Hearing those words, McCarthy smiles and starts to lower his hands. "Honey! What a pleasant surprise."

"I'm sure it is," she replies smiling. "And I have another surprise for you, too. Put your gun on the bar and step away from it!"

McCarthy is indeed surprised by her demand. He slowly places the gun on the bar and takes a couple of steps back.

"That's far enough." Michelle hands a large manila envelope to Julie and tells her to throw it to Joshua. Julie tosses the envelope at Joshua's feet. Then Michelle says, "Go ahead. Pick it up."

McCarthy leans over, picks up the envelope, and opens it. Inside are pictures of several of his conquests. While this catches him a bit off guard, there is a smug look on his face.

Suddenly, AJ hears a crackle on his com-link. "Mobile One to AJ. Mobile One to AJ."

"Miss, I hate to break up the party, but I've got a call on my com-link here, and if I don't answer it, there'll be a lot of agents here in a heartbeat," says AJ.

"Go ahead and answer it. But if I suspect any sort of code or anything else out of the ordinary, she dies. Understand?" AJ nods his head in agreement.

"Go ahead with your traffic Mobile One," he replies.

"We seem to have a problem trying to get into the security room," says Niles. "We've tried your access code, but it doesn't work. It acts as though it's been locked out."

"Tell Anderson and Lawson to hold their position until I get there."

"Roger that," says Niles. "What's your ETA?"

"I have no idea. I have a few problems of my own right now."

"Need any backup?" asks Niles.

"Negative. I just have a few loose ends to tie up. There's only one way into and out of the security room, and they've got it covered. Tell them to just hang loose, and stay out of view of the camera. I'll get there as quick as I can."

"Copy that. Mobile One, out."

TLC: Chapter 57

"Well, well, well. It appears that you've been doing a little spying of your own," says McCarthy.

Michelle begins to smile as she watches her husband gaze upon his conquests. Suddenly, his smile turns to a look of shock and horror.

Michelle says coyly, "What's the matter honey? Haven't you ever seen a dead woman before?" The pictures appear to show these same women to have been viciously murdered. Their clothes are torn, blood everywhere, and each victim has been shot in the head.

"Michelle! What have you done?"

"Me? Joshua, my love, I'm a victim, just like those women. You have used me, abused me, ignored me, lied to me, and above all, cheated on me. I even have the media to back me up. But fortunately, I'm still alive to take my vengeance upon you."

"Michelle, honey. You can't possibly believe that I…"

"Oh Joshua," she says coyly. "I know you didn't kill those women, because I did. Actually, I had it done. But it looks like you did it, and when the police perform the ballistics on your gun, they'll find it matches perfectly. Higgins? I guess giving us matching Walthers as an anniversary gift was a pretty good idea after all."

"This isn't possible. There hasn't been any word of it on the news. I would have heard something, anything!"

"Not if it happened today," she says with a Cheshire cat-like grin on her face. "And they've all met their end at places you've been seen with them before. Reservations were made by your 'secretary', with word you were not to be disturbed, and the victims picked up the keys at the desk, using your name."

"How were you able to get them all to show up?" asks McCarthy, stunned by his wife's actions.

"Oh honey, you underestimate your charm, your way with words, and gifts; very expensive gifts, I might add," she says seductively. "Each of your little conquests received a bouquet of white roses, a note, and a jewelry box. Some of them received diamond earrings, others got diamond bracelets, and a couple even got a diamond necklace. After all, owning your own shipping company has its perks, you know."

"Sorry, I digress," she says. "Anyway, you said in your note you wanted to meet them before the party and celebrate your announcement for the Vice Presidency in private. You have left me, and want to spend the rest of your life with them. Of course, you top it off by providing a limousine to take them to your secret rendezvous. What woman could resist such chivalry?"

"When they arrived at their destination, they found a beautiful silk nightgown draped on the bed, and of course they couldn't resist putting it on right away. But then, my man comes out of hiding, beats them mercilessly, shoots them in the head, silenced of course, takes a couple of pictures, then leaves. The bodies probably won't be found for another day or two."

"And why would I do such a thing?" he asks disbelievingly.

"Tying up loose ends, perhaps? After all, by the time their bodies are found, you will have announced your plans to run for the Vice Presidency, and you don't need any jilted lovers muddying the political waters. You obviously think you can eliminate almost anything or anyone without fear of reprisal. And literally in front of witnesses, you have murdered your own running mate!"

"I'm not dead yet!" says Higgins in a guttural tone. "Kill him and give me the antidote!"

"Antidote?" Michelle says innocently. "Did Joshua tell you there was an antidote? Oh, honey. There you go jumping to conclusions again. Remember? I said we thought we had an antidote, but we wouldn't know until we had finished testing it. It turned out our test subject had an unusual tolerance for alcohol. He died two days ago. I'm so sorry Bill, but there is no antidote."

"You son of a bitch! I'm going to kill you myself!" yells Higgins as he attempts to get out of the chair.

"Sit down!" yells Michelle in an authoritative tone, as she points her Walther at Higgins. "Increased heart rate, adrenaline, as well as alcohol, all play a part in how fast the toxin works. You need to remain calm if you hope to find a way to survive." Higgins calms down and settles back into the chair, but it's obvious that he's severely agitated.

"So where do we go from here?" asks McCarthy in a more subdued tone.

"Well dear, I could let AJ here shoot you in self defense. I could shoot you myself, and say it was an act of passion, as well as self defense," she says with a devious smile. "Or, AJ might decide to capture you and let the people know just how rotten you are, expose the Core, and make a name for himself."

"Your life would be a living hell as you wake up every morning in an eight by ten foot cell, wearing a prison uniform instead of your designer clothes and Italian shoes. Your daily routine would be extremely limited, and rigidly structured, and, of course, your love life would certainly take an interesting turn."

You can see that McCarthy is beginning to feel very uneasy and desperate, as his eyes start darting about the room, from Michelle, to AJ, to Higgins, his gun on the bar, and the pictures.

"Or, I could let you go," she pauses. "But only on one condition."

"And what would that be, my love?" he asks delicately.

"Higgins, take his gun, remove the magazine, and remove all of the bullets," she says authoritatively.

"What are you doing?" asks McCarthy.

"There's still a round in the chamber. It'll be your decision how to use it. You can try to shoot your way out of here and get yourself killed before you even get to the door, or you can walk out of here, find a quiet place, and..." Michelle pauses, smiling, savoring the moment. "Or I can let AJ make the decision for you."

You can see the rage in AJ's eyes. He's just waiting for an opportunity to present itself, so he can get his hands wrapped around McCarthy's neck.

"You don't honestly expect me to kill myself, do you?" he asks.

"Frankly Joshua, once you leave this house, I don't care what you do. As of tonight, your political career, our marriage, and your life in general, will be over. You'll have no money, no credit cards, no friends, and no future. When copies of those pictures hit the news, along with your assassination of Senator Higgins, you'll be hunted down like a dog. And I will finally be rid of you, forever." McCarthy can feel the world closing in around him.

Taking on a more compassionate tone, she says, "I had the Aston Martin driven up here for you. I felt like you should enjoy it one more time. After all, I'm not anywhere near as coldhearted and ruthless as you. The valet has it parked across from the front door. He's holding the keys for you. I'll give you a five-minute head start before I turn AJ loose. After that, you're on your own."

With that comment, McCarthy starts to feel a little more confident. But then Michelle says, "Oh, by the way. I wouldn't waste my time looking for anything of value in the car. I had it thoroughly searched, cleaned, and detailed. I took the liberty of removing everything except the owner's manual, and that includes the brown leather satchel hidden in the spare tire compartment with all those papers, credit cards and cash. I have the extra pistol magazines, too."

"I must admit I was a bit surprised to find all that information on the numbered accounts in the Caymans. You've managed to amass a sizable fortune over the past twelve years. It's a shame you didn't invest some of that time in our marriage. We might have accomplished some great things together. I guess it's a good thing I have that letter granting me Power of Attorney."

"What letter? I don't remember signing any letter," replies McCarthy with a puzzled look on his face.

"Tell me. Don't you remember signing all those papers about the proposed merger of BioGen with one of our pharmaceutical companies a few weeks ago?"

"And what does that have to do with granting you Power of Attorney?"

"Well, you were obviously focused on something or someone else, because you signed one page after another, just like I knew you would," she says, smiling.

"Oh! Did I mention the car needs gas, too? It's down to about a quarter tank. I hope you have some cash on you, because I reported my purse stolen, and since most of my credit cards were in it, all of them have been cancelled, and that includes those with your name on them as well."

406

"You're not leaving me with much of a choice, are you," he says with a disgusted tone in his voice.

"Joshua, your actions brought us to where we are right now. Don't try to put the blame on me, or anyone else," she says firmly.

"Well, at least I have the satisfaction of knowing Bill won't be running the country after I'm gone," says McCarthy while smiling at Higgins. With those words, Higgins points the gun at McCarthy and pulls the trigger. McCarthy flinches, but the gun doesn't go off. McCarthy snatches the gun away from Higgins as is about to strike him with it, when Michelle yells, "Stop it! That's enough!"

"But he was trying to kill me!"

"Even I know these guns have a built in safety that won't allow them to fire without a magazine in it." McCarthy grabs the empty magazine, jams it into the gun and points it at Higgins' head. "I said that's enough. Put the gun down now! You have just one round. If you shoot him, you'll never get out of this room alive."

Then he points the gun at AJ and says, "What if I shoot him instead? Then who will stop me?"

Julie says, "You know we're not the only Secret Service agents here. And we're not the only ones who know about you, Higgins, and the Core. If you fire your weapon, you'll have a half dozen agents here in seconds. Plus everything that's been said since we entered this room is on tape. AJ and I are wired. So, why don't you give yourself up? You know you can't get away."

"I don't believe you," he replies. "If the two of you were wired, there'd be agents all over the place, and AJ wouldn't have gotten that call a moment ago."

"I said everything's being recorded on tape," she says thinking quickly. "I didn't say we were being actively monitored."

"Well, according to my lovely wife, my life is over anyway. What have I got to lose?" he asks.

"Your five minute head start," replies AJ in a slow and deliberate tone, with a look that would strike fear in any man's heart.

407

"You're right, of course," says McCarthy while lowering his weapon. "Michelle? Any last words?"

"How about…goodbye?" she replies rather flippantly.

"What about a goodbye kiss?" he asks with a forced smile on his face.

Michelle points her gun at him and says, "Don't press your luck."

McCarthy turns toward Higgins and says with a smile, "It's a shame I can't hang around and watch you die."

"Get out of here, you son of a bitch!" says Higgins as he throws the bullets taken from McCarthy's gun at him.

McCarthy stares at Higgins for a moment, then AJ, Julie, and finally Michelle. "Well, I guess this is goodbye," he says as he walks by AJ, Julie, and Michelle. Once past the doors, he steps up his pace and hurries down the hallway toward the foyer.

Michelle manipulates Julie into the doorway, so she can watch him. Once he's out of sight, Michelle hands her gun to Julie, who instantly points it at Michelle. AJ reaches down and picks up his MP5 and is about to go after McCarthy when Michelle says, "Wait! He won't get far. Besides, I have someone following him."

"So what? He's a murderer and so are you!" says Julie in an angry tone.

"You can't begin to compare me to him. Besides, I haven't killed anyone," she replies as she reaches in her purse and starts to pull something out. Both Julie and AJ take aggressive postures to shoot Michelle.

"What's in the bag!" barks AJ. "Ease your hand out slowly, no sudden moves." Michelle slowly pulls out a long, slender, brown leather pouch. Inside the pouch is a loaded syringe.

"What's in the syringe?" asks Julie inquisitively.

"The antidote," replies Michelle as she removes it from the pouch and approaches Higgins. "Roll up your sleeve, and hold out your arm."

"But you said there was no antidote!" says Julie.

"I lied. Just like I lied about having all those women murdered," replies Michelle.

"But those pictures!" says AJ.

"Staged," she replies. "All of them."

"Why?" asks Julie.

"Isn't it the least bit obvious? I've known for some time that Joshua was having sordid little affairs here and there. But after some of them hit the tabloids, I decided to hire a detective and see just how busy he really was. There were several instances where he was seeing two, sometimes three women at the same time. It was amazing he found any time for work or me!"

"My detective was getting some very interesting and revealing footage of my husband and these women, and on many occasions, audio as well. It had gotten so bad, I would be doing my own work, while occasionally watching and listening to the recordings."

"Then one day, I thought I heard something about giving someone a TLC. That caught my attention. I stopped the tape and replayed it over and over again, until I was certain of what I had heard."

"Do you know what TLC means?" asks Julie.

"Of course I know what it means. My father was a member of the Core for almost forty years, as was his father before him. Joshua was given my place, because he was a man."

"When I found out Joshua was getting what I felt was my birthright, I asked my father why. He told me that a woman had never been a member of the Core, and he wasn't about to break tradition."

"My father and I rarely spoke after that night, until I showed him some of the pictures and videos of Joshua's blatant infidelity. My father was ready to have him picked up, tortured, then buried alive under tons of cement at one of our construction sites. But I told him I had a better idea."

"Rather than have him suddenly disappear under suspicious circumstances, I wanted to ruin him politically, financially, and personally, so the whole world would know who and what he really was. No matter where he went, I wanted everyone to recognize and scorn him. In the end, he would kill himself."

"What makes you so sure he would do something like that?" asks Julie.

"His entire life has been built around politics, money, and women," she replies. "He doesn't know anything else. As of tonight, his political career is over. Other than the clothes on his back, and the money in his pocket, he's penniless."

"What about the car? Couldn't he sell the car?" asks AJ.

"It's leased, and for some unknown reason, the last two payments haven't been paid," she replies with a devilish smile. "I have it on good authority the leasing company plans to repo the car tomorrow morning."

"Won't they have trouble finding it?" asks Julie.

"Not at all. You see, I've had GPS tracking units installed in all of our cars," she replies. "That's how we're tracking him as we speak."

"You really are pushing him into a corner, aren't you," says Julie.

"Let's get back to the other women," AJ says. "You're telling us they're all alive? How were you able to get them to go along with you on this? And how do we know you're telling the truth?"

"Haven't you heard the old saying, "There's no fury like a woman scorned?" asks Michelle. "Everything I said about the flowers, the notes, the gifts, even the limo are true. It's just that none of it happened today."

"I arranged all of it, in my husband's name, of course. But instead of an assassin waiting for them in the room, I was there instead."

"The first one was the worst. Yes, I wanted to scratch her eyes out, beat her senseless, maybe even kill her, but I didn't. Instead, I introduced myself as Joshua's 'aging' wife. Then I showed her some pictures of them in various degrees of undress, even played some of the audio."

"She was obviously embarrassed, hurt, and upset, but she still believed Joshua loved her and would eventually leave me for her. That's when I showed her pictures of the other women in similar, or even more revealing situations with Joshua."

"Once she crossed the threshold of self-pity and on to anger and revenge, it was easy to convince her to help me take care of Joshua once and for all. We exchanged phone numbers and even became friends, in an odd sort of way."

"After struggling through the first one, the rest became progressively easier. After the fourth or fifth one, it became more of a business proposition. I had become somewhat detached from the situation."

"At first, I had no idea how I was going to get even with Joshua, but whatever it was it had to be career ending and life threatening. I wanted to stick it up his ass, as he had mine."

"Then one day, as I was thumbing through a magazine, I saw an article about cosmetic special effects in the movie industry. Some of the pictures seemed so real! That's when I got the idea of faking their deaths."

"Most of these women are models or wannabes. Some of them hope to break into the movies, so I offered to set them up with my modeling agency or any agency of their choice. Plus, I would help set up screen tests, provided they helped me with my little venture. All of them were more than happy to cooperate."

"So those pictures weren't taken today," says Julie.

"Heavens no. That would have been quite impossible. No, each photo shoot took days, sometimes weeks to plan. The shoot itself would take several hours, as well as cooperation from the various hotels and resorts."

"One of them flatly refused to let us do a shoot on their property, but allowed us to take a few pictures of the room. We wound up making a copy of the room at a local studio, right down to the carpet, furniture, comforter, drapes, the works."

"Wow! That had to cost a chunk of money," says AJ.

"You have no idea," she replies while rolling her eyes.

"Well, you could have fooled me," says Julie.

"That was the idea," replies Michelle.

"But still. How do we know these women are alive?" asks Julie.

Michelle reaches into her purse, pulls out a small address book, and hands it to Julie. "You'll find a list of names written in red. Those are the women Joshua had affairs with. You'll find their home and cell numbers, along with their physical address, and the agencies they're currently working for. All of them are expecting your call."

"But what about Joshua?" asks Julie.

"He'll be dead before morning," she says rather coldly. "Just like you, Bill."

"What do you mean? You're holding the antidote. Give it to me!" he bellows.

"Before I save your meager, undeserving life, you're going to make a promise. No, two promises," she says with a devilish smile, as she holds the syringe upwards, slowly forcing the contents out of the syringe, into the air.

"Michelle! What are you doing?" he pleads.

"Why, Bill, I'm waiting for your answer. Hopefully I'll hear it while there's still enough of the antidote to save your pitiful life."

"AJ! Julie! Do something! Stop her!" he demands.

"I think you better tell Michelle what she wants to hear, or you're a dead man, Senator," says AJ.

"Okay! Okay! I promise! Anything! Anything!"

"Don't you want to hear my demands first, before committing?" she asks coldly.

"You know I'm in no position to bargain," he says reluctantly.

"That's more like it." She stands next to Higgins and wipes a spot on his upper arm in preparation to injecting him with the antidote. "Number one, you will make no mention of the Core in your speech, and you will cease any attempt to expose or discredit the Core."

"Now wait a minute," says Higgins.

"Shut up. I'm not finished. You will also resign from the Core and appoint me as your successor. By doing this, I will make certain no other attempts will be made on your miserable life. If you win the election, you will become President of the United States. But if you lose, you will retire gracefully and live out the rest of your life on the talk show circuit or writing your memoirs. I really don't care which. But if I *ever* hear of you mentioning the Core or TLC, you *will* see it coming, and I will personally guarantee it will be the most painful experience in your life. Do we understand each other?"

412

Higgins is silent. Michelle becomes impatient and starts to squirt the rest of the precious antidote out of the syringe when Higgins yells out, "All right! All right! I promise! I'll do anything and everything you say!"

"Oh, I think you're going to have to do better than that," she says. Michelle pulls an envelope from her purse, and hands it to Higgins.

"What's this?" asks Higgins.

"It's a contract stating what you just agreed to. Read it if you wish, but I'm going to count to three, and if it isn't signed by then, you're life will be over. Your body just doesn't know it yet."

"All right! All right! Give me a damn pen! I'll sign it!" says Higgins in disgust. Michelle hands him a beautiful rosewood pen, with Michelle's monogram inlaid in gold.

"There! Happy now?" asks Higgins.

"Very well, Bill," she says. "Now don't move. This is probably going to hurt a little. I'm not a nurse, you know."

"Hold it!" shouts AJ. "Before you stick it to the old prick, I have a few questions of my own I want answered."

"Damnit, AJ. Not now! Michelle? Give me the antidote!" demands Higgins. But Michelle backs away from Higgins, as AJ walks up and stands in front of him.

"If you haven't had too much to drink, another minute or two isn't going to make any difference, right Michelle?" says AJ, looking at both Higgins and Michelle. She nods her head in agreement. "Now then, I remember you telling me a story about Kent State. You told me you lost a niece that day. That was a lie, wasn't it."

"I don't see what that has to do with anything. Michelle. Give me the antidote!" barks Higgins.

"Answer the question," counters AJ.

"Okay! So maybe I didn't lose a niece there. What of it?"

"But you do have intimate knowledge of the incident, don't you?"

"So what?" he says flippantly, looking away from AJ.

"Well, I know why."

"That file means nothing," says Higgins. "While there are some names and dates in there, there's no way to substantiate

413

anything other than the end result. I have proof I was nowhere near Kent State the day the massacre occurred. You don't have the triggerman, you don't have the clothes either of the girls wore that day, and you don't have the name of the girl or the senator who was being blackmailed." Higgins shakes his head and lets out a light-hearted laugh. "And even if you did, it would be difficult getting a statement from a dead man."

"What do you mean, a dead man?" asks AJ. "Did the Core have him killed off after he helped the bill pass?"

"Come on, AJ. That was 1970, and here we are in 2011. He died of natural causes. We already had him by the balls. What was he going to do? We owned him! Christ! That was forty years ago!"

"Well, I'm sure we can find something that will stick," replies AJ in disgust. "What about the two men who died in a plane crash a week or so afterwards?" asks AJ.

"The FAA did their investigation. It was determined to be pilot error," counters Higgins. "There was no evidence of foul play. The case is closed, and the investigators are either retired or dead."

"Julie? Help me out here," says AJ, as he turns to Julie looking for support, only to see Julie has a gun pointed at her head again. "What tha... You!"

TLC: Chapter 59

"Drop your weapons. All of them. Now! Or she dies!" says the woman holding a gun on Julie.

"Who *are* you?" asks AJ as he slides the MP5 off his shoulder, easing it down by the sling onto the floor.

"Your sidearm, too! Do it!" she commands.

"Okay, okay," he replies. "No one needs to get hurt."

"Just shut up and do it!" she yells.

"Geez! Do you have a limited vocabulary or what?"

The woman pulls the hammer back on her pistol. "Now!"

"I'm doing it! I'm doing it. Just stay calm," he says, as he reaches under his left shoulder to retrieve his Beretta. He brushes against the pistol he had picked up from one of the assassins on the second floor, still in his coat pocket. AJ holds his coat open with his left hand to clearly show his right hand releasing the snap on his shoulder holster, and removing the pistol with only his thumb and forefinger. He holds it out front of him, slowly squats down, and lays the pistol on the floor next to the MP5. While the woman is focused on his Beretta, AJ checks to make sure the other pistol is secure in his waistband in the small of his back with his left hand. Even Higgins doesn't catch AJ in the act.

"Now stand up and back away from them," she commands.

"Good work Beth!" says Higgins smugly. "But what took you so long?" he pauses, then says, "Michelle? How about that shot? Now, if you please." Higgins grimaces as Michelle injects him with the antidote.

"Just as I thought!" says AJ. "But I don't know why."

"You can never have too many friends," replies Higgins, smiling.

"What's your name, and how did you get that Secret Service ID?" asks Julie.

"I work for the Secret Service, same as you," replies Beth. "I just work in a different department. And you already know my name."

"You were the one who attempted to steal Julie's briefcase, and tried to break into my apartment." says AJ.

415

"Well, you shouldn't talk about where you hide your key on an open line," replies Beth smiling. "By the way, how are the family jewels?"

"Why did you try to kill Niles and me that night?" asks Julie.

"I hadn't planned on killing anyone," she replies nonchalantly.

"Then why did you shoot Niles, and with my gun?" asks AJ.

"First of all, I didn't know it was your gun. Higgins gave it to me," she replies. "Secondly, I wasn't sure anyone was even in the apartment. I knew you were at Higgins' estate, so I thought maybe you had just left the TV on while you were away."

"But you shot Niles!" says Julie in an elevated tone. "Was that just a convenient coincidence, too?"

"What can I say? As I unlocked the door and started to go inside, I heard you calling AJ's name, then a man yelling something as he charged the door. I couldn't afford to get caught, so I blindly fired a couple of shots. I hoped I might scare him. I never thought that I'd actually hit him," she replies.

"Bullshit!" says AJ angrily. "There was a silencer on the gun. You were sent to retrieve the file and kill Julie!"

"That's a lie!" yells Beth as she takes the gun away from Julie's head and starts to point it at AJ. Julie seizes the opportunity and grabs Beth's outstretched arm with both hands, forcing the gun upward just before she pulls the trigger. AJ charges Beth and Julie while reaching behind his back to retrieve the other pistol. Before Beth can get off another round, AJ has his pistol positioned against her forehead.

"I think it's your turn to drop it," he says calmly. Julie takes her gun, then cuffs Beth's hands behind her back, and sits her down in a chair. Julie calls Niles on the com-link and asks him to send in an officer to pick her up.

"Now what?" asks Higgins as he rubs the spot where Michelle had injected him.

"Well, it's going to take at least forty-eight to seventy-two hours for the antidote to neutralize the toxin, so no alcohol for the next few days, okay?"

"You know? You could have made me offer you the Vice Presidency," Higgins says smugly as he rolls down his shirtsleeve.

"Now you know I couldn't do that. As a member of the Core, we're forbidden to hold the offices of President, Vice President and Speaker of the House. I was actually thinking more along the lines of Secretary of State or Attorney General. What do you think Julie, AJ?"

"Michelle. What about Joshua?" asks AJ adamantly.

"Don't worry about Joshua. As I said, the Aston Martin has a GPS tracking device on it. Avery knows exactly where he is, and I have a pretty good idea where he's going."

"And where might that be?" asks Julie.

"I'm willing to bet he's going to Chesapeake Bay."

"Why there?" asks AJ.

"Well, for starters, he has just enough gas to get there. Secondly, that's where his father's boat is moored, and he can see it from the bluff where he and I first made love," she says with a lump in her throat.

***

Sure enough, McCarthy has driven up to the bluff overlooking the bay. Hundreds of watercraft, from tiny sailboats to luxury yachts, are moored on the calm waters of the bay. He turns off the ignition, then the headlights. With ignition off, the interior lights turn on automatically. He picks up the manila envelope from the passenger seat, opens the flap and starts thumbing through the pictures, looking for one particular photo. Finally, he finds the one he's looking for, removes it, and lays the open envelope back on the seat.

With trembling hands and tears in his eyes, he whispers, "I'm so sorry, Elizabeth. I'm so sorry." Seconds later, the interior lights begin to fade until they turn themselves off. He pulls the Walther from his coat pocket, and places it in his lap.

Suddenly, the peace and calm of the bay are interrupted by a series of deafening explosions! Moments later, the night sky comes to life with a brilliant and awesome fireworks display. McCarthy is momentarily distracted from Elizabeth's picture, and a faint, forced smile slowly replaces the pain and heartache that had enveloped him.

417

But this diversion is short lived as McCarthy spies a pair of headlights, dancing wildly, in his rear view mirror. A car is charging its way up the hill behind him. As the vehicle closes the gap between them, he can also see flashing red and blue lights.

McCarthy gently lays the picture of Elizabeth on top of the envelope, picks up the gun, and raises it to his right temple. He pauses for a moment, and as he has one last thought of Michelle, he screams "Bitch!" then pulls the trigger. POW!

As Michelle's investigator pulls up behind the Aston Martin, he's close enough to see the flash of the gunshot briefly light up the interior. He's positioned his car so his headlights effectively blind McCarthy, just in case it might be a trap. After waiting several seconds, the investigator turns off the flashing red and blue lights, and puts on a pair of latex gloves. He gets out of his car and slowly approaches McCarthy's car on the driver's side.

He stops next to the rear wheel of the car, holding his Mag-Lite in his left hand, and his pistol in his right. When he turns on his flashlight, he can clearly see blood and brain matter splattered on the door glass, along with a bullet hole at the epicenter.

Confident that McCarthy is dead, he holsters his weapon and walks around to the passenger side, opens the door, and shines his flashlight briefly at McCarthy's head. There is sizable hole in front of his right ear. His face is distorted, exaggerated by his bulging eyes, and to the degree his mouth is open. A stringy mass of darkened blood is oozing from both his mouth and nose.

The investigator deftly opens the mouth of the manila envelope and removes the pictures of the women in their death poses, then inserts a letter from Michelle's attorney, advising him she has filed for divorce. A copy of the divorce papers is also added. He then makes sure the envelope and picture of Elizabeth are properly aligned to the surrounding blood spatter on the seat.

Satisfied that everything is at it should be, he gently closes the door, and returns to his car. Once back in his car, he removes the latex gloves, then starts to make his way back down the bluff. He takes out his phone and calls Michelle.

Michelle's phone rings. "Yes?"

Avery says, "It's done."

"Did you get the pictures?"

"Yes, and I took care of the divorce papers as well."

"Good," she says, then terminates the call.

"Well?" asks AJ.

"Higgins? It appears you're going to need a new running mate. My husband just killed himself." Michelle pulls a tissue from her purse, and gently dabs away a tear.

"Good riddance," grumbles Higgins.

AJ walks up to Higgins and says, "I'm going to enjoy putting you behind bars, you son of a bitch."

"Michelle! We have a deal here!" says Higgins gruffly.

"AJ," says Michelle, "He's right. What are you going to arrest him for?"

"I have proof he conspired to kill a number of people over the past forty years, treason against the United States, blackmail, and God knows what else," he replies.

"But to do that, you have to expose the Core, and that would include Weathers, too. I can't let you do that. Even if you were able to initiate an investigation, I doubt you would be alive by the time it reached court, provided it even got that far. AJ, the Core is far bigger and more powerful than you can possibly imagine."

"Maybe so, but I've got to try," he replies.

"AJ, do you love Julie?" she asks.

"What does that have to do with anything?"

"Do you love her?" Michelle asks again.

AJ takes a long look at Julie, then says, "Yes, I do." Julie immediately tenses up, and her eyes fill with tears of joy.

Michelle points to Julie and yells, "Kill her!"

"What? Are you out of your mind? I just told you I love her! Why would I want to kill her?" he asks disbelievingly.

"Because if you attempt to expose the Core, Julie will be one of the first to die. If they can't get to you, they *will* kill her. It will be ugly. It will be slow and painful. She will die screaming your name, begging you to save her. And you will have the video to relive her agony over and over again. Each time you watch it or think about it, a piece of you will die. You will eventually lose your desire to live, and will either kill yourself, or set yourself up to attempt something you know will end in your death. Is that what you want?"

AJ takes another long look at Julie, then down at the floor, starts shaking his head and says, "No, I couldn't bear losing her.

Not again." Then he looks up, stares coldly at Higgins, and says, "But I just can't let Higgins go. Where's the justice in that?"

"Right here in my hands," replies Michelle. "Higgins might very well become President. And if he does, he'll be inclined to do everything we ask."

"What do you mean by we?" asks AJ.

"We have the perfect opportunity here. If he wins, you will be Higgins' head of security, so you'll be able to watch his every move. I will have my place in the Core. You will be my direct link to Higgins and the White House. We will be on the inside track of everything that goes on both in and out of the White House. And I want you to be my senior operative."

"You can't be serious! I'm not an assassin, or some sort of indiscriminant contract killer."

"Nor do I want you to be. Weathers is an operative. Do you think he's killed anyone?"

"Of course not."

"AJ? I can assure you those days are truly numbered. It's time we steer the Core back to its roots, and by doing so, we can help turn this country around by running it more like a business. We will make members of Congress and the Justice Department more accountable for their actions. Over time, we will level the playing field."

"There's a lot to digest here. I need to give this some thought, before I make a decision of this magnitude."

"Well, here's one more thing to think about." Michelle walks up to AJ and whispers in his ear, "How would you like to have a hundred thousand dollars dropped in a numbered offshore account every year? Interest bearing, tax free. As she backs away from him, she continues, "And of course, I'm sure there will be other perks along the way."

"What about Julie? And Weathers?"

"You know Weathers is already involved with the Core, and as far as Julie is concerned," she pauses a moment, thinking. "Tell me Julie, do you really want to be a Secret Service Agent, practice law, or be Little Miss Suzie Homemaker? I could make you a partner in my law firm, and you can specialize in anything your heart desires."

"We cater to everything from national and international mergers and acquisitions, white-collar crime, insider trading, patent infringement, insurance fraud, high profile divorces, criminal investigations, and class action suits. If you can name it, we probably have a department for it. We have offices and clients around the world. We also have our own investigations division, which is one of the largest in the country. And with your military background and security clearance, you could add a whole new dimension to that department."

Julie is staring at AJ, her heart still singing from what he had said about her, and only half hearing what Michelle is saying.

"Julie? Julie."

"I'm sorry. What were you saying?" she asks, snapping back to reality.

"Nothing that can't be discussed at a later time," says Michelle smirking. "Why don't you come down to my office tomorrow, and we'll talk about it. Here's my card. Maybe we can discuss it over lunch, say around 1:00-1:30. Wait a minute. I'll be in mourning, won't I." She pauses for a moment, then says, "Let's make it Monday, the eleventh, okay?"

"Yes, I think I'd like that," she replies.

"Good. Now, since that's all settled, I think I should go home and wait for the police to call me about the death of my husband, don't you?"

"Michelle? Don't you think we should call an ambulance for Higgins?" asks AJ.

"Unless he feels a need for one, I wouldn't. There's a chance someone might notice the needle mark on his arm, and that might arouse some suspicion. Plus, I don't know if any anomalies will show up in his blood work from either the toxin or the antidote at this stage."

"I'm fine," says Higgins. "I've only had a couple of glasses of champagne tonight. Haven't felt the slightest buzz."

"So, you don't want to take a trip to the emergency room to get checked out?" asks Julie.

"No, I'm fine. Maybe just a little worn out from all the excitement," he says. "I guess the party's a bust."

"I'm afraid so," replies Julie. "Most of the guests began to leave when the first shots were fired."

421

"Well, I guess we're just going to have to throw another party!" shouts Higgins. "Michelle! Are you certain you don't want to run as my Vice President? With a woman like yourself running in the number two spot, we'd be a shoo-in!"

"Thank you, but no," she replies as she starts to turn and walk away.

"I'm sure we can work something out," he says with a sly grin on his face.

"I'm sure we will," as she walks out of the library.

"Michelle! Wait up!" yells AJ while trying to catch up with her. "How are you getting home since Joshua took the Aston Martin?"

"Eric, our chauffeur drove him up in the Bentley. He'll take me home," she replies.

"Oh, okay. Are you serious about this operative thing?"

Michelle stops and says, "I've never been more serious about anything in my life. You should know that if you weren't so in love with Julie, and she with you, I'd make a play for you myself." AJ is taken aback by her comment.

"AJ, you're a nice man. You're handsome, you're strong, you have a strong sense of right and wrong, and you'd lay down your life to protect those principles."

"But you also have a gentle, tender, and loving side. I saw it by the way you looked at Julie when I told you what could happen to her. It's a shame there aren't more men around like you."

"You see, when I first met Joshua, I thought he was a lot like you. But I was wrong. He was weak, greedy, and hungered for power. Do you see where it got him?"

"He took my rightful place in the Core. Worse! My own father gave it to him. Joshua used both of us, and he humiliated me in front of the world."

"But worst of all, he stole my heart and crushed it, without giving it a second thought. I'm glad he's dead."

AJ can see she's beginning to break down. Tears are streaming down her cheeks. "I'm glad he's dead!" Her voice has become broken, then suddenly, she begins to cry.

AJ wraps her in his arms, holds her close, and says, "Michelle, he can't hurt you anymore. Come on. We need to get you out of here." AJ takes her under his left arm and walks her out the main entrance of the house. "Do you have any idea where Eric might be?"

"He should be with the car. It's a silver Bentley Continental Flying Spur, U.S. Senate plate: J A MC 1," she sobs.

"I don't see it." About that time both hear Eric lightly tapping the car horn, then flashing the headlights. He's parked about four cars to the left of the entrance. He starts the car, and pulls up to the curb in front of them. The valet opens the passenger rear door, and AJ helps her into the car.

"Thank you, AJ," she says while trying to regain some degree of control. "Think about my offer."

"I will," he replies, "I promise."

"Good night," she says.

"Just get home safe and you'll be all right," he says as he closes the door and motions to the driver to take her home. She waves to him as they drive away.

As AJ watches the car disappear through the trees, Julie eases up behind him and says, "Is everything okay?"

"For the moment? Yes, but I don't think we're out of the woods just yet," he replies.

"What do you mean?" asks Julie.

"I'm not sure, but something just doesn't feel right. By the way, you realize I'm going to have to file a report on your lack of performance tonight."

"What are you talking about?" she asks with a surprised look on her face.

"Julie, you're my partner. We're supposed to be watching each other's back, and we got blindsided, not once, but twice, and both of them were women!"

"Now AJ, I don't think you're being very objective about the situation. After all, you didn't see them coming, either," she says.

"Julie, I was the primary, you were my back up. That means keep an eye on our backs," he says with a stern look on his face. "You know? If either of them had been hardened criminals, we might both be laying in pools of blood right now."

"Okay! Okay. I get it."

"I'm afraid if I tell Weathers about tonight, you could end up flying a desk, or placed on suspension, without pay!"

"All right, AJ. I get the point. I screwed up."

"Yes, you did. Now I've got to figure out how to unscrew you," he says, finally cracking a smile.

"AJ, you're an asshole. You know that?" she says, while giving him a solid shove to the shoulder, then turning away.

"I know, but you love me anyway, right?" he replies, waiting for a response. But Julie is silent. "Right?" he asks again.

Julie remains tight lipped for several seconds, but then starts to crack a smile, and finally, no longer able to contain herself, she starts to giggle. "Yes, I love you, in spite of all your faults."

"Mobile One to AJ. Mobile One to AJ," crackles over AJ's com-link.

"Niles? Tell them I'm on my way," he says.

"Copy that," replies Niles.

AJ looks at Julie, then makes a sweeping gesture toward the door, and says, "Shall we?"

"Why not?" she replies.

"After you," he says while taking a bow.

"You're such a gentleman," she says somewhat sarcastically.

"Hmmm. I must be losing my touch."

"And what's that supposed to that mean?"

"Never mind," he replies. "Let's see what's going on in the security office." As they're walking up the steps, he asks, "By the way, what did you do with Beth?"

"She's on her way to the Women's Detention Center, just outside Washington. I told him to call in the transfer by phone, and keep it off the air. The last thing we need is for the Core to find out where she is. They might try to extract or kill her. We'll keep her in solitary until we find out what her part is in all this."

TLC: Chapter 60

AJ and Julie find Agents Anderson and Lawson standing near the entrance to the security office, underneath the security camera, out of its field of view. "You two certainly took your time getting here," says Lawson. "Decide to stop for dinner and a floor show?"

"Very funny Lawson, very funny," replies AJ. "Have you heard anything from inside?"

"Not a peep, sir," says Anderson.

Suddenly, the door goes CLICK. All of them draw their weapons almost instantly. AJ motions for everyone to spread out. Several seconds pass without another sound. AJ eases up to the door and tests the doorknob. It's still locked. Then he keys in his code, the light turns green, and the doorknob is free. AJ motions for Anderson to kneel next to the door, opposite him, and Lawson to stand next to Anderson. He waves at Julie for her to take a position farther down the hall.

"Security Control to AJ. Control to AJ," comes over AJ's com-link.

"Jamison? Is that you?"

"Roger that. Ask your men to stand down. I'm not armed. Please come on in, alone."

"Why should I trust you, Brian?"

"Why do you think Weathers countermanded the order to kill me?"

"Because he wanted you alive, I suppose."

"There's a lot more to it than that, but you're going to have to trust me."

"Okay, I'm coming in alone, but I will have my gun drawn, and I will shoot if I have to."

"Roger that. Come on in. I'll be in the break room. Just close the door behind you."

"I'll be right with you. Just give me a minute."

"Actually, you've got about fifteen seconds before the door automatically times out."

"Here, hang on to this for me," says AJ to Lawson as he hands him his MP5. "You might need it."

"You sure about this, AJ?" asks Lawson.

425

"Give me about five minutes, then call me on the com-link. If I say, '10-4', that means everything's turning to shit."

"Then what?" asks Lawson.

AJ just shrugs his shoulders, then says, "Okay, Brian, I'm coming in." AJ opens the door just before the lock times out.

As he enters the room, the door closes behind him with a dull thud and then an electronic click. There's a red light blinking on the wall plate next to the doorjamb. "Nice touch, Brian. I hadn't thought of that."

"You mean the electronic dead bolt?" asks Jamison. "I figured that if we were going to upgrade the security around here, we might as well do it right."

"Is it activated by a key, keypad, or computer?"

"Primary operation is by this remote," says Jamison as he holds up the remote for AJ to see. "But it can be overridden by computer, once you know the access point and the five digit code."

"Okay Brian, what do you want to tell me?"

"I'm General Woolbright's senior operative," he says bluntly. "And up until a few days ago, my orders were to TLC Higgins."

"I thought General Woolbright was aligned with Higgins."

"Things aren't always as they seem."

"So I guess that means you didn't drive a truck in Iraq," says AJ.

"No, I was an Army Ranger, eighteen years. Two tours in Iraq, one in Afghanistan."

"When did your orders change?"

"When General Woolbright met with Colonel Weathers."

"Now I know why Weathers wanted you taken alive," says AJ. "Do you know why your orders changed?"

"No, my job is to follow them."

"What about your leg? Your injury, that is."

"Now that's real. That's why I only got in eighteen years. We ran over a mine on my last tour in Iraq. Cut through our Humvee like it was butter. Killed everyone but me. Luckily, it didn't catch on fire, so I stayed inside, and decided to wait them out.

A couple of them fired a few rounds at us, then about six of them pulled up in a beat up Toyota pickup. One of them got out, walked around the Humvee, peeking inside as he went. When he

426

came back over to my side and opened the door, I buried my Ka-Bar just below his bellybutton and pulled it all the way up to his sternum. While using him as a shield, I rested my M4 in between the door and the window frame, spraying everything in sight. I got all of them but the driver, and in his panic, he forgot about where all the mines were and managed to blow himself all to hell."

"So Brian, I'm supposed to buy this story over the other one?"

"While I wasn't truck driver, most of the other story was true, too. Terry was my half brother. He had been on the ground in Iraq for less than two weeks."

"Sorry to hear that Brian."

"That's okay. At least the Army let me take him home."

"How am I supposed to believe any of this is real rather than just another fabrication to keep me off guard?"

Brian raises his right hand, palm out, then slowly crosses his chest, reaches into his left shirt pocket and pulls out a cell phone. He lays it on the counter top and slides it over to AJ. "If you'll press Recall and Send, the voice you hear will be General Woolbright. He's expecting your call."

"Since I've never met General Woolbright, how will I know it's him?"

"You'll know."

AJ picks up the phone, opens it, and makes the call. The phone rings once. "This is General Woolbright. I'm assuming this is Marine Sergeant Thomas Andrew Jackson, now working for the Secret Service under the direction of Colonel Robert Monroe Weathers, U.S. Army Retired."

"Yes sir, General," replies AJ. "Begging your pardon sir, but how do I know you are, in fact, General Woolbright?"

"Well, I can't think of too many people with enough balls who'd dare call themselves by my name," says the general sounding a bit boisterous.

"You're probably right, sir," replies AJ. "But this is a rather unique situation."

"I agree," says the general. "Who's running your mobile command center?"

"Agent Wesley Niles, sir," AJ replies.

"Well, I've met Agent Niles, son. Ask him to open the door and identify who's standing in front of him. You needn't mention my name. He'll tell you."

"Yes sir, stand by. AJ to Mobile One, AJ to Mobile One."

"Mobile One, go ahead," replies Niles.

"I need you to do me a favor. Open the back door of the van and tell me who's standing there."

"Roger that. Stand by," replies Niles. Somehow Niles' mic is still open when he opens the door. "Holy shit! It's General Woolbright!" Niles attempts to stand erect and salute, but beans his head on the roof of the van. "Ow! Son of a bitch!" AJ and the other agents listening in are literally in stitches!

"Yep, it's Lieutenant Niles, all right," says the general chuckling. "Hasn't changed a bit."

"Well General, sir, can you tell me what's going on here?"

"I'll let Sergeant Jamison fill you in on his end, then I'll meet you at the hospital outside of Weathers' room. He's still in the emergency room, but they should have him squared away in a private room by the time you get there. Call me on this phone when you're heading that way," says the general.

"Since you're just outside, can't we talk here?"

"Higgins doesn't need to know I've switched my allegiance just yet. So, the last thing he needs to see is you talking to me."

"I understand, sir." With that, the general terminates the call, and AJ sticks the phone in his coat pocket.

"Okay Brian, I believe you. Would you mind telling me what's going on here? Why is Brandon tied up and unconscious? He was telling us about the two assassins on the second floor when you entered security."

"And he told you he had lost a visual on them, didn't he," says Jamison.

"How'd you know that?"

"Because I heard him on my radio."

"Our radio?" asks AJ.

"No, 'our' radio," he replies, as he pulls out a small transceiver from his right shirt pocket.

"Wait a minute. Niles said he was monitoring all frequencies, but hadn't heard a thing."

"Well, he's right, at least as far as his access of known frequencies go. These radios work in a unique bandwidth that only a couple of agencies are even aware of. And because of the encryption software, even if he could have picked it up, he wouldn't have been able to interpret what he was hearing. It would sound pretty much like background noise."

"What are you saying?"

"Those two men on the second floor weren't here to take out the senator. They were here to take out you and your team. It was a trap, and if I hadn't stepped in when I did, you and Weathers would have been killed the moment you hit the second floor."

"But Brandon said they had taken out the camera in that room."

"You mean *that* camera?" counters Jamison as he points to a monitor showing the room the assassins had been in.

"Son of a bitch," says a surprised AJ. "According to Higgins, there were supposed to be five assassins. We have one KIA in the sitting room, Brandon here, and you. That still leaves us with two unaccounted for. Any idea as to who they are or where they might be?"

"Well, I don't have an answer for you on that one," replies Jamison. "I just happened to hear Brandon telling someone where he had hidden the assault bag. That's when I knew he had to be one of the operatives. If I had to guess, I'd say they've probably left the estate by now. It's obvious the whole thing backfired," says Jamison. "As far as I know, McCarthy was the only one who knew who the five operatives were. Everyone trained in secret."

Brian continues. "Honestly, up until I heard Brandon on the radio, I wasn't sure Brandon was an operative. It was more of a hunch than anything else. Since he was the new guy, he got swapped around a lot from one shift to another. Plus he was working the weekend before you and Higgins were attacked on the expressway. I'd be willing to bet he's the inside man who sabotaged the limo, told them when you were leaving, and what you were driving."

"That sounds reasonable. Do you think anyone else might be working for Senator McCarthy or other members of the Core?"

429

"I've been watching everyone on my shift pretty closely, and other than Brandon here, I haven't seen anyone else acting out of the ordinary," says Jamison. "But who knows? After all, there are six shifts."

"Then maybe we should wake up Brandon and see if he can answer any of these questions," says AJ.

"Sounds good to me," says Jamison cracking a smile. "I haven't interrogated a prisoner since April of '09."

TLC: Chapter 61
Higgins' Estate
Tuesday morning
July 5, 2011, 0758 hours local time

Tuesday morning looks like it's going to be a typical day. AJ arrives at the gate and presses the button on the intercom. Someone in security responds in a tone similar to what one might hear at the drive-up of a fast food restaurant, "Good morning! Senator Higgins residence. How may I help you?"

AJ decides to play along. "I want two Egg McMuffins, an order of hash browns, and a large coffee, three sugars, two cream. Oh! And make it to go."

"I'm sorry, but this is not McDonald's. This is a residence," replies the lyrical voice.

AJ responds in a much more aggressive tone. "Thomas Andrew Jackson, Secret Service, ID number Sierra, Sierra 55191. I'm Senator Higgins' bodyguard. Who is this?"

"Hey, AJ! It's me man, Jeffrey!"

"What are you doing in security?"

"A couple of the guys were showing me some video from the action last night! Man! You were smokin'!"

"Very nice. Thanks for the compliment. Now, can you have someone open the gate?"

"Oh! Sure thing, AJ. Comin' right up. By the way, you want fries with that?"

"You know? That expression was real hot. Last year."

As the gate starts to open, Jeffrey says in a deep voice, "Open Sesame!" AJ smiles and shakes his head, as he passes through the gate.

Pulling up to the front door, he sees Jeffrey walking down the steps to meet him. "Man! The video of you taking out those dudes was so cool! It was almost as good as a movie. Except there was no sound, of course."

"Jeffrey, I know you mean it as a compliment, but that wasn't a movie," AJ says in a somber tone. "None of them were actors. Those bullets were real. When I shot them, they died. No chance for a reshoot, or a reset. One take."

"Guess I was just caught up in the moment. I'm sorry, AJ."

431

Forget it," says AJ as he pats him on the back. "But, tell me. What's gotten into you today? You seem to be all wired up?"

"I guess I'm still workin' off the high from last night. I couldn't believe I was seein' all those big shots, celebrities, government big wigs, and stuff. I was just warming up when your fireworks started. The next thing I know, I'm duckin' for cover like everybody else!"

"Well, that was one very expensive party that didn't happen last night. I'm sure the Senator is pretty steamed about that."

"Actually, from what I heard, the old man has been on the phone since a little after seven this morning. He's been calling restaurants and stuff, trying to find a home for all that lobster and prime rib."

About that time, AJ's phone rings. It's Higgins. "Good morning Senator. I'm just down the hall talking to Jeffrey."

"Good. I'm glad you're here. Meet me in the library. We've got a lot of things to discuss."

"I'll be right there, sir."

"Well? Duty calls," says AJ. "Guess I'll see you later, Jeffrey."

"Look man. I just wanted to tell you again, I appreciate you tellin' the senator about my side gig. You know, he's still gonna pay me."

"Jeffrey, friends take care of friends. I saw an opportunity and thought both of you could benefit from it. That's all."

"Hopefully, I'll be able to do the same for you some day."

"We'll see. Gotta go. The last thing I need to do is keep the senator waiting."

"I hear ya. Take it easy, AJ."

Nearing the library, AJ notices the doors are closed. He stops and knocks on the door.

"Come in, AJ." He opens the door and enters the library. "Please close the doors behind you and have a seat." AJ complies with his requests. Higgins is standing in front of the window, holding a large mug of hot coffee. "Care for some coffee? There's plenty in the urn on the bar, along with cream and sugar."

"Thank you sir, but three's my limit, and I had that before I left home this morning."

"Very well. Just thought I'd ask."

"I appreciate the offer, sir."

"Look, AJ. I know you and Michelle have me over a barrel. What I want to know is, how long have you two been working together?"

"Who? You mean Michelle and me?"

"Who else would I be talking about?" Higgins replies sarcastically.

"Sir. Just so we understand each other, I've never lied to you about anything, and frankly I don't feel the need to start now. I don't like you. And under normal circumstances, I wouldn't even associate with you. But Mr. Weathers has assigned me to you, and I've made a commitment to do my job to the best of my ability. Now, to answer your question, up until last night I had never met Mrs. McCarthy, nor was I aware of your intention to have Senator McCarthy as your running mate until a few days ago."

"So, you're telling me, there's no mention of McCarthy in those files."

"No, sir. Nothing."

"Hmmm. Interesting." Higgins pauses for a moment then says, "I've decided to announce my intention to run for the Democratic nomination for President at the Watergate Hotel, just as I had originally planned. I've already talked to them, and they have an opening next Friday."

"Sounds like we're working with a short fuse again."

"I've also called the temp service, and they'll have most of the same girls out here again before noon. Hallmark came through with five cases of blank invitations in parchment. My secretary is whipping up the words as we speak."

"You're not going to try to go all out like last night are you?"

"No, not at all. We'll just have a dinner, a couple of speakers, some floral arrangements for the tables, a couple of banners, and balloons. I might even get Jeffrey to play some music for us, although it would be nice to hear "Hail to the Chief" from a live band."

"In due time, sir. In due time." AJ pauses a moment. "Have you given any thought of who you might want as a running mate?"

"Yep. Got it all planned out. It's gonna be a doozy, too!"

"Are you going to let me in on it?"

"Nope. You'll find out the same time as everyone else. At the dinner."

"What about security, sir?"

"You can handle it."

"Four agents, plus the mobile unit?"

"Yes, and hotel security will be at your beck and call as well. I've already cleared it with the hotel. You'll find the phone number and contact person for Watergate's security on the corner of my desk."

"That's good. Thank you, sir," says AJ as he picks up the note.

"No problem, AJ. I understand you may have captured a Core operative working security last night. Who was it?"

"He gave his name as Brandon Lee. We're checking him out now."

"Did he tell you who he's working for?"

"No sir. He clammed up on us as soon as he came to, but we're pretty sure he was working for McCarthy."

"What about Beth?"

"She's safe, sir."

"Where is she?"

"As I said, sir, she's safe."

"Has she said anything?"

"We haven't gotten around to asking her anything, yet. But Julie will probably handle the interrogation. She's an excellent interrogator and attorney."

Higgins smiles and shakes his head. "You know? When Bob told me he wanted me to let you bring her in as part of your security team, I smelled trouble. Looks like I was right."

"Sir, your troubles began the day you decided to help the Core kill and maim a bunch of innocent kids," says AJ with an air of resentment in his voice.

"AJ, that was over forty years ago, and…"

"And you've never looked back, have you? Did you ever try to look at things from the perspective of those parents? What about the others who witnessed their friends killed or wounded? What about the ones who have the physical scars from that day?

434

Have you ever thought of what those kids might have become? How many lives do you think were ruined that day, just so the Core could get a bill pushed through Congress? Do you even remember what the bill was for?" Higgins doesn't answer. "That's what I thought."

"Look, AJ. You and Michelle have me on a short leash. If I screw up, I'm a dead man. You know it, and I know it. So let's drop the history lesson and move on, okay?"

"Fine," replies AJ rather coldly.

"How's Bob and the other agent doing?"

"Mr. Weathers should be released sometime today. Luckily it was just a flesh wound. No bones or arteries involved, although I doubt he'll be running track anytime soon. And as for Agent Rollins, the bullet passed through just under the collarbone, fracturing it, rather than shattering it. The surgery was a success. He'll be in the hospital for a few days, just to make sure there's no infection. But he won't see active service for probably six weeks or so. He'll either be stuck behind a desk or transferred to investigations for awhile."

"Well AJ, you should be proud of yourself. You've eliminated four out of five of the Core's senior operatives, and put a serious dent in its ability to carry out future TLC's," says Higgins with a smug look on his face.

"Actually, I think we only got two out of five, sir."

"You killed one in the sitting room, two upstairs over the library, and captured the one in security. That's pretty simple math, even for you, AJ."

"Sorry sir, but the two men upstairs weren't for you. They were here to take out my team and me to clear the way for the other assassins to get to you."

"How do you know that?"

"As I said, we believe Brandon worked for McCarthy. We also know Brandon was in direct contact with the two assassins on the second floor. He tried to lure Weathers and me into a trap up there by saying they had knocked out the camera. Once we were able to gain access to Security, we discovered Brandon had the same transmitter as the two assassins, plus the camera he said had been knocked out was still fully operational. We suspect all three worked for McCarthy."

"Speaking of that son of a bitch, are you sure he's dead?"

"Well sir, I haven't personally viewed the body, but according to the coroner's office, and a visual by Mrs. McCarthy?" He mimics putting a gun to his temple and squeezing the trigger. "Yes sir, he's dead."

"Good. You know? I can't believe he'd betray me like that. I helped bring him up the ranks in the Core. Hell! I even wanted him as my running mate. Why in the hell would he want to kill me?"

"How about money, power, and greed? Isn't that what it's all about? The reasons predate written history. And it'll probably still be with us long after you and I are gone."

"So where does that leave us? You and me, that is."

"Should you actually win the election and become President of the United States, and Weathers and Mrs. McCarthy want me to stay on as your head of security, then that's what I'll do. I won't like it, but I'll still do the job. But if you lose? I have no idea."

"I guess that's a fair answer," replies Higgins.

"Now, I have a few questions for you," says AJ.

"Go ahead."

"Do you have any idea who wanted David's sister murdered?"

"Who's David?"

"He was one of the men who tried to take us out on the expressway."

"If I had to guess, especially after everything that's transpired over the past twenty-four hours, I'd say Joshua was probably behind it."

"Any way to find out?"

"Not anymore. Remember? I've resigned from the Core," he says smugly. "All of my connections have been severed."

"Well, if he's the one who ordered the TLC, and he's dead, does that nullify the previous order?"

"That's hard to say. I don't think it's ever come up before. Your guess is as good as mine."

"Okay, what are your plans for the next few days?"

"The Senate is in recess now through next week, so I guess I'll be staying close to home, and getting things organized for the dinner at the hotel. I'll need the time to rewrite my speech, too, since Joshua's out of the picture."

"In that case sir, I'd like to go to the hospital and visit with Mr. Weathers and Rollins, if you don't mind."

"Please, be my guest. I'm not going anywhere anytime soon. I'm not sure just how safe it is outside these walls right now, anyway."

"If you change your mind, just give me a call, and if I hear anything, I'll do the same."

"Fair enough."

***

AJ drives out to the Bethesda Naval Hospital to check on Weathers and Rollins. He arrives just in time to see Weathers about to be wheeled out of his room by Mrs. Weathers and an orderly. "Well this is a pleasant surprise. Checking out?"

"Good morning, AJ. No, not quite yet. They're still shuffling papers downstairs somewhere. Betty and I thought we'd go upstairs and visit Rollins for a few minutes. Lisa's already up there."

"She is? What about the boys?"

"Our neighbor, the one whose husband works at Walgreen's, is watching them for us," says Mrs. Weathers. "Lisa really needed to get out of the house for awhile, and away from the boys, too. They're really little darlings, but sometimes... Sometimes you just need to take a break, you know? Oh! Did Robert tell you that Lisa made a perfect score on that Civil Service Exam? You should have heard her when she found out she passed."

"Normally, you either pass or fail," says Weathers. "But the board sent her a letter stating she's one of about a hundred people in the country who have made perfect scores in the last ten years."

"I'm sure she was happy to hear that." says AJ.

"Honey! That child's feet haven't touched the floor since she got that letter!" replies Mrs. Weathers.

"Well, let's go up and check on Rollins and see how he's doing," says AJ.

When they get to Rollins' room, AJ is surprised to see Lisa sitting on the side of the bed. As they enter the room, Rollins looks over and says, "Hi guys! You're not going to believe this, but Lisa and I went to school together."

"How about that," says AJ.

"Actually, I didn't know Lisa at the time. I mean I met her a few times, but I was older, Tim's age. Four years doesn't seem to mean much now, but in high school, that was a lifetime. I hated seeing Tim fall in with the wrong crowd and quitting school. And I really felt bad to hear he had died the way he did. David was just starting to hit his stride with the football team my senior year. The coach made a smart choice making him quarterback his junior and senior years."

"Why didn't you say something at the morgue that day?"

"AJ? I played ball with David my senior year. We didn't hang out or anything. I was a senior, and he was a sophomore. I hadn't seen him in almost ten years! Besides, it's a lot different to see someone alive versus stretched out on a slab."

Lisa starts to get upset. "Sorry guys, but can we talk about something else?"

"My apologies Lisa," says AJ. "You're right, of course. So Rollins, have you heard all the news?"

"About last night? Only what I saw on the news. Sounds like Higgins' party was a bust. And why would he want a playboy as his running mate? I thought we'd had enough of that kind of excitement with the Clinton Administration."

"Well that's a moot point now, since he shot himself last night."

"What's Higgins' next move?"

"He's going to have a dinner party at the Watergate Hotel a week from Friday."

"That's not giving you much time to get a team together," says Weathers.

"Well, I'm assuming I still have Lawson, Anderson, Julie, and Niles. I really only need one more. You're going to be there for moral support, aren't you, sir?"

"If I can walk, I'll be there," replies Weathers.

TLC: Chapter 62
The Watergate Hotel
Friday evening
July 15, 2011, 2100 hours local time

The main banquet room at the Watergate Hotel is packed to capacity. A large table is set up on a platform at the front of the room. Senator Higgins, Robert Weathers, Michelle Marston-McCarthy, General Woolbright, AJ, and a handful of other dignitaries are seated up there. Behind them is a huge American flag.

After dinner appears to be completed, and the stewards have started clearing the tables, Senator Alex Burgess walks over to the podium and says, "Good evening ladies and gentlemen. I'm sure you know why we're all here, and that's to bear witness to Senator William Henry Higgins' announcement of his bid to run for the President of the United States!"

As the crowd applauds and cheers, a large banner of Higgins unfurls in front of the American Flag. "For those who may not be familiar with Bill, he's been on the Hill for almost forty years, representing the great state of Nevada. He's been on practically every committee worth mentioning, along with a few that aren't."

"Prior to coming up here and creating a stir, he was also a state senator, and before that, he served our country in Southeast Asia. Bill has fought the hard fight in the Senate, either writing or supporting bills that have helped make our country what it is today. So without further ado, here he is, the next great President of the United States, William…Henry…Higgins!"

Jeffrey takes the cue and starts playing 'Hail to the Chief', as the crowd stands, applauding and cheering wildly. Senator Higgins stands up, smiles at the crowd, then walks over to the podium, and shakes the hand of Senator Burgess. He then raises both arms with his hands fashioned in the 'V' for victory sign. He leans toward the microphone and says, "Thank you! Thank you!" As the applauding and cheers start to subside, and the people begin to take their seats, he says, Thank you, Doo Whopp, for that colorful rendition of 'Hail to the Chief'." Jeffrey stands and takes a bow, then Higgins continues. "You know this place

is filled with history, hidden cameras, microphones, wire taps…"
A wave of laughter ripples through the room.

"And a lot of famous speeches relate to this place. One in particular from a former President comes to mind, and that is: 'I am not a crook'! And let's not forget, 'How would I know anything about eighteen minutes of silence in the middle of the tape'?" The crowd cracks up over that one.

"But you know? This country has been through a lot over the last five hundred years. Christopher Columbus thought he had found a new trade route to the Far East. Boy! Did he take a wrong turn! But he had a good excuse. No gas stations, and Magellan wouldn't loan him his GPS unit." Again the crowd breaks up with laughter. "I think Magellan said something about it not being waterproof…I don't know."

Higgins pauses a moment, then continues. "We've beaten back tyranny, slavery, disease, and ignorance…" He gives that comment a moment to sink in, then says, "Well, two out of three ain't bad…" Again, laughter permeates through the crowd.

"What?" He points to a lady at one of the tables near the podium who doesn't seem to get it. "You can't count either?" Some of the guests are starting to howl with laughter. "Hey! Somebody call the CDC and get 'em down here right away! This lady's sufferin' from two very serious diseases! She's both blonde and a Republican!" He leans closer to the microphone and says in a softer tone, "Don't worry, sweetheart. I don't think either one is fatal."

"Seriously folks. The last two hundred and thirty years, haven't been a picnic either. But it's kinda like a marriage, except there's no such thing as divorce. Well, we did have that little thing called the Civil War. I guess you could call that a trial separation." Again, there is laughter in the crowd, but not as intense, while others aren't smiling at all.

"Aha! That one wasn't quite so funny, was it. That one hit a little closer to home, didn't it. Civil War. Let's attack this thing in reverse order, shall we? War. When someone says war, we have a pretty good idea what they're talking about, right? This guy puts his army together, and they go after the other guy's army. There's a whole lot of shooting, fighting and dying going on, right? Okay, now that we agree on the definition of war, let's move on. Civil from the dictionary means, polite or courteous… Hmmm. Nope. Well, how about citizens in their ordinary capacity or way of life. Don't think so. Strike two. Okay, here's another one. Social order or organized government; civilized. Somehow, I don't think so. Folks, let me tell you something. There was nothing civil about the Civil War." Higgins isn't smiling anymore.

"Thousands, and I really mean thousands of people, not just soldiers, but women, and children were killed or maimed. Families were destroyed, literally torn apart!" Higgins pauses a moment, takes out his handkerchief and dabs his forehead.

"Most of what you read today about that time, tells you it was about the slavery issue, and with that, everyone's focus is on the Black population, our African Americans. But folks, there were other nationalities who were slaves, such as the Chinese, even White nationalities, who suffered many of the same atrocities as the Blacks."

"Some of you are aware of the economic issues that were involved. The Southern states felt that laws being introduced in Congress favored the industrial North, and further hindered the agricultural South. Animosity and hate grew between them."

"But do you know what really caused the Civil War? Communication. Or more to the point, the lack of it. Oh, there was talking, bellowing, and saber rattling, but you see, that's not communication. Communication means I talk, you listen, you interpret, and you comment. Then I listen, I interpret, and I comment. And, eventually, through this give and take process, we come to an agreement. Hmmm. Now, to me, that's what I think civil is all about." Higgins is starting to sweat profusely and dabs his forehead with his handkerchief again. It's also obvious he seems to be suffering some discomfort.

"Folks, in a lot of ways, we're still fighting that Civil War. There is hate, distrust, resentment, and fear still running rampant in this country. And because we are so focused on spreading democracy around the world, feeding the world's hungry, shoring up other countries' economies, and God knows what else, we have stopped communicating with ourselves!"

"We're spending billions of dollars to feed wars in foreign countries, yet we have millions of people, right here in America, who don't have enough to eat, a roof over their head, or jobs with which to support themselves, much less a family. Health care is out of reach for millions of others. And while the media has many of you believing that White America is doing its best to oppress the Black and Latino population, it's a lie.

The media thrives on unrest. It glues you to the TV, or radio. It's what sells newspapers and magazines. If one network is talking about White police officers beating up innocent Blacks or Latinos, another network is telling us about Black and Latino gangs killing Whites. And let's not forget about being inundated with the exploits of millionaire socialites, movie stars, and recording artists, or the inappropriate behavior of our state and federal government officials."

"Tell me, how many of you know the names of your neighbors? When was the last time you had them over for coffee, or a barbeque? You know? It's funny how we know so much about what's going on around the world, but we haven't got a clue as to what's going on in our own backyard.

Communication...Communication. We're more concerned about foreign oil effecting gas prices, North Korea and Iran's growing potential of developing nuclear weapons, or some hotel heiress' inability to drive a car, while primping her hair, touching up her makeup, and texting her boyfriend after hitting her favorite night spot. Wait a minute. Did I say hitting?" A wave of giggles and muffled laughter floats around the room.

"You see? You know exactly who I'm talking about, and I didn't even have to mention her name."

"Our country is on the brink of imploding. Thirty years ago, we were a country that led the world in practically everything. We were the most industrialized nation in the world. Today, we're the leading consumer oriented country in the world. Most of what we buy and use today is made in another country, even though it might have an American brand name on it. Japan, South Korea, and even a number of European manufacturers are making automobiles in this country, with some models having a higher 'Made in America' content than automobiles from Ford, General Motors, and Chrysler. Imagine, a Honda that's more American than a Chevrolet." Higgins pauses a moment to catch his breath and dab his forehead again.

"Our trade deficit is spiraling out of control, and if something isn't done to pull us out of this tailspin, our economy is going to crash. This great nation has survived two World Wars, the Korean War, the Vietnam War, the Cold War, and War in the Middle East. But the war on ignorance, hatred, greed, jealousy, and selfishness will ultimately be our undoing, unless we wake up and start communicating with each other. Communication…Communication."

"This is why I'm running for President. I believe in this great country of ours, and I believe that by working together, we can fix it. I can only hope you feel the same way." The crowd goes wild!

"Ladies and gentlemen!" The crowd continues to applaud and cheer. "Ladies and gentlemen! Please! Please take your seats. I have a few other things I'd like to say." The audience starts to quiet down and return to their seats. "Thank you for your vote of confidence and enthusiasm. Thank you."

"I'm going to do something that's a little unorthodox, so please bear with me for a few moments. As I'm sure most of you are aware, Senator Joshua McCarthy took his own life about ten days ago. While he had an illustrious career in politics, he was not without fault. He ignored one of the most precious things a man could ever hope for, and that is a wife who loved and supported him, and even did her best to ignore those faults."

"Mrs. Michelle Marston-McCarthy has made a name for herself on her own terms. She is a Harvard graduate, the top in her class. She's an accomplished model, having been on the covers of Vogue, Cosmopolitan, Elle, People, Women's Day, Elegant Dining, Metropolitan Home, along with countless others."

Michelle senses that Higgins is about to introduce her as his running mate, and begins to feel uneasy. Out of the corner of her eye, she notices Senator Long, sitting almost directly in front of her, smiling, and nodding his head in approval. She gives him a questioning look, and he continues to smile, and mouths the words, *"It'll be okay,"* as he makes a gesture with his hand, as if he's smoothing something over.

Higgins continues his introduction. "There have been articles about her, and the corporations under her control, in the New

443

York Times, Forbes, Business Week, Working Woman, and Time magazine. This woman has not only survived in what has long been considered a 'man's world', she has thrived in it, and literally taken it by storm."

"She now runs one of the largest law firms in the country. And within the last ten years, she's literally built up New York's second largest accounting firm from scratch! And because of her successful modeling career, she owns one of the fastest growing modeling agencies in the country, with offices in LA, Houston, Miami, Atlanta, Chicago, and New York. She is also credited as being one of the strongest influences for women jumping into corporate America."

"She is a beacon of hope to thousands of women who have the guts to go out and pursue their dreams. Gentlemen…and ladies, let me warn you. If her law or accounting firms ever call on your business, I suggest you have all of your ducks in a row. Because I can assure you, any irregularities will stand out like a sore thumb to them! So, ladies and gentlemen, I take great pleasure and consider it an honor and a privilege to introduce to you, Mrs. Michelle Marston-McCarthy as my running mate for Vice President of the United States of America!"

The women in the room literally jump from their seats, clapping and chanting, "Mi-chelle! Mi-chelle! Mi-chelle!" She looks down at Senator Long, who is standing, clapping, and cheering along with everyone else in the room. Again he nods his head in approval, then motions her to go to the podium.

Michelle walks over to the podium, shakes Higgins' hand, and says under her breath, "This was not part of our agreement."

He replies, "I'm sure you've heard the old saying, 'keep your friends close, but your enemies closer'. Well, Michelle, I don't think I can get you much closer than as my Vice President. Do you?" He then backs away from her and begins to applaud as well, and the applause swells in the room.

Michelle steps up to the podium, clears her throat, and says, "Thank you! Thank you!" The people continue to cheer, and it's obvious the women in the audience are elated about having a woman running for Vice President. "Ladies and gentlemen, please, please." The audience finally starts to settle back into their seats.

444

"Let me tell you something. This is as much a surprise for me as it is for you!" She turns to Higgins as says, "You could have at least given me a little warning." Then looking back into the audience, she says, "Just like a man, waiting until the last possible moment to make a decision that a woman would have planned for weeks on end. The speech, the dress, the shoes, the jewelry…" Then, as she turns back to look at Higgins, she continues, "We're definitely going to have to work on your organization and planning skills. It's amazing you've lived this long without me!" The women in the audience burst out with laughter, followed by moderate applause.

"Honestly, ladies and gentlemen, I had no idea Senator Higgins was going to put me on the spot like this tonight. And since I wasn't aware of his plan to offer me the Vice President's position, I have no speech prepared for the occasion."

"However, I am both honored and humbled by his recommendation, and yes, I believe it's time a woman ran for this office. Ladies…and gentlemen, Senator Higgins and I need your support for the coming months ahead. We have a lot of ground to cover, and we're not going to be able to do that without your help. Tell your friends, your neighbors, your business associates, everyone you meet. It's time for a change in this country. We've been traveling down the same path far too long, and if we don't get out of this rut pretty soon, we're going to become the late, great, United States."

She stops momentarily, then with a serious, yet determined look on her face, scans the crowd and says, "Personally, I'm going to do everything in my power to make sure that doesn't happen. What about you?" She pauses once again, then says, "Thank you." As she turns and starts to walk away from the podium, the audience goes wild with applause, and the women are chanting, "Mi-chelle! Mi-chelle! Mi-chelle!"

Higgins stops her and says, "We're going to win this election by a landslide! I'm tellin' ya! A landslide!" Suddenly, he grabs his chest.

"Bill? Are you all right?" she asks with a concerned look on her face.

"I'm fine, fine. Just a little heartburn, that's all," he replies, although he's obviously in a lot of pain.

Michelle reaches for his glass of champagne and says, "Here, drink some of this. The carbonation in the champagne should help release the gas."

"Thanks."

The audience is still applauding and chanting when Higgins steps back up to the podium. "Thank you! Thank you! Ladies and gentlemen, please. Another moment or two of your indulgence. Please! Please!" Once again the audience quiets down and take their seats.

"Now, I don't know if you've been following the things that have been happening to me recently, but I'd like to introduce you to someone who's been instrumental in taking care of me." Higgins looks over to AJ, and motions for him to stand by him at the podium.

"Ladies and gentlemen, I'd like to introduce you to Secret Service Agent Thomas Andrew Jackson." AJ walks over to Higgins side. "AJ, here, was assigned by the Secret Service to be my personal bodyguard and driver. I've gotta tell you, he wasn't exactly overwhelmed about being a chauffeur for an old codger like me, but through his training and experience, he's saved my bacon more times than I care to count. Over the past several weeks, I'd like to think that we've even developed a sort of bond that goes beyond just a job. In fact, I've begun to think of him more like a son."

"Earlier today, I informed his supervisor that once I'm elected President, I want AJ to stay on and be my head of security." Again the crowd cheers and applauds. Higgins reaches out and shakes AJ's hand, then reaches over with his left hand and pats him on the shoulder. Suddenly, AJ feels a slight prick and a stinging sensation. He backs away from Higgins, to see him smile and mouth the word, "Gotcha!"

AJ strengthens his grip on Higgins' hand, then smiles back. "Sir, I think you should know I've read a lot of very interesting and revealing things about you, courtesy of some of your colleagues within the Core. You evidently believe I've been drinking tonight. I hate to disappoint you, but the only thing I've had this evening has been ginger ale." Higgins smile quickly changes. "And since I haven't consumed any alcohol, it will be a simple matter of taking the antidote."

446

"Plus, you just named me head of your security team in front of all these people. Any sudden decision to replace me would certainly draw a lot of attention, especially since you've told them I'm like a son to you. And let's not forget your comment about the number of attempts made on your life. It wouldn't take much for a member of *my* security team to stand slightly out of position and allow something or someone to get through. I'm sure you've heard the old saying, 'shit happens'."

Higgins suddenly realizes he's essentially played into both AJ and Michelle's hands, painting himself into a corner. AJ hasn't been drinking and knows many of his secrets. And Michelle is now in position to take his place if something should happen to him.

Without warning, a sharp pain hits him, literally taking his breath away. "This can't be happening to me! Not now! No! Not now!" Higgins begins to stagger, then starts to collapse. Both Michelle and AJ catch him, lowering him gently to the floor. The audience evidently can't see what's happening, because the applause and chanting continues unabated.

AJ calls out on his com-link, "AJ to Mobile One! AJ to Mobile One! Medical emergency! Medical emergency! Blackjack One is down! Blackjack One is down! I repeat! Medical emergency!"

"Copy that, AJ. What is your location?"

"We're near the center of the stage, almost directly behind the podium," yells AJ. "It appears the Senator is having a heart attack. He has pain in both his chest and left arm. Breathing is shallow and rapid, pulse is very high. Your best bet in getting to us will be to come in from the service entrance."

"Roger that. Paramedics should be on scene in less than two minutes. Hang tight."

Michelle leans over Higgins, smiling and says, "Two minutes is about all you have Bill. The toxin is already breaking down the muscle tissue in your heart."

"What? What are you talking about?" he says with panic in his voice. "I know for a fact nothing touched me when I pricked AJ. Besides, you gave me the antidote ten days ago. And I haven't touched a drink, until tonight."

"AJ? Is it true? Did he prick you?"

447

"I'm afraid so."

"Have you had anything with alcohol in it within the last 24 to 48 hours?"

"No, I'm not much of a drinker, Michelle, never have been."

"That's good, you're safe for now." Michelle turns her attention back to Higgins. "Well Bill, there are a couple of problems with your theory. First off, I never gave you the antidote."

"Yes you did! Right there in front of AJ and Julie in the library! The damn thing hurt like hell!" Higgins is getting agitated, and red faced. Plus the pain in his chest is getting worse, and it's becoming more difficult to breathe.

"Sterile water."

"What?"

"The syringe was loaded with sterile water," she says coldly. "Nothing more."

"Why? What did I do to you?"

"You're an evil man, Bill. You've killed innocent people for personal gain. And you helped corrupt Joshua."

"What are talking about? You don't know anything! AJ! Help me! Please!"

"What do you know, Michelle?" asks AJ inquisitively.

"I know that you and Weathers are missing two files on him."

"How do you know that?"

"Let's just say that we have a common ally, and leave it at that, for now."

"And what's that supposed to mean?" asks Higgins, wincing from the stabbing pains in his chest.

"I know who broke into Weathers' house and left the files."

"Tell me who betrayed me! Tell me! I want to know, so I can curse their name before I die!" His left arm is starting to become rigid and distorted. Higgins wrenches from another sharp pain in his chest.

"First, you're going to tell AJ why you asked for him specifically. He has a right to know."

"Fuck you! I'm not telling him anything!"

"Suit yourself, Bill. Then I'll tell him."

"Tell me what?" asks AJ.

"I'm sure you remember Bosnia, right?"

448

"How can I forget? It was the first time I got hammered by friendly fire," he says disgustingly. "I lost three men that day, two of them had been in my squad almost three years. I trusted them with my life, as they did me with theirs, and I let them down. Some yahoo ordered a battery to fire on us, even after one of their men warned them we were trying to communicate in Morse code with both the headlights and horn."

"That yahoo was my son, and you killed him! You son of a bitch!" Higgins cries out, wrenching in agonizing pain.

"What are you talking about? We never fired a shot!" says a resentful AJ. "After we got hit, I was in the hospital for almost five weeks! I had to undergo three separate operations to get all the shrapnel out of my arm and leg!"

AJ leans directly over Higgins' face and growls, "And up until I started protecting you, I've never shot anyone who's *ever* worn an American uniform. While I'll freely admit I would have loved to have taken your son out behind the barracks and rearranged his outlook on life, I wouldn't have killed him. I don't know where you got your intel about me killing him, because it never happened. In fact, the court martial never materialized, so I never had the opportunity to meet him or the Base Commander."

"But you know what happened to them!" The veins on Higgins face and neck are standing out. His face is almost beet red, his eyes are bulging, and his entire body is starting to shake.

"The Base Commander got transferred to a non-combat zone, and my son got demoted and sent to Alaska…Alaska!" Higgins pauses for a moment, waiting for the pain to ease up a bit. Finally the wave begins to subside, he sighs and continues. "His military career was in the shitter, and his political career was over before it started." Each sentence, each word is becoming more difficult for him to assemble.

"One day, he got in a Humvee and drove out to a desolate region of the base, and he didn't come back. The next day, an aerial search found the Humvee, his pistol, and blood spatter in the snow where it appeared he had shot himself." Higgins begins to break down, with tears streaming down his cheeks. "But very little of his body was found, because a pack of wolves had fed on his remains, some of it dragged almost a half mile away." Higgins begins to whimper and cry.

AJ softens his tone a bit, and says, "Higgins, I'm sorry. I didn't know."

Higgins' anger returns as he says, "You might not have been there to pull the trigger, but you killed him just the same."

Suddenly, Higgins' eyes and mouth open wide. He takes in a deep breath, as his back arches upward. Then, just as suddenly, he collapses and goes completely limp.

AJ checks for a pulse. Nothing. He leans over his mouth to check for respiration. Again, nothing. He tilts Higgins' head back, holds his nose closed, and gives him two quick breaths, followed by a series of chest compressions. The paramedics arrive just as he's starting the compressions and take over for him. Both AJ and Michelle slowly rise to their feet, and step back, allowing them room to work.

Michelle says, "He's dead, isn't he."

"Yes," he says, as they start walking away, "I'm afraid so. I guess that takes care of you running for Vice President. You can't draw a cart without a horse." He stops and faces Michelle. "I need to know something. Is this toxin going to kill me?"

"When was the last time you had a drink?"

"Julie and I had some wine with dinner over the weekend."

"How sweet," she says flippantly. "I don't think I need to remind you that you shouldn't consume any alcohol until you meet me at my office tomorrow morning. Is that a problem?"

"No, but how will I know whether or not you've actually given me the antidote? No offense."

"None taken. I have no grudge against you, AJ. Besides, you're a hero now."

"What are you talking about? I haven't done anything."

Michelle smiles and says, "Trust me, this isn't over yet. You'll see."

"Don't you think someone needs to tell everybody Higgins just died?"

"Technically, he's not dead yet, at least until a doctor or coroner says otherwise. At this point in time, he's unconscious and unresponsive. Besides, everyone is having a good time right now. There's no need to spoil it for them. They'll see it on the news or read it in the newspaper tomorrow morning. It'll also give us some time to come up with Plan B."

The two of them are standing by the table when Michelle notices a light flashing on her cell phone. She reaches into her purse, pulls it out and says, "Hello?"

"Plan B?" asks AJ, as his phone starts to vibrate. He looks at the display, and all it shows is a row of 9's. "Who is this, and how did you get my number?"

"I have you, Michelle, and Weathers on the line. Come up to room 713. Use the service elevator. We want to have a word with all of you." Before any of them can answer, the line goes dead.

"What's going on?" he asks with a perplexed look on his face.

"AJ?" says Michelle. "I think you're about to meet some key members of the Core."

As the elevator doors open on the seventh floor, two tall, muscular men step in front of the opening, displaying an imposing posture. In the blink of an eye, AJ's pistol is out of its holster and in firing position. Both men start to back away when AJ bellows, "Freeze! Nobody move! Hands behind your head!" Both of them stop, but neither of them raise their hands. AJ takes a step closer to the man in front of him and places his pistol within inches of his forehead and says, "Do you have selective hearing or something?"

"Sir, if we raise our hands, there's a sniper in the building across the street who'll shoot the first person who steps out of the elevator."

"Then tell him to stand down."

"I can't. There's no communication between us and the sniper units, only standing orders. Sorry sir, no can do."

"Well then, drop your weapons."

"Sir, we're not armed," he says as both men open their coats to show they're not armed."

"What?"

"No sir, we're not armed. That's why we have snipers. I'd suggest putting your weapon away. No one's going to hurt you up here."

"That's easy for you to say."

"If you'll follow us, we'll take you to the meeting," and both men start walking down the hall.

AJ and Weathers stare at each other for a moment, then AJ shrugs his shoulders, holsters his weapon, and holds out his arm to escort Michelle down the hall.

As they approach room 713, there are two more bodyguards standing in front of the door.

One of the bodyguards says, "Agent Jackson, we need to collect your weapons."

"AJ? Please do as they ask," says Michelle softly. "I assure you, no one will harm you."

"I'm not in the habit of surrendering my weapon to anyone," he replies, as he concentrates his focus on the two men at the door.

Weathers says, "AJ, I'm asking you to surrender your weapon. They're not going to hurt any of us."

"You're willing to bet your life on that Mr. Weathers?"

"Yes, I am."

"Very well," says AJ, as he hands over his Beretta. "Here ya go, fellas. Knock yourself out."

"Both of them, sir," says one of the bodyguards.

"Excuse me?"

"That includes the Centurion you have in the small of your back, sir."

"Oh! That…Sorry," says AJ rather flippantly. "And, if that's the case, I guess you'll want this, too," as he pulls out his pocketknife.

Once they're satisfied AJ is disarmed, they open the doors and allow them to enter the room.

The drapes are drawn, and the room is dimly lit. As they pass the corner, they find seven men sitting behind two long tables, among them are General Woolbright and Senators Burgess and Long. There are also three chairs in front of them.

General Woolbright says, "Mrs. McCarthy, Colonel Weathers, Agent Jackson, please have a seat. We'd like to have a word with you." The three of them take their seats. "Mrs. McCarthy, may I call you Michelle?"

"Yes General, I'd prefer it."

"Thank you. Michelle, we know your late husband had injected Bill with the toxin developed by your firm, and we are also aware of your delivery of the supposed anti-toxin. While we were suspicious as to whether you had given him the anti-toxin or a placebo, we decided to give him a little boost tonight."

"I'm sorry, but I'm not exactly sure what you're trying to say," replies Michelle.

"We've had some time to do a little research of our own, and discovered that if you add the toxin directly to alcohol, its potency more than doubles and death occurs within twenty to thirty minutes after it's ingested."

"So, you're saying someone spiked his champagne?" asks AJ.

"Precisely," says Senator Long.

"Why are you telling us this?" asks AJ.

453

"Bill did a fine job of introducing Michelle to the world tonight," says Senator Long. "She's endured the humiliation caused by her late husband's infidelity."

"She's a grieving widow," pipes in Mr. Connelly.

"She's a woman who's made serious inroads in a man's world," says Senator Burgess.

"She's an icon by which all women want to emulate," says Woolbright.

"She's beautiful," says Weathers.

"And she's my daughter!" says a voice from the shadows.

"Dad? Is that you?"

"Yes, my dear, it's me," says her father as he emerges from the darkness.

"This is such a surprise!" she gets up and rushes to his side, with tears streaming down her face.

"After you showed me those pictures and videos of that son of a bitch, I started doing a little snooping on my own. Our, actually, I should say your investigations division provided me with a wealth of information on his investments and bank accounts outside of the country, along with his under the table business deals. I came to the realization that I stole from my only child, giving him what was rightfully yours. I was foolish to think you couldn't do the things you've done. I've watched you make our businesses grow and prosper, while he pissed away millions of dollars. I looked the other way when he openly cheated on you. I helped create this monster, and I want to make it right."

"Dad, he's dead. He can't hurt me anymore."

"I know, but you've been denied your seat here within the Core, and today we're going to remedy that."

"But Dad, I'm getting confused. At first, it sounded like the Core was going to want me to run for public office, and now it seems you're telling me I'm going to be a member of the Core."

"Honey, you *are* a member of the Core, if you want it. But we don't want you to run for just any public office. Tomorrow morning, on national television, you're going to tell the world of Senator Higgins' passing, and that his dying wish was for you to take his place, and announce your plans to run for President of the United States."

454

"Dad! Even you know I can't do that and be a member of the Core."

General Woolbright responds to Michelle's comment. "Over the past few months, the Core has been going through some radical changes. In a way, we owe the late Senator Higgins a debt of gratitude. His desire to run for President, along with his plan to take control of the Core, told us it was time to review our purpose, our focus, and our strategy. We now have a Board of Directors that doubles as a Tribunal."

"The Board consists of nine members who will serve for three years, although three of the members on this Board will serve two years, and three other members will serve only one year. This will eliminate the complete turnover of the Board every three years. From that point on, all members will serve three years, unless they decide to run for the top three government offices, those being the President, Vice President, and Speaker of the House. From this day forward, a member of the Core can hold one of the nation's three highest offices. However, they forfeit their voting rights, and they cannot sit on the Board during their period in office."

"With these changes in place, why did you TLC Higgins?" asks a puzzled AJ.

"Higgins was a dangerous liability," replies Woolbright. "Besides, he still might have tried to overthrow the Core once he got in White House. He had a lot of friends both in and out of the Core. We just needed to keep him alive long enough to introduce Michelle to the world as his running mate."

"What made you so certain he was going to pick me?" asks Michelle.

"While we weren't completely certain of it, we had been monitoring all of his calls and emails, and he never offered the position to anyone else. It was a bit of long shot, but as a group, we were comfortable with it," says Senator Long.

"Do you honestly think I have a chance of getting the Democratic nomination for President?"

"Mrs. McCarthy, just who do you think is the Chairman of National Democratic Committee?" asks Senator Burgess.

"I believe you are, Senator," she replies. Senator Burgess nods his head in agreement. "Dad, are you sure about this? Do you think I'm ready to run for President? Do you think this country is ready for a woman as President?"

"Baby, you're going to take this country by storm! Your professional and personal life is going to thrust you ahead of any and all comers. You've endured the humiliation of an unfaithful husband, and built three empires! You have grace and poise, intelligence and compassion, all without a hint of ego."

"Well, can I at least go back to my maiden name? My stomach churns every time someone calls me Mrs. McCarthy. In my mind, I've always been Michelle Marston."

"Michelle," says General Woolbright, "right now, one of our biggest trump cards is playing off the infidelity and death of your late husband. Millions of women are going to vote for you, because of what your husband to you. It's women striking out at men in general. Your beauty, innocence, and compassion will also have an effect on millions of men who will find it hard to believe why your husband would want to cheat on you. If you drop his name, we'll lose some of that momentum."

He adds, "While you have had significant successes in the business world, you have virtually no public political history. We are prepared to use every tool at our disposal to bring the Michelle Marston-McCarthy story to the public."

Then her father chides in, "And once you become President, then we'll play up the part where you want to cleanse yourself of your late husband's name and notoriety, declare your independence, and reinstate your maiden name. The public will eat it up! We may even have it broadcast on national television!"

"Eat your heart out Desperate Housewives!" says Mr. Connelly with a wicked smile on his face.

"Michelle, we're going to get you on every major talk show across the country, from Oprah, the View, Leno, Letterman, Larry King, and what's the name of that morning show with that cute Latin girl? Oh! I remember! Live with Regis and Kelly!" says Senator Long. "We'll contact all the major women's groups and set up meetings with them, too!"

"You're going to go after the self interest groups, wasteful spending, frivolous government contracts, programs with constant cost overruns, etc. Then you're going to focus on the problems of the needy, work programs, health care, housing," adds Senator Burgess.

"But more importantly, you're going to appeal to providing tax breaks and incentives for families in the middle income bracket. We can't continue to bleed them dry. At the current rate, there'll be no middle ground, just the ultra rich, and the ultra poor. Next will be anarchy or the total collapse of our economy, our way of life," says General Woolbright. "It'll make the Civil War look like a backyard barbecue."

"Gentlemen, these are all very important issues, certainly worthy of discussion. But are we going to address these issues, and make an honest effort to solve them, or is it just whitewash to cover up what every other President has done in the past? If we're going to discuss these issues, then I want to offer true workable plans to fix them, or at least improve them. I don't want band-aids, or pitiful excuses. No porcelain dolls, gentlemen."

"And what's that supposed to mean, Michelle?" asks Senator Burgess.

"Pretty on the outside, empty on the inside," she replies.

Mr. Connelly leans over to General Woolbright and mumbles, "Sounds like we've got a tiger by the tail."

"Mr. Connelly, I heard that, and you have no idea what I can do when I set my mind to it," she says with a determined look on her face.

"Well, Michelle. Do you want to run for President of the United States?" asks Woolbright.

"I'd like to think about it."

"Mrs. McCarthy, Michelle. Higgins' body is already en route to the hospital, and they'll be announcing his death on the news in less than an hour. You have the opportunity to be the first woman President of the United States. The Core is willing to help you achieve that goal. We need an answer, now," says Woolbright.

Michelle looks over to her father, who's smiling and nodding his head. Then she looks at each of the men sitting at the table in front of her, and finally at AJ and Weathers. Then she asks, "Do you really think they'll elect me President?"

457

"Honey, you're gonna kick their ass at the polls! I guarantee it!" says her father confidently.

"Okay, then you've got yourself a candidate!"

Woolbright stands and says, "Michelle, you've just made history on several levels. You're the first woman to be brought into the Core. You're the first person to be counseled by the Core's Board of Directors, and you're the first person, man or woman, the Core will be actively supporting to become the next President of the United States. And before this is over, you'll be the first Madam President of the United States, in addition to being the first woman to aspire for the Presidency with no previous political background!"

"Hear! Hear!" cheers the Board.

Michelle's father hands her a glass of champagne, and Connelly gives both Weathers and AJ their glasses, as General Woolbright proposes a toast, "To Michelle Marston-McCarthy, the next President of the United States!" Everyone turns up their glasses.

Then Burgess chimes in, "To two terms!"

"Hear! Hear!" cheers the Board.

"Long live the Core." toasts Michelle, as she tips her glass to her father.

"Long live the Core!" cheers the Board and her father in unison.

"Okay, okay," says Woolbright. "We have a few other things to discuss. Let's move on, shall we? Colonel Weathers. It has come to my attention some papers were lost prior to your retirement from the United States Army."

"I wasn't aware of anything out of the ordinary, sir," replies Weathers with some concern in his voice.

"It was nothing on your end, Colonel. It appears the paperwork recommending your promotion to Brigadier General, prior to your retirement, was somehow lost in transit, and completely overlooked."

"I was not aware of any such promotion, sir."

"Well, Colonel, I'm happy to report those papers have been found, and I'm proud to be the first to congratulate you, General Weathers. We'll make the necessary adjustments in your retirement pay, and of course it will be retroactive."

"General Woolbright, I don't know what to say."

"How about, thank you?" says the General as he reaches over the table to shake Weathers' hand.

"Thank you, General." says Weathers as he shakes his hand. "Thank you very much."

"Robert, you've earned it, and I'm very happy for you. I'm personally aware of the work you did for us during your military career. Your diligence and perseverance helped save thousands of lives with the intelligence you and your department provided over the years. For that, I'm truly grateful."

"Thank you again, sir," says Weathers with a tear in his eye.

"Please, call me James," he replies. "One other thing Robert," says Woolbright. "Over the past couple of weeks, we've lost two key members of the Core. Michelle, of course will replace her late husband. The Board, including me, would like you to fill Higgins' seat."

"General Woolbright, James," he pauses, "I'm flattered by your and the Board's recommendation, but considering the history of the Core over the past forty or so years, I'm not so sure I want to be that close to it. I hope you understand."

"What if I told you the Core is in the process of completely restructuring its role influencing the current and future history of this great country of ours? This Tribunal is just the first step in that direction. You could help us get back to what the Core was all about, back when it first came into being."

"You're serious?" says Weathers disbelievingly. "No more TLC's?"

"That would certainly be one of the goals, Robert."

"I would want to make that a priority, James."

"Well, the only way you can make it one, is to become one of us," says Connelly.

Weathers looks Woolbright straight in the eye and says, "Okay, I'm in."

"Well, that leaves just one more thing to discuss, and that's what are we going to do with our man, AJ here?" says Woolbright.

"I don't suppose you found some lost papers making me a general, too, did you?" asks AJ rather flippantly.

"Do I need to?" asks Woolbright in a similar fashion.

"I think it would arouse more than a little suspicion within the Corps, sir. The Marine Corps, that is."

"I imagine it would, son," replies Woolbright. "I've looked over your service record, AJ, and I've never heard of a Marine, or anyone else in the United States Military for that matter, turning down, not one, but two Battlefield Commissions. You've earned over a dozen medals, and citations, ranging from two Purple Hearts, three Bronze Stars, two Silver Stars, the Navy Cross, and the Distinguished Service Medal. Son, by all rights, you should have been at least a Captain by now. Why?"

"While I've sworn an oath to serve and protect my country, I wanted to be with my men, sir. I wanted to make sure they all got in, and more importantly, I wanted to make sure they got out, preferably in one piece. I couldn't do that sitting on the sidelines, sir."

"That's very commendable and admirable, AJ. But that doesn't help me in determining what I should do with you," replies Woolbright.

"Who says you're supposed to do anything with or for me, sir? I gave twenty years of my life to the Marine Corps. And the only days I regret, are those when I lost a member of my team, or we were unable to fulfill the job we were sent out to do. Otherwise, I'd do it again in a heartbeat."

"Now I'm a Secret Service Agent, ID number Sierra, Sierra 55191. My supervisor is Brigadier General Robert Weathers, US Army, retired, and my job, up until about twenty minutes ago, was protecting the late Senator William Henry Higgins. I suppose my future will hang in the balance until a review board makes a determination as to whether or not I could have prevented the Senator's untimely demise."

"AJ, the coroner's office will confirm Higgins' death was caused by a heart attack, nothing more. The performance of your duties has never been in question here. In fact, Senator Higgins recommended you for the National Security Medal shortly after the incident on the expressway. While it's still going through channels, I'm confident it will be approved shortly," says Woolbright.

"Okay, where does that leave me?" asks AJ.

"As a formality, the National Democratic Committee will ask the President to grant Mrs. McCarthy Secret Service protection," says Senator Burgess. "Of course, her being a recently widowed, seemingly helpless woman, we're confident the President will see that it would be in the nation's best interest to make sure she is properly protected."

"In other words, you want me to be her personal bodyguard."

"Actually, I think we'll be able to convince them she'll need a proper security team to protect her. You'll be her head of security," says Woolbright.

"Isn't that up to Michelle?" asks AJ.

"I have no objection. Actually, I look forward to it," she replies.

"Then it's settled," says Connelly.

"Wait a minute!" says AJ firmly. "Don't I have a say in this?"

"It appears that Higgins took one of the rings loaded with the toxin over the weekend. Have you any idea what he planned to do with it?" asks Woolbright.

"I'm afraid I do," replies AJ sadly.

"He didn't use it on you, did he?" asks Weathers.

"He tagged me at the podium, sir."

"AJ! You just drank champagne!" says Michelle.

"AJ, are you in or out?" says Woolbright with a serious look on his face.

"Do I have a choice?" AJ turns, looks at Michelle, and asks, "How long have I got?"

"I don't know. It depends on your tolerance to alcohol," she replies, obviously concerned for his safety.

Woolbright reaches under the table and pulls out a briefcase, lays it on the table, and opens it. Inside, among the papers and files, is a long and narrow pouch, similar to what Michelle had at Higgins' estate. He opens it, pulls out a syringe, and holds it in front of him. "AJ, you're a good man, and a fine Marine. I'd trust you with my life. But you also know too much about the Core. So, I'm asking one last time. Are you in…or out?"

TLC: Chapter 64
AJ's apartment
Friday morning
July 29, 2011, 1100 hours local time

"I still can't believe Weathers talked you into being Michelle's personal bodyguard," says Julie with the sound of disappointment in her voice. "I thought after you got such a bad taste in your mouth dealing with Higgins, you'd put up a decent fight." she says while packing her suitcase.

"I did, but I lost," replies AJ, while picking out a few shirts and slacks from the closet.

"Who are you trying to kid?"

"Since the Department of Military Records found those papers promoting Weathers to brigadier general, you'd think he was a direct descendant of General George Patton," he says.

"Well, you have to admit he really does have a good heart," she replies. "I'm sure it took a lot of work and more than a few favors to have David, and the rest of the Core operatives, cleared of any wrong doing, and allowing their bodies to be buried at Arlington. I'm sure it'll help give a lot of families closure."

"Yeah," he sighs.

"Do you think Higgins really died of a heart attack?"

"Well, that's what the coroner's report said."

"And you know? It was one thing for Higgins to help get your Hummer replaced, but then to turn around and list you as his sole living heir, splitting his wealth between you and a handful of charities? All in less than a week before his death? I guess he wasn't such a bad guy after all!"

"I admit he had his moments," says AJ as he folds his slacks and shirts, and places them in his suitcase. While gathering up his toiletries in the bathroom, he catches his reflection in the mirror and stares at it for a moment. He doesn't appear to be very happy. "I'm thankful Weathers is allowing us some time off to check this place out, aren't you?"

"Of course! It's not every day someone you know and love inherits a ranch. How far out is it from Vegas?"

"About twenty miles or so," he says as he returns to bedroom. "Look, there can't be much too it. According to the deed, it's only about a hundred sections."

"How big is that?"

"I don't know. Section is probably just a fancy word for acre or something," says AJ as he tosses in some boxers, T-shirts, and socks.

"Well, I guess we'll find out soon enough, won't we?" she says while trying to squeeze her suitcase down enough to zip it closed.

"I reckon," he replies with an exaggerated Western drawl, and smacks her butt as he walks by.

"Hey! That smarts!" she yells while trying to rub the sting out of it.

"I'll bet your suitcase is about as full as those jeans," he says with a smile.

"You just wait! You'll get yours!"

"Come on. Get the lead out. The cab's going to be here any minute." About that time the door buzzer goes off. "I wonder who that could be?" he says sarcastically, while walking over to the intercom. "Yes?"

"Somebody by the name of AJ up there? He ordered a cab to take him to the airport."

"That would be me. We'll be down in a minute."

"No problem. But just to let you know, the meter's running."

"Julie. Let's go!"

"I'm coming! I'm coming!"

The trip to the airport is uneventful, as is their flight to Las Vegas. After a two hour layover in Chicago, their flight finally arrives at McCarran International late in the afternoon. As they pick up their luggage in the baggage area, they can see the sun beginning to set in the west.

They pick up a rental and luckily, it has an onboard GPS system. AJ keys in the address, and everything seems to be a go. Once they reach the outskirts of town, they decide to stop and grab a bite to eat.

After recharging their batteries with a filling, western style meal, they hit the road again. A good twenty minutes passes when Julie asks, "Are you sure it's only supposed to be about twenty miles out of town?"

"Well, that's what was written on the directions."

"You've been driving between sixty and seventy ever since we left that truck stop, so we're well past twenty miles. Do you think we're lost?"

"According to 'Mr. Magellan' here, we're heading in the right direction. We've got to be getting close though, because it says we're going to be turning right…right…about…here!" He stabs the brakes and whips the wheel to prevent overshooting the turn.

"Hey! Mario Andretti! Next time, scrub off a little more speed before you try to make another turn like that! Okay?"

"Yes, dear."

"How much farther?" she asks.

"I don't know. It doesn't look far," he says, squinting at the GPS display. "Is that a gate I see up ahead?"

"Yes, and it's closed."

AJ pulls up to the gate, and grabs his flashlight to check it out. It's secured with a padlock. There's no keypad, nor intercom. About a quarter mile down the road, he can see what appears to be a house with its porch light on. AJ gets back into the car.

"Are you sure we're on the right road?" she asks.

"All I know is this is where the GPS system says we should be."

"Is there someone we can call?"

464

"The only number I have is for the attorney's office, and I'm sure everyone is long gone for the day."

"So, what should we do?" she asks.

"Well, there's a light on about a quarter mile down the road. I could probably walk down there and see if anybody's home."

"And considering we're out in the middle of nowhere, and you would be technically trespassing, especially after having climbed over a locked gate, you might get yourself shot!"

"I suppose that's a distinct possibility, and I didn't think to pack my vest."

"Me either," she says. "Let's go back up the road and find a place to spend the night. I'd feel better checking this place out in the daylight anyway."

"Fine by me. There's probably not much out here but an old bunk house, a couple of barns, and a lot of tumbleweeds and scrub brush." As AJ is about to put the car in reverse, he looks into the rearview mirror. In the distance, he can see a pair of headlights coming toward them. "Well? Looks like someone else might be lost."

"What do you mean?"

"Someone's coming down the road." He gets out of the car, and stands beside it, while waiting for them to arrive. As the vehicle gets closer, he can tell that it's a truck, and it's stirring up a fair amount of dust.

Finally, the vehicle comes to a stop a short distance from AJ and his car. A man gets out, and says, "Are you lost? Since you left the highway back there, you've been on private property." He's dressed in conventional western garb, boots, jeans, denim shirt, and a sweat stained cowboy hat. He appears to be in his late fifties to early sixties. His face and hands are tanned and weathered.

"Is this Senator Higgins place?" asks AJ.

"Do you know the senator?"

"Yes sir. Well actually, I guess I should say we knew him. You see, Senator Higgins died two weeks ago."

"Yep, I saw that on TV. That's a shame, truly is," he says sadly. "So, what brings you folks out here? You reporters or somethin'? Ain't much to see, really. In fact, the senator hardly spent any time out here at all, at least over the last six or seven years or so. He always seemed to have somethin' cookin' in Washington, New York, places like that, you know. Say, I didn't catch your name."

"Sorry. Everyone calls me AJ. Actually, my given name is Thomas Andrew Jackson, and this is my girlfriend, Julie, Julie Robinson."

"Well, everybody calls me Dusty. I keep up the place," he says with a grin. "So, what are you doin' out here in the middle of nowhere, after dark? Sight seein'?"

"Actually, Dusty? I'm the new owner," he replies, as he reaches out to shake Dusty's hand.

"You're funnin' me, aren't ya."

"No sir, I'm afraid not."

"The old man never told me he had the place up for sale. He'd a told me somethin' about that." It's obvious Dusty is a bit upset. "Now that's a damn pisser!"

"I'm afraid you don't understand, Dusty," says AJ, trying to calm him down. "The senator didn't sell it. He left it to me in his will."

"What?" he says with a surprised look on his face. "Now, why in the hell would he do a thing like that?"

"I'm not exactly sure myself. You see? I was assigned by the Secret Service to be his bodyguard."

"So you're the fella that saved his hide out there on the expressway, and then again at that shindig on the Fourth of July!"

"Well Dusty, I had some help at the shindig. Tell me. Is there a place out here where Julie and I can stay the night, or do we need to go back into town?"

"Me and a couple of hands are sleepin' in the bunkhouse. Not much privacy in there, if you know what I mean, for missy here. But there is a guesthouse you could sleep in tonight, then I'll show the rest of the place tomorrow. I'll warn you ahead of time. It ain't been used in awhile, so the air's gonna smell a little stale in there. But as cool as it is tonight, you can open up a few of the windas, and you'll be fine. Sheets and all should be clean, might have a little dust on things though. You're out in the desert, you know."

"Sounds okay to me," says AJ. "How about you, Julie?" Julie nods her head. "We're game. Let's go."

466

"Let me get the gate, then you can go on through. Once you get past it, pull off enough so I can pass you, and you can follow me on in. How about that?"

"Fine by me," AJ says with a smile, as he gets back in the car. AJ looks over to Julie and makes a funny face. She just rolls her eyes, then looks straight ahead.

Dusty pulls up to the front of the bunkhouse, and the other two ranch hands come out to help Dusty unload groceries from the truck. "Hey fellas! Come over here for a minute. There's someone I want you to meet." Dusty motions to AJ to get out and meet the two men. "Fellas, this here is AJ. He was the senator's bodyguard. According to him, the senator left him the ranch, so he's our new boss." AJ reaches out to shake their hands. "This here is Chuck, as in 'chuck wagon'. He's our cook, and a damn good one, too! He makes a mean ass steak that'll melt in your mouth."

"Nice to meet you, Chuck," says AJ.

"Same here, Mr. AJ," he replies, smiling.

"Please, just call me AJ."

"Yes sir, AJ."

"Now, you *do* need to be careful with his chili. You might want keep a pitcher of beer within arm's reach! If you know what I mean," Dusty says with a smile. "He's also the ranch's vet. Not registered, mind ya', but he don't cost as much, and I'd put his abilities up against any of them fancy doctor types." Chuck blushes a bit with that remark.

"This here's Brad."

"Hi Brad," says AJ.

"Pleased to meet you AJ," replies Brad, shaking his hand like a pump handle.

"Now Brad, he's kind of a jack of all trades. He can rope, break horses, even do a little mechanicin' on the tractors, equipment, and stuff. He spends a fair amount of time ridin' the fences, and checkin' on the water and cattle.

Once, I seen him take out a coyote at better than fifty yards, free hand, in the saddle, and the damn thing was runnin' through the rocks at the base of a bluff. One shot...POW! Right behind the shoulder blades!"

"What were you using?" asks AJ.

467

"My old Winchester. It's an 1894, lever action, 44-40, carbine. Finish is gone, but it still shoots good. Used to belong to my father, and his father before him. It's over a hundred years old. Made back in 1905."

"Impressive!" says AJ. "Look fellas, I just want you to know that I'm not the type that likes to jump in and start rocking the boat. Dusty calls me your new boss. Well, I may be the new owner, but as far as I'm concerned, Dusty's your boss. You don't need to be worrying about trying to second-guess me. Dusty and I will sit down and talk about what's going on down here, and together we'll figure what needs to be done, if anything. So, enjoy your evening, and go about your business just like you would any other day. Okay?"

"Sounds good to me," says Dusty. "Whatcha say I take you up to the guest house?"

"That sounds like a good idea. We've been on the road or in the air since 11:00 this morning. I'm beat, and I'm sure Julie is too."

"All right then, follow me."

"Nice meeting you fellas. Good night," says AJ, waving to them as he gets back in the car.

"Somehow, I get the feeling this place is bigger than a hundred acres," says Julie.

"Well, I'll ask Dusty when we get to the guest house. How's that?"

"Fine, fine."

The guesthouse is about a hundred yards farther up the road. With the exception of the stars, it's pretty dark out. AJ and Julie can barely make out the shape of the house from the road.

Dusty gets out of the truck and starts walking back to AJ's car. "Need any help unloadin'?"

"Sure, if you don't mind." AJ hands him Julie's suitcase and overnight bag, while he carries his two bags.

Dusty's struggling under the weight of Julie's bags, when he asks, "Mind if I ask how long you plan on stayin'?"

"Just a couple of days, really. The last few months have been pretty hectic, and I've just been assigned as Mrs. McCarthy's head of security. She'll be hitting the campaign trail sometime next week."

468

"Wasn't she the one who was going to be the senator's runnin' mate for Vice President?"

"Yep. Now the committee has decided to give her a shot. While she doesn't have much of a political past, she's got a pretty strong following in both the professional and business communities. And of course, being a woman, she's going to have a strong feminine presence."

"Well, maybe it's time to have a woman for President. We've already had an actor, a playboy, and a peanut farmer. A woman's touch might be what this country needs!" Dusty's grinning from ear to ear.

"Now folks, wait here at the door for a moment, while I flip the main breakers, and get some light in here. Dusty drops Julie's bags at the door and disappears into the darkness of the house. AJ and Julie hear him bump into a few things, then hear him say, "Found it!" A couple of lights come on in the house, along with the outside lights.

Dusty makes his way back to the entry, and says, "Okay folks, I'll give you a quick tour, then leave you to it." He shows them the kitchen, the hall bath, then the bedrooms. At the end of the hallway, he says, "Now this here's the master bedroom. Ya got your walk-in closet over there, and your master bath over here."

"Now before ya do any washin' or bathin', I'd let the water run a little while. There's probably going to be some rust in the lines. No one's been in here for at least a year or two. Oh! And since the power's been off, it'll be at least a half hour or so, before you get any hot water. So, unless you're into cold showers, I'd wait a bit, if I were you."

"Now look, I know you probably didn't bring any food along with ya, so you're more than welcome to have breakfast with us. Bein' it's the weekend, we usually sleep in, so Chuck won't start makin' breakfast until, oh, somewhere around 6:30, maybe 7:00." Julie turns away from Dusty and AJ and snickers. "Does that sound okay by you?"

"Sure! Great!" AJ says smiling. "We'll be there."

"We normally eat out back behind the bunkhouse. We have a table and some chairs back there, under the tree. It'll still be cool out, and the air'll be fresh, with just a hint of a breeze. I think you'll find it relaxin'."

469

"I don't suppose there's a working phone here, is there?" asks AJ.

"We have one in the bunkhouse, but nothin' down here. Like I said before, no one's been in this house for a while, but you should be able to get a signal on your cell phone, though."

"Right," says AJ, sounding a little disappointed.

"Like I said, if you'll open up some of the windas, you'll have this place aired out in no time. Now, it gets pretty cool out here at night, so if it gets too cold for ya, there's some blankets in the hall closet."

"Thanks, Dusty," says Julie.

"Well, AJ?" Dusty tips his hat and says, "Miss Julie, I'll leave you two alone for the night." Dusty and AJ start walking down the hallway toward the front door. "If ya need anything, just holler. It's pretty quiet out here. You might even hear a coyote or an owl maybe, but other than that…"

Standing just outside the front door, AJ says, "Good night, Dusty. We'll see you in the morning."

"Come to think of it, if ya sleep with the windas open, you'll probably be able to smell Chuck makin' breakfast. Especially his coffee, sausage, and homemade biscuits."

"Homemade biscuits? Yum!" hollers Julie from the bedroom.

"Julie loves homemade biscuits," says AJ. "Oh! I have a question."

"Go ahead. Shoot." says Dusty.

"Just how big is this place? When we first met out there on the road, you mentioned we had been on the property since we had gotten off the highway."

"Yep. That's right."

"Well, the paperwork I saw, said that Higgins, I mean me, I own about a hundred acres of land."

"Nope, it's a hundred sections. The property covers most of the land between this side of the highway and the base of those mountains behind ya."

"That sounds a little bigger than a hundred acres," says AJ.

"Miles," says Dusty.

"Excuse me?"

"Miles, AJ. A hundred square miles."

"You can't be serious!" says AJ disbelievingly.

"AJ? A section is six hundred and forty acres, or one square mile. You're standin' in the middle of a hundred sections, which is about sixty-four thousand acres, or one hundred square miles."

"There's about ten miles of frontage that runs along the highway, and it's about ten miles deep, give or take. Some of it runs up into the foothills, a little farther west of here. While most people might see it as nothing but scrub and desert, it's actually pretty country. That's one of the few things the senator seemed to understand about this place."

"Any idea what his plans were to do with it?"

"We never really sat down and discussed much, other than just keepin' it up, mendin' fences, keepin' a few head of cattle on it, and stuff. You see, to call it a ranch, and take advantage of those tax benefits, there has to be cattle on it, so we try to keep a few hundred head on hand at any given time, just to keep the Feds and state boys off our ass."

"Dusty, I'm not sure I follow."

"Look, AJ. This property lies on the outskirts of Las Vegas, the gamblin' and entertainment paradise of Nevada, smack dab in the middle of the desert. That road up there is one of the main arteries between Las Vegas and California. Ten miles of frontage. Do the math."

"So, you're saying he eventually planned to develop it?"

"Like I said, we never really talked about it, but I ain't stupid. This place isn't makin' any money. Hasn't for years now. Me and the boys get our checks in the mail once a month from some law firm in New York. All the bills go up there, too. And there's an account at the bank we can draw from for emergencies. Otherwise, we're pretty much on our own."

"Sounds like a nice setup, neat and clean," says AJ.

"Tell me somethin'," says Dusty with a serious look on his face.

"Sure."

"Are me and the boys out of a job?"

"No, nobody's out of a job. I just got here. It's late, and I'm pretty beat. And up until just a minute ago, I really had no idea how big this place is. In fact, I think it's going to take a little time for all this to sink in!"

AJ continues, "Look, Dusty. You and I could probably stay up half the night talking about this. Let's both call it a night, and get a fresh start in the morning. Whaddaya' say?"

"Fair enough, AJ. Goodnight. Goodnight, Miss Julie!"

"Good night, Dusty," she yells back.

AJ reaches out to shake his hand, and says, "Goodnight, Dusty. See you in the morning." The two of them shake hands, then Dusty walks back to his truck. Once Dusty heads back toward the bunkhouse, AJ closes and locks the door, then turns off the outside lights.

As AJ enters the bedroom, he can see that Julie has turned back the covers and fluffed the pillows. The windows above the bed are open, and the drapes are gently waving in the cool evening breeze.

He hears the sound of water running in the bathroom, and as he rounds the corner, he finds Julie standing in front of the mirror in her bra and panties, cooling herself off with a damp washcloth. Standing just outside of her peripheral vision, he stares at her, taking in her beauty. His eyes follow her every move as she dampens and caresses each and every part of her body. His heart feels as though it's about to burst, because of the love he has for her. But his heart is also heavy, because of the secrets he will have to keep from her.

AJ joins her in the bathroom, standing behind her, staring at her image in the mirror. She dampens the washcloth again, then hands it to him over her left shoulder. While he gently sponges her neck, she reaches behind and unfastens her bra, then slowly crosses her arms across her chest, sliding the straps off her shoulders. As he continues to work his way down her back, she closes her eyes and tilts her head back, softly brushing her head against his. He lays the washcloth down on the vanity, wraps his arms around her waist, then slowly glides his hands up her body, and caresses her breasts. As she moans with pleasure, she turns her head, and begins to kiss his neck, then his cheek. Slowly, she turns around in his arms, reaches up around his neck, and draws his lips to hers, and they begin to kiss.

TLC: Chapter 66
Saturday morning
July 30, 2011, 0630 hours local time

Morning breaks, and sure enough, the aroma of Chuck's coffee, bacon, and biscuits, are wafting in the air. AJ is the first to awaken, and finds Julie laying on her side, with one arm laying across his chest, and a leg draped over his.

He lays there for a minute trying to decide how to escape this situation without awakening her, when he comes up with a devilish idea. He takes a lock of her hair and softly tickles her nose. She unconsciously brushes her nose a couple of times, then rolls away from him. He takes the opportunity to ease out of bed, and slips into the bathroom. After tapping the kidneys, he washes his face, then quietly slips over to the closet, grabs a change of clothes, and leaves the room, closing the door behind him. He dresses in the bedroom across the hall, then slips out of the house and heads down to the bunkhouse.

Dusty and Brad are already sitting under the tree, enjoying their morning coffee. "Morning Dusty, Brad," says AJ.

"Good mornin' AJ," they reply pretty much in unison.

"How do ya' like your coffee?" asks Dusty.

"Black's fine," he replies.

"Are ya sure?" asks Chuck, as he sticks his head out the back door. "We got real cream and that artificial stuff if ya want it."

"No, black is fine, thanks."

"Did ya sleep well last night?" asks Dusty.

"I must have. I barely remember my head hitting the pillow."

"Yeah, it's amazin' what a little fresh air, along with some peace and quiet can do for the body and soul," says Dusty. "Where's Miss Julie? She still sleepin'?"

"Yes, still out like a light."

"AJ? Last night you mentioned about checkin' the place out. How do you want to do that? By truck or horseback?"

"I'm still trying to get a handle on how big this place is. Did I hear you right about it covering about a hundred square miles?"

"Yep. Let me put it to you like this. If you want to go by truck, I can show you a good portion of the place in a few hours. But if you want to do it by horseback? Well, we'll need to set up a couple of pack mules with food and campin' supplies, because we'll be gone a day or two."

"Well, I guess for Julie's sake and mine, we'll do it by truck this time."

"Considerin' we're in the middle of summer? That's probably best. The sun can be a real killer this time of year. It's even tough on cattle, especially the young ones. If they don't get enough nourishment, they dehydrate and die. Doesn't take long, either. And between the buzzards and the coyotes? Well, there ain't much left after a day or two."

"What are your plans for the day? I don't want to mess up your routine," says AJ.

"Bein' it's the weekend, we generally don't have much in the way of plans. Once in a while, we might go into town to catch a show, go to a rodeo, or somethin'. But most of the time, we stay right around here.

Now, if you want to check out the place, we should probably think about gettin' a move on before the sun gets too high in the sky, 'cause it's only gonna get hotter, if you know what I mean."

"I suppose I should get sleepy head up, so we can have breakfast and get the day started," says AJ as he starts to get up from his chair.

"Well, I don't think that's gonna be necessary, 'cause unless I'm seein' a mirage, I believe I see Miss Julie walkin' this way," says Dusty.

"Wow!" shouts Brad as he almost tips over his chair. "She really knows how to fill out a pair of jeans!"

Julie's wearing a pair of form fitting jeans, flared a bit to fit over her boots, a western belt with a large, silver, oval shaped buckle, a brightly colored kerchief, and a bleached, coarse linen, long sleeve shirt, turned up at the cuffs, and open to the point you can clearly see some cleavage. Her hair is pulled back into a ponytail, and she's wearing a pair of aviator style sunglasses. She's gorgeous!

Dusty reaches over to Brad, lifting his jaw, and says, "Son, it's impolite to stare. Besides, you're drawin' flies."

"Huh?" asks Brad, still star struck.

"Never mind," says Dusty shaking his head and smiling.

"Good morning, boys," she says with a smile.

"Julie, this is Brad," says AJ.

Brad jumps up, and tips his hat. "Mornin' ma'am!"

"Good morning Brad."

"And in the kitchen is Chuck," continues AJ.

"Hi Chuck!"

"Good mornin' Miss Julie!" he says. "Coffee?"

"Yes please, and black is fine."

"How do you like your eggs?" asks Chuck.

"Over easy, if you don't mind," she replies as she takes a seat next to AJ. "It's so beautiful out here this morning! The air is fresh and it's so pleasant out."

"Just give it another hour, and you'll be huntin' some shade in no time!" says Dusty.

"I know what you mean," she replies. "I was born and raised in Texas."

"Really? Where abouts?" asks Dusty.

"Just outside of Galveston. My dad was in the Navy."

"Did you ride horses much?"

"During the summer months? Almost every day."

"Saddle or bare back?"

"A little of both, actually," she says smiling as she remembers those times. "But that was a long time ago, almost twenty years."

"Dusty and I were just talking about taking a tour of the property after breakfast. Are you up for that?"

"Sure! Can't wait!"

After bouncing around in Dusty's dually for the better part of the morning, they're on the way back to the bunkhouse to rest and grab a bite to eat.

Julie says, "You know, this is actually a pretty place. A little desolate maybe, but still it has a unique look all its own. It certainly has character."

"What do you think about it, AJ?" asks Dusty.

"I'm with Julie. It's a little desolate, but I like it. It's peaceful."

"Well, there's still more to see, but we'll save the rest for later."

Dusty's cell phone rings. "Hey Brad, what's up? Hang on a minute and I'll ask 'em. Say, are you folks expecting company?"

"No. Do you know who it is?" asks AJ.

"Who is it?" There's a long pause. "Okay. Hold on a minute. She says her name is Michelle. Say. Isn't that the lady you said is runnin' for President?"

"What's she doing down here?" asks Julie in a rather suspicious tone.

"Don't look at me. I'm just as surprised as you are." says AJ. "Dusty? How far out are we?"

"We should be back at the bunkhouse in about ten maybe fifteen minutes."

"Then, I guess you better tell him we're on our way."

"Ya got that Brad? Okay, see you in a few minutes. Bye."

***

As Dusty pulls up in front of the bunkhouse, Brad rushes out to meet them. "Dusty? I ain't believin' this! Not one, but two beautiful women out here at the same time!"

"Where is Mrs. McCarthy?" asks AJ.

Brad stops and does a double take. "Did you say, Mrs. McCarthy?" he asks as though he might have committed some unpardonable sin.

"You can relax, Brad," says AJ. "Her husband's dead."

476

"Oh! That's good, ah, I mean, ah, I'm sorry to hear that." Julie turns her head and tries to hide a giggle.

"Brad? Where is she?" AJ asks again.

"She's in back, underneath the tree drinking some of Chuck's lemonade."

"Thank you," says AJ. "Do you think you could get the rest of us some lemonade, too?"

"Sure thing, Mr. AJ! Comin' right up!" Brad rushes in the front door of the bunkhouse shouting, "Hey Chuck! Everybody wants lemonade!"

"Well Brad? The pitcher's in the fridge, and you know where the glasses are." replies Chuck.

As Dusty, Julie, and AJ round the corner of the bunkhouse, Michelle starts to stand up. AJ says, "Hi Michelle, please don't get up. I'm sure you remember Julie, and this is Dusty."

"Hi Dusty," replies Michelle.

"He's the foreman of the ranch. We were taking a tour of the place when Brad called us. Sorry we took so long getting back."

"It's not a problem, AJ," replies Michelle.

"So, what brings you all the way out here?" asks AJ. "Change of plans, itinerary?"

"Well no, not exactly," she replies. "I have some information for you that I'm sure you'll find interesting, and I have a few surprises for you myself."

"Really?"

"Yes. Is there any place around here we can talk in private?"

"Sure. We're staying in the guest house right up there, if you don't mind walking."

"Sorry, AJ. But these heels aren't exactly made for walking in terrain like this."

"AJ? I don't mind givin' you a lift up to the house," says Dusty.

"That would be great," replies AJ. "By the way, how did you get here? I didn't notice a car out front."

"I took a limo from the airport."

"Oh, okay. Shall we go?" The four of them load up in Dusty's truck and ride up to the guesthouse.

"Thanks for lift, Dusty," says AJ as he drops them off at the guesthouse.

477

"No problem, AJ. Nice to meet you Mrs. McCarthy, and good luck on your campaign. Ya got my vote."

"Thanks Dusty, I appreciate that."

Once inside the house, Julie starts, "Well, Michelle? What's the scoop?"

"We really haven't had much of chance to chat since Higgins' death, funeral, and the reading of his will. Everything's been such a blur."

"Yes, it has," replies Julie sounding a little frustrated.

"I'm willing to bet you've reread your paperwork on AJ's court martial and haven't been able to tie things out, right?"

"That's correct. According to my records, the Officer of the Day was a Captain William H. Marshall. In fact, there was no one by the name of Higgins even in Bosnia at that particular point in time. It sounds like Higgins was trying to throw AJ a curve ball just before he died."

"Julie, Captain Marshall was Higgins' son. Don't you think it's a bit odd for both Higgins and Marshall's names to begin with William H.? If you check Marshall's records, H. stands for Henry."

"I agree that both of them having the same first and middle name is pretty unusual, but his military records clearly showed a Walter Marshall as his father."

"Walter Marshall adopted William. Higgins met Ellen Atkins shortly after he returned from Southeast Asia in 1967. They were married in 1969. Though both of them were eager to begin a family, Ellen suffered through two miscarriages, before finally giving birth to William, Jr. in 1971. However, there were complications with the delivery, and she almost bled to death on the delivery table. An emergency hysterectomy was performed. The surgery was a success, but emotionally, she was a wreck."

"Ellen left him in 1972, taking William, Jr. with her. She filed for and got a divorce from him in 1973. A short time later, she met Walter, and they were married in 1974. Since Ellen could no longer bear children, she pleaded with Higgins to allow Marshall to adopt William, Jr. Higgins agreed, provided they only changed his last name to Marshall. He would still be allowed some degree of visitation with William, Jr., and he would see to it that his continuing education would be covered, provided his grades warranted it."

"William, Jr. was an above average student in high school, and because of Higgins' participation in the war in Southeast Asia, William, Jr. was allowed to enroll at West Point, where his grades were about mid-pack. He entered active service in 1994 as a second lieutenant. In 1996, he was promoted to first lieutenant, then just before being transferred to Bosnia in 2004, he was promoted to the rank of captain."

"His service record was unremarkable. While he performed his duties well, he was not insightful. His leadership skills were less than stellar, and his desire to succeed and move forward was found to be lacking. It is suspected that Higgins pulled some strings to affect his last promotion."

"Contrary to what Higgins said as he lay dying on the floor, William's military and potential political career were far from certain. He lacked his father's drive and determination."

"Well, if he lied about his son's potential political career, do you think he lied about how, or even if he died?" asks AJ.

"No, everything else he said about him was pretty much true, particularly his suicide and his body being dismembered and consumed by wolves."

"You said his body was dismembered by wolves?" asks Julie.

"Yes. Didn't AJ tell you about that?"

"No, and frankly, I'm glad he left that part out."

"Well, he was already dead, so it really didn't make any difference."

"It would to me," replies Julie.

"Anyway, I'm sure you remember Beth, right?" asks Michelle.

"How can I forget?" says AJ while giving Julie a disappointing look. "Yes, of course. Why?"

"First, her name is Bethany Hathaway, and she worked in the records division of the Secret Service."

"So, Higgins had a backup in the Secret Service over Weathers," says Julie.

"Not really. Most of the materials she handled were not considered high security. I'm not really sure what her purpose was, other than maybe keeping an eye on Weathers, or possibly keeping track of certain investigations. But again, her security clearance didn't allow her to look at much in the way of sensitive material. However, there was another connection with Higgins."

"What was that?" ask AJ.

"She was William, Jr.'s fiancée."

"Great," says AJ sarcastically.

"And I'm sure you haven't heard the latest about her either."

"What's that?" asks Julie.

"In the process of transferring her to another facility, the vehicle transporting her was involved in a fender bender. While waiting for an alternate vehicle, Beth managed to escape."

"When did that happen?" asks AJ.

"Yesterday, early morning."

"Who authorized the transfer?" asks Julie.

"That's another weird part of the story," says Michelle. "Somehow, during the course of her transfer and escape, all of the related paperwork disappeared with her. Not only that, but no records could be found at the facility from which she was released, nor the facility she was being transferred to. There was also no information found in the prison database regarding her admission on the Fourth of July, nor the transfer."

"I would willing to believe that maybe, just maybe, Beth might have been able to escape on her own. After all, she gave both of us the slip once," says AJ with a look of disgust. "But for the paperwork and computer data to disappear, too? No, other people were involved, and the only ones I know of who could pull off a stunt like that would be someone within the Core."

"You could be right, but it might have been one last play set up by Higgins, you know," replies Michelle. "He might have told his operatives to get her out, prior to his death. Remember he had over a week to set it up."

"Well, at least we still have Brandon as a backup," says AJ.

"I'm afraid not," replies Michelle. "He was found hanging from a sprinkler head in his cell yesterday morning."

"How'd that happen?" asks AJ while becoming more agitated.

"It appears he had ripped his T-shirt, braided it into a noose, and it's assumed, rolled off the top bunk, snapping his neck. Death was probably instantaneous."

"Now that just doesn't sound right," says AJ shaking his head. "I know the kid was around one fifty, maybe one sixty, but to roll off the top bunk and snap his neck? No way! The sprinkler head would have snapped first. Somebody killed him, then hung him up to be found."

"That may be true, but that is what's on the coroner's report, and they're calling it a suicide."

Suddenly, a semi's air horns can be heard, and a large, white, unmarked eighteen-wheeler can be seen coming up the road, leaving a cloud of dust hanging in its wake.

"Now what?" asks AJ.

"Oh, that's my surprise!" replies Michelle.

"And what kind of surprise requires a semi to deliver?"

"Come on out, you'll see!"

The truck pulls up in front of the guesthouse, and a short, stocky man with a balding head and round face, punctuated with a well-chewed butt of a cigar, climbs out of the passenger side of the truck. "Are you Mrs. McCarthy?" he asks.

"Yes, I am."

"Well, my name's Buddy, and I have a delivery for ya."

"Actually, the delivery is for him," she says pointing to AJ.

"You are?" asks Buddy.

"Thomas Andrew Jackson."

"Well, Mr. Jackson, where do you want 'em?"

"What?"

"The cars, Mr. Jackson. The cars!"

"I'm sorry, but I have no idea what you're talking about," says AJ with a confused look on his face.

Dusty pulls up in his dually. "What's goin' on?"

"This guy says he's got some cars for me, courtesy of Mrs. McCarthy."

"What kind of cars?" asks Dusty.

"Expensive ones!" says Buddy. "And I've got to get 'em off here and start headin' back to New York, pronto! So, where do you want 'em?"

"There's a pretty good sized metal building we keep some of the farming equipment stored in right over there."

"Mind if I check it out?" asks Buddy.

"No, go right ahead," says Dusty.

"Hey Joe! Start getting' ready to unload, will ya? I want to be headin' back east in less than an hour. Got it?" shouts Buddy to the driver of the semi.

"Yeah, yeah, yeah," mumbles Joe as he climbs down from the cab.

"How many cars are we talking about Michelle?"

"I only had them bring four out here this time."

"Four cars? What's this about?"

"Joshua had a thing for buying and collecting expensive cars, and since I was moving, I really didn't want to be bothered with trying to maintain or sell them. I don't drive very much, and since most of these cars are equipped with manual transmissions, I'm never going to drive them. The first person I thought might be interested in them was you. You do like cars, don't you?"

"Definitely, Michelle, but I can't afford a bunch of expensive cars. I just found out I've inherited a hundred square miles of desert, along with a foreman, a cook, and a ranch hand, plus a few hundred head of cattle, and a handful of out buildings! I haven't got a clue as to how much it's worth, or how much it's going to cost to maintain!"

"AJ? My law firm has been managing this ranch for Higgins for the past twelve years. A trust was established to maintain it, along with handling the salaries of the men who work it. There's really nothing for you to do, other than to enjoy it."

"Michelle, I really can't accept them. It's not that I don't appreciate what you're doing, but I think we'd be violating some rules or laws about accepting gifts from your employer."

"AJ, I'm not your employer. The United States Government is your employer. And until Mr. Weathers makes your assignment to me official, and in writing, I can give you whatever I want. They're a gift. Besides, they weren't purchased for you to begin with. My late husband bought them, and considering he's no longer among the living, they're in need of a new home. Plus, I'm sure you would appreciate them much more than he ever did. So please, don't make this anymore difficult than it already is."

"Okay, Michelle. You win. Thank you. Thank you very much."

"You're welcome, AJ."

Buddy comes back and says, "Yeah, there's plenty of room in there. It's a little dusty though."

"Buddy," says Dusty, "this is a cattle ranch in the middle of the desert. Of course things are going to be a little dusty!"

"Whatever," says Buddy smugly. "Hey Joe! You think these cars are gonna unload themselves? Move it! Move it! Move it!"

From inside the trailer, all of them hear the first car fire up. VaROOM! VaROOM! VaROOM! Buddy helps guide Joe down the ramp. It's a silver Mercedes Benz SL65AMG Black Series. Its V-12 is purring like a kitten, except this kitten has some pretty serious claws!

Once Joe clears the ramp, Buddy climbs into the trailer and fires up the second car. VaROOM! VaROOM! There's an occasional crackle and pop in its exhaust note. The sound is definitely that of a spirited V-8. What begins to emerge from the trailer is a replica of the Ford GT 40 Mk I, built by Race Car Replicas out of Michigan. It's a medium silver metallic with a black racing stripe down the center. It's powered by a 427 cubic inch fuel injected Windsor block bumping 550 horsepower! Buddy really has to pay attention, because rearward vision is almost non-existent in this car, but he's able to make a clean exit.

Once Buddy clears the ramp, Joe starts pushing and pulling hydraulic levers, and the cars on the upper ramp are lowered to the trailer floor. Joe quickly clears the chains and blocks, then fires up the next car. VaROOM! VaROOM! Its note is characteristic of a very high-strung V-12. As Joe starts to back the car out, AJ almost has a heart attack! The rear of the car is obviously a Ferrari, and of course, it's red. While Joe eases the car down the ramp, AJ discovers that he's the proud owner of a rare 575 Barchetta! Joe wastes little time clearing the ramp, as Buddy makes his way back up the ramp and disappears into the cavernous trailer. There's a long silence, then VaROOM! VaROOM! It's the distinctive sound of a V-12, but it is much more refined than the Ferrari, very similar to the Mercedes, yet different. The last car is also silver, but it doesn't appear to have a nameplate on it. It has a very distinctive shape, very sleek and powerful looking.

"Well? What do you think?" asks Michelle.

"I can't believe it! These are all beautiful and desirable cars.

Michelle, you could put these on the market and make a lot of money. I feel like I'm stealing from you."

"Nonsense! They belong to me now, and I want you to have them, plain and simple," she says flatly. "What time is it? My watch is still on New York time."

Julie says, "It's 12:45."

"I'm going to be late! My flight leaves at 2:30! There's no time to call a limo either! AJ, could I persuade you to give me a lift to the airport?"

"Sure! But the semi has my rental blocked."

"Hey mister!" says Buddy. "This one has a full tank. If you know how to drive a stick, I'll bet it'll get you there in no time!"

"Do you mind, Julie?" asks Michelle.

"Not at all. Let's go!" she says.

"I'm sorry Julie, but it's just a two-seater." Julie quickly realizes she's been set up. She's already agreed to let AJ take her to the airport, and she's willing to bet Michelle planned it this way.

"No problem, I'll just hang around here with Dusty and the boys. I'll be all right," Julie says, trying not to look disappointed, but she's more than a little suspicious.

"You sure you don't mind, Julie?" asks AJ. Julie can see in his eyes he's dazzled by the cars Michelle has given him.

There's a long pause, as she looks at AJ, then Michelle, then AJ again. "No, you go on ahead. I'll be here when you get back."

"Thanks Julie, I shouldn't be long," he says jumping into the car without kissing her goodbye. The two of them buckle up and head out toward the highway leaving a trail of dust as far as you can see.

Dusty can tell Julie is very unhappy and tries to cheer her up. "Miss Julie?"

"Yes, Dusty?" she says, while watching the car's dust cloud fade in the distance.

"I didn't have a chance to show you and AJ somethin'."

"What's that?"

"Well, you know I told you last night you were stayin' in the guest house, right?"

"Uh-huh…" she replies while still looking out in the distance.

484

"Well, while we're waitin' for AJ to get back, why don't I show you the main house," he says with a devilish grin on his face.

"Did you say the main…house?" asks Julie inquisitively.

TLC: Chapter 68

Once out on the highway, AJ starts picking up the pace. The sound of the engine is exhilarating as he shifts through the gears. The ride and handling are incredible. The seats are form fitting, yet very comfortable, and the aroma of the leather is almost intoxicating.

AJ turns toward Michelle to comment about these sensations, but he can see her eyes are closed, and she has a very provocative smile on her face. Up until this moment, he hadn't noticed how revealing her blouse is, or the slit up the side of her skirt that ends almost at her waist. It's more than obvious Michelle is teasing him. AJ revs her up and finds another gear.

"I bet Jeffrey would die to work on a car like this. He's more into cars than I am. I'm gonna miss him. George, too," he says with some sadness in his voice.

"I guess I forgot to tell you about that little fiasco," she says without opening her eyes.

"What fiasco?"

"Higgins didn't own that estate, he was leasing it. He had a five-year contract, plus an option on another five. He was well into the fourth year of the first contract, when he decided to renew the lease in advance. When we notified the owner of Higgins untimely demise, they claimed the lease wasn't directly with him, but with a trust set aside by Higgins. Considering the lease on the property is just over fifteen thousand a month, they weren't very enthusiastic about canceling the lease. In fact, they were going to sue for damages! In case you haven't noticed, the market is a little soft right now."

"Since I was looking for a new home anyway, I decided to take over the lease. And that includes Jeffrey and George," she says, smiling. "I'll probably keep most of the staff on hand, since they're familiar with the place."

"Are you serious?" asks AJ in disbelief.

Michelle opens her eyes, looks directly into his, and says, "AJ, you've asked me that same question once before when we were leaving the library that night." She reaches over and places her left hand on his leg, perilously close to his groin, and continues, "I don't say or do anything I don't mean."

"Sorry, I wasn't trying to offend you."

Michelle smiles at him, then settles back into her seat. She closes her eyes again, but leaves her hand resting on his thigh.

"Something's bothering me, though," he says while staring out the windshield, scanning for anything out of the ordinary.

"Really?" she asks. "And what would that be?"

"Since you've publicly announced your intent to run for President, and the President has authorized the Secret Service to provide for your protection and safety, who's supposed to be protecting you right now?"

"Aren't you up to the task of taking care of me?" she asks sheepishly.

"You know what I mean. Who guarded you on your flight from Washington to Vegas? Who checked out the limo before you got in, and who, in their right mind, would leave you out in the middle of the desert without any sort of protection?"

"Why are you being so melodramatic?" She pauses momentarily, sighs, then says, "Yes, the President has given his approval for the Secret Service to provide for my protection, but I asked Weathers to hold off appointing you to be in charge of my security detail until you returned from your little vacation."

"That's not the point, and you know it." Michelle doesn't answer. "Michelle, what airline did you fly on?"

"American."

"Any layovers or a direct flight?"

"Direct."

"What was the flight number?"

"I don't know, 1140, I think. My secretary handled the arrangements."

"What was the gate number?"

"Departure or arrival?"

"Both."

"AJ," she says as she sits up and faces him again. "What are you trying to accomplish with this, this vigorous interrogation? If we were in a courtroom, with you as an attorney, and me on the witness stand, I'd say you were badgering your witness."

"You didn't fly into Vegas on American or any other commercial airline, did you," he says in an accusatory tone. "You arrived by private jet, probably owned and operated by one

487

of your firms. The same goes for the limo, too. And that means there's no real rush to get back to the airport to catch a flight back to Washington, either."

"Is that an accusation or an invitation?" With a demure look on her face, she begins to massage his thigh. "From the first time I saw you in Higgins' library, I could tell you weren't your typical grunt."

"Grunt's a slang term for Army ground troops," he replies in a stern voice. "Marines are known as leathernecks."

"Point taken, my mistake," she says coyly.

Without looking down, he says, "I'd be lying if I said what you're doing isn't arousing me to some degree, but I'm in love with Julie, and there's no way in hell I'm going to jeopardize our relationship."

"Tell me, AJ, does she know about your new arrangement with the Core?"

They're running right around a hundred when he spots a black and white in the distance, on the side of the road. "Oh shit!" Suddenly, AJ is downshifting and nailing the brakes, but it's too late. The officer clocks them at ninety-seven miles per hour. AJ is able to scrub off enough speed to pull over to the curb directly in front of the officer, before he's able to even merge into traffic.

The officer eases his squad to within a car length of AJ, and turns on his emergency lights. AJ lowers his window, kills the ignition, and has his driver's license and Secret Service ID ready for the officer's inspection.

From his rear view mirror, AJ can see the officer talking on the radio, probably calling in his location, and the car's tag number, before leaving his vehicle. When the officer finally exits his squad, he approaches them slowly, checking traffic over his left shoulder. Once he reaches the driver's side of the car, he stops just behind the open window. With his right hand on his side arm, the officer leans over and says in an authoritative voice, "License and registration, please."

"Here you are officer," replies AJ as he hands him his license, ID, along with the paperwork on the car.

AJ's Secret Service ID immediately catches the officer's attention. "Secret Service, huh?" says the officer. "Think you're James Bond or something?"

"I beg your pardon, officer?"

"You know, Casino Royale, James Bond, Aston Martin DBS…"

AJ suddenly realizes this must be the car Joshua shot himself in! He looks over at Michelle, and she's smiling.

"Would you believe the leasing company wouldn't take it back because of what Joshua did? I had the car thoroughly cleaned and sanitized, and they still wouldn't take it back. So, we worked out what I considered to be an amicable deal and bought it. You're not superstitious, are you?"

"Sir," says the officer. "This paperwork says this car belongs to a Mrs. Michelle Marston-McCarthy."

Michelle leans toward AJ and replies, "Officer? That would be me."

"Ma'am, do you have any identification?"

"Yes, officer. Here you go," as she hands him her license and her firm's business card.

While the officer walks back to his car to call in and verify their credentials, AJ says, "Right or wrong?"

"Right or wrong about what?" she asks.

"Did you fly commercial or private?"

"Oh. That. Private of course," she replies rather flippantly. "I enjoy my privacy, and I prefer to travel when the time suits me, rather than the other way around. Plus the food is better, too."

"So, don't you think you need to tell me where I should drop you off?"

"Certainly. Hangar 19, where Hard Eight Air Freight and Charter Service is located."

"Well, since this is my first time in Vegas, I have no idea where that might be."

"Can't you just enter that information into the GPS system?"

"I would if I knew how," he replies with an air of sarcasm in his voice.

About that time, the officer returns to AJ's side of the car and hands AJ their credentials. "Tell what I'm going to do. I'm going to let this one pass. Partly because you didn't make me chase you, so there was no real risk to the public, and partly out of professional courtesy. But I'll be honest with you. I had no idea the Secret Service pays enough to justify buying one of these babies. I might have to try my hand at getting on."

"Thank you, officer. May I ask you a favor?"

"Sir, I thought I just gave you one!"

"Yes sir, you did," says AJ apologetically. "But you see, Mrs. McCarthy is running for President of the United States, and I need to get her to Hangar 19 at McCarran as quickly as possible. Since this is my first time in Vegas, and I have no idea where Hangar 19 is, would you be willing to give us an escort?"

The officer leans over to get a good look at Michelle, then says, "Think you can keep up?"

"I don't think that'll be a problem, officer."

"Then follow me!" The officer rushes back to his car, hits the siren, and they're off!

***

Minutes later, they're on Airport Road. The officer kills the siren, but leaves his emergency lights on to alert any surrounding traffic. Once past the main entrance, they turn onto a service road that takes them to the freight and charter hangars. The officer pulls over, just inside the entrance to Hangar 19.

A large weathered sign on the side of the hangar shows a pair of red dice, with each having four white dots facing up. Arched over the top of the die are the words, "Hard Eight". Arched below the die is, "Air Freight", and below that are the words, "and Charter Service, Serving the West Since 1953." AJ is convinced he's seen this sign and logo before, but exactly when and where escapes him for the moment.

Rounding the corner of the hangar, he's suddenly confronted with the nose of a glistening white Gulfstream G200, swept wing, corporate jet, its twin engines idling, and its warning beacons flashing. A uniformed officer, dressed in black slacks, white short-sleeved shirt, black tie, and aviator style sunglasses, is standing by the stairway leading into the cabin, awaiting Michelle's arrival. Two other men, dressed in business suits, and similar aviator style sunglasses, are standing just inside the open hangar, trying to shade themselves from the blistering afternoon sun.

As AJ pulls to a stop near the jet, one of the men makes his way to Michelle's door, while the other man maintains his vigil, looking for any possible threats to her safety.

Before AJ can find his door handle, Michelle is already swinging her legs out of the car. As she walks around to his side of the car, AJ lowers his window. She leans over and crosses her arms on the windowsill, providing him a teasing bird's eye view of her ample breasts. With a provocative look on her face she says, "You never answered *my* question."

"What's that?" he asks.

"Are you superstitious?"

"I don't think so, why?"

"You know Joshua killed himself in this car."

"Yeah, but it wasn't the car's fault, now was it?"

"I like your attitude, AJ," she says with a seductive smile. "I think we're going to get along just fine." As Michelle starts to back away, she notices something in a seam of the upholstery on the door. "What's this? Looks like they missed a spot." She scratches at it with her index fingernail, finally working the dark speck loose. She picks it up with her pinkie fingernail, holds it up near AJ's face, then touches it to the tip of her tongue. "Hmmm. Tastes like. Yes, I believe it is." She stands up, turns, and starts to walk away. But after taking a couple of steps, she stops, turns back toward AJ one last time and says, "Take care AJ. I'll see you next week."

AJ waits until Michelle and the three men enter the aircraft, then he slowly backs away, allowing the pilot ample room to maneuver. He watches them fall into line with the commercial traffic and await their turn for takeoff. Once Michelle's jet aligns itself on the runway, he can hear the shriek of the engines reach their peak, and within seconds, they're in the air.

Much to his surprise, as he rounds the corner of the hangar, AJ discovers the officer is still parked at the entrance. When AJ pulls up next to him, the officer says, "I kinda figured you might need me to help get you back on the expressway."

"Thanks, I appreciate that," AJ replies.

"I also called in to see if the highway patrol had any speed traps outside of town, just in case you wanted to see what that

491

baby can do. The corridor is open for at least fifty miles outside of Vegas."

"You're not trying to bait me, are you?" AJ asks a bit suspiciously.

"No sir, but this is a onetime offer, you understand? Besides, once I take you back to the edge of town, my shift will be over, and I'll have to head back to the station to file my reports."

"I appreciate the heads up. Maybe I'll be able to return the favor someday."

"How about when I apply for a job with the Secret Service?"

"No problem. You've got my information. Just drop me a line or give me a call. I'll help you out any way I can."

The officer glances at his paperwork, then says, "Will do, Thomas."

"My friends call me AJ."

"AJ it is. Now, why don't we get you back out on the highway so you can stretch your legs," says the officer with a devilish smile.

"After you," replies AJ.

***

While weaving their way through the afternoon traffic, AJ puts in a call to Weathers.

"Don't you know what time off means?" asks Weathers.

"I could ask you the same thing. After all, you're the one who picked up the phone. I was expecting voice mail," replies AJ.

"How's the weather out there?"

"Hot! Guess who paid me a surprise visit today?"

"Jesse James? The Clantons? Little green men from Mars?"

"No, Michelle."

"Now that *is* a surprise!"

"I need to jog your memory about something."

"Go ahead. Shoot!"

"Do you recall seeing the name Hard Eight Air Freight and Charter Service in any of the files on Higgins? Seems like I saw an older black and white photo with four or five people standing in front of a sign with that name on it."

492

"That name does sound familiar. I'll do a little digging and see what I can come up with. Any rush?"

"No, no rush. Remember? I'm on vacation."

"It sounds like it. I'll get back to you when I find something."

***

Once clear of the heavy afternoon traffic, the officer pulls off to the side of the road, and waves to AJ as he passes by. AJ downshifts to third and accelerates away. Just as he shifts into sixth gear, his phone rings. It's Weathers. "That was fast."

"I was lucky. In fact, Hard Eight Air Freight pops up in at least four different places. The first entry shows up as the name of a business started by Higgins' uncle shortly after returning from Korea in 1953. He picked up a few war surplus cargo planes under the GI Bill. Next, when Higgins flew for Air America out of Thailand in the 60's, he named his plane "Hard Eight Air Freight." The next entry is when Higgins sabotaged the plane chartered by the late Senator Wooten and Andrew Carlson in 1970. The company that owned the plane leased hangar space from Hard Eight Air Freight. And finally, when Higgins' uncle passed away in the early 80's, Higgins was the sole surviving heir and inherited Hard Eight Air Freight and Charter Service, lock, stock, and hangar."

"Sounds like this place has a lot of interesting history. But I don't think that's the end of the story," says AJ. "I'm willing to bet Hard Eight Air Freight is now owned by one of Michelle's companies, or some dummy corporation owned by them."

"I'll see what I can find out."

"Sir, it's the weekend. Shouldn't you be spending it with your wife? It'll keep until Monday."

"You're a big one to talk! After all, you're the one who asked me to look into this mess to begin with. By the way, what's Julie doing right about now?"

"Probably plotting my demise. She wasn't in a very good mood when I drove Michelle to the airport and left her high and dry back at the ranch."

"Sounds to me like you've got a lot of sucking up to do when you get back."

493

"Don't remind me. If I don't show up for work on Wednesday, send out a scouting party. They'll probably find what's left of my carcass out in the desert somewhere. After all, I'm the proud owner of over a hundred square miles of desert, brush, and foothills."

"See you Wednesday, and tell Julie I said hi."

"I will. Have a good weekend."

"Goodbye, AJ."

"Goodbye, sir," he replies. As AJ ends the call, it suddenly hits him. While the chapter of William Henry Higgins has drawn to a close, a new one is already on the horizon…

**In Memory of
Brian John Edgerton
a man whose courage and determination
to live life on his terms
despite insurmountable odds.
11/19/1943-2/28/2011**

**In Remembrance of
Lesley Jane Rion/Moretti
Mother, Sister, Daughter, Companion
And Friend
An Endless Source of
Life, Light, Love, and Happiness
6/30/1966-7/16/2013**

The Birth of
TLC: Terminate Life Cycle

If you've gotten this far, I hope you enjoyed reading TLC: Terminate Life Cycle. And if that's the case, I'd like to share with you how TLC was born.

Getting the cart before the horse
Sometime in 1998, while my wife, Ginny, and I were living in the suburbs of Chicago, the topic of a television talk show was "tender loving care" or "tlc". Although I wasn't actually watching the show, I could hear the term "tlc" being repeated over and over again to the point of distraction, as well as some degree of aggravation.

Suddenly, my twisted sense of humor kicked in and posed a question. "What would be the polar opposite of tender loving care, yet use the same three letters?" It only took a couple of minutes to come up with the term Terminate Life Cycle. Mission accomplished, and that should have been the end of it, right?

There was just one problem. My version of "tlc" became stuck in my head and wouldn't go away. After several days of trying to erase the term from my mind, I finally surrendered and began to think of a story that could use Terminate Life Cycle as its title. U.S. Senator William Henry Higgins was the first character to come to light, followed soon after by U.S. Secret Service Agent Thomas Andrew Jackson, aka: AJ. And as their back stories began to gel, AJ's former love interest, Julie Anne Robinson, and his supervisor, Robert Monroe Weathers, began to come into focus as well. Senator Joshua Abrams McCarthy would round out the initial characters. Oops! I almost forgot the Yellow Hummer H2.

Problems, like misery, love company
In 1998, I had very limited experience using a computer, and the one we had in our home was owned by the company my wife worked for. Its programs were primarily accounting based, so I had no idea if any type of word based programs was installed, or

how much memory a novel might require. In short, my ignorance got the better of me. Computer: 1, Pat: 0.

While I had learned to type in high school, I knew I would be making numerous corrections, coming up with new ideas, plotlines, and improvements were to be expected as the story progressed. I would probably need to buy stock in White Out before I started the first page. I knew similar problems would occur if I were to write it long hand.

Above it all, I feared these and other frustrations would eventually lead to dumping everything in the trash, and abandoning the project entirely. My solution was to write down my ideas in a notebook and hang on to it until I acquired sufficient knowledge to work with a computer. At least that was my intention.

Fast forward to July 16, 2005
Ginny and I moved to Mississippi in early 1999, where I began to build our dream home. Since I am originally from Mississippi, I had experienced a number of hurricanes, one of which was Hurricane Camille in 1969. The devastation was the worst I had ever seen, and it was one of the reasons I wanted to design and build homes that could withstand hurricane force winds as well as protect the people inside. Ours was the first home I designed and helped build that met my personal goals and expectations.

One of the features in our great room is a built-in dual computer station. Ginny and I have our own computers, complete with satellite internet access, and we share an all-in-one printer situated between us. While I'm definitely no expert in regards to computers or the Internet, I can usually find my way around with minimal hassle.

TLC had been more or less out of sight, out of mind for at least a year, probably more. However, something completely out of the ordinary happened the morning of July 16, 2005. While taking a shower, I was suddenly inundated with ideas about TLC! It wasn't a culmination of words, but more like having a series of movie clips running in my head. Yes, I know that sounds crazy, but it's the only way I know how to describe it. They were so vivid! And while this "download" occurred in mere seconds, it contained an enormous amount of information.

496

I jumped out of the shower, made a cursory attempt to dry off, put on a pair of shorts, forced my damp feet into my house shoes, and rushed to the great room to tell Ginny what I had just experienced. I'm sure I was a sight, sitting in my chair, my hair still soaking wet, and a damp towel draped over my shoulders. Well, that's probably description enough without embarrassing you or me.

Ginny was looking at me like I'd lost my mind, but says nothing. I told her about what I had just experienced. And I needed her to tell me if I had somehow transposed something she had told me about one of the books she had read, or was it possibly part of a movie we had seen together. She agreed to listen to what I had seen. As I began to tell the story, she started to smile. She didn't interrupt me, but allowed me to continue without turning away. When I finished, I waited for her response. Her first words were, "It sounds to me like you're ready to start writing your book."

With the information I have, I start with what I called chapter two (in TLC's current form, it's chapter four), or the point where AJ and Higgins are attacked on the expressway. It takes about five hours to complete. The time it took to write this chapter, was proof my hunch was right about the number of corrections and rewrites it would take to get it down the way I wanted. Had I been trying to type or write it down in long hand, TLC would have probably died the first day.

I hit the sack around 11pm, satisfied with what I had accomplished, and I'm out like a light. But around 2am, I'm awakened by another string of information. At first, I thought to myself, "I'll remember it and start on it first thing in the morning."

Luckily, it kept gnawing at me to the point I relented, got up and began writing chapter three (again, in TLC's current form, chapters five and six). I completed chapter three in about three hours. In fact, from July 16 through August 28, 2005, I would complete nine chapters, or 105 pages in typical single spaced, letter style and sized format. The storyline was continuous and fluid, with one chapter leading to the next.

Hurricane Katrina, August 29, 2005

To say that Hurricane Katrina threw a monkey wrench into TLC would be an understatement. Living approximately sixty miles from the Mississippi Gulf Coast, plus living dead center of Katrina's inland path, meant we would experience much of her wrath. Winds reached over 140 mph for an extended period of time in our area. We would lose over sixty trees on our property. Many were pulled out by their roots, while others were snapped off from twenty to thirty feet above ground. Fortunately, our home suffered minimal damage. Some water seeped around the French doors in our two guest rooms, and one 36-inch wide section of our metal roof was lifted slightly at the eave.

Our storage shed wasn't so lucky. It was tossed on its side and blown approximately five feet west of its original location. And as luck would have it, the only wall with a door and windows, lay on the ground. Part of the roof had to be removed to gain access.

We were without power for about ten days, and it was about three weeks before we had limited phone service. We were quite lucky and fortunate, especially in comparison to many of our neighbors.

Near the end of October, most services, and life in general, were back to normal. Almost two months had passed since I last worked on TLC. I decided it was time to start writing again. But I soon discovered it would prove to be easier said than done. I was drawing a complete blank. I decided to back up and read the last chapter written, but when I reached the end, nothing new came to mind. So, I decided to go back to the beginning and read it all, but when I came to the end... Nothing.

I was beginning to think I had lost the story. The harder I tried, the worse it got. That was the point I decided to focus on what I had already written. Polish it up. Clean up the dialog, find the proper sentence structure, etc.

At Last! The Patient has a heartbeat!

It would be almost ten months before TLC developed a heartbeat again. But while TLC had been in "cryo-sleep", something changed. TLC developed a twisted sense of humor of its own.

When TLC first came to life, everything came to me in order

498

or succession. There was a distinct continuity from one chapter, one scenario, one scene, to the next. Call it a constant, if you will.

However, this time around, she gives me a paragraph, a new character, a new scenario, a new plot. And while I am confident these new pieces are a part of TLC, they don't seem to fit anywhere within the current framework. I decided to go ahead and write them down and let them play out. When they ended, I gave them an arbitrary number and a tag line as to what it was about, with the hope they would eventually find their place in TLC. There would be a lot of these tidbits scattered all over the place.

Hallelujah!

Finally, in April 2007, TLC gets back on track. We're back to the point where flow and continuity prevail. I recall one instance when I wrote over twenty-five pages at a single sitting, and another, when I started getting emotional while writing the scene about Tony getting blown up.

But one of the biggest surprises was how all of those snippets, with their arbitrary numbers and tag lines, literally started falling into place. Most of them required little or no modification whatsoever. The first draft of TLC: Terminate Life Cycle was completed July 3, 2007. However, that was not the end, but just the beginning.

Perfection is elusive

TLC: Terminate Life Cycle continued to evolve, and continues to do so to this day. Being a novice writer, there were many mistakes from grammar, punctuation, etc.

I was also guilty of providing TMI (too much information) on occasion. I'm sure many women have very little interest in cars or firearms, along with various types of ammunition and related items, at least to the depth I described them in earlier manuscripts.

Plus I'm sure some men would have been a bit disappointed (disgusted?) with some of the sappy dialog between AJ and Julie, especially since AJ had been in the Marine Corps.

And my in-depth medical questions regarding Julie's possible injuries, caused by slamming into the concrete column at the entrance of the parking garage, would have everyone yawning before the ambulance finally hauled her away to the hospital.

Patience is a virtue

As I mentioned earlier, the first manuscript of TLC was completed in July of 2007. I also mentioned the completion of TLC was just the beginning.

As an unknown writer, finding an agent or publisher to represent or publish my work proved to be a daunting task. After sending out a number of letters, synopses, and/or chapters, my efforts yielded little to no interest. In fact, I rarely received any sort of response. Self publishing or print-on-demand seemed to be the only solution.

My first experience with a print-on-demand publisher was not a good one. However, seeing my book in print for the first time gave me a sense of accomplishment. It also proved to be an important and valuable learning experience. That lesson led me to CreateSpace.

CreateSpace offers a myriad of options and opportunities for both novice and experienced writers alike. They provide you with the tools and assistance to help make your work the best it can be. Professional and personable assistance is just an email or phone call away, and they're available well past normal business hours, too.

Opportunity knocks

So, if you have a story hidden away in your closet, drawer, shoebox, or embedded in the back of your mind, contact CreateSpace. Who knows? You could be sitting on the next Best Seller!

Coming soon

Oh, there's one more thing. If you enjoyed TLC: Terminate Life Cycle, you might want to keep an eye out for TLC II: A New Era. Where? CreateSpace, of course!

13288488R00281

Made in the USA
San Bernardino, CA
17 July 2014